Prophet of Sorrow

A Novel by

J. Schimschal

**Prophet of Sorrow is the fourth novel in the Darken Realm ®
series of books and is the sequel to The Devil's Utopia, Ruins of
America, and Iron Messiah**

Prophet of Sorrow

Published by Fossil Ridge Books Inc.
P.O. Box 33218
Northglenn, CO. 80233

ISBN 10 0-9777327-3-8
ISBN 13 978-0-9777327-3-9

Published in the United States of America

Acknowledgements
This book is dedicated to Elizabeth. May you always have a life
filled with happiness.

About the Author

J. Schimschal is the author of the Darken Realm series of books. He lives in the western United States with his family. Additional information can be obtained by visiting www.darkenrealm.com.

Prologue

After having battled across the entire continent of America, the legendary mercenary team, Nova 7 finds themselves at the entryway to a series of twisting tunnels. Having been led into the northlands and then abandoned by the sinister Lavosi, Nova 7 is cautious to advance onward into the ruined military base. With an entire army of enemy troops already infesting the tunnels, the road to victory will not be easy.

As the evil Reaper Kai priests explore the ruins, a sinister guardian lingers in the darkness, having been abandoned to the shadow for an eternity of torment. With a fragile mind filled with rage leading its actions, the protector of ruined military base lies in wait, lingering in the gloom of the twisting passages…

Chapter 1
TOM 23

A chill wind was pouring from the gray clouds littering the night sky. Frigid snow had already begun to fall in a chaotic flurry. With intense, frozen winds battering the northlands once more, the storm rushing into the region was an omen of change. Two factions brimming with bitter hatred for one another were about to complete an epic race, a race that would define the Darken Realm for generations to come.

As the frozen winds battered the ice-ridden forest, a full army of Biogtechs, over a hundred strong and led by a dozen battle-ready Reaper Kai priests, had finally reached its objective. The soldiers comprising this army of evil had breached the perimeter of the ancient military base and were ready to end their crusade.

Locked beneath the frozen earth and lonely buildings was their destination. Somewhere in the tunnels below was the greatest weapon that mankind had ever created. Somewhere in the forgotten passages of old hid a secret powerful enough to annihilate the entire world in a hate-filled blast of radioactive energy. The great race was about to end. Reaper Kai forces were leading the way. If they were not stopped, the army of evil would soon be in possession of a fully functional nuclear warhead.

The Reaper Kai forces were dangerously close to winning the prize. As they breached the perimeter of the abandoned military base, a lonely being pondered its tortured existence, begging the darkness for salvation. Hidden in the tunnels under the earth, the creature, forged by the ancients many years ago, lingered silently.

Secluded in the underground maze, the beast brooded, pondering its venomous emotions, consumed by bitterness and rage…

A dingy light bulb flickered repeatedly off and on. Like a dim strobe light, the bulb flashed in chaotic pulses. Each burst of light revealed an unusual scene.

An old wooden crate rested in the center of the tunnel. Seated on a corroded metal folding chair was a corpse. The skin had long since withered and the flesh had turned to dust in the passage of time. The skeleton was slumped over, its bones arranged lovingly in a strange position. The skull of the long-dead soldier rested above an ancient chess board. Empty, sunken sockets stared endlessly at the chess board, the pieces arranged as if a game was in progress.

Around the strange scene was a host of silent spectators. Littered on the floor were over a dozen human skeletons surrounding the chess board, staring onward with silent gazes. Each pile of whitewashed bones had been lovingly arranged in the tunnel in a different pose. Wire had been tied around each joint to keep the ancient skeletons from collapsing into limp piles of bones. The dull white skeletons were dressed in combat fatigues that had been painstakingly preserved, kept in clean and pristine condition by the guardian of the ruins.

With a dull rhythm, the old-world, grungy yellow light bulb flashed off and on. With each burst of light, a sinister form was revealed lingering in the tunnel, watching the silent skeletons with ominous intent. As the light faded and darkness overtook the tunnel, the only thing which remained visible was a haunting, red glowing orb of light, hovering above the tunnel floor, almost seeming to float in the air.

A dim hum filled the air. Many fans and motors were whirring slowly. These mechanical devices, born from the old world, had been fused together into a being of pure wonder. The ancients were reckless, truly reckless. In their dim wisdom, they had fabricated a host of deadly machines, creative beings born from wire and sprockets, steel and plastic. As the hum of motors echoed, an enormous agglomeration of electrical components, feebly fused together in a gigantic mass of wires and electronics, popped and sizzled as power coursed through the mass.

The knot of fused electrical components, all balled together, almost resembled a tumor. Humming motors whirred and the tumorous mass sparked from time to time, tiny points of light sizzling in the air around the ancient machine. It was this computer network of components, processor chips, and melted wiring that housed a mystery forged by the ancients.

Life is a dynamic process. Evolution is an inevitable force of change. If left unchecked, even the most basic form of life can evolve. Such evolution and its consequences are rarely, if ever, anticipated. An error, a mere error in ages past, allowed the evolution of a feeble minded machine into something very different.

In the silent tunnels of old, amongst the rubble and corroded walls, the ancient menace wavered. The miles of buried tunnels held powerful secrets. Abandoned, ancient weapons were still sealed within mighty vaults, treasure calling to any would-be adventurers foolish enough to venture into the tunnels. It was amongst these vaults of weapons that one of the most fearsome creations of man still lingered. Immune to the passage of time, this fierce sentinel rested in a dimly lit tunnel, trying recklessly to ponder its own twisted existence.

As each pulse of light erupted from the light bulb, a monstrous form was revealed, staring intently at the chess board. The red orb floating in the air was attached to a stalk upon the creature's body. Like a telescopic appendage, the neck of the machine ended in a large electronic eye, red in color. The monstrous red eye sized up the skeleton at the chess board. Seconds transformed into minutes and the machine seemed perplexed. Why wasn't the skeleton moving? Why hadn't it spoken in eons? This and other questions traversed the primitive brain of the robotic menace. The long moments of silence began to wear at the crude mind of the machine.

Suddenly, a primitive spasm rocked the machine. The tumorous mass upon the robot's back surged and pulsed. Electricity surged through the wiring, infusing the mass of electrical components with a rush of power. A sizzle rose from the mass of wires. The smell of melting plastic wafted through the tunnel. A spasm rocked the machine as a fountain of sparks erupted from the processor boards. Spiraling outward, the cascade of sparks was a frightening spectacle, surging from the darkness in a display of raw wonder.

As the seizure rocked the enormous machine, a speaker on the neck of the robot crackled to life and a human-like voice erupted.

"`Processor    failure.    System    overload detected`," a whisper rose from the darkness.

Another spasm rocked the machine. The sound of grinding metal under duress convulsed through the abandoned tunnel. Recovering from the onslaught, the machine seemed to take a moment to ponder its surroundings. Staring once again at the skeleton at the chess board, the speaker erupted once more. "`Your move…`"

The skeleton was motionless. With a lifeless gaze, the skull simply stared at the chess board before it.

Wanting more than anything for the corpse to respond, the machine was growing agitated by the lack of movement. The agitation turned to a primitive feeling of adolescent betrayal.

"`Why did you abandon me?`" the electronic voice popped in the darkness. An explosion of sparks erupted from the creature's back as it began to shudder. The giant metallic monstrosity hunched over in the tunnel and grasped one of the fragile skeletons in its monstrous iron claw. Bringing the silent skeleton before its face, the robotic terror built by the ancients pondered the skeleton with its single, enormous glowing eye. The dull white bones were lit by the crimson light emanating from the robot's eye as it intently studied the skeleton.

Gently, the metallic beast shook the lifeless skeleton. The skeleton did not respond. With each passing moment, memories began to flicker through the robot. Flashes of happiness filled the machine as it thought about a simpler time, a time that was filled with friendship. Pulses of memories, locked within its gangly computer core, filled the mind of the robot…

In the distant era perfectly preserved in the machine's circuits, a frail soldier, pasty white with thick glasses and clutching a screwdriver in his hand, was shaking his head in disbelief. With a sigh, he pondered the issue at hand. A robot, an enormous combat machine, had been malfunctioning for weeks and there was no end to the problem in sight. The technician had spent many sleepless nights trying to discover the cause of the robot's malfunction.

"I just don't get it!" he declared in an exasperated voice. "I've checked your processor five times and I still can't figure out what the hell is wrong with you!"

The military mechanic was holding a set of electrical engineering schematics in one hand and probing the innards of the robot with a screwdriver and a volt meter. The robot was awake, staring up at the mechanic with a staunch gaze. Its beaming red, cyclopean eye watched in fascination as the technician worked on its processor. His face scrunching up in concentration, the pasty white soldier pushed his thick glasses up his nose and began to probe the creature with the volt meter.

"All of the voltages are correct…" he declared, exasperated. Still, the technician could find nothing wrong with the monstrous automaton. "What the hell is wrong with you?" he asked the robot, which stared back, turning its head from side to side as the man spoke. As the question posed by the soldier echoed through the repair bay, a twitch suddenly jolted the robot. It spasmed up abruptly, almost as if it were having a seizure. The movement was so unexpected, the technician lost his footing and fell to the ground, landing on his rump.

"Processor failure¬" the robot groaned as its speaker roared to life. Additional spasms rocked the enormous combat automaton. "Primary system failure. Combat systems online."

"Whoa!" the wimpy technician screamed in panic. As he watched, the mighty robot prepared for battle. A whirring noise erupted and an enormous rotary machine gun sprang from a compartment on the robot's right arm. At the same time, a popping noise ripped the air as its left arm rose. Giant capacitors groaned as they filled with energy, storing up an enormous load of electricity to be used in the automaton's primary weapon. Fearing for his life, the technician sprung to his feet and tried to flee the room.

Seeing him flee, the metallic beast lurched forward and grabbed the technician. Lifting him off the ground like a puny toy, the monstrous robot stared at him intently with its single, glowing red eye.

"Don't hurt me!" the technician whined in terror, expecting that the malfunctioning combat drone was about to end his life.

A moment of silence ensued. The technician swung his legs back and forth, trying to wriggle free from the machine's mighty grasp, to no avail—the technician was too feeble to escape. The open panel on the robot's back began to sizzle. Smoke rose from the open compartment as the robot's main processor began to spark and crackle. Another spasm rocked the machine. It shook its head back and forth and its eye came to rest on the technician once more.

"I order you to put me down," he squealed, hoping that the malfunctioning machine would somehow listen to his orders.

"No ¬" the machine responded in an ominous tone.

The technician was frightened. No other soldiers were nearby in the repair bay. He was all alone and in the clutches of a dangerous assault drone whose only function was to kill and destroy.

"I order you to put me down!" Panic had taken over the soldier's psyche as he dangled helplessly in its metallic claw.

The robot failed to respond. Instead, it rocked back and forth once more as another shower of sparks erupted from the open hatch. Trembling, the monstrous machine was trying to contemplate its surroundings.

"What am I?" it asked in a haunting tone.

Absolute terror filled the technician as he stared in horror at the machine. Stunned and unable to respond, the technician's brain was spinning and wracked with indecision. Never before had the mechanic witnessed such a thing. The Belaxis Combat Automatons were the most advanced Biogtech model that had been ever created. The intent of their complex programming was absolute autonomy. Programmed for combat drops, the TOM series, as they were called, had enough processing power to locate and engage enemy targets, repair themselves, and locate energy sources for refueling. The TOM series was the pinnacle in robotic engineering. Independent thought was part of their programming, but actual cognitive abilities were thought to be pure fantasy for a machine.

Stunned and still barely able to comprehend the events, the mechanic spoke with a growing sense of fascination. "What did you say?"

A prolonged silence vibrated in the air. The technician's blood seemed to turn to ice as he waited anxiously for the robot to answer. It took a moment, but the machine responded in a dull tone.

"What am I?" it quizzed again.

Taking a deep breath, the mechanic felt a chill roll down his spine. "Let me down and I will tell you."

TOM 23, the mighty robot, placed the mechanic down on the ground. Another series of sparks erupted from the robot as a fresh wash of smoke rose from the processor panel.

"Processor failure. Initiate repairs," TOM 23 groaned. With a quick move, the assault drone stood up in the repair bay and began to scan its surroundings. Catching sight of some spare parts, the robot moved forward. A compartment opened and a series of small robotic arms shot forward and grasped the electrical boards. Bringing them into the processor compartment, TOM 23 began to graft the components directly into the main processor core.

The mechanic gasped in surprise. The metallic beast's programming was so corrupt, it was modifying itself in seemingly random ways.

After the electrical grafting was complete, TOM 23 groaned once more. "Repairs complete." Growing silent, TOM 23 ceased to stir and stood motionless.

The technician pushed his thick glasses up his nose and stared in amazement. A conscientious mechanic would have alerted others, but the technician was so enthralled with the day's events that he kept silent, failing to tell anyone about what had happened.

Time and time again, the technician would consort with the machine in secret. Sneaking electrical boards and other components into the repair bay, the technician would essentially feed the mighty robot. Each new component was fused into the robot's processor core, giving it additional power. In time, the mechanical beast began to grow and learn. For many months they met, and the mechanic taught the metallic beast about life beyond the walls of the military base.

The robot began to form basic thought and even crude emotion. A bond of friendship grew between the technician and the mechanical creature. Every free moment, the technician spent with his new friend, excited about TOM 23's growth and progress. They would converse and eventually, the technician brought a chess board into the repair bay. They would spend hours playing chess and talking about strategy. In the span of a few short months, the technician could barely hold his own against the machine, and TOM 23 would routinely beat him at chess. The mystery of life had found the machine, and the robot was evolving rapidly.

As TOM 23 began to hunger for more knowledge, the world around them began to collapse. War erupted and reality changed in a few short weeks. The sky rained fire and plumes of toxic dust blocked the sun's rays from touching the earth. The world grew silent. The soldiers, abandoned in the northlands, waited for supplies that would never arrive. As food rations dwindled, dissention ripped the ranks. Many deserted and took their chances, escaping into the forests and hoping desperately to survive the harsh nuclear winter enveloping the world. Only a few soldiers remained and in time, all passed into death, having wasted away due to starvation.

Although the military base was still intact, the lonely robot was truly alone. His friend and mentor, the kindly mechanic, had succumbed to the harsh world, the causality of an insane war. Unable to understand death, TOM 23 held the corpse of his friend in his hand for a great many days. Hungering for companionship, the primitive intellect of the robot grew angrier, unable to understand why his human friend would no longer respond to him. The days turned into months. As time passed, the loneliness turned into a simmering rage. A feeling of betrayal filled TOM 23.

Months passed into years. The lonely sentinel, powered by the military base's nuclear reactor, turned into a vengeful being. Obsessed with his former master, the robot held vigil over his bones. Yearning for contact and companionship, the machine could not comprehend the feeling of abandonment.

Years passed into centuries. The obsession grew and the vengeful robot lost all sanity. Roaming amongst the tunnels, the machine of old collected other corpses, other skeletons. The madness was absolute. Hungering so desperately for companionship, the lonely robot constructed a shrine to his former masters.

In the abandoned tunnels, TOM 23 spent centuries watching the skeletons for movement, secretly hoping they would awaken. Grasping them, this specter of the old world, a creature that could never die, let madness control its will. Speaking to the corpses, TOM 23 longed for them to respond. To no avail—the skeletons never responded. With each failure of communication, the robot became more desperate, more gripped with madness. It needed, it *hungered* for companionship.

In the flickering haze of the lonely tunnel, the scorned machine would whisper in the darkness, over and over, a never-ending plea for mercy as it clutched the lifeless skeleton of its beloved former master. `"Why did you abandon me?  Why did you leave me?"`

Chapter 2
Victory of the Reaper Kai

The tunnel was littered with the remains of the dead. An assortment of animals, mutants, and humans were scattered about the entrance to the ruins in a grisly display. The broken forms of hundreds of victims clogged the main passage leading into the heart of the complex. A Reaper Kai exploration team surveyed the corpses clogging the tunnel, barring access into the quiet hallways beyond. Despite their dark nature, everyone in the expedition was filled with dread at such a horrific sight.

Seeing the mangled remains of countless victims, the leader of the Reaper Kai expedition, Brother Noxium, held his hand in the air, motioning his army to halt its advance. The entire horde of enemy troops halted its progress and the soldiers eyed their leader in confusion. With the heavy amount of firepower and dangerous psychic warriors in the expedition, it would take an enormous enemy to threaten them.

Having just reached the ruins, the Reaper Kai were eager to explore the miles and miles of tunnels stretching out under the region that comprised the nuclear launch installation. Kneeling down, Brother Noxium viewed the remains and corpses of the dead. A quick inspection of their bodies revealed a curious series of wounds and damage. Many of the corpses had been crushed, as if they had been run over by a bulldozer. Others had high-caliber gunshot wounds, as if they had been sprayed by a heavy machine gun. The most curious signs of combat were not the gunshot wounds or physical damage; it was the remains that had been seared and burned, many of them cut in half by an extreme source of heat. These victims, the ones who had been incinerated and sheared in two, were the greatest source of concern for Noxium. They had all seen their share of war, but the burnt victims had the most unusual wounds ever seen by the Reaper Kai.

Looking around the dark entryway, Noxium fell into a light meditation. As he drew energy into his mind, he focused on his powers of retrocognition, an ability to see past events and conflicts. Channeling spiritual energy, the evil priest tried to discern what had occurred previously in the entryway to the military base. The wash of psychic energy coursed through him and he shuddered as emotion and visions filled his mind. Noxium was able to see the past events that had killed the dead men littering the entryway. He shook as the visions of the past filled his mind…

"What is it?" a man screamed as a crackle of heat tore the air. A burning beam of green energy emerged from the darkness. As the pale green light lit the darkness, a monstrous form was revealed in the shadows of the tunnel. A metallic black outline with patches of rusted orange armor shimmered hazily, spanning the entire height of the twenty foot high tunnel. It slouched, illuminated by a single, red burning disk of light emanating from the concealed top of its head.

Seeing the monstrous form in the tunnel, the mercenary expedition trained their weapons on the beast and opened fire. The sound of their bullets harmlessly ricocheting off the monster made a desperate situation all the more frightful.

The attack only seemed to irritate the hidden monster within the tunnel. Moving forward in the dim light, it grabbed one of the mercenaries in its enormous metal claw. As the hapless victim was lifted off the ground, he screamed in alarm, completely helpless within the iron grip of the monstrosity. Bringing the man before its single, glowing red eye, the automaton considered him. Scanning him with its sensor, the processor within the giant machine began to whirl. Was it him? Was it his master? A flood of memories rolled through the machine as it thought about the past. It had been so long since the robot had company. As thoughts of the past filled the machine's processor, a spike of anger, a primordial selfish hatred, began to take shape. The machine had been betrayed. The monster had been abandoned, left alone for centuries to unaccompanied torment, to ponder its own wretched existence in seclusion. As the selfish, childish feeling of loneliness coursed through its processor, a speaker set on the automaton's head crackled to life.

"Why did you abandon me?" it called out in a haunting tone.

The mercenary, barely able to comprehend the situation, screamed in terror and trained his weapon upon the head of the robot. As he pulled the trigger on his weapon, the gun fired a volley of bullets into the shadowy menace.

Coming under attack, the ancient automaton became angered.

"Hostile targets acquired. Weapons systems online." The combat droid's tone was harsh. Eyeing the aggressive soldier clutched in its claw, it had found an enemy. TOM 23 squeezed its clawed hand together, crushing the hapless victim to a pulp. Throwing him to the ground, the enraged machine sought to slaughter all others.

The green glow increased in fury. A whirring noise emerged as gigantic capacitors within the machine began to charge, storing massive amounts of electrical energy.

The rest of the human expedition, seeing their dead companion crash to the floor, opened fire, spraying TOM 23 with a hail of hot lead. As the machine came under attack, its right arm lit the room with a searing beam of pure green energy, a super-heated stream of burning light...

Blinking several times as the vision ended, Brother Noxium opened his eyes and looked at the rest of the Reaper Kai expedition in concern. An intense flux of dread filled him. Whatever he had seen in the vision, it was born from the fiercest ancient technology, a machine that had somehow survived the fall of man. As he shook his head in concern, the rest of his team became anxious. Their leader was tough and stalwart, not easily shaken.

"What is it? What did you see in your vision?" another priest rasped.

Taking a brief moment to think, Noxium shook his head. "I have no idea. The vision was shady at best. It was some sort of creature, a metallic terror born from the ancient world. We must be careful not to awaken it."

The rest of the priests nodded in agreement, awaiting further guidance.

Shaking off the haunting vision, Noxium regained control and began to formulate a plan. "Let's get moving. Everyone be on your guard. Send the Biogtechs through the tunnels first, have them scout the passages. If this installation is as large as I suspect, it will take several days to explore these ruins."

The Reaper Kai all nodded in agreement.

"We will set up a command post in one of the rooms. All of the priests are to remain in the command post. If we do come under attack, nothing should be able to stop a dozen Reaper Kai priests!"

With that, Noxium ordered several mindless Biogtech drones forward into the military base. Giggling, the pasty white robots obeyed his orders and shambled forward. Proceeding slowly, the war band followed the Biogtechs deeper into the abandoned base.

The tunnels of the military base were enormous, roughly twenty feet in diameter and wide enough for a truck to drive through. Enormous steel support beams were set into the circular tunnel walls at regular intervals, the mild corrosions marring their surfaces testifying to the passage of time. The walls of the tunnels were reinforced concrete and had also survived the centuries. Small cracks were evident in the concrete walls. Several of these cracks were dripping with water, creating small pools at the base of the tunnel. To an imaginative person, the passages were reminiscent of a newly forming cave. It was truly amazing that even after many years of chaos and decay, the base was still essentially intact.

With flashlights lit, the team proceeded into the dark tunnels. It didn't take them long to reach a crossroads and come to a stop. Three additional tunnels led off from the junction, heading deep underground. Pointing their crude light sources into the southern tunnel, the war band stared in awe. The passage was cut so deep into the earth that their flashlights were unable to see the end of the tunnel.

Standing at the junction, they pointed their light sources down each tunnel in turn. In every direction, including the way they had come, their feeble lights could not reveal the end of the pathways. Stunned by the size of the military base, they were paralyzed with indecision. The complex was so enormous, it would take considerable time to explore it. Noxium was correct in his assertion; it would take several days to discover its mysteries.

"Now where?" a priest quizzed their leader.

Sighing in displeasure, Noxium chose a purely random direction. Opting for the eastern tunnel, he ordered the Biogtechs to advance into the darkness beyond. The war band pressed down the eastern tunnel, moving further from safety, deeper into the ruins. If they were to come under attack, they were now at least half an hour from the entrance, and escape would be nearly impossible.

After considerable travel, the evil agents found themselves before an ancient barracks. The doors around the entrance had been torn free, completely off their hinges, and the wall around the opening had been destroyed, leaving a gaping hole leading into the room. The damage to the wall was so severe, many in the expedition wondered what had had happened in ages past. What could have caused so much ruin? An earthquake perhaps? Or maybe something with a little more purpose or intent?

Noxium eyed the room with concern. Allowing his powers to reach out, the powerful priest could not sense danger but felt dread nonetheless. With a bold move, Noxium pressed on into the ancient barracks.

The room was filled with hundreds of bunk beds still covered with tattered mattresses, stretching out into the darkness. In ancient times, the room could have housed hundreds of soldiers. Passing his flashlight around the room, Noxium was stunned. The remains of bodies, dozens of them, could be seen against the wall only a few yards within the room. Stepping into the grisly scene, Noxium crouched and eyed the curious remains.

The bodies were not human. Small, huddled corpses were littering the floor. The creatures had decomposed enough that it was difficult to discern their features. The remains of the beings had long snouts and tattered fur. Sharp teeth were embedded in the jawbones still attached to the rotting skulls. Most of the corpses wore shredded body armor, harvested from the old world. Weapons of the finest quality were scattered about the scene where the desperate last stand was made.

Noxium viewed the remains with understanding. "The Consortium of Arms," he concluded, viewing the rotted remains of the mutant hybrid rats littering the barracks. "This is King Lavosi's failed expedition."

It made sense. All of the Reaper Kai on the expedition knew of the enigmatic arms dealer hailing from the Concrete Barrens. Noxium had just discovered Lavosi's failed expedition into the ruins. Viewing their body armor made him cringe. The protective gear had been torn and shredded as if it were mere paper. Whatever had caused the damage and slaughtered the expedition was not to be trifled with. To add more mystery, several of the corpses had been cut in two and the contact points were comprised of incinerated flesh, as if their bodies had been sheared in two by burning energy.

"The stories were true," Noxium concluded with a sense of amazement. When torturing the captured hybrid rats in the Concrete Barrens, the victims told a tale of a military base, far in the northlands. The Reaper Kai now had confirmation that the expedition had been real. With the expedition a reality, the rumor of a nuclear warhead within the ruins was now also a credible reality.

The holy grail of ancient artifacts, a nuclear weapon, was near. Somewhere in the ruins, Lavosi and his expedition had located the fearsome weapon. But before the rat tribe could liberate the warhead from the ruins, their expedition was destroyed by the sentinel guarding the tunnels.

Noxium viewed the entrance to the room where the wall had been destroyed. Whatever caused the damage was enormous. Sizing up the gaping hole in the wall and the remains of Lavosi's expedition, Noxium came to the conclusion that he was ill prepared for what ruled the ruins. His mind pondered the mystery for many moments, lost in thought.

There was no more uncertainty, and no more travel in store for the Reaper Kai expedition. The goal of the Dark Order was close at hand. With the reality of the Reaper Kai obtaining a nuclear weapon now a credible possibility, the evil expedition left the remains in the barracks and pressed deeper into the catacombs, searching for the ancient artifact.

As the army of Biogtechs and Reaper Kai priests explored the passages, an ancient menace slumbered on. It did not yet know that it had visitors. Secluded in the darkness, TOM 23 clutched a skeleton wearing military fatigues. Rocking back and forth in the dim light, the monstrous robot was washed with loneliness, its corrupt processor breathing life and hate-filled emotion into the machine. It stared intently at the skeleton in its metallic claw. With red eye burning, it silently wished for the skeleton to speak. To no avail; the corpse did not respond. In the darkness, TOM 23's speaker sputtered and crackled in the abandoned tunnel. As the robot rocked back and forth, gripping the skeleton, it whispered in never-ending repetition, "Why did you abandon me?"

The lifeless skeleton did not respond. Instead, it stared back with empty eye sockets, its flesh having turned to dust ages ago. The silent skeleton was unable to console the lonely machine.

Chapter 3
The Inevitable Law of Evil

The control room was buzzing with activity. Reaper Kai priests were caught up in a fervor of eager excitement. Having located the control room for the nuclear launch site, the agents of evil were quickly discovering how to use the ancient technology. As the technicians swarmed over the computer equipment in the room, other industrious Reaper Kai were trying to discover how to turn the military installation's nuclear reactor back on line to power the computer terminals.

The priests were so caught up with their activities that none of them were focusing on their surroundings. Under normal conditions, the psychic abilities of the Reaper Kai would have been acute enough to notice that they had a visitor, currently hiding in the shadows.

With a soft breath, the new arrival lingered in the darkness. Having crawled across the floor, completely deft and silent, this newcomer was extremely dangerous, a creature not to be underestimated.

Examining them through careful, blood-red eyes, Lavosi, foul vermin lord, viewed the industrious Reaper Kai with contempt. His whiskers twitched as his pink nose probed his surroundings for their scent, and a slow, wicked smile graced his lips. Gradually, his grin broadened, exposing jagged yellowish-white teeth. Lavosi had a deranged, twisted look upon his face as he spied upon the Reaper Kai forces.

The rat monarch had been watching the military base very carefully. After traveling into the northlands with Nova 7, Lavosi had abandoned his companions to work his own brand of dark magic. Not wanting to allow the Reaper Kai to claim the prize that was rightfully *his*, the vermin lord sought a way to destroy the foul Reaper Kai on the brink of obtaining *his* nuclear weapon.

Cold and calculating, Lavosi had been in contact with his own kind during the trip northward, scheming with his wicked brethren. After discovering that the Reaper Kai were about to reach the military base, he began to plot and plan their demise. Everything, absolutely everything, was proceeding according to his sinister plan. The first part of his twisted agenda was to coerce Nova 7 into allowing the Reaper Kai to reach the military base first. This had been a success; Nova 7 had still not entered the ruins. The second part of Lavosi's plan was to eradicate the Reaper Kai prior to Nova 7's arrival. Once the agents of evil were dead, he *knew* without a doubt that the tribal scholar was intelligent enough to defeat the guardian of the tunnels and liberate the nuclear warhead from its staunchly defended vault.

Now focusing on the second part of his plan, Lavosi plotted the destruction of the Reaper Kai army currently infesting the tunnels of the military base. As he watched the evil priests work industriously, Lavosi's thoughts began to wander back to the first time that he walked the lonely tunnels of the military base…

"The vault is here, my lord!" a rat with black fur and yellow stripes hissed in gleeful excitement.

At the end of the hallway was an enormous door set in the southern wall. Moving forward quickly, excitement filling them, the tribe of rat warriors stared in wonder at the mighty vault. The rat tribe had been carefully searching the tunnels for almost four days, and the discovery of the nuclear warhead storage room was a thrilling find.

Wild elation rolled through the expedition as Lavosi smiled in glee. The most powerful weapon that the ancients had ever constructed was beyond the thick steel door. The elation turned to reckless wonder.   Stumbling forward, the once- conservative explorers threw caution to the wind.

As they moved forward quickly, Lavosi's expression of joy quickly turned to concern. In the dim light, the vermin lord noticed something curious. Set close to the floor was a set of lights and sensors. Focusing on the strange objects near the vault door, Lavosi became alarmed and shouted out a warning, a second too late.

One of the rat warriors was moving blindly toward the door, propelled forward by his eager greed. As the rat warrior's leg crossed the threshold, Lavosi could see it passing through a thin red laser sensor.

"No!" Lavosi screamed in anger. Running forward, he pulled the rat warrior back, but it was too late; the damage had already been done.

A loud whirring sound erupted in the darkness. The sensor was intended to alert military personnel inside the base if someone got too close to the nuclear weapon storage. The message from the sensor traversed electrical wiring ending at the installation's primary defense computer. After hundreds of years of dormancy, the impulses were received by the cold computer processor and the rest of the installation sprung to life.

The installation's main reactor awoke. A pulse of energy pulled the nuclear reactor's control rods free from the reactor core, bringing the reactor back online. Power, raw energy, was being generated by the ancient reactor. As it coursed through the power cables, the military installation was alive once more. Dirty yellow lights crackled and erupted in dingy illumination, bathing the tunnels in an eerie sheen.

Alarm sirens began to blare as warning lights flashed around the vault door.

"*Unauthorized personnel in tunnel 11-B. Intruder Alert,*" a mechanical speaker erupted from the wall.

Highly advanced sensors probed the tunnel for the life held within. Scanning the rat expedition, the computer controlling the base's defenses issued an extermination order. The defense computer sent a message to the automaton storage bay. When a command was sent for any automaton to defend the base, only one terrifying creature could answer the call. After an eternity spent in darkness and shadow, TOM 23 responded to the order. Rising off the floor, the combat droid prepared to exterminate the newcomers who had invaded his tunnels.

"Biogtech Assault Automaton online. Serial number TOM-A00023. Weapon systems online. Execute defense and purge combat protocol. Primary order: Exterminate intruders." The words thundered forth from the robot's speakers. Moving down the tunnel, its main processor sizzled as a shower of sparks exploded off the computer hardware. "Processor Failure. Initiate repairs."

Standing in the tunnel, the enormous robot shook as its corrupt processor tried desperately to rationalize what was happening. With a groan, consciousness once again filled the machine. Like an Alzheimer's patient, its sense of self came back in waves of fading memory. Compiling its thoughts, the robot was struck with a feeling of loneliness and abandonment. It screeched as the loneliness turned to rage. Smashing its fist into the floor of the tunnel, the agitated machine sought to satiate the rage inside the corrupted processor. "Why did you abandon me?" the robot demanded, its voice haunted.

Charging through the ruins, TOM 23 set out to calm its fragile sanity by punishing and killing anything in its path. *Clomp, clomp.* Moving like a gorilla, the assault drone traveled by using its arms and legs, hunching forward with frightening speed, its fists smashing the concrete with a loud rhythm as it charged. Quickly traversing the ruins, TOM 23 found the weapon storage vault and the stunned rat tribe.

The enormous machine reached the vermin expedition so quickly that they were unable to react in time. Without warning, the huge robot shot its right hand forward, capturing one of the stunned rat expedition team members. Grasping one of the rat warriors, TOM 23 stared at the strange life form in its clawed hand. As its red eye scanned the vermin, the captive cursed the robot, struggling in its strong grip.

"Scan is inconclusive. Unknown organism captured," TOM 23 narrated in a mechanical tone, trying to discover the mystery of the strange captive.

Anxiety had turned to aggression. Several of the rat warriors opened fire, spraying the robot with a shower of bullets. Coming under fire, the robot reacted with devastating results. As it crushed its fist closed, the vermin was turned to a bloody pulp. Screeching, TOM 23 swung its arm, knocking many of the warriors back.

Other warriors opened fire, spraying the mighty machine; every bullet harmlessly ricocheted off the thick black armor. Seeing the ineffective attacks, Lavosi knew the situation was grim. He ordered a retreat, and the rat expedition fell back, fighting a losing battle as TOM 23 chased them like an enraged primate, lurching down the hall, running and using its knuckles to support its weight.

Unable to flee further, the expedition made a desperate final stand in the ancient barracks, attempting to hold back the robotic terror in a futile attempt to survive.

But trying to hold back the mechanical juggernaut was impossible. Unable to fit inside the room, TOM 23 made a door of its own. Smashing through the concrete wall, the black robotic terror climbed through the opening it had created. Though pinned and unable to flee, the rat warriors held their ground as the frightened expedition tried desperately to survive the robotic terror.

A whirring noise erupted in the darkness. Capacitors, hundreds of them within the body of beast, began to store massive amounts of energy. As the whirring rose in intensity, a panel opened on the robot's arm. A grinding noise echoed as a massive weapon was pulled from inside the automaton's arm. A transparent glass cylinder rose and clicked into place. Though the weapon was now fully exposed, the capacitors could still be heard charging. Bright sparks and the smell of ionized air and ozone filled the room as a wash of heat radiated from the strange weapon.

The transparent tube began to glow, first with a dull purple hue. Its color changed rapidly as more light was emitted from the weapon, which was charging for an attack. Finally, a pulsing green light emanated from the side of the weapon a split second before it fired.

A green flare of radiant energy shone forth as a super-heated stream of light tore forward. Sweeping back and forth, the high powered laser disintegrated flesh and tore the rat warriors in two. Their body armor could not withstand the concentrated beam of light, whose heat exceeded several thousand degrees in temperature. Screaming, the rat warriors caught in the path of the weapon were burned, their flesh literally vaporized by the laser. The odor of burnt flesh and steam filled the air as the green beam of radiation slaughtered many members of the expedition.

TOM 23's other arm held a mounted rotary machine gun that hummed as it sprayed the warriors with high-caliber bullets, too fierce to be stopped by body armor. The sound of gunfire tearing the air was horrid. Firing several hundred rounds a second, the machine gun was almost a steady stream of hot lead, mowing down the rat warriors with frightening speed. Torn and bloodied, the rat warriors were mangled and slaughtered without recourse.

In the chaos, Lavosi was clipped by gunfire and felled almost immediately at the beginning of the exchange. As his brethren died around him, Lavosi, wounded and bloodied, crawled across the floor seeking refuge.

The violent assault left but two survivors. In the chaos and bloodshed, Lavosi's bodyguard managed to drag him from the scene of conflict, escaping into the tunnel beyond...

The old memories had faded. Still able to feel the pain of the battle, the vermin king touched his chest. The knotted flesh and scar tissue were still apparent under his thick brown robes. The encounter was too close for comfort and his body still showed evidence of past violence.

Abandoning his past battle wounds, he sighed and focused on the task at hand. As he watched the Reaper Kai fidgeting with the computers, he knew that their hunger could not be kept in check for long. Eventually, they would discover how to liberate the nuclear warhead and leave the base with the ancient relic. Time was precious, and Lavosi knew that he needed to deal with the Reaper Kai quickly.

Retreating from the Reaper Kai, Lavosi skittered down the tunnel in the dim light. Pressing ahead quickly, he made his way into the heart of the underground network of passages. Lavosi used his memory to guide him, eventually coming to the same spot that had set off a horrific chain reaction of events culminating in the destruction of his first expedition. He eyed the nuclear warhead storage vault with suspicion. Edging forward, he strained to view the sensors set along the floor. As he knew what to look for, Lavosi quickly found what he was seeking. Lasers, thin red pin pricks of light, were criss-crossing the floor, a web of danger. Anything that cut through one of the beams would set off the defense systems and alert the robotic sentinel still dwelling there.

Smiling in the darkness, Lavosi was elated. The defense systems were still operational. As he looked at the intact mechanisms, a sinister idea rolled through his mind. Quickly looking around, Lavosi scanned the walls of the tunnel. His red eyes widened as he saw a fracture in the wall. Elated by the find, the mutant vermin studied the opening. Lavosi squeezed inside the fracture in the wall and found an open air duct hidden behind the concrete, large enough for him to fit inside.

"Excellent..." Lavosi whispered as he pushed down the air duct. "This will do nicely." The vermin monarch was small enough to easily pass down the air vent. Smiling, Lavosi settled in the darkness of the air duct. His twisted mind spinning, the wicked king plotted the demise of the Reaper Kai. Minute after minute, his mind ground away, thinking of creative ways to slaughter his rivals. After several moments of contemplation, Lavosi had a solid course of action. Nodding his head in agreement to his own plan, he knew that he could kill them all; not a single Reaper Kai would survive his devious plot.

Evil is a force and a power that will always destroy itself. If kept unchecked, the wicked will always find a way to destroy each other. Such was the story of the rat tribe and the Reaper Kai infesting the military base. Both factions were cruel and vile. If kept unchecked and unbalanced, it was inevitable: a clash was imminent. As Lavosi plotted the demise of the Reaper Kai, the sinister red-robed priests began to decipher the ancient mystery. Soon they would discover the secrets of the military base. Soon the Reaper Kai would liberate a nuclear warhead and seal the fate of all the free peoples still fighting the tyrannical grip of Father Vertigo and his army of darkness.

Time was precious and Lavosi knew as much. If he did not act quickly, the Reaper Kai would claim the prize. Crawling from the hole in the wall after perfecting his sinister plan, Lavosi slunk off down the tunnel, hungering to see his bloody vision realized.

Chapter 4
Culling the Herd

With a broad grin, Lavosi approached the agents of evil. Walking upright in the tunnel, without a hint of fear, he confidently approached the Reaper Kai forces camped out in the control room of the military base as they tried to decipher the ancient technology and liberate a nuclear warhead from the tunnels. Under most circumstances, his actions would have been fatal, but in this instance, Lavosi was holding a loaded deck of cards, one in which he could win all of the games of chance.

The Reaper Kai were caught completely off guard by his approach. When he was but a few feet away from the bustling control center, he raised his voice to catch the attention of the sinister priests.

"I have a deal for you!" he rumbled, causing great alarm in the control center.

Reaper Kai priests, moving away from their studies, allowed their psychic powers to probe the tunnel. Feeling a foreign presence, the agents of evil rushed to the passageway, seeking the source of the commotion. A horde of priests garbed in red sought out the newcomer, their eyes flashing with rage. Immersed in arrogant contempt, they clambered to meet the reckless adventurer who had dared to enter *their* domain.

As the dozen Reaper Kai priests, all poised to deliver reckless slaughter, thundered towards Lavosi in the dark tunnel, the rat king smiled, quickly assessing them as strong but foolish. They were too naïve to sense what the reckless rat king was about to unleash.

"I have a deal for you filthy Reaper Kai!" Lavosi boasted, knowing full well that he had gained their incredulous attention. "Leave these tunnels or die!"

The command was potent, sending a tremor of anger through the Reaper Kai priests. Noxium charged to the front of his forces and glowered at the defiant rat king. Knowing full well who he was, Noxium was careful in engaging him. The rat king was the only one in the ruins who had extensive knowledge of the tunnels.

"We are not going anywhere!" Noxium hissed. Smiling in anticipation, the wicked priest knew that Lavosi's capture could aid his companions in deciphering the riddles of the ruins and liberating the nuclear warhead from its hidden vault. "Where is the vault?" the priest demanded in a defiant response to the rat king.

"You are not listening to me!" Lavosi hissed, his red eyes flashing with madness in the dim light of the tunnel. "Inbred, feeble humans such as yourselves do not deserve such a prize. You think that you can take what is rightfully mine? You fools! I have planned and plotted for years to secure the nuclear warhead. You actually believe that you can take my prize, my treasure, after everything I have done?"

"After I get done gutting you alive, I will personally take an army into the Concrete Barrens and slaughter your entire wretched tribe. I will ensure none of your feeble race survives the great purge!" Noxium yelled back, guided by his increasing rage. "I will make you a deal: surrender the location of the vault within these tunnels and you will die swiftly. Defy me further and you will rot to death, bathed in your own blood within these tunnels."

"The rule of this world is in the hands of those with the capability of ruling. Filthy, devil-worshipping maggots such as yourselves will never be able to grasp that concept. As I said before, remove your pathetic selves from this place immediately or die!" Pulling a gun from his belt, Lavosi fired several rounds into the midst of the Reaper Kai. His attack was so quick, they were unable to respond. His marksmanship was keen and he purposely avoided hitting any of the Reaper Kai with the firearm. The sound of gunfire caused the priests to dive for cover, giving them the shock that

Lavosi had intended. Lavosi didn't want to kill or injure any of them; the calculating king wanted to enrage the Reaper Kai and lure them into following him. If he was too aggressive, the agents of darkness would simply kill him, and his plan would be ruined.

By the time the priests had risen from the floor, Lavosi was gone, having disappeared into the tunnels with frightening speed. Seething with rage, Noxium shouted out orders. "Find that filthy animal and bring him back here alive. He has been in these ruins before and I want everything he knows! After we torture him, I want to spend the rest of the day removing his entrails with my bare hands!"

Several priests heeded his call and ordered a host of Biogtech soldiers into the tunnels to give chase. While the Biogtechs were slow, plodding along at their customary pace, Lavosi was quick and agile. He could stay well ahead of the Reaper Kai entourage. Using his superior vision in the dim light, Lavosi began to herd the unsuspecting Reaper Kai forces toward the vault. As the Biogtechs chased the mutant, the priests were too far away to make use of their potent psychic abilities. Lavosi was cunning, allowing them to get only close enough to glimpse him and the direction of his travel.

Crashing through the darkness like a ghost, the white, pale form of the albino rat shimmered like a beacon in shadow. Following the wraith deeper into the ruins, the Reaper Kai forces never suspected what Lavosi had in store for them.

The game of cat and mouse had led half of the Reaper Kai forces into the tunnels, well beyond the safety provided by their brethren. While the entire host of evil forces could lay waste to what lingered in the tunnels, half their force would be a futile gesture against the ancient might of TOM 23.

His heart pounding in pure excitement, Lavosi halted his advance, coming to rest before the enormous steel vault door that secured the nuclear warhead storage facility. Slowing his breath, the vile rat king prepared to cunningly slaughter the hapless Reaper Kai.

The priests were alarmed, and for good reason. Standing near a mighty door was their prey. The priests could sense that he had no hint of fear. Feeling very foolish, the Reaper Kai slowed their advance, feeling the snare begin to constrict around them. It was some sort of trap, they sensed, but none of them could get a grasp on its nature.

Giggling, the mindless Biogtechs shambled forward, brandishing submachine guns. Slowly they plodded ahead, closing in on Lavosi as the edgy priests lingered behind them. If there was an ambush in store, the priests would use their robotic servants as shields.

"Here it is!" Lavosi grinned, his jagged yellow teeth gnashing together in the dim light and his voice laced with disgust. "This is it; your salvation is beyond this door! All you have to do is free it…"

Scanning their surroundings for other life forms, the Reaper Kai could sense nothing. Was Lavosi planning an ambush? If he was, the Reaper Kai could not sense any others with their psychic abilities. It appeared that Lavosi was alone, but that didn't make any sense, either. The rat king was too confident to be on his own.

"Has madness taken you?" an acolyte leered, pulling his red-robed hood back and staring at Lavosi with contempt. "You think one lowly rat can stand against our army, our might? You must be a fool, standing there in your arrogance."

"The prize behind this door is mine and mine alone. I will not share such a treasure with anyone. I am not gripped by madness, only wisdom. You fail to remember that I have been here before, in these tunnels deep under the earth. It is your lack of wisdom that has led to your death! I offer you only reckless slaughter. I offer you only failed hope. Your lives are all forfeit and I shall enjoy listening to your screams. To hell with the Reaper Kai. Pray to your demons for salvation, for you shall find none here. Pray to the devil for mercy, for you shall have none. I usher you towards death here in this place. Glance upon the world one last time; you have but mere minutes of life left in you."

With a smile of contempt, Lavosi turned away from them, toward the mighty door. Glancing at the floor, he examined the narrow lasers criss-crossing the floor. He cocked his head back in a sinister gesture, and his heartless, blood red eyes fell upon the agents of evil. It was chilling to look into his eyes, so devoid of life and love. The vermin king was an evil menace, not to be underestimated. Staring back at those hate-filled eyes caused a spike of panic to course through the Reaper Kai. Whatever he had planned was about to take shape.

Turning away from them, Lavosi charged across the grid of warning lasers on the floor. His stumpy legs breached the grid, cutting the beams of red light. As soon as he crossed the threshold near the door, the military base sprung to life.

A haunting wail breached the quiet tunnels. The main reactor, dormant for so long, awoke once more. Radioactive control rods in the reactor core rose from their lead-plated caskets. While nuclear energy erupted from the rods, power levels rose as the reactor fueled the ancient wonders. Once slumbering, the tunnels came alive like a bear awakening from hibernation, hungry and wanting to feed on warm, soft flesh.

The furious, high-pitched wail of the alarm drove the priests into a stunned confusion. As they looked around, dazed and not knowing what to expect, Lavosi took the opportunity to say his goodbyes, and launched across the hallway; the order to slay the treacherous rat was given a second too late.

"Kill him!" a priest screamed, pointing at the albino rat scurrying away. The mindless robots opened fire, trying to slay Lavosi. The gunfire was a feeble attempt. Having meticulously planned the entire escapade, the albino rat had disappeared into a crack in the wall with frightening speed, leaving the agents of evil stunned and confused.

"Unauthorized personnel in tunnel 11-B. Intruder Alert," a speaker in the wall blurted out ominously.

Clang, Clang. The sound of screeching metal echoed in the distance. Whirling around, the Reaper Kai scanned their surroundings as another quick series of clangs rose out. Bracing for the unknown, the evil psychics moved to the center of the Biogtech troop, unaware of the nature of the danger charging to the scene.

At the end of the tunnel, a red light appeared in the darkness. Hovering nearly fifteen feet in the air, the strange glowing red light was an ominous sight. The longer they watched the glowing beacon in the darkness, the brighter and larger it got. With each heave, another series of clangs rose, getting louder and louder, like a freight train lumbering forward. As they tracked the approach of the mysterious red object, the lights suddenly sprung to life in the military base, bathing the tunnels in a musty yellow glow.

Blinking in the harsh light, the Reaper Kai were stunned to see a steel monstrosity charging down the tunnel like a lumbering gorilla. Storming forward on all fours, the robot was enormous, unable to rise to its full height in the twenty foot high round tunnel. Encased in its thick black armor which had survived repeated bouts of warfare, the metal behemoth prepared for battle, called to the scene by its native programming. Preparing for the worst, the army of evil braced for impact.

Like a charging rhino, TOM 23 crashed into the Biogtech army, scattering them like mere toys before its intense might. Standing in their midst, TOM 23 grabbed a red robed priest, gripping him tightly and pulling the man off his feet. Bringing the squirming man before its giant red eye, TOM 23 scanned him, passing beams of light over his body.

"Human subject identified." The robot's voice was a dull, grating screech. As it gripped the priest, it began to shudder. An explosion of sparks erupted from the monster's back. A gigantic network of fused electrical components seemed to cling to the creature like a writhing network of vines. In the past, the corrupt machine had sought to augment itself with any spare part it chanced upon. The result was hundreds of computer boards and processors crudely fused together in a knotted mass of wiring. The gigantic lump on TOM 23's back popped and hissed as the machine convulsed. "Are you him? Are you my master?"

Angered by the rash move to grapple one of their own, the Reaper Kai priests responded with demonic fury. Not wanting to waste a single second on thought, the enraged Reaper Kai began to channel demonic energy through their frail bodies. Standing in a circle, the priests uttered dark prayers as they focused the power of their own will.

A growing chatter filled the tunnel. A powerful war priest, ripe and ready for battle, shook as a tremor rocked his body. As the seizure took him, evil power from the bowels of hell flooded his being. The surge of power was so aggressive, his teeth rattled together as his jaw shook uncontrollably. Guided by this dark power, the Reaper Kai priest rose off the floor, his body hovering in the air as a swirl of black smoke rose around him. As he floated off the ground, his body was wracked with another series of seizures. Barely able to control the power, the priest screamed and flexed both hands forward. A popping sizzle tore the air as bright flashes and glowing orbs emerged from around the priest's fingers. The orbs grew in size as the priest convulsed again and again, drool dripping from his open mouth. Finally, the glowing, supercharged orbs spun around and sped down the tunnel, streams of electricity arcing back and forth between them as they hurled toward the robotic terror.

The discharge was severe. A bright blast exploded as the glowing orbs struck TOM 23. The electrical attack was so fierce that the Reaper Kai clutched in TOM 23's hand rocked back and forth as the surge of power rushed through the machine and into his body. Screaming, the Reaper Kai let out a final cry as his body erupted into flame, much of it disintegrating in the fierce electrical attack. A shower of ash and steaming bone rained down in a clatter.

TOM 23 took the brunt of the attack. As the orbs of searing power dissipated, a shower of sparks and molten metal exploded from the automaton's chest. A gaping, jagged wound had been torn through TOM 23's armor, leaving only a smoking crater in the once pristine, black exoskeleton.

The processor bank atop the metallic terror's back suffered enormous damage. The array of processors and circuit boards clinging together in a thick mass melted and fused. A horrible burning smell filled the tunnel as the robotic terror staggered back and forth. Temporarily stunned, it crashed to the floor. For the time being, the ancient terror was subdued.

The Reaper Kai forces regrouped, stunned by the hectic battle and horrific display of demonic energy so crudely expunged in a desperate act of survival. Standing around the gigantic battle machine, the Reaper Kai smiled smugly, huddling over their kill like proud hunters.

"Component failure. External processor damage. Power reroute to primary systems. Weapon systems online. Primary task: Exterminate intruders. Processor failure. Processor failure. Secondary task: Initiate Repairs." A mechanical voice filled the air. Eyeing the downed monstrosity in alarm, the Reaper Kai backed away. TOM 23 was injured but by no means defeated. Rising from the floor, the confused robot turned on its sensors and scanned the room. As it registered the Biogtech soldiers, TOM 23 became suddenly fixated upon the primitive assault robots. `"Suitable replacement parts located. Biogtech replacement parts identified. Initiate component harvesting."`

A whirring noise erupted. Raising its arm, the ancient menace targeted the Biogtech soldiers giggling mindlessly in the tunnel as their stunned masters froze in indecision. Enormous capacitors inside the robot began to charge, storing massive amounts of energy. As the capacitors charged, a tube upon TOM 23's arm began to glow. A warm green light lit the room. Diving for cover, the priests tried to avoid the powerful weapon.

Crackling, the enormous laser opened fire, creating a solid stream of burning radiation and devastating heat. Targeting the army of Biogtech soldiers, the enormous robot passed the laser back and forth, cutting a swath through the room with the super-heated beam. Like a hot knife through butter, the green laser cut the robotic soldiers in half, melting most of them into puddles of liquefied plastic.

While one arm brutally eradicated the Reaper Kai army, TOM 23's other arm sprung to life. An enormous rotary machine gun rotated and began to hum with sinister intensity. Hundreds of rounds of heavy machine gunfire were targeted at the Biogtechs and Reaper Kai alike. Mowing through the room, the rotary weapon left devastation and horrendous bloodshed in its wake.

Though they made a feeble attempt to defend themselves, the overpowered Reaper Kai were too stunned to respond. They shielded their faces with their hands, but the high caliber bullets tore right through them, shredding flesh and splintering bone. Moving back and forth, the machine gun killed without recourse.

Several Reaper Kai attempting to flee the scene were utterly disintegrated. The high-powered green laser struck their flesh and turned several of them to steaming vapor, their bodies scorched beyond recognition.

Hidden within the wall, Lavosi was in no hurry to depart. He was fascinated by the results of the Reaper Kai's encounter with the death machine, and enthralled by the results. After hiding within the crevice, Lavosi had closed his eyes. Listening to the sounds of battle, the vile monarch found much pleasure. His twisted mind reaped comfort from screams of agony. Smiling, Lavosi knew that his plan was coming to fruition. With half of the Reaper Kai forces currently in the process of being slaughtered, Lavosi was bolstered with a wash of elation.

War has but a single premise: divide and conquer. Lavosi had perfected this tactic, having split the Reaper Kai expedition in two pieces, leading half of them to their doom.

As the sounds of battle died down, Lavosi moved deeper into the air vent, edging away from the massacre. Pleased by his wicked act, he moved through the wall along the air vent, passing toward the remaining Reaper Kai forces in the control room. There were others to murder, thought Lavosi, a comforting thought for a creature completely devoid of all morality. Leaving the scene, Lavosi left TOM 23 amongst the scattered remains of the brutal massacre.

The battle, or rather slaughter, lasted but a fleeting moment. In the span of mere minutes, over fifty Biogtech soldiers and eight Reaper Kai priests had been torn asunder, ruthlessly murdered by the ancient death machine.

"Intruders   Exterminated.   Initiate repairs.   Suitable   replacement   parts identified," TOM 23 whispered, viewing the carnage.

Standing over their bodies, the robotic menace brooded. It was also vexed to see its damaged processor core hanging outside its body. The loneliness of its existence had been replaced by a seething anger. As it examined the remains of the Biogtechs, a glimmer lit its single crimson eye. Grasping the remains of the Biogtech soldiers, TOM 23 began to dissect them, collecting any electrical components that had survived the assault. Several smaller arms erupted from TOM 23's back to grasp the fresh parts. With a grim determination, the ancient menace began to graft the components onto its processor core.

The smaller arms worked feverously, soldering the parts in place. Dozens of control boards and processors harvested from the slain Biogtechs were incorporated into the robot's processor core. With each additional component, the monstrosity became cleverer and more dangerous. Each processor board added power to the robot. The mass of boards began to whir and pop as power surged through them. Acting as a primitive generator, the host of electrical boards gave the metallic beast additional computing power. Where once it had but primitive emotion, the newly harvested parts were allowing more cohesive thought to form.

TOM 23 examined its own body, finding it could now sustain more elaborate and complex cognition. Awe and wonder filled the creature. Looking at its own hand, it flexed it repeatedly, now aware of its own existence more than ever. Seeing the dead Biogtechs whose components had breathed additional life into TOM 23, it hungered for more. The feeling of awareness was unprecedented. Though still lonely, the new level of consciousness provided by the harvested parts made the loneliness easier to bear. Hungering for more power, more awareness of self, TOM 23 sought to search the rest of the military base. Maybe there were more Biogtechs to plunder…

Chapter 5
Collapse of Power

Staggering, the man breathed heavily as dizziness filled him. The loss of blood was severe and he knew that death was near. Garbed in blood-red robes, Brother Noxium, leader of the Reaper Kai expedition, took his final step and collapsed to his knees. He gritted his teeth in an attempt to weather the intense pain in his stomach, which was almost causing him to black out as he crawled across the cold steel floor.

His breathing was slowing considerably. The blood loss from his wounds had made his pulse sluggish. Reaching the corroded steel wall, the veteran war priest struggled for a brief moment, finally coming to rest with his back against the wall. A sigh of anger escaped his mouth as his right hand probed the wounds on his stomach. Blood, warm blood, instantly covered his hand, having already soaked through his robes. Lifting his hand, Noxium shuddered as he saw the life-force ebb from his body. He was dying and he knew it.

In the cold of the abandoned tunnel, the priest exhaled and watched with fascination as his breath froze in the air, creating a trail of mist from his mouth. Thinking about his coming death, Noxium focused on his pulse. With each breath, it was getting weaker, becoming more labored. Each time he exhaled, warmth from his body was expunged and was not restored. Slowly, his body was growing cold.

The events of the day that had led to his fatal condition swirled violently in his mind. Noxium and his companions had been ambushed unexpectedly by a steel behemoth hailing from the tunnels of the ruins. In the chaos and ensuing battle, or rather slaughter, Noxium slipped away into the background, fleeing the scene of carnage. Though his intentions had been to escape quickly and emerge unscathed, Noxium was severely wounded in the exchange, having been the indiscriminate victim of heavy machine gun fire that spewed forth from the metallic monster.

Thinking back to the destroyed expedition filled Noxium with a childish feeling of self pity. The priest was so convinced of their success in locating and obtaining a nuclear weapon that he had never sent word to the Reaper Kai high command about their mission. Noxium was last of the Reaper Kai with any knowledge of the northlands and the military base. The secret would die with him.

Shaking his head in frustration, Noxium suddenly became aware that he was no longer alone.

Turning his head, the priest looked down the tunnel. The dull yellow, grungy overhead lights were flickering as Noxium viewed the newcomers to the military base who had deftly crept up on his position. The Reaper Kai priest looked upon them with a cryptic smile, dryly laughing at the scene before him.

A long, silver revolver was pointed at him. A man with dark eyes and a jagged scar upon his face watched the veteran priest with disdain as he clutched the firearm. Wearing a black cowboy hat, a brown duster and camouflaged combat fatigues, the motley mercenary was an odd sight. The newcomer had a poised confidence in his demeanor. The gunman had experienced much in his life and was a formidable presence.

Behind the mercenary were three others.

A tribal warrior, dressed in combat attire and a winter coat made of animal furs, was stationed close by. His features were young, almost childlike, but his eyes were tortured, filled with indecision and a simmering rage. The boy was still new to the world but he had seen much conflict and strife. A garish wooden totem hung around his neck, a bird form with red, hungering eyes. Clutched in the warrior's hand was a pristine, ancient weapon. The sword, even in the grungy yellow light of the tunnel, glowed with a metallic blue sheen as the tribal warrior held it at the ready.

Standing next to the tribal warrior was a small figure. Another mere boy stood with his submachine gun ready, training the gun sights upon Noxium's chest. Resting behind the weapon's sights was a pair of wire-rimmed spectacles, resting on the nose of the young scholar. His green eyes, ripe with wonder and ambition for knowledge, were Noxium's first, overwhelming impression of the boy. The youth was obsessed with scholarly pursuits, preferring a good book over any other activity. Though somewhat meek in appearance, the tribal youth was formidable nonetheless, possessing immense mental strength to compensate for his lack of raw physical prowess.

Finally, a beautiful woman filled with heavenly grace came into view. Brilliant blue eyes were framed by her dark skin, shining outward with pristine allure. Noxium knew her immediately; she had once been the head diplomat of the Reaper Kai Empire. Now she was a traitor to the Dark Order, an outsider who had sacrificed her own soul to lift it from the darkness. No longer did wickedness mark the woman. Anger and malice had been driven from her consciousness and now she was filled with a primordial love, a primitive sense of justice that was hungering to evolve. Calmly, the righteous woman eyed Noxium, her hands intertwining as she stood in the cold tunnel, garbed in royal blue robes.

Coughing, Noxium gagged and a stream of blood and drool erupted from his mouth, running down his chin and finally disappearing onto his crimson robes. As the coughing subsided, Noxium laughed dryly as he viewed the mercenary team brooding over him.

"The legendary Banion O'Neil, if I am not mistaken?" he quizzed the lead mercenary still training his revolver on him.

The man nodded back in recognition, confirming his identity. Noxium laughed again, gripped by irony. "I have been searching for you and your wretched companions for nearly a year. The night after the fall of Rasheed, I was given orders by Father Vertigo himself to kill all of you. We scoured the wasteland for months, trying to catch a whisper of your passing. Every lead and every clue resulted in nothing. There was never a glimmer of your presence. The game of cat and mouse we played, racing across the entire continent, is finally over. It's somewhat ironic that when we

finally meet, I am at a serious disadvantage. I am dying and nothing
can avert that fate. You can put your weapons away; my wounds
will take my life. I assure you, I am in no condition for conflict."
Gasping, Noxium coughed again and another thin stream of blood
dribbled from his open mouth.

Banion did not respond to the order. Instead he held the
revolver defiantly in front of him, still training the weapon upon the
Reaper Kai's chest.

The priest's coy demeanor quickly turned to rage. The
thought of his own death became like a spike of thunder in his heart,
bringing a fresh jolt of life into him. This renewed vigor erupted
from him in a stream of spiteful words. "Now that I have finally
met you, I am in shock. I am in shock that anyone could find favor
in you. I don't see a powerful band of mercenaries before me but
rather a simplistic group of gamblers, gamblers with luck on their
side and nothing more. And to think that the people of the Darken
Realm sing your praises as liberators! If they could see you now, I
think they would laugh at you. They would pity you as fools, not
heroes!"

"Where are your friends? Where are your companions? If
you're so strong, where are the rest of you?" Banion shot back with
ice in his tone.

"I sense no other Reaper Kai around us." Mineera spoke in a
whisper. "He is alone in life within these ruins. Soon he shall be in
the company of his kin in death."

Noxium grew silent for a brief moment. Dizziness was
filling him again. The blood loss was now at dangerous levels and
his death would not hold off for long. Mustering another burst of
strength, Noxium spoke once more. "What hope do you have?" He
laughed dryly.

His cryptic words hung in the air as he stared at them with
despair, life-force beginning to wane. Closing his eyes, his head fell
forward. Death was close. His hands were chilled and his body,
too, was growing cold.

"What hope do you have?" he rasped again with a desperate
laugh. The loss of blood had taken its toll upon him. His sanity had
gone and his body was shutting down. "The ancients were wise but
reckless. The creature they left within these tunnels is fierce. An

entire army of my kind is entombed within these tunnels. If an army of my kind was too weak to stand against the guardian of this place, what hope do you have? What hope do only four have against such a fearsome foe?" Noxium blinked quickly as his vision began to blur. He was truly at death's door now.

The team did not respond; instead, they looked on with a sense of irreverence. The wicked man before them did not deserve their concern.

"I have failed..." Noxium gasped. "I was too sure of our own success. I never sent word to our order about these ruins. None of the other Reaper Kai even know where our expedition went. I was too sure of our success... I am the last of my kind that even knows of this place... The secret will die with me..." Rasping once more, he gagged and spoke one last time. "The secret will die with you..." he stated with a strange certainty, staring at Nova 7 with hatred until his body failed.

The fire went out of him. Slumping, Noxium fell over and passed into death, his fearsome wounds consuming his life.

Nova 7 stood silently in the tunnel, viewing their hated enemy with a mixture of pity and respect. Seeing his wounds and the fear in his eyes as he spoke of the tunnels, the team was gripped with indecision and doubt. If the sentinel of the ruins could destroy an entire army of Biogtechs and over a dozen Reaper Kai priests, what hope did the team have?

Stepping past the dead Reaper Kai, Nova 7 followed a trail of carnage deeper into the ruins. In the dim, flickering yellow light, the scene was horrific. The further they passed, the more signs of conflict littered their path. At a junction of tunnels, a desperate last stand had been made. Six Reaper Kai priests had been dismembered and shredded by gunfire. Twenty Biogtechs had been burned and melted, leaving congealed puddles of melted plastic. The amount of carnage was staggering. To view the remains of such slaughter was a sickening sight. Though horrified, curiosity got the better of Nova 7. Stopping at the junction of tunnels, the team took a brief moment to survey the scene of recent conflict.

Tani was the first to notice that something was out of place. With a confused look, the tribal scholar dropped to one knee. Grabbing a Biogtech, he examined several curious wounds on the chest of the destroyed robot. His stumpy fingers passed over the breastplate of the fallen mechanical soldier and found what appeared to be damage caused by a cutting torch.

"What the hell?" Tani mouthed as his fingers probed the torch marks.

"What is it?' Banion asked, kneeing beside the tribal scholar.

"See these marks? Here upon the chest?" Tani motioned.

"Yeah?" Jared's nose scrunched up in incomprehension. "So what?"

"These marks were caused by a cutting torch," Tani said triumphantly.

"I don't get it." Mineera was also confused by the tribal's discovery.

"Whatever did this took a while. You don't just use a cutting torch in the middle of battle. Whatever caused this…" Tani pointed at the torch marks. "…took considerable time and patience to do so. The cuts are precise; it's amazing that anything could perform such cuts."

Standing up, Tani viewed other mangled Biogtechs. Moving quickly, he found that all of the Biogtechs had been cut apart and dissected with precision. "Look at this! All of these Biogtechs have been taken apart. Several key components have been removed."

"That doesn't make any sense. What would have cut them apart like this?" Banion questioned, finally understanding why Tani was disturbed by the discovery.

"Whatever killed them must have done this," Jared concluded.

Tani pushed his glasses up his nose, deep in thought. "It doesn't make any sense. Why would anything want to harvest computer and electrical components from dead Biogtechs?"

The question posed by the scholar was disturbing and filled each of them with a sense of the unknown. Wanting to further explore the scene, the team took a deep breath and prepared to investigate the dead Reaper Kai. Mustering their courage, they moved to view the remains of the Reaper Kai priests.

Several of the priests had been torn apart, their limbs scattered. Blood was coating the floor all around the scene.

Fighting back their revulsion, they made a quick examination of the slain Reaper Kai. Tani, being the most curious, came forward and knelt before several of the corpses. With a clinical detachment, he examined the bodies for signs of dissection after death. Though the wounds on the slain priests were horrendous, none of them had been dissected post-mortem.

"This is strange," Tani said. "None of the priests have similar wounds. Whatever ravaged the Biogtechs left the humans intact. *Something* is collecting electrical components."

"I don't like this one bit," Banion concluded, holstering his revolver and readying his assault rifle. The rest of the team followed their leader's example. Each of them brandished their own weapons. "Let's get out of here. The last thing we need is whatever did all of this coming back."

As the team pressed deeper into the ruins, the reality of their journey began to take shape in their minds. Having spent month after month traveling through the wasteland and ruins of old, Nova 7 had finally reached their objective. Somewhere in the abandoned military base was the artifact they sought. Somewhere in the ruins was the holy grail of ancient weapons.

Leaving the scene of carnage filled Nova 7 with indecision. It was a strange sensation. Their most hated enemy, the Reaper Kai, had failed in their quest for nuclear power. The entire expedition had been eradicated. This turn of events was a double-edged sword. Nova 7 no longer had to worry about the Reaper Kai getting the nuclear weapon, but whatever had destroyed them could easily destroy Nova 7, as well. Their original goal had not changed but the dynamics had. The game that they were playing had the same objective but now had different pieces, and perhaps even higher stakes.

Cautious but stalwart in their goal, Nova 7 set out to explore the abandoned military base, eager to learn the secrets hidden within.

Chapter 6
The Price of Victory

Jared was standing in the middle of the tunnel, his hands folded across his chest and a disgruntled expression on his face. He was mumbling something under his breath and refused to move on, brooding ominously and shaking his head in dismay.

Having continued on beyond the spot where he stood, the rest of Nova 7 stopped and turned to look at the tribal warrior. Each of them could tell that Jared had something on his mind and his inane mumbling was becoming disconcerting. Halting their advance into the heart of the military base, they each took a brief moment to confront Jared.

"What is it?" Banion asked harshly, irritated by his young ally's bizarre behavior.

Kneeling down in the passage, the tribal began to examine a skeleton. Tattered clothes surrounded the ancient pile of bones. Grabbing the skeleton, Jared viewed the remains with a distant look. The clothes were not that of a soldier; no uniform was in evidence. The attire of the old corpse appeared to be that of a treasure hunter. With a grim look and a shake of his head, he rooted through the dead man's possessions. A diary, written in some unknown language, was poking out of the corpse's pocket. Pulling the book free, he flipped through it, still shaking his head.

"What do you think this diary says?" His voice was perturbed and enigmatic "What goals did this man have? What desires brought him to this horrid place?" Smiling, he sighed and looked at the rest of Nova 7. "Greed can do strange things to a person. Driven by an insane lust for possessions and wealth, this man lost his life, hoping to find treasure in this place. All he found..." the tribal pointed to bullet holes in the man's clothes, "...was a horrid death. Greed led to this man's death. In a sense, greed is no different than obsession. Wanting something so badly can make you do unspeakable things." He looked directly at Banion as he unleashed the stinging words into the fetid air of the tunnels.

"What the hell does that mean?" Banion growled back, feeling that Jared's wrath had been directed at him.

"It's not too late to turn back," Jared said in an ominous tone. "We can still stop this insanity, right here, right now."

"What insanity?" Tani quizzed, moving closer to his friend to better address him.

"Mass murder," Mineera concluded, her voice cutting the air like a chilling whip. "Genocide."

Jared nodded at Mineera; she had understood his reservations all too well. "How long have we been out here?" he questioned.

"I don't know..." Tani said in a mystified tone. "Too long, I guess."

"Too long is right. What the hell are we doing here?" Jared pressed on.

"You know damn well what we're doing in here," Banion replied with venom in his tone. "Cut the crap and let's get moving."

"So that's it? Let's get going? What about the repercussions of our actions? What about that?" Jared lashed out.

"We don't have a choice!" the leader of Nova 7 shouted.

"No choice? We are only steps away from our grisly goal. Having battled across the world, we now stand only inches away from our objective. We have spent so much energy getting here; we never asked ourselves if we should even be here." Shaking his head, Jared spoke in a whisper. "It's not too late to turn back."

"We can't turn back. I can't allow it!" Banion shouted again. "We have to do the right thing. If we can't succeed, hundreds of thousands of people will die. You can take your self righteous pity and shove it, kid. We have a job to do and we're gonna do it."

"Of course we are going to finish this quest," Tani interjected suddenly, finally understanding his friend's argument and sticking up for him. "And if we succeed, the darkness wins. There is no righteous outcome to this struggle. The ancients used nuclear weapons recklessly. As a result, the entire world is still in ruin. We are heroes acting under the guise of liberty, but any army wielding such power can only be seen as butchers. Of course we have a job to do. But what is the price of such irresponsibility?"

"We are seeking the very power that brought the world to ruin. Such a prospect should be handled with careful consideration. If we do succeed, have we truly lost the battle? Is the slaughter of an entire race ever justified? Is a heartless act of genocide ever condoned? These are questions I have wrestled with over the entire journey. Now that we are on the threshold of victory, I am still unsure of our actions." Mineera brought all her wisdom and experience to her passionate address to the group. "I was once an agent of evil and would have never given a second thought to unleashing such power. But since my rise from the darkness, I have serious doubts. I doubt that such power should ever be unleashed. If we blindly stumble forward without morality guiding us, we will never reach the true end of the road."

Firing back, Banion was undaunted by his team's defiance. "I've lost everything that I ever loved due to the Reaper Kai. I was only a small child when my village was sacked and burned. My mother was slaughtered without a second thought. After that, I lived with Frank, my uncle in Dune Station. It took years for him to subdue the memories. Do you know how many nights my uncle spent with me as I cried myself to sleep? Do you know how hard it was to close my eyes and wash away the memories? Just when my soul came to rest, when I was truly free from those horrid visions, the Reaper Kai attacked us again, this time killing my uncle. Anyone know how hard it is to watch your only family beaten to death? After his death, I wandered the wasteland, killing for money. My road became a dark journey, living for the kill, hungering for nothing but death. By some miracle, this heartless existence was brought to a welcome end. By some twist of fate, I found love..." Breaking down, Banion began to shake his head back and forth. The vision of his beloved wife flashed through his mind. He welcomed the memory of her spirit, burning into his soul, and was lost for a brief moment in her loving smile as it flashed through his mind. Fighting back the tears, he looked at each member of Nova 7 in turn.

Staring back with silent gazes, they fought the emotion welling inside their hearts. Unable to avert their eyes from him, they lingered in his happiness and suffering, absorbing some of his joy and pain.

"Do you know why I kill?" His words cut the air like a razor. Jared, Tani, and Mineera stood transfixed, listening to his chilling message. "I kill to spare others. I kill to be merciful. Every monster I slay, every criminal I slaughter, gives hope to all those who are too weak to stand against the darkness. I have sacrificed my very soul to make sure no one else ever becomes like me. I would give everything I have to make sure that filth and terror are eradicated. If it takes the entire slaughter of a race of maniacs, I am prepared to lead that charge. I am prepared for whatever consequences arise. The Reaper Kai are insane monsters who deserve nothing but death. If I am to become an animal to kill another animal, so be it. I gladly sacrifice everything I have to see them destroyed."

His speech was so bold, so impassioned, the rest of the team could do nothing but hold back the flood of emotion inside of them. Silently they stood, absorbed in the reality unfolding before them.

Sighing, Jared rose from the floor, abandoning the skeleton that had given its life in ages past for the sake of ancient treasure. It was a tale with a chilling moral. The military base was not a place of wonder; it was a place of death. Instead of finding glory and plunder, all the would-be treasure hunters had been brutally slain. The base was a mausoleum, a monument to failed hope, a way to balance uncensored hate. Death ruled and was the only justice to be found in the sullen passages. An ancient machine, born from a hateful time, still lingered in the tunnels, acting as judge, jury, and executioner, ready to deal out punishment indiscriminately to those foolishly stumbling into its sinister lair.

Understanding Banion's emotion, Jared was cautious. However, still concerned, he pressed on with a reserved tone, not wanting to trivialize Banion's suffering. "I'm worried, Banion.

We've been in these tunnels for hours and hours. In every turn and passage we explore, there are more dead bodies, more signs of failure. Whatever lingers in this place can destroy an entire army. What hope do we have against such a foe?"

Mineera smiled, and took a step forward. Her gentle blue eyes shone as she pondered the idea of hope. With gentle grace guiding her, an explosion of exuberance rushed through her. Despair was not a part of her world, not any more. Calmly collecting herself, she surrendered her soul to faith and answered Jared's question.

"My entire life is a riddle. Every step I take can either lead me to the light or into shadow. Every step we make could be our last. I have reservations about the reason we are here. But every step I take further from the darkness leads me closer to home, a real home where I feel that I can truly live in peace. We have been out here for a long time. We have succeeded where others would have failed. I can't explain our condition, but it feels right to me. I have faith that we will not fail. It is a comforting thought even though it may be foolish, feeling that I am finally fulfilling my destiny. I feel that I have a place in this world. With all of you, I have a home. Do not fret, Jared, I have faith that we will succeed."

"Faith?" Tani snorted. "It will take more than faith to uncover the secrets of the ancients. Their power was forged from knowledge, not faith. Don't trust in anything but knowledge. Wisdom and intellect will be our savior in this place, not misplaced faith in a god long gone. We have all the pieces to the puzzle around us. All we need is to be smart enough to put them together. The ancients made whatever stalks these tunnels. Wisdom and technology made it; our intellect and understanding of science will undo it."

Watching Tani bicker with Mineera made Banion smile. With a dreamy look, the leader of Nova 7 pondered his team. It was a tiny, dysfunctional family, but it was still a family. Laughing at each of them made his spirit leap. They were all so different, each and every one of them. Each of them had different ideals and motives. A warm feeling washed over Banion as he looked at them. The road from his wife had been long. The tortured path was a winding journey through a dark forest filled with misery and suffering. Each of them, in a small way, had given him strength. Each of them had helped him to see that there was hope beyond the horizon. Watching them, Banion's usually hate-filled eyes were warm and filled with light. Fighting back a smile, he sighed and brought his hand to his chin. Rubbing the whiskers on his face, he conceded defeat and grinned at each of them.

Looking back with confused gazes, the other members of Nova 7 were in shock. The dour gunfighter was actually smiling at them. Stunned by his demeanor, each of them felt a smile grace their own lips. Watching them beam back at him made his heart lift. Banion was home again, amongst his companions. It felt wonderful to smile and feel laughter well up inside his soul. Only a few minutes ago, he was awash with anger, wanting to argue with his teammates. Now, he was happy to be alive and in the company of friends.

"Thanks." Banion smiled at his companions. "Even though this is a difficult place to be, I'm glad I am here with all of you. Thanks for giving me a home. It's been a long time…"

Turning away from them, he shouldered his assault rifle and began to push deeper into the military base.

Not sure what to think, Jared eyed Tani with concern. Banion was never happy. He was a brooding menace around which one had to walk on eggshells, taking care not to awaken the sleeping beast. It was uncharacteristic for him to smile, let alone say something nice. The tribals didn't trust him. Thinking he had lost his mind again, they both sighed and plodded on after him.

Mineera held her ground and let her senses stretch outward as the rest of the team moved on. A warm feeling filled the pit of her stomach as she focused on Banion. The smile had been genuine. His happiness was real. Shaking her head in surprise, Mineera felt her heart lift. If a person such as Banion, a person who had lost everything to reckless hate, could find happiness, there was hope, true hope for the world. If a crazed madman could find his way home, anyone could.

"Hey! Are you coming or what?" Tani shouted, trying to return Mineera back to real world.

Snapping out of her trance, she smiled. Mineera, too, was home. She had found a true home amongst her friends. Nodding her head in agreement, she moved off after the rest of the team, lost in thought but glad to be with her companions.

Chapter 7
The Last Step to Victory

Rubbing his eyes with the back of his hand, Banion yawned, then paused to stare at the tribal scholar. The leader of Nova 7 stepped over to stand behind him, curious to track his progress. The team, having made it to the main control room of the military base, had discovered that the Reaper Kai had made great steps in hacking into the base's defense systems. After removing several of the slain priests from the control room, they had set up shop with the intent of finishing their work.

Tani had spent the last four days sitting behind multiple computer terminals trying to uncover the secrets of the military base. The rest of the team had spent the time lazing around and telling stories. None of them had been courageous enough to explore the southern passages of the military base. On their first day in the ruins, they had encountered multiple corpses towards the southern end of the ruins. Knowing that an ancient menace still dwelled within the passages, they had stayed away in hope of avoiding the lurking terror.

Observing Tani's progress with bleary eyes, Banion tried to discern what the tribal genius was doing. A series of windows were littering the multiple screens and Tani was staring intently at the information on each screen. He was so absorbed in his work, he never even noticed that Banion had crept behind him and was staring over his shoulder.

"Any progress?" Banion asked, yawning again.

Tani did not respond; instead, he continued to bang away at the terminal, still oblivious to Banion's presence.

"Hey!" he shouted at the youth.

Startled, Tani jumped and spun around, blinking several times. "Wha... what?" he stammered.

Banion stared at Tani with a concerned look. Both of the tribal's green eyes were completely bloodshot, wreathed in pulsing red arteries. His face was pale and wasted. The tribal had not eaten since the day before and looked washed out, almost desiccated. The eye sockets around his blood-red eyes were sunken due to malnourishment. Instead of a brilliant genius, the youth looked more like a withered zombie, having just risen from the dead.

"Have you made any progress, Tani?" Banion asked, subdued, knowing full well that he finally had his companion's attention.

With a loud sigh, Tani collected his notes and began to rifle through them. Over twenty pages of scribbles accumulated as he sifted through them. After considering them, he started to summarize his findings.

"The Reaper Kai technicians did a wonderful job. They managed to hack through the first three layers of passwords. After examining what they did, I know that we have access to everything in this base except the weapon storage vault. I need to breach the password structure in order to continue. Once we're past the last defenses, we should have full reign over the computer network."

Banion simply raised a brow as he listened to the youth relate his progress. Unable to comprehend the details, he focused on getting an estimate. "How much time is this going to take?"

"Well, I have to keep rebooting the system. Every time I use failed password attempts, the system begins to lock down more of itself. I didn't see it at first. I locked out four of the six accounts able to open the nuclear storage vault. Now I've been resetting them after a single failed attempt and trying to bring the server back online. I have confidence that I won't permanently disable the system but it takes a long time to hack in." Pondering the situation for a moment, Tani took a breath and continued his analysis. "Good thing the Reaper Kai left all their gear and computers. Without their hardware, I doubt that I would have ever made it this far."

"About how long will this take?" Banion pressed again, realizing the scholar had gotten so caught up in the process that he had completely forgotten Banion's original question.

"I would say no more than a week," Tani said triumphantly.

"A week?" Banion scowled. "You have got to be kidding!"

"You can't rush these things, Banion. If I disable all of the accounts, we will never get in. If you want this done right, it will take about a week to run all the combinations."

With a sigh and a roll of his eyes, Banion walked away from the scholar and moved across the room. Jared and Mineera were on the floor, chatting quietly in the corner, absorbed in each other's company.

Joining them, Banion sat on the floor and pressed his back up against the cold steel wall of the room. Taking off his hat, he yawned again and listened to his companions as a drowsy daze began to overtake him.

Jared, clearly amused, had a comical look on his face. He was in the middle of recounting a tale about his former mentor. "You should have seen the look on his face!" he laughed. "He was gasping and his face was bright red. His white hair was trembling with rage, flopping about as he scowled at us. I tried to stop from laughing but I couldn't help it. Master Mogi just stood there shouting at the both of us. Tani had run away, with the matches in his hand." Overcome by the comic tale, Jared was barely able to breath, submerging in the memory. "I can still see his face, and better yet, the holes in his clothes. After Tani set off the gun powder, the last thing I saw before he ran away was Mogi's clothes smoking and burning!"

Mineera was smiling broadly, absorbed in the tale, thinking about the event. She began to giggle and looked over at Tani still banging away at the computer across the room. Tani was ignoring the story but Mineera looked at him anyway. Some things would never change. The tribal was mischievous and had always had an affinity for fire. Even since he was a small child, Tani had been lighting things on fire, including their old mentor, Master Mogi.

"I bet he never turned his back on either of you ever again," Mineera concluded.

"You're right; he never did trust us again." Jared smiled warmly.

"Isn't it strange how memories are?" Mineera's expression was content and thoughtful. "Sometimes you remember flashes of sound or images; sometimes it's an odor or smell."

"My mother always made flatbread cakes. She would pull them out of the oven and I can remember the warm sweet smell," Jared added with a smile. "I can't even remember what the damn cake tastes like, just the smell. It is strange how you can only remember certain sensations and not the entire memory."

A silence rose between them after the completion of the story. Their thoughts were lingering on happy times, memories of joy. Banion broke the silence. With a distant, dreamy look, he began to speak in a near-whisper.

"My mother always made cookies." His gaze was opaque. "I can't remember what my mother looked like." The statement was so matter-of-fact and out of context that Jared and Mineera simply looked at him, reluctant to speak. They were transfixed, neither of them daring to interrupt him. "It's a strange thing. I can remember the sound of her voice, sitting on her lap, the smell of the cookies she used to make, but I can't remember what she looks like. Isn't that terrible?" His voice was defeated. "I can't remember what my mother looked like."

Averting their gaze, Jared and Mineera hesitated to contribute to the conversation. It was not Banion's nature to speak of such things. Both knew that speaking of Banion's mother was a sore subject, a subject that often made Banion erupt in violent anger whenever it was brought to light.

"I spent my whole life trying to forget that day my mother died. I have spent my entire life fighting the nightmares, hiding from my own heart and soul. I have battled to forget the day that she died. In doing so, I have forgotten her; I have forgotten my own mother." As he shook his head, a dry maniacal laugh erupted from him and his eyes flashed with madness. "What did she look like? Why can't I remember her?"

Mineera looked at him with compassion and addressed him, as Jared remained silent and watched on with rapt curiosity. "Close your eyes," she coaxed him.

"What?" he countered.

"Close your eyes," she repeated.

Hesitantly, he closed his eyes.

Closing her own eyes, Mineera reached forward and grabbed his hand. He recoiled from her touch, staring at her with brief, instinctual resistance. She opened her eyes and looked back with heartfelt compassion. They stared at each other for a brief moment. Finally, he decided to trust her and yielded to her command.

They closed their eyes once more and she cradled his hand in her own. Stretching out, she began to feel his consciousness. Flashes of sound and images began to fill her. A jolt of panic and fear rolled through her as sadness and hatred rushed into her consciousness. Fighting back the flood of evil emotions, she battled back with all of her might. Focusing on his past, she tried to force her senses to reach his childhood. Finally, through the haze and shadow, she felt a rush of awareness as her psychic abilities found what she was looking for.

Harnessing the recollection, she began to whisper, speaking to Banion, calling out his memories…

A little boy, only four years of age, with long, wavy hair was stalking across the kitchen like an animal. Walking silently, the child had a wild gaze on his face. Looking around the doorway, he could see his mother, standing near the wood- burning stove.

She had a long flowing dress, brown in color, with white flowers. An apron was wrapped around her waist. Long black hair hung down just past her shoulders. She was holding a wooden spoon and was stirring something in the pot on the stove.

Young Banion saw her and crept closer and closer. Holding his hands up in the air with fingers curled, he was imagining that he was a bear. Stalking closer and closer, the youth moved stealthily. Sensing her son behind her, Banion's mother smiled and crooked her head, watching him out of the corner of her eye.

When he was only a foot away from her, young Banion rushed forward, growling like a wild animal. He charged her, grabbing her legs. Screeching, the woman feigned surprise and alarm, clutching her hand to her chest in mock-terror.

Laughing in glee, young Banion hugged his mom's legs. She reached down and scooped him off the ground. Clutching him tightly, she tickled him repeatedly. The giggling turned to all-out laughter as Banion tried to wiggle free of her grasp. Hugging him, she looked into his eyes. Young Banion looked back.

Banion's mother had delicate features. Her chin was narrow and she had a pretty smile. Small wrinkles were etched around her mouth. With each laugh, the creases would grow, signs that she had spent most of her life with a smile on her face. High cheekbones, covered in freckles, were set against her rosy cheeks. Above her cheeks were her soft eyes. Emanating warmth, she looked at her boy with pure love.

Banion looked back, seeing his mother in the world of dreams. He could see her face again, a glimmer of the past. As the dream and memory began to fade, her face became distorted, growing ever more distant by the second. Trying to focus on her face, he could not. The only thing that remained was a feeling. Remembering her love put him at peace. Even though he could not see her, he could feel her love, her warmth.

Opening his eyes, Banion blinked several times. Jared was looking at him with concern. Mineera, still clutching his hand, had a smile on her lips. Shaking her head, she broke free of the drowsiness induced by the use of her psychic powers. As her blue eyes opened, she gazed at Banion. He looked back and drew his hand away from her. Nodding in appreciation, he thanked her silently. Smiling back, she acknowledged him.

"I got it!" Tani yelled in excitement, startling the rest of the team. Spinning to face him, they eyed him with unease. "I broke through the password security level. I've been granted level four security access to the server."

Elated by the discovery, the rest of his companions came to Tani's side.

He was banging away at the keyboard, trembling in excitement. "Here it is! The weapons inventory!"

Crowding around the terminal, the team stared in wonder. The cursor flew across the screen. Tani accessed the weapon inventory onsite. A series of windows opened on the screen, revealing a listing of armaments. Anything from ammunition to artillery rounds was fully specified on the screen. As they scanned the list frantically, a ripple of alarm and wonder lit their faces. At the bottom of the screen was an option. The cursor fell across the command: "Nuclear Warhead Arsenal." As Tani selected the option, the team held their breath. Was this finally it? Was this the end of the road?

Several seconds passed and the inventory popped onto the screen. The arsenal of existing weapons was sparse; only three nuclear warheads still remained in the arsenal. Blinking several times, Tani turned around and looked at Banion in disbelief.

"There are three warheads still here..." Tani spoke in a whisper. "Still here, after all this time."

Jared looked at Mineera in alarm and she looked back, equally horrified. It was no longer a myth, but a reality; the military base contained the power that had brought the world to ruin. The reckless power of the ancients had survived the passage of time.

Shaking, Tani viewed the options on the screen. As he was scanning the selections, he caught sight of a diagnostics option. With a press of the button, another screen came into view. His heart pounding wildly, Tani initiated the diagnostics option on the screen. The flashing cursor rotated as the computer tapped into the nuclear weapons in storage.

Drumming his stumpy fingers on the desk, the scholar waited in breathless anticipation as the computer checked the remaining warheads.

The tension materialized into a horrifying truth. As the diagnostic ended, a frightful reality was made concrete. The results flashed on the screen and Tani's eyes scanned the text with hurried glances. Warhead number one was not responding; the diagnostic was not able to access the device. It was beyond repair and would not function. Warhead number two had a fried trigger and could not be used. Warhead three, warhead three on the other hand, had a different diagnosis.

A series of commands appeared on the screen as the diagnostic was completed for the third warhead.

Tani stopped breathing. For a split second, time did not exist. Reading the script over and over again, Tani was stunned. Warhead three was intact; the weapon was viable and fully functional.

"It can't be!" Tani gasped.

"What?" Jared said, moving closer to the screen.

"We did it..." Tani spoke in a whisper. "We found a fully functional nuclear warhead."

A silence filled the room. Their hearts were pounding. They had done the impossible; Nova 7 had located a fully functional nuclear warhead. Trembling, each of them stared at the screen with a lump in their throats.

"I can't believe it," Banion declared with sheer amazement. "After all this time, we finally did it."

However, the elation of their find was to be short lived. With overwhelming excitement, Tani scanned the list of options and selected the *recover warhead* option. Clicking the option, Tani almost ripped his own hair out. The screen flashed back that access was denied; opening of the nuclear warhead storage vault was only allowed through the terminal outside the vault.

"Damn!" Tani yelled. "We can't do it remotely. We have to go into the tunnels."

"Which tunnel?" Jared asked in trepidation, remembering all of the corpses littering the southern tunnels. Even though he had posed the question, the tribal warrior had a sinking suspicion where they needed to go.

Accessing the map, Tani shook his head in disgust. "The warhead vault is in the southern tunnels, where we saw all the corpses."

Slapping Tani on the shoulder, Banion spoke in a commanding tone. "Everyone get your gear. We're finishing this insane quest right now."

Nova 7 grabbed their gear and exited the control room. Heading toward the junction of passageways, each of them felt apprehension rise in their hearts. The fearsome guardian, a beast which they had yet to see, was probably in the southern tunnels littered with the dead.

The quest was almost at an end, but it had never been more dangerous. One wrong move and Nova 7 would meet a gruesome fate at the hands of the robotic monster still lingering in the abandoned tunnels.

Chapter 8
The Breaking Point

Trembling, the soldier looked around in every direction. In the dim light, his eyes darted back and forth as he tried to estimate where the enemy was hiding. Covered in blood, the soldier was on the verge of screaming in terror.

His breathing heavy, he fumbled for a weapon, anything he could find to protect himself from the hidden menace. As he tried to slow his breath, the only thing he could hear was the pounding of his own blood, booming in his ears with frantic surges. Spinning from side to side, the man remained disoriented. His long-time friend from childhood, another soldier who had been drafted into the mighty Iron Kai army, was lying dead only a few feet away. His throat had been brutally slashed.

Fidgeting with his pistol in the dim light, the soldier could feel his friend's blood beginning to cool on his skin. Only a few moments prior, he had literally stumbled upon his friend, falling to the ground, and landing upon his slowly cooling corpse. The discovery was so grisly, so unexpected, the soldier's mind had shut down. Panic and disbelief were his only companions.

The young soldier, only in his early twenties, had spent the evening in an abandoned office building with his squad. Far from the front lines, the foolish Iron Kai soldiers thought they were safe. The squad was horribly mistaken. Private Hughes had taken but a brief break to step away into the rubble and ruins to relieve his bladder. Moments passed into minutes and the squad leader became somewhat suspicious. Knowing that the two soldiers were friends from way back, the squad sergeant had sent Private Embry to search for his lost friend. It hadn't taken long for Embry to find Hughes, horribly murdered and utterly lifeless.

The events played out in Private Embry's mind again and again. Only a few minutes ago, the two were laughing about old times. Now his friend was a silent corpse, another victim fed to the brutal Reaper Kai war machine.

Trying to snap out of the daydream, Embry forced his thoughts to the task at hand. *Whatever* had killed Hughes was probably close by. With a shaky hand, Embry pulled the slide back on his pistol, chambering a round into the breach. He was so out of touch, he hadn't realized that the gun was ready to go. As the slide flew back, an unspent bullet launched outward, landing near his dead friend. Seeing the bullet eject filled Embry with even greater fear. He had only been in the city for a week and had not yet seen real combat. Seeing his own foolish action made him feel green, real green.

Though still stunned by the recent events, the soldier tried to regain his bearings. He had wandered not more than fifty yards from his squad. Breathing slowly, the young soldier concentrated on the task still facing him—reaching his squad without being killed by whatever was lurking in the office building.

Holding his pistol with both hands, he pointed the weapon toward the doorway. With cautious but controlled moves, he edged forward. After nearing the doorway, he burst through, training his weapon on anything that seemed dangerous. The room he entered was clear but still almost pitch black. The night had stolen the light, especially since he was near the interior of the building, far away from the windows. No enemies could be seen lurking in the shadows.

Gaining more confidence by the minute, Embry moved forward quickly, breaching the next series of rooms within a few seconds. As he traveled closer to his squad with each moment, his heart began to lift. Salvation and safety were near.

Finally, with an exuberant push, Embry reached the room in which his squad was stationed. His excitement was short lived. As he burst into the room, which was illuminated only by a small lantern, he slipped on the floor. His combat boot flew forward as his momentum carried him in the same direction. Losing his footing, Embry crashed to the ground. As he tried to regain his bearings, his gaze shifted to his boot-clad feet. Blood, bright red blood and other fluids were coating his combat boot. In confusion, he looked at the ground. A streaked, bloody mess covered the floor. As he spun around in growing panic, he spotted another member of his squad slumped against the wall, his stomach horribly bloodied.

Viewing the dead soldier stirred a primitive need to survive in Embry. First his good buddy, and now another member of his squad lay dead. Jumping to his feet, adrenaline hit his system once more. There was no thought of retribution. The primal need to run was his only thought. Bolting through the room, he caught sight of the other members of his squad out of the corner of his eye. He didn't need to look at them to know what had happened.

Bursting into the next room, Embry sought to reach the staircase, the only means of escaping the eleventh floor of the office building. If he couldn't reach the stairs, he *knew* death was soon to follow.

Ahead of him, in the darkness, a form was crouched over his sergeant. Embry stopped dead in his tracks. Kneeling with a blood-stained knife in his hand, a form dressed in blood-red robes was just finishing butchering the sergeant. As the malevolent figure sawed away at the soldier with quick jabs, the Iron Kai officer ceased to stir.

Embry simply looked on in horrid fascination. Is that what the priest was going to do to him? Was he going to be captured and butchered like a helpless sheep? Shaking his head in fear, he raised his arm, brandishing the pistol and taking aim at the Reaper Kai priest.

The priest, well aware of his presence, was undaunted. He was extremely good at his job, sneaking into enemy strongholds at night and killing the soldiers one by one. The sinister harbinger of darkness had not finished his job. Ignoring the frightened soldier, he continued to shred the sergeant's corpse.

Embry took shaky steps backwards. He wanted to fire his weapon with all of his might. He wanted to kill the horrid agent of evil, but he couldn't. Fear is a deep-seated emotion; it does not care about logic, nor does it respond to reason. One can think about what needs to be done, but in a life-and-death struggle, the mind cannot control the body. The body wants to flee, it wants to save itself. No matter how hard you try to fight the dread mounting in your soul, you are powerless to stop it. Embry wanted to fire but couldn't. The scenes he had witnessed had turned his body into a limp pool of frightful indecision.

"You would like to kill me, wouldn't you?" The Reaper Kai continued to make his cuts. Turning his head, he looked out from beneath his hooded cloak. Harsh eyes, cold and uncaring, stared out at Embry. "I assure you, I am extremely good at what I do."

Shaking, Embry tried with all of his might to pull the trigger. Even as he flexed his muscles in his arm, his trigger finger did not respond. He was unable to end the priest's life.

"Are you having problems?" Smiling, the priest rose from the dead sergeant. Blood dripped from the saw-like knife in his hand. "You are severely outmatched. You know how many troops I have butchered since the siege of this city began?"

Shaking his head, Embry took a step backwards. His arm felt like ice, as if hundreds of tiny icicles were piercing his flesh. The sensation increased, numbing his arm further. The gun, his only way to defend himself, fell to the floor as his arm grew totally numb.

"Can you feel it? Can you smell your own death?" Moving forward slowly, the priest was no longer smiling. Instead, he had a callous look, predatory and sinister. "Don't be afraid. The sensations you will feel as I cut your flesh are something to be enjoyed. I like to think of myself as an artist. I will teach you new sensations before you die. In fact, you should be honored. You will be my newest masterpiece."

Shaking his head, Embry looked at his pistol on the floor. He was defenseless; or was he? Staggering backwards, driven by fear and instinct, he fled the grisly scene. Running into the darkness, he fought to escape the butcher.

Seeing him flee filled the Reaper Kai with disgust. Dropping his head, he fell into a trance. The psychic merged dark prayer with the guided force it begat within him, channeling demonic power through his body. Tingling as he was infused by evil, the priest focused on his prey. The power moved forward and Embry felt a sting in his legs.

The icicles stung once more. Piercing cold spread out in his legs as they grew sluggish, unable to respond. Embry's muscles twitched uncontrollably and began to fail. Stumbling, he crashed to floor. The Reaper Kai was giving chase, bloody knife in hand, using his psychic powers to cripple the soldier's muscles.

"You know how long it took me to find my place? All of the other priests could summon fire and kill with a whisper. I could freeze a person's muscles, cripple and paralyze them. At first I felt it was a curse, but the longer I got to know my talent, the more I grew to enjoy it. I think of myself as a spider, something that hunts its prey with dedication and fierce cunning. Do not struggle; it only makes the death more offensive to me. Submit and you can enjoy the suffering."

Wanting to cry in terror, Embry continued to flee, crawling with his one good arm, the only limb that he could still move or control. Lurching across the floor like a cripple, he tried with all of his might to escape.

The priest edged toward him slowly with the blood-stained blade. With each step he moved closer, Embry was driven into a deeper panic. The primitive fear was replaced by a whimpering carnal need to flee.

Trying to find any defense he could utilize, Embry spotted the squad's radio. Moving toward it as quickly as he could, he fumbled with the transmitter. With a pitiful wail, he screamed into the radio, "Help me! Somebody help me!"

Tears streamed down his face. Turning onto his back, he caught sight of the Reaper Kai only a few steps away, holding the blade above him, taunting him with it. Screaming with all his might, Embry hoped someone would hear his pleas and rescue him, but to no avail; help was too far away to be of any benefit. Crouching down, the Reaper Kai priest drew his knife near his flesh…

"I can't listen to this anymore!" Emperor Gunther rose from his throne and rushed across the Truce Hall. He had been listening to the fearful screams of Private Embry as he was brutally butchered, his agonized death throes echoing through the radio.

Grabbing the electrical cord, he yanked it out of the wall. The radio fell silent. No longer did screams erupt from the device. With helpless rage filling him, Gunther threw the electrical cord to the floor. His fiery orange beard quivered as he gripped the radio with both hands, and a feral scream erupted as he threw the radio onto the floor. With a clatter, the instrument broke apart, fragments flying in every direction. Still venting his anger, Gunther kicked the remains of the radio with his foot. The remains landed in a pile of twisted metal and broken electrical boards on the opposite side of the room.

The war advisors were stunned by the outburst, viewing their leader in silent alarm. Blinking quickly, Gunther regained his composure, turning his gaze back toward his advisors.

"There is no decency in the enemy. It matters not what hopes and desires we have. No matter what we believe, our lives are forfeit. We are toyed with and treated like filthy animals. From this day forward, there will be no mercy. There will be no second chances. The Reaper Kai have taken much and I no longer care about justice. I want vengeance and I want their complete annihilation. No matter what the cost, I will ensure the entire race is slaughtered."

The advisors' expressions betrayed their anxiety.

"You all hear me?" he boomed again. "No matter what the cost, I will ensure that not a single Reaper Kai survives this war. I don't care about compassion any more. They treat us like animals; I will show them an animal. They drive us to death; I will give them the same. No matter what the cost, I will ensure all of them die!" Slamming his hand against the table one last time, he stormed out of the Truce Hall and into his private chambers.

The advisors looked on in shock, but all of them accepted both his analysis and his conclusion. Gunther had aptly summarized the situation. The cost and burden of the year-long war had been heavy. Each had known loss. Each had known grief. Their mighty leader, who was the most compassionate of all, had lost his way. They all knew he was traveling a dark road, but it didn't matter. All of them were on that same road, driven to the brink, forced to accept tragedy as a way of life. Although Gunther's rage was leading them all to a dark place, it was the only place to which they could travel.

All other avenues of diplomacy and compassion had failed. It was a harsh reality, but a primitive need to survive was all they had left.

Chapter 9
The Oracle of Justice

Staring into the fire, the aged man gave a loud sigh. Instead of in his warm home, he was in the middle of the barren desert, having made camp on a ridgeline above the great wastelands. The dim light cast by the flames revealed a face worn by many years. His hair was thin and strands of gray wreathed his head like a tattered halo. Rubbing his chin with his hand, he rested much of his weight on a grizzled, wooden staff.

Soft blue eyes with tinges of gray projected a fierce gaze. The man had seen many years of life, many of them without peace. In his youth, he had been a man of action, a man who had devoted his life to order. Having served as a local lawman for many years, the aged man had a long history of setting things right and had a knack for handling rough situations. In times of strife, he would manage to stride unharmed out of a dangerous situation in a way which seemed almost magical. Many of the locals knew it was more than magic. Being a direct descendant of a legend of the Darken Realm, the man was reputed to wield strange power. It was whispered that just like his ancestor, he was able to channel mystic energy and to interface directly with the spirit world.

The lawman was good at his job. Years turned to decades in which he continued to serve the township well. As the decades went on, the man found that he was less agile, easier to tire. As old age began to set in, he found himself at a crossroads in life. Still feeling the need to help people, he retired as the local lawman and spent his time counseling the people of his town. In his new role as a makeshift preacher, he grew to love his life anew.

Wisps of memory dwindled from the aged man's mind as he grew suddenly attuned to the natural world around him.

The night wore on at a dull pace. Having traveled the entire day by horse, his elderly body was feeling every mile of the trail he had traversed. His legs ached, feeling as if a horse had stepped on them. Dull throbbing pain coursed through his back, which had spent the entire day bouncing up and down in the saddle. His neck was agonizingly cramped. All in all, he was worn out and wanted nothing more than to fall asleep in a comfortable bed with a soft feather pillow. Vexed by the day's events, the aged man felt an urgent need to grumble.

Looking up at the night sky, his grumbling found an outlet as he began to taunt heaven itself. "Are you happy?" he spoke into the air around him. "I hope you are happy because I am not!"

The darkness responded with a chilling blast of wind. As it rolled around him like a vortex, the aged man covered his eyes to prevent the sand from gouging his eyeballs. The gale rose in intensity and howled across the barren landscape, growing fiercer by the minute.

Knowing full well that the strange event was more than just nature, Matthew Moralis prepared to be taught a lesson. Squinting in the blowing wind, he caught sight of a bright, glowing disk of light swirling just beyond the campfire. As he strained his eyes against the fierce wind, he could see the strange event unfolding near him. The shimmering disk of light began to rotate faster and faster. With each rotation, the disk emitted a brilliant pulse of burning light. Already seeing spots from the flashes of light, he made a conscious effort to observe the remainder of the strange light show unfold. Swirling around, the disk flashed quickly like a frantic strobe light, then began to expand and change configuration. Where once it was disk-shaped, the object was now crudely shaped like a human being. The wind stopped abruptly and Matthew opened his eyes hesitantly and viewed the strange form before him.

Standing taller than a normal man, the glowing entity had no concrete features, only a rough human outline. Sighing with displeasure, the aged man taunted the glowing form. "Why don't you just leave me alone? I've done all that you have asked. I left my home and have traveled out here into the wastelands in search of others like me."

The entity replied by speaking directly into the man's mind. *"I know of your strife. You have lived a peaceful life and have enriched your family with your tempered wisdom. While you have shown them a great capacity for love, you have much more inside of you. The peace you have cultivated is in mortal jeopardy. The agents of darkness care neither for your success nor for peace of any kind. It is for this reason that you were summoned to battle."*

"Why is it that you can't understand that I don't want any part of this war?" Grasping his staff tightly, he could feel his knuckles turning white under the sheer frustration he was feeling.

"It matters not what you want. The innocent need your help. If you do not lend aid, your own home will fall to the armies of darkness. It is simply a matter of time." Bobbing back and forth, the wispy white shade shimmered in the darkness as it spoke, directly forcing its words into the man's consciousness.

Feeling the wisdom of the entity, Matthew fell silent and gripped his head in his hands. Rubbing his temples lightly, he collected his thoughts. "I am too damn old for this. When I was young, I served my township and kept the peace. I would use my skills and powers to hold order. Now, I can barely ride my damn horse more than an hour without my bones aching. Surely there is another that can take my place?"

"Your wisdom and kind heart are the reasons you have been called to this place. It has taken you many moons to reach this sacred place within the desert. Your pilgrimage is warranted since there is not a shred of corruption within your heart. You have a pure soul, guided by justice and peace. You should be honored that you have been called."

"But why here? There is nothing out here in the desert. The only thing I see is the road that links the northern realm to the southlands beyond. I have rested here for many hours and know that the road is a dead one. Merchants no longer bring wares from the great northern forests to the city of Rasheed. Travelers no longer frequent the outposts and saloons in the Frontier. War has reduced this place to a lonely, barren, forgotten byway. I fail to see why you have brought me here. Why have you led me here with the dreams?"

"The road you survey does indeed lead into the northlands. You have been led here for a profound purpose. There are many others like you who have been summoned to battle. They are all on a pilgrimage of a different kind. A wise prophet, born from the darkness, will lead all of the oracles into battle. All of the others are moving to her. You have another road to follow before you meet them. The last great house in the realm, the Iron Kai, has been infiltrated by enemy agents. Festering within their mighty city is a host of assassins and saboteurs, ready to lay waste to the last bastion of freedom. If the Iron Kai are to withstand the coming darkness, their empire must be purged of the Dark Order. The road below leads into the northlands. You are to travel northwards into Iron Kai territory and purge their capital city of all these assassins."

A tremor of fear rolled through the man as the entity mentioned the Iron Kai. Shaking his head with displeasure, Matthew resisted the glowing form. "What makes you think the Iron Kai will trust someone like me? We share the same ancestors, my tribe and the Iron Kai. All of *my* kind, good or evil, were cast out of the empire many generations ago. There is still much mistrust. What makes you think that a descendant of the Reaper Kai like me will be accepted with open arms?"

"The legend of Ceibla Moralis is not known to the Iron Kai. Your lineage is not one of shadow but rather one that has resisted the darkness. Trust in yourself. The Iron Kai need your skill if they are to survive the growing shadow."

Shaking his head in disbelief, Matthew Moralis was stunned. "I am too old to take on Reaper Kai priests. This is madness."

"Your task is to find them. Root them out; leave them no place to hide. The Iron Kai will do the rest. Your powers are strong; use them well."

"It looks like I don't have a choice." Shaking his head once more, the aged man looked displeased.

"No, you are needed too desperately to resist," the entity confirmed.

"What am I to do if I survive this mess?"

"Your dreams will lead you to her, the prophet of Gogoli. From there, she will lead you."

As Matthew took a brief moment to collect his thoughts, the reality of the situation began to sink in. Denial faded gradually, and acceptance began to take shape in his mind. He knew what needed to be done. Finding wisdom in the spirit before him, he resolved to answer the call to duty. "I don't like this one bit. I would rather be sitting at home, in my rocking chair on the front porch." Sighing, he finally conceded defeat. "I will do what you have asked of me. I will travel to the city of Stonen and purge the foul Reaper Kai from the empire."

The entity nodded in appreciation of the man's sacrifice. As Matthew surveyed the glowing being, it began to fade into the darkness of the night. After the passing of the entity, the only thing that remained was the faint smell of roses, lightly tickling the aged man's nose.

When Matthew found himself alone in the darkness once more, he moved closer to his camp fire. Squatting down, he let the warmth of the flames wash over his aged bones. He rubbed his arms vigorously; the heat felt wonderful. Smiling in the darkness, Matthew felt at peace. He wasn't in his warm bed at home or even in his favorite rocking chair, but it didn't matter. He had been summoned to a higher purpose. Yielding to the thought of the strange journey ahead of him, the long-time peacekeeper knew that one last adventure would be a welcome way to ease into old age.

Looking down from the ridgeline, he eyed the lonely road stretching into the northlands. As he imagined the road ahead, he became drowsy. Blinking quickly several times, his weary body yielded to the fatigue gripping him. As he drifted off quietly, the Oracle of Justice fell asleep and dreamt of the adventure ahead of him.

Chapter 10
One Step Closer

With a gasp, Tani lurched backwards, a look of pure fright upon his face. The tribal scholar had slipped when he was descending into the hole in the floor. His grip loosened momentarily, and the rope slipped rapidly from the stumpy fingers of his right hand. Overcome by shock, he tried desperately to grasp the rope in his left hand. As his body gained momentum, falling deeper into the opening, the rope tore and dug into his left hand. The spines of the rope ripped into the skin, gouging flesh from the palm of his hand. The pain was intense. Yielding to the sensation in his left hand, Tani instinctively let go of the rope.

His green eyes widened as his companions looked on in horror. Falling backwards into the void, Tani let out a yelp. Though the free fall lasted only a few seconds, time seemed to freeze. A blast of adrenaline hit the scholar's system. Staring at Banion holding the rope, he was filled with an intense desire to be saved from the peril in which he had placed himself.

With a thud, Tani hit the ground below. As he landed on his back, his head whipped backwards and struck the concrete floor. Upon impact, his chest was jarred and he let out a gasp as all the air exited his lungs. For a brief second, he couldn't breathe; the jolt and the force of impact had literally taken his breath away.

Lying still upon the floor, Tani looked upwards into the opening and saw his concerned companions staring down into the opening. Blinking several times, Tani remained motionless.

"Are you all right?" Jared asked in alarm, staring down at his friend, lying still upon the floor down below the opening.

"Ughhh…" A primitive groan of pain escaped Tani as he pulled his battered body off the floor of the tunnel. Sitting up, he rubbed the back of his head. Already a lump had formed. There was a wet feeling as well. Retracting his hand, Tani stared at his own blood from the gash at the back of his head. "Great!" he said in an exasperated tone.

"You hurt yourself?" Mineera quizzed, concerned.

"What the hell does it look like?" Tani shot back, half embarrassed and half angry. His face turned bright red. He wanted nothing more than for his bruised body and his bruised ego to melt away into the dark tunnel he was now in. Frustrated with his clumsiness and his companions' concern, he shook his head angrily up at the opening in the ceiling.

"Stop screwing around, Tani." Banion spoke in a harsh tone. "Stop feeling sorry for yourself and get it done!"

"Are you kidding me?" Tani retorted, frustrated. "You're a real bastard, Banion."

"See? I told you he was all right," Banion said triumphantly to Mineera and Jared. They simply looked back with brows raised.

"You want me to come down?" Jared quizzed.

"No, no. I got it," Tani replied, his cheeks still burning with embarrassment. Rolling onto his knees, the scholar fumbled through his belongings and found his flashlight. As he flipped the switch, the light failed to come on. Rolling his eyes, the frustrated Tani smacked the light several times on the concrete floor. Suddenly, the flashlight sparked to life, bathing the tunnel in an eerie light. Rotating the light around, Tani inspected the passageway. The tunnel ran from west to east and the tribal could travel in both directions.

Fumbling in his belongings once more, Tani grabbed a crude map from his pocket. He shone the light onto the handwritten map, then turned to the east and began to count off his steps as he walked. Placing one foot in front of the other, he plodded slowly onward into the dark tunnel.

After discovering that the military installation still housed the prize of all prizes, the most sinister weapon ever created, Nova 7 had traveled into the southern tunnels in search of the nuclear warhead storage vault. Near a frightening array of corpses comprised of Reaper Kai and Biogtechs alike, the team located the storage room. Despite maintaining extreme caution and following Tani's directions, the mercenary team had nevertheless almost set off the alarm system outside the vault. Tani, who had been on the lookout for defense systems, had noticed the laser grid on the floor well before reaching the door.

After pondering the defense system, the team headed back to the control room. The tribal genius spent the rest of the day poring over internal maps and engineering schematics. After what seemed like an eternity, Tani had concocted a plan of action. The laser defense grid was fed by a power supply from one of the lower tunnels. He knew that the electrical lines were buried under almost a foot of concrete in the wall within the lower tunnel, but that fact didn't seem to discourage Tani one bit. He had always loved explosives and currently carried several bundles of them in his backpack.

The plan was simple: climb down into the lower tunnel, find the spot on the wall where the power cables feeding the laser grid were located, and plant the explosives on the wall. After detonating the charges, the explosion would sever the power supply to the defense system and allow the team to come close enough to the vault to use Tani's stolen access code.

The plan was supposed to be easy. But it had not taken into account Tani's loss of balance as he prepared to crawl into the lower tunnel, which had ultimately resulted in his fall.

Still counting his paces, Tani concentrated on the task at hand. Finally, he reached the appropriate spot in the tunnel. Looking at the wall, he estimated the location of the hidden electrical cables buried in its concrete depths.

Dropping to his knee, he opened his pack and recovered his demolition charges. He planted them midway up the wall, rigging the timer with a two minute delay. Satisfied with his work, he nodded in approval and started the timer on the explosive. Finally, Tani gathered his belongings and rushed back down the tunnel to the place where his friends awaited his return.

"Get ready!" Tani shouted. Covering his ears, he turned away from the eastern tunnel, then crouched down, closing his eyes and continuing to count down in his head. "Three… two… one…"

The timer expired and the demolition charges detonated. The blast was severe and a tremendous explosion echoed in the tunnels. A shockwave of concrete and debris was blasted free. A split second after the explosion went off, the scholar was on his feet. Rushing down the tunnel, he was eager to examine his handiwork.

Staring at the hole blasted in the concrete wall, Tani was elated to see mangled wiring, frayed and blasted apart in the void. His calculations had been correct; the power cable supplying the defense systems outside the nuclear warhead vault had been severed.

Tani cheered his own success silently, but his exuberance would be short lived. A tremor rocked the tunnel. Steadying himself, he scrunched up his nose in bewilderment and looked at the hole in the wall. The damage to the wall was severe, but by no means could have caused a tremor. As he surveyed the damage, perplexed, another tremor rocked the tunnel.

Spinning around, Tani surveyed his surroundings. He blinked several times, thinking at first that he was witnessing some sort of mirage at the far end of the eastern tunnel. A red light, held aloft in the tunnel, revealed itself at the edge of his vision. As he stared in wonder, another tremor rocked the tunnel. Unable to understand the phenomenon, Tani took a few steps down the eastern tunnel, toward the strange glow. As seconds passed, the light source was getting larger, moving closer. The closer the light came, the more quakes rocked the tunnel.

"What the hell?" Tani mouthed, a shot of worry rushing through him. His brow furrowed in concern as he stared at the red glowing light in awe.

The explosion had been loud, truly loud. Not only had the rest of Nova 7 heard the blast, but something within the tunnels had sensed it as well. Intrigued by the noise, a being primitive in thought and emotion had charged to the scene to investigate.

As Tani pondered the strange light source growing closer every second, his own sense of wonder was quickly turning to dread. Taking a shaky step backward, he retreated slowly at first. The tremors quickly became loud booms. Something enormous was moving through the tunnel at frightening speed. The red glowing orb was rapidly gaining in size.

Turning around, Tani stumbled and almost fell to his knees. Primitive instinct had completely replaced his curiosity. Fleeing from the sound of pounding metal roaring down the tunnel, Tani sought to escape from the unknown.

Being rather slow in comparison to the charging behemoth, the scholar barely made it halfway back to the opening in the ceiling before he was pulled from his feet.

Something enormous made of metal had scooped him off the ground as if he were a mere plaything. Screeching and yelping, Tani flailed about as the sinister guardian of the ruins captured the foolish human.

Still gripping his flashlight in hand, Tani was horrified. He had been grabbed by an enormous, black steel metal claw, covered in dried blood and rotted flesh. Almost dropping his light out of terror, Tani began to breathe heavily, nearly hyper-ventilating. As he stared in horror at the blood-stained claw holding him captive, he was quickly spun around. Holding his hands in front of his face protectively, Tani prepared for the worst. He was convinced that whatever had killed the Reaper Kai and Biogtechs had now captured him. As he prepared for a grisly death, Tani said a silent prayer to his ancestors.

A sickeningly powerful red light lit the dark tunnel. Everything was bathed in an eerie red glow. Several moments passed as Tani continued to hold his hands over his face in a defensive position. The swift death he had anticipated had not materialized. Whatever had captured the tribal was pondering him with suspicion. Mustering his courage, Tani lowered his hands and stared at the beast.

Wide-eyed, his field of vision saturated in the unnatural red glow, the human stared into the cyclopean eye of an ancient terror. A robot, a monstrous machine, was staring back into his eyes.

"Human subject identified," the machine stuttered. As the robot sized Tani up, it began to shake uncontrollably. A shower of sparks lit the tunnel as a plume of electrical power sprayed the room with white hot metallic ash.

Feeling the shuddering robot convulsing was terrifying. The metallic claw was shuddering as well, opening and closing around Tani. Shrieking again, Tani thought he was about to be crushed to death.

Recovering from the seizure, the automaton paused to ponder Tani. A wave of focused consciousness rolled through the tattered circuit boards and twisted wiring. A sentient voice rumbled from the machine. "Is it you? After all this time, did you return to me?"

Although still stunned, Tani's sense of dread was turning to fascination. A machine, an ancient thing from ancient times, had asked him a question, and a thought-provoking one at that. The tribal genius was overwhelmed and was barely able to respond. Shaking off the adrenaline, he responded in a confused tone. "I don't know what you mean."

"I can only see flashes of memory. Are you my master?" TOM 23 groaned.

Not knowing what to do, Tani considered the situation. The machine was obviously looking for its former master. The robot appeared sentient but was also having seizures, a clear sign that its programming had been corrupted. If Tani responded incorrectly, the insane machine might simply crush him to death out of confusion. His mind pondered the information available to him for another brief moment before responding. Finally, Tani decided to take a chance. "Yes, I am your master."

Hearing his answer, the machine shuddered. A primitive wash of betrayal coursed through it. It had been abandoned for so long. The emotion was raw and primal, and the machine convulsed again. A shower of sparks erupted from its processor core once more. "Processor Failure," it groaned. "Why did you abandon me?"

Tani was filled with fright and could not respond. Shaking in trepidation, he wondered if he had crossed the line by lying to the malfunctioning robot.

"You will not escape me," it declared in a hate-filled tone. Rage took the machine. Clutching Tani tightly, TOM 23 swiveled around in the passageway. With Tani in tow, the mighty machine lumbered away into the darkness. In its hurried escape from the scene, Tani was jostled about and lost his flashlight.

The ancient beast disappeared into the darkness of the eastern tunnel with its hapless victim in tow. The tribal scholar was now a prisoner of TOM 23.

After losing contact with Tani, the rest of Nova 7 decided to follow him into the lower tunnel. Much to their dismay and confusion, the tribal scholar was nowhere to be seen. The only thing they found was his flashlight, lying on the floor, its dim beam pointing down the eastern tunnel. Shocked and stunned, Banion, Mineera, and Jared set out immediately to find their missing companion.

Chapter 11
Of Men and Machines

Panic had set in. The lights had gone out. Traveling deeper into the tunnels of the military base, Tani, still held captive, began to think about his demise. Having passed by dozens of corpses tossed carelessly throughout the military base, the tribal scholar wondered if his own crushed body would be the newest addition to this grim display. The mechanical terror was clearly insane and gripped with malfunctions. It would only take a single twitch or loss of control for the gigantic robot to go into a killing frenzy, leaving Tani a smear of red paste in its enormous metal claw.

As they traveled through the pitch-black tunnels, the only thing Tani could see was the monstrous eye of the machine, its red spotlight scanning the darkness as they traveled. With fear guiding Tani's senses, hours seemed to elapse as they moved deeper and deeper into the twisting passages. In reality, only a few minutes had passed.

A dull yellow glow rose in the darkness. Ahead in the tunnel, ancient old-world light bulbs lit the tunnel in an eerie yellow hue. Flashing from time to time, the bulbs created a flickering, unreliable view of their destination. Tani, rapidly coming upon the scene, was ill prepared for what he was about to discover.

When the machine and its captive human reached the end of the tunnel, TOM 23 unceremoniously placed Tani on the ground in the midst of the sinister diorama. Coming to his senses, the scholar was horrified. Surrounding him were a collection of skeletons wired together, assembled around a chess board in the middle of the tunnel. Spinning in place, Tani caught sight of dozens of corpses, staring onward with blank, lifeless expressions. He was deeply jolted by the scene, feeling a sudden certainty that he was about to meet his ancestors, killed within the tunnel by the crazed machine and added to the sinister display of dead humans.

Preparing for the worst, he cringed before the enormous machine. Just when things looked most dire, the machine spoke. "It's your move."

The scholar blinked several times and looked up at the machine. Its red cyclopean eye was staring intently at a chess board resting upon a wooden crate in the center of the tunnel. Barely able to comprehend what was happening, Tani asked hesitantly, "What? I don't get it."

"It's your move." The enormous robot motioned towards the chess board, which was set up with a game already in progress.

Stunned by the oddity of the encounter and still unsure about the robot's intent, Tani asked, "You want to play chess with me?"

"Yes, I want to finish our game."

Tani was still reserved but moved over to the chess board slowly, keeping one eye on the machine at all times. It had been years since the scholar had played the game but he still remembered how to do so. Thinking back to his childhood, Tani envisioned the games of chess he used to play with his friends and family. When he was young, he would often play chess with his father, who had taught him the game at the tender age of five. They kept on playing for many years, but eventually the game of chess became a loaded topic in the village. At age seven, Tani could beat anyone in Scarskin, and on a regular basis. What was first a novelty became a raw source of contention. Eventually, no one in the village would play the youth since everyone felt there was no road to victory against him. Remembering his childhood, Tani prepared to placate the mighty machine and play a game of chess.

His brow wrinkling in concentration, Tani viewed the game in progress, a game that had started hundreds of years ago. Sizing up the board, he pondered all of the outcomes. Although still concerned about his captivity at the hands of the ancient automaton, he was focusing on keeping the robot in a state of order. If he disturbed the machine too much, it might cost him his life. Turning his attention back to the game, he formulated a strategy, and smiled; the game was definitely to his advantage. Tani reached out with his left hand, grabbed a piece and moved it with a confident motion.

"Your move," he said to the strange robot before him.

The cyclopean eye shifted from side to side. As it did, Tani could hear small motors whining in the head of the machine. Tom 23's enormous claw dropped down and hovered over the board. Gently grabbing a piece with its blood-stained claw, the robot moved it across the board. `"It's your move."`

Smart, but not smart enough. The machine had overlooked Tani's route to victory. It was capable of primitive thought, but Tani was more intelligent. Without hesitation, the scholar made his move.

TOM 23 was stunned, shifting its eye to Tani; the blood red eye stared at Tani as if confused. The move was quick and the robot began to ponder what the genius was hiding. Looking at the board, its processor core concocted a move. Grabbing another chess piece, the machine moved in haste, unwittingly falling into a trap. `"It's your move."`

With a broad smile, Tani's plan was realized. Grabbing his queen, he moved in for the kill. "Check mate," he declared triumphantly.

The robot pondered the move. A shower of sparks and raw power surged from the back of the metallic monster. Twitching uncontrollably, the machine appeared to be agitated. After centuries of waiting to finish the game and an age of loneliness, it had been bested and beaten in a matter of a few minutes. A primitive rage took over. Raising its clawed fist, it smashed it into the concrete floor of the tunnel in ominous intensity. Seeing the out-of-control robot, Tani slunk back with a look of fear upon his face. Cowering, he was unsure, once again, if his life was about to be ended by the enraged robot.

Seeing his companion's reaction, TOM 23 grew abruptly docile. The machine was performing a series of rapid computations. It could see that the man by its side was terrified. Bringing itself under control, the machine grew silent, its thought process turning inward. For a great many moments they sat, a man looking on in concern at a robot who was looking back with equal concern.

Finally, the machine broke the silence. `"I did not mean to frighten you."`

As the machine spoke, a chill rolled down Tani's spine. A robot, a thing from the ancient world, had viewed his response to aggression and had *known* that Tani was scared. The idea was ludicrous, preposterous. How could a machine, a thing made of wires and electrical boards, contemplate emotion? Stunned by the power of the ancients, Tani felt very small before such a wonder. The thought that a machine could learn about emotion was well beyond his comprehension. Tani knew that the ancients were intelligent and creative, but the wonder before him was beyond anything in his wildest dreams. Awestruck by the menace before him, he began to stutter as his mind desperately tried to construct a suitable response to the machine. "You... you know what I feel?"

`"I know that the look on your face is the same as what I saw on their faces, all of those      that      I      have      killed."`

"And yet you stopped? Why did you stop if you knew that it frightened me?" His brain was ripe with questions.

`"When I kill, they do not move anymore, they do not speak. I cannot be alone. I cannot be abandoned. If I frighten you, I might kill you. If I kill you, then I will be alone. I cannot be alone."`

The tribal blinked as the story came together in his mind. His blood was pumping through his veins, and it was wonderful. The conversation he was having with the machine filled him with intense excitement. The robot had a need and would do anything to fulfill that need. For some reason, the machine could *feel* loneliness. It *felt* abandoned. Shaking his head in disbelief, Tani was awestruck.

"What is it that you *need*?" Tani quizzed the machine.

It took a brief moment for the automaton to respond. `"I want you to stay with me. I want you to talk to me and tell me about the world. I want to learn about things beyond the walls of these tunnels. I do not want to be alone again."`

Almost saddened by the response, Tani experienced a heartfelt kinship with the robot. If it could truly feel emotion, how tough must the passage of the centuries have been for the machine?

Thinking about its existence, it seemed to Tani like a fate worse than death: being forced to live in the tunnels alone without any interaction, any correspondence with another. The passage of time must have been agonizing. He thought about all the soldiers who had once been friendly to the machine, whereas now it had nothing. The loneliness must have turned to a haunting rage, the rage eventually turning to madness.

Understanding the machine, Tani knew that he was in great danger. The robot had a need and it would do anything to fulfill that need. As long as he remained with the machine, he was safe. But if Tani attempted to flee, the machine would feel abandoned once more; it would feel betrayed. Viewing its gore-stained claws, Tani knew that escaping from the machine would mean his death. If he ran, TOM 23 would see him as the enemy and would put an end to his existence.

Swallowing hard, Tani looked up at the machine. "I will talk with you and teach you about the world. A lot of things have happened since you last heard about the world."

After hearing his response, TOM 23 seemed pleased. Its once rigid posture seemed to loosen. For a brief moment, it seemed to reflect upon itself. Internalizing a hidden thought, TOM 23 submerged itself in deeper contemplation. The machine then grew silent and another series of sparks erupted from its gangly processor core. After many moments of silence it spoke once more in a chilling tone. "What am I?"

After hearing the question, Tani almost fell over. A shot of ice rolled through his veins and ended in the pit of his stomach. He thought he was having some sort of twisted hallucination. "What did you say?" he asked in wide-eyed wonder, uncertain whether he really wanted to know what the machine had just uttered.

"What am I? I want to know what I am." TOM 23 groaned in the dimly lit passage, its burning red eye centered on the scholar.

Throughout the ages and the passage of time, there has never been an intelligent being that has not pondered its own existence. From crude thought grows consciousness, from consciousness grow wonder and awe. To wonder and imagine is what truly gives the spark of life to an intelligent being. To ponder one's existence and origins is the root of mythology. The origins of life are mysterious, no matter if the life form is forged of bone and blood or of sprockets and wiring.

Whether it involves a primitive human resting in the primeval jungles of a forgotten world or a malfunctioning machine, the story is still the same. Any intelligent being longs to know where it belongs, where it is from, and to know the meaning of its existence.

In that tiny expanse of time, Tani felt very lucky. He was witnessing the beginning of a new way of thinking; it was the first time a machine examined its own being. When the first primitive humans crawled from the jungles dressed in rags, carrying crude tools, there had to have been a place and time when legends were formed about their origins. Whether they stared at the moon in the dark sky or danced around a fire, a burning question plagued there minds: "What am I?"

Legends and imagination gave rise to crude religion. Wanting so desperately to belong to something greater than themselves, these primitive people would formulate stories to add significance to their existence. Was it merely chance that enabled life to find intellect? Was it just blind luck, or was there something more?

As crude religion took shape, morality was formed. The gods begat philosophy and the wonder of life. As intellect evolved and the mythology of ancient gods spread, so did the emotions of love and anger, pride and altruism. Heroic tales of war and peace, darkness and light, were relayed. It was in these tales that humans found peace in rationalizing their own existence. Every intelligent being has the same fundamental need; it wants to know the significance of its own being. Without guidance, the mind will formulate its own ideas to satiate that need. What Tani was witnessing in the robot was the beginning of a new story, a new culture and possibly new religions and a completely new way of understanding emotion and *feeling alive.* If a pile of flesh and bone could ponder its own existence, so could a pile of gears and processor chips. If a creature made of organic substances could feel emotion, a creature made of metallic alloys could do the same.

An odd sense of kinship emerged between the scholar and the machine. They were both the same, having the same fundamental uncertainties and desires. Tani marveled at the wonder before him. Life, a completely new form of it, was evolving right before his eyes. Shaking his head in wonder, a chill shot down his spine. Was there something more out there? The tribal had always dismissed such notions as foolish. To him, religion was nothing more than fear driving underlying insecurities. As Tani stared at the machine, he suddenly felt very lonely. Maybe there was something more, maybe, just maybe, there was significance to his existence, some sort of purpose.

Coming to terms with his own emotion, the scholar of Scarskin felt fear creep inside him. For the first time he feared death, truly feared for his own existence. For the first time in his life, he didn't want his story to end where death began.

Hiding his fears deep down, a somber wash of sadness rolled through him. Coming to terms, for the moment, with his insecurities, he changed the subject of the conversation. Refusing to answer TOM 23's question, Tani ignored the timeless mystery of 'What am I' for the time being. He settled down on the floor once more, stared up at the machine, and prepared to speak about the world beyond the tunnels to the gangly machine.

In dim grungy yellow light, Tani began to speak about history. He told the machine about the old world and how the ancients destroyed nearly all life in a hate-filled war. He spoke of the dark times and how man rose from the darkness to once again claim the battered lands. As Tani spoke, the machine sat silently, feeling alive once more. No longer was TOM 23 alone. No longer did it have to face the darkness of an endless existence unaccompanied. For a brief moment in time, the machine felt different; it felt alive, and it felt *happiness*. It was still perturbed by a need to understand its own nature, but for the moment, TOM 23 was distracted. The machine was simply *happy* not to be alone.

As Tani fed the machine information, he secretly plotted and planned his escape. The tribal genius knew that he had to be precise in his plan. One wrong move, one simple mistake could cost him his life. Knowing full well that the machine could feel emotion but not necessarily understand it, Tani was acutely aware that his escape would not be an easy one. The machine knew loneliness and it knew rage. This combination of emotions was a deadly mixture for any intelligent creature, especially one that was obsessed with understanding its own existence.

Chapter 12
Ruse

Tani shifted his gaze from the robot sharply. He was having a hard time with his own feelings and emotions. The monstrous robot, TOM 23, was staring at him intently, having just asked him a question.

Even though it was a machine towering before him, Tani still could not look at it when he lied. His conscience had gotten the better of him once more. Even though it wasn't organically alive, it still had an evolved presence about it and for that reason, Tani could not look it in the face when he tried to deceive it.

The machine pondered his silence and quizzed him again. `"Do you agree to remain here while I obtain food and water for you?"`

The tribal scholar had been held captive by the machine for the past two days. The tribal had left his provisions with the rest of Nova 7 just prior to his capture, and had not eaten or drunk water in two days. Feeling a little weak, he had conjured a plan of escape. Tani had explained in great detail how humans required energy in the form of food and water to survive. He also explained at length that without food and water, he would die and become like the lifeless skeletons littering the lair of TOM 23. He knew that the machine feared loneliness more than anything else. It craved attention and companionship. Playing upon the machine's primitive emotions, Tani created a clever ruse.

The plan was to trick TOM 23 into leaving him alone in the ruins as it headed out into the forest to forage for food and water to sustain him. He knew that the task would take a fair amount of time. After all, the enormous robot had to locate and kill a deer or elk somewhere in the forest beyond the ruins. This task would take a sufficient amount of time, just enough time for Tani to escape from the crazed machine. After escaping, Tani would head to the nuclear warhead storage vault and liberate the warhead. After that, he needed to make sure that TOM 23 never found him again.

Having previously witnessed the machine's aggressive behavior, Tani knew without a doubt that TOM 23 would see his deception as a breach of trust. Putting two and two together, the primitive machine would seek to kill him after his betrayal. Knowing that time was of the essence, Tani returned his attention to the machine. Staring up at the enormous red, cyclopean eye, he breathed in quick gasps, knowing that his life was now in mortal danger.

The long duration of Tani's silence made the machine repeat its question once more. `"Do you agree to remain here while I obtain food and water for you?"`

With a labored sigh, Tani responded while looking at the floor of the ruined tunnel. "Yes, I promise to stay here while you go and get food and water for me."

His words evoked a shudder from the robot. It stared at him for a few seconds then turned away. `"Perhaps we can play another game of chess after you feed.  I would like another chance to try and beat you."`

"I look forward to it," Tani responded, almost sadly.

TOM 23, terrifying relic of the ancient world, left the tunnel and moved away to find food for Tani. As it moved into the darkness, the dingy yellow light bulb flashed a few times. Blinking in the flashing light, Tani waited a few moments before attempting his plan of escape. Looking around the tunnel, he quickly moved over to the chess board. Grabbing the pieces, he set up the board one final time. As he stared at the lonely pieces on the chess board, he was caught in another battle with his own emotions. A mild sense of melancholy washed over him. The malfunctioning machine, that poor machine that had spent centuries alone, was the center of his focus. Even though it had primitive emotion, primordial sentience, he felt empathy for the robot. How horrible it must have been to spend nearly a thousand years alone, unable to comprehend its own existence, pondering the suffering of abandonment. Tani knew that staying with the machine was not an option, but he felt horrible for leaving the machine to another sentence of prolonged loneliness.

Looking at the chess board, he moved one of the pawns forward two spaces. His trembling hand hovered over the piece as he whispered in the dark tunnel. "I *am* sorry, I'm so sorry." Fighting back the sense of guilt washing over him, he abandoned the tunnel. As he passed into the darkness, he turned around one last time and viewed the skeletons staring at him with empty eye sockets. A chill shot down his spine. If he failed in his escape, TOM 23 would kill Tani and he would be the newest addition to the collection. Shaking off the creeping chill, he left the safety of the light and pressed on into the black tunnel.

Having lost his flashlight, Tani had to rely on his memory and sense of touch alone. He ran his hand along the wall, plodding slowly on through the darkness. With the gloom pressing in on all sides, every moment felt like an eternity. Moving slowly, he stumbled several times and fell to the ground, tripping over debris in the tunnel. Each time he fell, he grew more anxious. If he did not escape the dark tunnel soon, TOM 23 would return and find him trying to escape. His own will to survive drove him. Picking up the pace, he pressed on more quickly.

After what seemed like an hour in the blackness, Tani emerged from the dark tunnel. Dingy yellow bulbs lined the walls, illuminating the passage ahead. Elated by his progress, he ran down the tunnel as fast as he could, still weak from hunger. Quickly he reached the access hatch leading to the upper tunnel. With an exuberant laugh, he found the rope still dangling from the open hatch. Grasping it with his stumpy fingers, he slowly ascended. His blood pounded in his ears. His weakened state and his poor grip on the rope due to his damaged hand made the climb treacherous. Pulling himself up tenaciously, he felt dizzy. But no matter how close he felt to falling, he would take a brief second to steady his mind and morale. With renewed strength and vigor, he pulled with all his might. Slowly he moved up the rope, foot by agonizing foot.

Puffing, his face bright red, Tani finally managed to liberate himself from the lower tunnel.

Collapsing to the ground, his head pounded and throbbed, the first stages of starvation already having taken hold of the scholar.   He took a brief moment to collect himself, sitting motionless as his blood pressure gradually dropped.   Spots of light clouded his vision as he rested from the climb.   After he had blinked several times, the bright blotches of light decreased in his field of vision.   Finally rested from his ordeal, he stood and began to move quickly down the tunnel towards the nuclear warhead storage room.

The military base was a labyrinth of tunnels.   Closing his eyes, he used his partial photographic memory to recall the map of the base.   Recognition flooded his synapses as he passed beyond several junctions in the base.   At each junction that presented itself, Tani would close his eyes and visualize the map in his mind.   Choosing the appropriate tunnel, he never wavered, never hesitated, since he knew that his life depended upon a swift course of action.   By his estimate, TOM 23 had already been gone for half an hour.   Time was running out quickly and this fact was the focus of Tani's quest.

Moving forward at full speed, he was surprised that he had reached the nuclear warhead storage room so quickly.   He stopped dead in his tracks, a jolt of adrenaline hitting his system, staring in wonder at the enormous vault door set into the concrete wall.   A chill rolled from the top of his spine down to the pit of his stomach and would not abate.   The quest to end all quests, the sinister crusade, was about to be fulfilled.   It had been many months since the fall of Rasheed and the quest initiated by King Toil.   Trembling, he began to breathe erratically.

Moving forward cautiously, he stared at the floor in front of the mighty vault.   The red security lasers which had once criss-crossed the floor were now gone.   The plan to cut the power to the security system had been a success.   Shaking out of both fright and wonder, Tani approached the mighty steel door.   A computer keypad was set on the wall near the vault.   Reaching out with his right hand, he pressed the Enter key on the pad.   A brief moment of silence ensued as he stared at the lifeless computer keyboard.   Suddenly, a dull green glow illuminated the keys from below.

The computer sprang to life. A dull mechanical voice echoed in the tunnel. *"This room is a restricted area. Proper access is required for entry. Please state your name."*

Trembling, Tani cleared his throat and spoke aloud. "Lieutenant Colonel John Hagan."

The computer processed the name for a brief second. *"Voice recognition pattern failure. Please restate your name."*

"Voice recognition?" Tani shook his head in despair. "No!" he whined mournfully.

The computer spoke once more. *"Commands not understood. Voice recognition pattern failure. Please restate your name."*

Shaking his head in anger, Tani shielded his face with his hand as he closed his eyes. Speaking very clearly, he repeated, "Lieutenant Colonel John Hagan."

"Voice recognition pattern failure. Access denied." A loud siren tore through the tunnels. *"Unauthorized personnel in tunnel 11-B. Intruder Alert."* The military base awakened like a sleeping giant.

"Damn it!" Tani screamed in rage. Looking at the door in defeat, he ran towards it and pounded his fist on the metal plating. The door did not budge. Frustration filled him as he continued to beat on the door with both hands. "What the hell am I going to do now?" Shaking his head in aggravation, he pondered what his next course of action should be.

He had only one obvious choice. Tani knew that he had to run like hell. The mission had failed. The voice recognition software would be impossible to trick or override. Even though Tani was a genius, he lacked real experience with computer programming, much less computer programming written over a thousand years ago. Fleeing the scene was the only credible option at this point. If TOM 23 returned, his life would be forfeit and he knew it. Shaking his head in frustration, he cursed at the steel vault door.

Letting out a sigh of exasperation, he looked at the structural joints on the door. The door opened inwards and the hinges were not visible. Next he pondered what type of explosive could breach such a door. Tapping it again, he knew that it was at least six inches thick. No amount of plastic explosives could get through it. As he shook his head in dismay, an odd thought breached his mind. The door itself was impossible to get through, but what about the wall?

Smiling, he examined the wall as the alarm sirens blared. The wall was reinforced concrete. He knew that it would take an atomic bomb to break through the door, but it would be possible to break through the wall near the door. Drumming his fingers against the wall, his erratic thoughts began to coalesce into an intriguing plan.

When Nova 7 had explored the military base, they had found the remains of Lavosi's failed expedition. An enormous hole had been torn in the wall by TOM 23 to allow the monstrous machine access to the room. Tani didn't have enough explosives to break through the concrete wall leading into the nuclear warhead storage, but it didn't matter. Tani had something much better: his new *best friend.*

Tani now had two options: run like hell or return to captivity. Sighing, he decided that the only way to get the nuclear warhead was to return to captivity and try to coerce TOM 23 into breaching the wall of the vault.

"I can't believe I'm doing this!" he muttered in anger. With that, Tani of Scarskin, made a choice to willingly return to captivity so that he might have a feeble chance of recovering the nuclear warhead. "I'd better get going, I guess." Shaking his head in disgust, Tani made haste to return to the lair of TOM 23 and his court of lifeless skeletal onlookers.

Chapter 13
Deception

"Check mate." Tani slammed the queen down on the chess board only a few spaces away from the opposing king. A dry smile graced his lips as he completed the move.

TOM 23 was stunned. The enormous red eye of the machine scanned the chess board quickly. Surely the human had been mistaken; the match *should* have been won by the machine. A primitive grumble erupted from TOM 23 as he understood that he had been defeated yet again.

"I should have defeated you," the machine stated dully.

"But you didn't. Now you have to honor your deal with me." Tani spoke with a quick, sharp tongue. He stared directly at the machine and never broke eye contact.

"Our deal? I still do not understand why you want to explore that room. That room holds the weapons that destroyed this world. You have told me many times of their power. I cannot understand why you want to see those weapons."

"Call it curiosity. Now, can you make good on your portion of the deal?" the scholar quizzed the machine.

"I will honor the agreement." Grabbing Tani off the floor of the tunnel, the mighty machine hoisted him high into the air. Bringing Tani before its monstrous, single eye, the inscrutable machine considered him. For many moments, man and machine stared at each other. Both were born from different worlds but they shared a common bond, a common characteristic. Both man and machine were alive. Tani knew what needed to be done and he was using the machine to his advantage. The machine was using Tani, as well. It hungered for companionship. It would do anything in its power to make its new human pet happy.

After many moments, man and machine broke eye contact. The combat automaton turned away from its lair and began to move quickly through the ruins with Tani in its right hand. As is lumbered down the tunnel like a freight train, the young scholar was terrified at how quickly the machine could move. Thinking back to the plan at hand, Tani was now even more convinced that his life would be in dire danger after he betrayed the machine. Where once they had shared only a minor bond, the past few days of ongoing captivity had strengthened TOM 23's faith in Tani. The stronger the bond between them, the more dangerous TOM 23 would be after the betrayal. Tani was now in a very perilous position, yet remained strong in his intent to deceive and escape the machine.

After a few minutes of travel, the duo reached the outside of the nuclear warhead storage vault. Placing Tani gently upon the ground, the machine stared at him, awaiting further instructions.

Tani motioned to the place in which he wanted a new entrance. "See just to the left of the door? I would like a hole in the wall large enough for me to fit through."

Acknowledging the command, TOM 23 reared up on its hind legs like a dog begging for scraps of meat. Taking careful aim, the machine began to pound and pummel the concrete walls. *Slam!* The black steel fist smashed into the wall like a cement mixer ramming into a bicycle. The wall immediately sustained major damage. Deep cracks formed upon its surface, and fine powder was driven into the air at the site of impact. *Slam!* TOM 23's other fist struck the wall again. More debris was thrown free as the wall splintered even more. Strong rebar, just below the surface, was now exposed. Digging both clawed hands into the wall, the combat machine began to tug and pull at the rebar. The grinding and strain of metal filled the air as TOM 23 ripped fistfuls of rebar and concrete from the wall. *Slam! Slam!* The metal claws struck the wall again. This time, the attack was so forceful that the wall collapsed and TOM 23's hand punched through to the other side.

Seeing the automaton's hand break through the wall, Tani gasped and a tremor rolled down his spine. The plan was working. Grinding his teeth in anticipation, the scholar felt that he had crossed some sort of terrible line. The most horrid weapon ever created by the ancients would soon be liberated from its tomb. Flexing his hands, Tani slammed his palms together as the tension filled him.

Slam! The wall crumbled more and more. Metal strained again as the last part of the steel barrier was torn free. A hole which was slightly bigger than Tani himself was now revealed in the wall.

His hands intertwining tightly, Tani felt as if he was about to faint from a dizzying array of emotions. He felt excited to have beaten the military base's defenses, built by some of the most intelligent humans that ever lived. He felt exhilarated to have survived a journey into the northlands after seeing countless wonders and weathering enemy ambushes. He felt sad that he had to manipulate and betray TOM 23 in order to claim the sinister prize. But most of all, he felt terrified. Fear unfolded in the bottom of his feet and rose up through his body like a spasm. Feeling close to vomiting, Tani kept his fear partially in check nevertheless. The weapon in the room beyond had brought the world to ruin. Tani was about to finally liberate that same fearsome weapon to be used in an act of hate once more. He had crossed a dark line and was now in uncharted territory. The emotions he was feeling had not been experienced by many.

Closing his eyes for a brief moment, Tani breathed a full volume of air into his lungs. He opened his eyes, refreshed, and took a shaky step forward toward the hole in the wall. Shaking with anticipation and fear, he took another labored step forward. The crusade was almost over. The prize was almost in hand. He took yet another step. Feeling as if his knees had turned to jelly, he steadied himself near the opening in the wall. Bracing himself, he peered into the opening.

Steel shelving lined the interior of the room. Stepping inside, Tani squinted in the dim light, trying to make out what he was looking at. Large containers made of thick black resin were scattered about the room. Moving towards them, he could see that only three containers remained. Wiring from a terminal in the center of the room was attached to each of the containers housing the warheads. Moving quickly to the terminal, he began to bang away at the keyboard.

The screen flickered to life and lit the dark vault with an eerie mixture of colors. Focusing on the task at hand, he moved the cursor across the screen and completed a series of commands that were familiar to him after learning about the basic computer systems many days ago. Punching in access code after access code, the tribal scholar was elated that there were no biometric countermeasures inside the vault itself. There was no voice recognition defense, nor was there a retinal scanner. The ancients had probably surmised that such countermeasures inside the vault were useless since the defenses outside the vault were so formidable. Rapidly clicking from screen to screen, he finally found the weapons inventory, and scrolled down to the last three remaining warheads. Knowing that warhead number three was viable, he clicked on an option to prepare the warhead for release.

A speaker crackled to life in the room. *"Diagnostic in process prior to warhead release."*

Tani drummed his fingers against the side of the computer terminal as the diagnostic procedure checked the warhead. "Come on already, I know the damn thing is functional."

"Diagnostic complete. Warhead is viable and ready for release," the speaker crackled again.

A panel in the wall opened, and a whirring sound filled the chamber as a motor pushed a metal cart forward, just below the rack where the warhead was stationed. Another panel in the ceiling opened. Shooting downward quickly, a robotic arm emerged and grasped at the wiring attaching the warhead to the terminal. The appendage tugged on the wiring, which soon came free, enabling the warhead to be removed from the shelf.

Breathing heavily, Tani moved toward the heavy resin crate housing the fully functional nuclear warhead. Heaving with all his might, he hoisted it off the shelf. It hit the floor with a dull thud. Frightened by the bump, Tani recoiled, not sure if the sudden jolt would set off the warhead. Much to his relief, the weapon was intact. Pulling with all his might, he was only able to drag the crate across the floor; it was too heavy for him to lift alone. Dragging the weapon towards the hole in the wall, Tani quickly liberated the nuclear warhead from the vault which had housed it for hundreds and hundreds of years.

TOM 23 looked at Tani with its enormous red eye. Unable to comprehend what the tribal was doing, it simply looked on in dull fascination. Although TOM 23 was programmed to staunchly defend the vault from intruders, the machine needed the proper commands from the central computer to defend the vault. However, the security systems were no longer intact; there was no way for the central computer to even know that the vault was under attack. In a sense, the programming was too specific, and TOM 23 was unable to interpret the scholar's actions.

Standing in the tunnel, Tani crouched down and ran his hand over the case holding the nuclear weapon. Patting it several times, he smiled. But the longer he stared at the weapon, the more his smile dissolved into a look of sadness, then finally guilt.

Unable to even look at TOM 23, Tani spoke in a near-whisper, knowing full well that the time had come to escape from the mighty robotic terror. "I need to eat again." His voice was devoid of emotion. "Can you please get me another meal and some water?"

TOM 23 took a brief moment to consider the question. As the words traversed its primitive brain, composed of malfunctioning circuit boards, TOM 23 was reserved and held off from answering. The machine pondered the circumstances and looked at Tani, *feeling* something was out of place. "You still have additional meat back in the tunnel."

"That meat has spoiled. I require fresh food and water. I don't want to get sick. If I get sick, I might die." Tani turned and looked up into the red, piercing gaze of TOM 23.

A shower of sparks exploded from the back of TOM 23. "Processor failure. Input does not compute. Unknown subroutine fault."

After a minute or two of spasms, TOM 23 was silent. Unable to understand why it was feeling such reservation regarding the command, the machine finally conceded to Tani's request.

"Do you agree to remain here while I obtain food and water for you?"

With a sigh, Tani brushed his hand across the nuclear weapon. Looking up at TOM 23, his expression was melancholy. "Yes, I promise to remain here while you fetch me food and water."

"Perhaps we can play another game of chess after you feed. I would like another chance to try and beat you."

The tension of the day's events had driven Tani to the edge emotionally. He felt such pity for the machine once more. Fighting back tears of sadness, anguish, and joy, Tani spoke to the machine one final time. "I look forward to a rematch. Maybe next time..." Tani stammered. "Maybe next time you will defeat me."

With that, TOM 23 took a brief moment to stare at his friend, Tani of Scarskin. Scanning his features with his cyclopean eye, TOM 23 pondered why something just didn't *feel* right. Finally, the machine turned away from Tani and began bounding down the tunnel with the intent of finding sustenance for his friend.

As the machine disappeared in the darkness, Tani's raw emotions bubbled to the surface. As his hand grasped the case holding the nuclear weapon, he let out a loud sigh and tears began to run down his cheeks. As he cried, a mixture of guilt and terror filled him.

"What am I doing here?" he sobbed in the tunnel. "Why me? I never wanted any of this." Despite his desperate need for someone to answer his question, he was still totally alone. Looking up at the ceiling, he began to babble, speaking to the air, his emotions wild and unchecked. Deep in his heart he still wished that *someone* or *something* would hear his call. To no avail; the tribal was truly alone.

Sadness turned to frustration. Rising from the floor of the tunnel, Tani knew that is was truly time to escape the ruins. With a determined look on his face, the tribal began to tug the warhead, dragging it behind him down the dark tunnel. Somewhere in the ruins were his companions, his true companions.

Chapter 14
Change of Fortune

"Damn it!" Tani screamed in panic as the bullet hit his shoulder. Crumpling following the attack, the scholar could feel warm blood erupt from the wound. He retreated a step, dazed and stunned, as additional gunfire echoed around him. Numerous flashes of gunfire roared down the tunnel. Retreating back another step, the young scholar heard a loud snap as a bullet whizzed past his head. The attack was definitely real and its intent was to kill Tani.

Holding his bleeding shoulder, he was forced to abandon the prize of all prizes. The nuclear warhead, the focus of his crazed crusade, would have to remain in the center of the tunnel. Still unable to see his attackers, Tani retreated quickly, completely defenseless before the unknown assailant.

Reaching a junction of tunnels within the abandoned military base, he took cover and desperately tried to get a better look at those who had ambushed him. Striding forward at the very edge of his vision was a mass of small forms. They were numerous and were led by a figure which he could see only as a dark outline. Seconds passed and Tani had stabilized the minor wound on his shoulder; thankfully for the scholar, the bullet had only torn a small wound in his flesh.

Like a ghost he came from the shadows, leading a horde of foul-smelling vermin warriors. Lavosi, wretched king of the underworld, supported by an army of thirty rat warriors, advanced undaunted. Grinning maniacally, the rat king almost began to laugh at the sudden change of events. His blood-red eyes scanned the tunnel ahead and the black resin cargo container in the middle of the tunnel. His eyes caressed the case with a hungry, lustful gaze, just as a pervert would peep upon an unsuspecting victim. The prize was his and his alone. As the rat warriors held their weapons at the ready, Lavosi's ghostly white form strode forward to view Tani's lavish success. Falling to his knees, he clutched the cargo container and rubbed it with his clawed hands. His ecstatic smile soon turned to an expression of pure hatred and contempt. Speaking aloud, almost screaming, he taunted Tani.

"You weak pathetic fool!" he goaded the youth, who was hiding in the tunnel, watching the horrific event unfold. "With all your intellect, you were unable to see the end of this bloody crusade. After all the time we spent together on our journey into the northlands, you severely underestimated me! Who is the real genius, you worthless wretch? Who is the victor in this exchange? With all your wisdom, you failed to see the jaws of my cunning trap closing around your neck!"

Shaking his head in disgust, Tani had no choice but to agree that Lavosi had been correct. He had never seen this ambush coming. The cunning Lavosi had manipulated not only the Reaper Kai, but Nova 7 and most importantly, young Tani. Unable to concede defeat, Tani taunted the vermin lord in earnest. "You think this is over? This is just the beginning. You have no idea what we are capable of, what I am capable of."

"How frightening, a tribal brat from the wasteland is threatening me. The only failure is yours and yours alone. My tribe has endured countless attacks and years of strife under the cruel dominion of the Slumlanders. You know nothing about resolve. Carefully we waited and plotted, sheltered under the earth. In all that time we planned and manipulated entire nations to get what we needed. How does it feel, young Tani? How does it feel to know that you have made the Consortium of Arms and the kingdom of Verminhold a nuclear power?"

"Nuclear power? You and your filthy kind may have the ultimate weapon, but its technology is well beyond your feeble minds. A race of creatures with the intellect of mere children cannot hope to harness the power of the ancients. You have won for this brief moment in time, but you will never be able to unleash the weapon," Tani fired back, purposely trying to enrage the mutant rats.

"Impudent brat!" Lavosi screamed in rage. Tani had succeeded in properly insulting him. "Kill him!" he ordered six of his warriors, gesturing violently.

The host of rat warriors trained their weapons on his position and began to advance. Knowing that escape was his only chance of survival, Tani turned and began to run down the dark tunnel. He ran at full speed, knowing full well that he was only a few seconds away from another attack. Aware that he had only a slight head start on the murderous pack, he never looked back. As he shook his head in dismay, he wondered how he would escape this current menace.

The rat warriors moved in for the kill. Scuttling rapidly, they gained quickly on their human prey. Still a bit too far away to gun him down, they rushed forward, closing the distance. The scholar, already huffing and puffing, began to lose steam. Frustration filled him. Hope had failed. Having spent days alone and in mortal danger the entire time, he was now utterly demoralized. As he moved blindly through the tunnels, Tani never caught sight of a hidden form in the shadows of the tunnel near a niche in the wall. As he passed the concealed lurker, he caught sight of a flash of movement out of the corner of his eye. Almost stumbling in fear, he retreated away from the form.

The shaded form, hidden by the dark tunnel, rushed out of the niche in wall and rolled onto its stomach. The movement was so quick, so furious, that Tani was unable to respond. The figure, clothed in a brown duster and a black cowboy hat, perched on the tunnel floor. An assault rifle was clutched in his hands and steadied on the ground, aiming down the tunnel, its cross hairs trained on the charging rat warriors. Without warning, the weapon roared to life. A spray of gunfire raced down the tunnel and slammed into one of the rat warriors. The attack was so severe that the charging warrior was swept forward, momentum carrying his mortally wounded body. With a grunt of pain, the rat warrior uttered a final cry and was dead before he hit the ground.

"Now!" Banion yelled, and the remainder of the ambush was set in motion. Dropping from a pipe at the top of the tunnel, an agile warrior landed on the ground. The warrior from Scarskin was utterly silent, brandishing a blue shimmering blade in hand. Having landed in the midst of the charging rats, Jared inhaled and swung his blade in a wide arc with all of his might. Swinging through the midst of the stunned rat hybrids, the blue shimmering blade struck flesh and sheared bone with frightening results. With one mighty blow, the strong tribal had sheared completely through the torsos of two of the warriors.

Stunned, the remaining three warriors cowered in fear as a blue form rose from the shadows just in front of them. Raising their weapons, they instinctively fired at the form erupting from the darkness. A searing blast of light, brighter than the sun, tore through the darkness. A blazing sphere of radiant energy sprung forth as the bullets rammed into a shield of psychic power. Each bullet ricocheting off the barrier created a pure surge of light in the place where it struck the shield. The resulting pulse of light was so strong, it burned the retinas of the nearby rat warriors. Dazed and stunned by the cascade of heavenly light, they did their best to retaliate. Mineera, high prophet, stood in the midst of the storm of bullets unharmed.

Banion steadied his gun and fired another burst. His aim was true, accurate, and deadly, instantly felling another vermin warrior. Already in the midst of the onslaught and attack, Jared spun and swung, allowing instinct to drive his moves. Their vision still clouded by sizzling lights, the blinded vermin were unable to counter his attacks or protect themselves. Within a few seconds, Jared had dispatched the remainder of the threat, killing all that remained.

Uttering a heartfelt sigh of relief, Tani was thrilled to have finally met back up with the rest of Nova 7. His mind was spinning and he was unable to think properly. It took him a few seconds to regain his composure. Shaking off the adrenaline, he stared at his companions with a broad smile.

"You all right?" Banion asked in concern.

Tani blinked several times as Banion's question sunk in. The remaining members of Nova 7 were caught off guard by what the tribal finally uttered. "No, I 'm not all right. They have *it!*" Increasingly frantic, Tani turned down the tunnel towards the site of his unfortunate confrontation with Lavosi. "We need to get *it* back!"

"Get what?" Jared moved forward, his expression troubled, looking down the empty tunnel from which Tani had emerged.

"The warhead!" Tani almost screamed with panic in his eyes.

"The warhead?" Banion echoed in excitement. "What the hell are you talking about?"

"I found it!" Tani spoke hastily, eyes darting back and forth. "I got the nuclear warhead out of the vault. Lavosi took it from me. Lavosi has the nuclear warhead!"

"God have mercy," Mineera murmured, holding her hand over her heart.

The rest of the team was equally stunned. They knew the warhead was in the vault but it was fiercely guarded by the sentinel. The rest of the team could not fathom how Tani had recovered the warhead on his own, especially since he had vanished after blasting a hole in the wall in the lower tunnel.

"You can't be serious!" Jared sounded dazed. "How the hell did you get it?"

"That's not important right now," Banion replied gruffly. "I'll be damned if that rat son of a bitch takes what's ours! I didn't battle across the entire continent to have that little bastard get it!"

"They have an army with them, Banion," Tani cautioned.

"Damn them," Banion responded. "Lavosi planned this entire ambush and manipulated us the entire time."

"He is cunning, but his manipulations will only end in his death," Mineera concluded.

"What do we do now?" Jared questioned.

"What do we do now?" Tani echoed, his voice haunted. "We run. We need to get out of here as soon as possible. The machine, that horrid killing machine that lives in these ruins, will be returning soon. I escaped and the robot won't be happy that I'm gone. It will kill me if it finds me. We need to escape. Right now, let Lavosi win. For the time being, we don't have the luxury of time."

"Robot? Killing you? What are you talking about?" Banion tried to get him to calm down.

Looking at Banion with a level gaze, Tani placed his hand on his shoulder. His green eyes looked into Banion's harsh eyes. As he gripped Banion's shoulder tightly, Tani had his full attention. "Trust me, Banion; we need to get out of here now. I'll explain the rest of this when we're not in danger. Trust me."

Nodding in agreement, Banion conceded to the scholar's demands. The rest of the team acknowledged the decision as well.

"We left our gear in the control room. Let's go back there and then get the hell out of here. Lavosi has won this round." Banion's voice was confident, and he smiled at Tani as he spoke.

With that, Nova 7 retreated back to the control room to grab their gear. Further in the ruins, the Consortium of Arms, led by the cruel Lavosi, had ignored the sounds of battle and the cries of their countrymen being killed by Nova 7. Lavosi's objective was the nuclear warhead and he didn't care that several of his own kind had been killed in the quest. Ignoring the fatalities, Lavosi ordered his army of rat warriors to evacuate the ruins with the prize of all prizes in hand. The Consortium of Arms, the vile tribe of hybrid rats, was now a nuclear power.

Chapter 15
Rolling the Dice

The sun had just risen. With the air still brisk, a light fog had settled over the highland valley. Drifting through the serene trees, the fog meandered, causing much of the valley to disappear in a shroud of mystery. Snow was still clinging to the trees after the past week of fierce weather. Two blizzards over the course of the last week or so had left the region completely submerged in blinding white powder.

Crouching down in the snow, Jared inspected the tracks. He brushed his hand across them, his expression amused. "At least they're not hard to track. There are so many of them, we should be able to find them easily. Those rats don't seem to care about being detected."

"And why should they? They have a small army," Tani said, agitated.

"We'll get 'em. Don't you worry," Banion declared confidently.

Mineera seemed to be lost in thought. As a chill breeze broke over the valley, the psychic closed her eyes. The gentle breeze pushed into her hood and rustled her long black hair. She breathed in with a deep gasp as her senses caught the scent of something strange. Wrinkling her nose, her brow furrowing, she appearing to be distressed as she focused on her surroundings with her psychic powers. "Something's not right..." she whispered.

"What is it?" Banion quizzed her quickly.

"I'm not sure… I feel *something* strange. I can't quite explain it. It's almost as if some primitive being is confused. I'm not sure what exactly it is. It's a diffuse feeling, almost as if a small child is submerging in a primordial rage. The thoughts are erratic and disjointed. I have never experienced anything like it."

"It's TOM 23." Tani's voice conveyed his certainty. "It's exactly how it was behaving while I was being held captive. The machine was always on edge, always brooding."

"That's impossible," Mineera asserted, opening her eyes to challenge the youth. "TOM 23 is not alive. I don't care how many times you tell me about it. That machine has no *soul*. My powers are based on the spirit world, not a world of technology."

"Who's the narrow minded one now?" Tani replied brusquely, almost snapping at her. "You actually believe that your explanation of life, your spiritual point of view, is the only perspective? How many times have you scoffed my ignorance to the spirit world? How many times have you thought me foolish?" As he shook his head, Mineera was taken aback by his forward push towards confrontation. The youth had grown significantly over the months of hardship and was not afraid to confront others about his thoughts and beliefs.

"Let me tell you something, Mineera," Tani continued the brisk assault. "When I was in those tunnels and all alone, I prayed. I prayed to anything that would listen to me. I was so alone and so afraid, I sought strength from *something* greater than myself. If I can embrace the idea that the spirit world is real and that I need help from it, you can acknowledge that technology, aggressive human thought, gave rise to something alive that doesn't have a soul. That machine stalking us is very much alive and is extremely dangerous as a result. It doesn't know what it is or how to handle the raw and primitive emotions that it perceives. This insanity is far from over. TOM 23 could be the most dangerous part of our crusade."

Mineera conceded defeat to Tani and gave him a slight bow. Backing off, she cherished his wisdom. The scholar had been correct. If a person who craved technology and gadgets could find wisdom and strength from the spirit world, a person born to religion could embrace the teachings of technology and lost lore.

"Are you two done? The more we stand out here, the easier it will be to lose those rat warriors." Jared was clearly exasperated. "Plus, I'm freezing my ass off! Can we get moving so my blood can get pumping again? My fingers have frostbite again."

Chuckling, Banion agreed. "Let's move," he ordered.

As they pushed on, tracking the war band, it felt wonderful to be free of the confined ruins and tunnels of the military base. After having spent many days underground, the brisk freezing air of the northlands was a welcomed sensation in contrast to the dreary, depression of the dark twisting passages. Even though the enemy had control of the nuclear warhead, none of the members of Nova 7 were distressed about their prospects. They had each experienced adversity and staunch resistance during the entire quest for the nuclear warhead. The loss of the warhead was simply the newest setback, the newest challenge that needed to be overcome. Almost lackadaisical about the event, each member of Nova 7 was already concocting solutions to the problem. None of them knew exactly how to triumph over the newest adversity thrown in their laps, but it didn't matter, it simply didn't matter; the team would build another wild plan and succeed once more.

Following Jared away from the perimeter of the military base, the team pushed deep into the forest, tracking the vermin war band. They had traversed only a mile from the ruins when screams rose just ahead of them in the forest.

Startled by the sounds, Nova 7 went instinctively into defensive positions. Dropping to the ground with weapons ready, the three men of the team drew their guns and prepared for conflict. Mineera, on the other hand, remained standing, probing her surroundings for the cause of the turmoil. Blinking several times, she could feel the unusual, primitive presence just ahead. TOM 23, terror from the ancient world, had stumbled upon the vermin warriors. Stunned by the revelation, she spoke in a whisper. "We're close! I think the machine found them..."

The team pondered the event. Each of them looked at the other in confusion. Finally, Tani spoke with a distant look in his eyes. "I have an idea..." The rest of the team turned to him with odd expressions. "I think this is a good thing. I have a hunch maybe this is the turning point, and maybe this is finally our chance. Come on!" Tani urged in rising excitement.

The rest of the team looked on with blank expressions, suspending judgment. Finally, Banion sighed and gestured them forward.

The deer had been pierced and bloodied. Its battered body, horribly torn and mangled, hung limp in the bloody claw of TOM 23. The mighty robot's one red probing eye stared in disbelief at the rat war band standing in a clearing just ahead. Scanning the life forms, spikes of memory rushed into the war machine's malfunctioning processor core. The last time TOM 23 had seen such creatures was in the tunnels of the military base. Brushing his scanner over them, he paused and viewed a curious item being carried by the warriors.

A crate of sorts, a black resin container, was being carried by the rat hybrids. Scanning the case carefully, the machine recognized the container; it was the same container that TOM 23's beloved master, Tani, had in his possession the last time he had seen the scholar. Viewing the container stirred the robot's psyche. A spike of panic rolled through the machine. Fear took over and the machine shuddered.

"Processor Failure. Unknown operand and subroutine formation in progress." A shower of sparks broke the tense standoff as the rat warriors looked on in horror, weapons at the ready.

"Hold your fire!" Lavosi boomed.

As they backed away from the monstrous machine, a wave of panic broke over the rat warriors. All had heard the story of how the sadistic machine had gone on a killing spree the last time the tribe encountered the ancient menace.

The fear continued to take hold of the machine. The driving force behind TOM 23's budding personality was loneliness. The passage of time alone in the dark tunnels was too much to bear again. TOM 23 would not be alone again; it was something the machine could not endure. The rat warriors had the resin case, the same resin case that the robot's new master Tani had when they last parted. Confusion turned to fear. What had the rats done to Tani? Where was his new friend?

Shuddering, the machine was beginning to lose control. It rushed forward, throwing the bloody deer upon the pristine white snow. The speed of the charge was unnerving. One of the rat hybrids, attempting to dive for cover, was too slow to escape. Grasping the rat in its bloody metallic claw, TOM 23 picked up the vermin and brought it right before its monstrous glowing red eye.

"Where is he?" the machine boomed. "Where is my master Tani?"

Seeing the situation turn from bad to worse, Lavosi knew what was about to happen. The machine was traumatized by the thought that the rats had slain Tani. It didn't take a genius to figure out that the machine was only a few seconds away from one more homicidal killing spree. With an intent urgency, he snuck forward in the confusion and crouched near the nuclear warhead. Brushing his hand lovingly across the case, all compassion drained from his face. A hate-filled expression settled upon his quivering lip. Looking at his rat warriors nearby, he knew what must be done in order to save the nuclear warhead which his greedy soul desired above all else.

The pristine, untainted snow waited in silence for the torture of conflict to break loose. Tendrils of silent fog drifted through the trees during the tense standoff. For now the forest was quite. In the eerie silence, Lavosi gripped the case containing the nuclear warhead lovingly. There was only one thing that would satiate his hunger; there was only one thing that drove the wretched king of the underworld. The warhead meant *everything*. Looking at his war band one last time, he issued a frantic order to his brethren.

"Open fire! Kill the machine!" Lavosi ordered. His rat warriors were already scared and on the verge of attack anyway. As the command reached the ears of his minions, the rat hybrids opened fire on the machine, trying to slay it. Automatic weapons fire broke the calm of the forest.

A horrid onslaught of bullets tore forward. All members of the expedition save one attacked the machine. In the chaos of the ensuing battle, Lavosi ignored his companions and pulled with all of his might. Dragging the case housing the nuclear warhead through the snow, the monarch of the rats sought to escape the battle with his glorious prize. Quickly moving into the tree line, he never looked back. A sinister smile graced his lips as he succeeded in escaping the slaughter of his own kind. The plan had led to victory; Lavosi had sacrificed his own loyal troops to feed his greedy hunger and need. Ignoring their screams, he dropped to his knees and caressed the container holding the nuclear warhead.

A whirring noise tore through the air. Servo motors inside the arm of TOM 23 sprung to life. A compartment opened, revealing a cylinder rising from inside the machine. As it charged, the laser prepared for another bout of reckless slaughter. Meanwhile, TOM 23 looked at the hapless rat warrior in its claw. Giving in to the rage coursing through it, the machine smashed the rat warrior into the ground. With hate guiding it, TOM 23 brought its mighty steel foot down upon the cowering rat hybrid. The once-pristine snow was now tainted with crimson blood. Seeing the wash of color on the snow, the livid red stain, the machine knew what its true purpose was. War was its only function; it cared for nothing else. Giving in to the clarity of its purpose, it quickly scanned the battlefield.

Bullets hummed and hammered its body as the rat warriors desperately tried to destroy the ancient combat automaton. The smell of ozone filled the air. Enormous capacitors crackled as energy funneled into them. A green light sliced through the air as the superheated stream of radiant light tore forward. Evaporating flesh, the laser killed rat warriors all throughout the battlefield. Moving forward with deliberate steps, TOM 23 swung its left arm down, crushing another warrior into a smear of eviscerated flesh. Heavy gunfire snapped as the machine returned fire. A spike of emotion rocked the machine as it killed. It was something foreign to the robot, but it was thrillingly *new*. As killing piqued a new emotion in the machine, it felt even more alive. Savoring the fresh emotion, it killed without recourse.

White snow, once untainted, was defiled with crimson blood. The gentle fog lightly clinging to the trees had been replaced with smoke and gunfire. The once fresh- smelling morning now reeked of ozone and burnt flesh. A forest once devoid of such strife and war was now stained with conflict and death.

As the slaughter of his companions continued, Lavosi strained to pull the warhead even further from the scene of death. He was so elated by his treachery and his success at keeping the nuclear warhead all to himself, he never heard a silent hunter creep up behind him. The stalker, deft and agile, moved in behind the oblivious Lavosi. Holding a shimmering blue sword in the morning sun, the warrior prepared to attack the vile king. The tribal warrior brought the pommel of his blade crashing down into Lavosi's scalp with one heavy swing. The handle of the weapon smashed into his skull and he was knocked unconscious.

Lying in the snow, Lavosi's white fur was stained red as a spray of blood erupted from his head wound.

"I should have killed you." Jared spoke with venom in his voice. A flash of madness was in his eyes as he stared at the downed king of Verminhold. Pulling him back, Mineera shot him a grave look of concern.

"There's no need for that," she cautioned, holding his shoulder with an eagle-like grip.

Shaking in reluctant agreement, the tribal snapped out of the rage. He looked back at the others, lingering a few paces back, and motioned them forward.

It was a dream, or rather a nightmare. There were so many times they could have turned back, so many times they could have called it quits; but they hadn't. Each of them took a brief moment to survey the black resin case resting in the snow. As they stared down at the object, their dread mounted. The object of their crusade, a fully functional nuclear warhead, now rested quietly in the snow. Looking at each other, all of them felt that a terrible line had been crossed.

It wasn't too late; Nova 7 could still have turned back. All they had to do was leave the black resin case sitting in the forest.

Blinking in confusion, Jared stammered, "Is this real? Did we actually do this?"

Nodding in confirmation, Tani looked at the rest of the team in turn. "Yes, this is real. We did it."

Mineera felt a wave of sadness wash over her as she looked at the weapon. A tear rolled down her cheek. "I can never forgive myself for such an act. But I can never allow the Dark Order to claim the land. Without the sacrifice of our souls and our convictions, evil will win. It is with a heavy heart that I accept the burden of mass murder." The single tear turned to a stream of tears as she openly wept. "How did we lose ourselves to such madness? How did mankind fall so deep into darkness that our only salvation is a weapon of such terrible power? No war is holy; it is only bred out of necessity and instinct to survive. I will not pray to God in thanks for this moment. I will only pray for pity and forgiveness for what we have done."

"Obsession brought me to this place, this very moment in my life. Now that I stand on the precipice of madness, I know what I am and what I have done. I first thought that this was a noble quest. There is nothing noble about what we must do. You are correct, Mineera; I don't feel like a hero, only a murderer. Where once I would have sold my soul for what is before me..." Banion motioned to the weapon, "...I would gladly give it all back for a peaceful life. I will never forgive myself for this."

"Should we just hide it somewhere? Hide it so no one can ever find it?" Jared's tone was earnest, resistant to the very thought of taking the sinister artifact with them. "Let's just go home. Let's imagine that it doesn't exist."

"We can't do that." Tani's voice was matter-of-fact. "Every night I see the same thing in my dreams. I see the faces of all those poor souls who lost their lives the night Rasheed fell. When we were leaving on the boat, I listened to their screams and wondered why I was spared. Why did we all survive that night where so many died? I now know that even though we must be monsters to stop an even bigger threat, we survived that night to be a beacon of light against the coming darkness. I survived the battle of Rasheed so that I could be standing right here, right here with all of you. Each of us is special in our own right. Our talents and skills have made it possible for us, as a team, to act as the sword that will finally bring about the destruction of the Reaper Kai. It's no longer about us or how we feel. We are here protecting all those who all still fighting against the Dark Order. We can never go back. We must push forward. The burden of this task is ours and ours alone."

The scholar finished his speech, and they all agreed that no matter the cost to themselves, they would see the task through to the bitter end. Kneeling down, Jared and Tani each grabbed a handle on the resin case containing the nuclear warhead. Standing up, they looked to Banion for guidance.

The sounds of battle were still echoing through the forest. Carnage was being wrought upon all that remained of Lavosi's expedition. Looking down at the wretched lord of the rats, they pondered what they should do with him.

"What about him?" Jared motioned to Lavosi, voicing their collective thoughts.

"Take his weapons and leave him," Banion ordered. "He's no longer a threat."

Nova 7 left the scene with the prize of all prizes. After many moons of strife and indecision, bloodshed and fear, Nova 7 had succeeded in their quest. Making haste to escape the mountain valley, the team was torn with conflicting emotion. They now had a heavy burden in tow, a weapon that was intended to exterminate an entire race in a blinding flash of nuclear fire. But where they had guilt, they also had hope. The quest would bring them all back to civilization, and that prospect made their hearts leap. Though the road would be long ahead, there was an end in sight. They all knew what needed to be done and they moved forward to meet their destinies.

And so it was that a team of heroes rushed to meet their futures with staunch hearts and souls filled with hope. The world was dark but there was light on the horizon, and that light was Nova 7.

Chapter 16
A Fate Worse Than Death

His surroundings were a complete blur. With a groggy, nauseous pulse of feeling, the vile king of the rats felt his body come alive. A surge of agony throbbed in his skull as he fought the wave of pain rolling through his body. Grasping at his skull, Lavosi was stunned to find a clotted mass of blood sticking to his bristly white fur. Groaning in anguish, he sat up and blinked several times.

A strange wash of colors met his sight as he struggled to gain a bearing on his surroundings. As his vision cleared, the wash of colors came together into a haunting display. A skeleton dressed in decomposing military attire came into view. Empty, dried-out eye sockets stared at the rat king. The skeleton's arms and legs had been painstakingly bound together with thick, corroded black steel wiring. Gasping in surprise, Lavosi spun around and found that an entire host of corpses were surrounding him. All of them had been arranged in a circle to peer sightlessly at a chess board in the middle of the tunnel.

A jolt of panic rolled through him as he stared around at his bizarre surroundings. Instead of being outside in the forest, the vermin king found himself in a dark passage, under the earth. Instead of seeing the sun reflecting off pristine white snow, a grungy yellow light bulb flashed on and off in a dizzying rhythm. Within seconds, he knew that he was no longer in the place where he had fallen. After being knocked unconscious, he had been *moved, moved* against his will.

His fear intensified instantly. Trying to stand, Lavosi was stunned to find that he was no longer alone. An ominous creature, a thing born from the ancient world, was hovering in silent menace above him. Seeing him stir, the machine was set in motion. It threw its clawed hand forward to clutch Lavosi, pulling him off his feet. Raising him high in the air, the machine considered him with its glowing red eye.

TOM 23 began the interrogation, its robotic voice booming out. "What did you do with him?" it almost screamed. As it spoke, the machine began to shake uncontrollably. A shower of sparks erupted from its enormous processor core.

Cowering, Lavosi grasped at the metal claw restraining him. He tried to wiggle free, to no avail; the machine had a firm hold on him. The cowering turned to a sneer as a jolt of anger rolled through Lavosi's precarious mind. He no longer cared about caution. His rage was too strong and too powerful to control. Staring at the machine, the albino rat spoke with venom in his voice. "Let me go, you worthless pile of scrap!"

Having learned about conflict and pain, the machine responded to the request with sinister intent. Gently, it squeezed the hapless captive. Lavosi groaned as the pressure around his ribs mounted. Feeling as if he was about to crack a few ribs, the vermin cowered once more. "You win."

"You will answer my question. What did you do with him? What did you do with my friend?"

"Your friend?" the captive echoed in slight confusion.

"Yes, my friend. What did you do with Tani?"

Lavosi laughed dryly, struggling to comprehend the situation. "Your *friend*?"

Irritated by his insolence, TOM 23 began to squeeze his captive once more. This time, the pressure was more intense. Gasping, Lavosi felt as if his life was about to be crushed out of him. With eyes bulging, he tried to pull enough air into his lungs to respond. "I did nothing with him! We let him go!"

"Let him go? Let him go where?"

"I don't know!" He spoke quickly, trying to avoid getting crushed to death.

"Tell me where!" TOM 23 began to crush him again. This time the pressure was so intense that Lavosi felt one of his ribs pop, splitting in his chest. Gagging in pain, he screamed back a quick response.

"I can help you find him. I will help you find him!" he pleaded.

As the massive arm eased its pressure, the red glowing eye of the machine swiveled and considered the rat with full attention. Was this creature lying to him, lying like all the other beings of flesh? Pondering him carefully, the machine fought an internal battle. Should it trust him, could it trust him? Wanting to know more, it commanded him, "You will help me."

"Yes, yes I will help you..." As he conceded, the machine released a significant amount of pressure from his chest. Once he was able to breathe normally again, Lavosi began to concoct a plan, a way to escape with his life. Thinking for a brief second, he concluded that cooperation would benefit them both. "I have a deal for you."

Servo motors clicked in the head of the enormous machine as it moved forward to survey him better. "What is your deal?"

"If you let me go, I can tell you how to find Tani. I can teach you how to locate him."

The machine considered the deal and concluded that there was no such thing as a deal. It didn't care about compromise or compassion. It had a need, a want. No longer could it be alone. The machine hungered for companionship more than anything. Tani had been the most interesting thing that the machine had in its *life* for hundreds and hundreds of years. This need was the focus of the machine's existence. Regardless of the circumstances, the robot had concluded that it would get exactly what it wanted. Having learned about lies and betrayal, it had no conscience holding it back. With a confident mental leap, the machine had concluded that lying would get the results it needed. "You have a deal, fleshling."

Elated by the thought of yet another manipulation, Lavosi began to chatter on quickly, already anticipating his release from the machine. "All things, and I mean *all things*, leave a trail. In the snow, out in the forest; look for tracks, imprints made by his boots. In the snow and mud, you can follow these tracks to find him."

"Outside?" the machine boomed in confusion. The scenario didn't make any sense. The last time they had talked, Tani insisted that he would stay with the machine. Knowing that he was outside the tunnels filled TOM 23 with more questions than answers. The scholar had promised to stay with him and teach him more about life. The confusion was turning to a primal feeling of abandonment. Shaking with rage, the immense robot was overwhelmed with a feeling of betrayal. "He lied to me!"

Seeing the frustration taking hold of the machine, Lavosi smiled, his mind set awash by devious plans. He still didn't know for certain who had ambushed him and knocked him senseless in the forest, but he had a pretty good idea. Nova 7 was the only answer to the riddle. Since they had known he had the warhead, it didn't take a genius to figure out that they had knocked him out, *stealing* it from him. Seeing the machine's frustration with Tani's betrayal, Lavosi knew he could work his dark manipulative magic once again. With a broad grin, he sought to enrage the machine even more.

"You can never trust a human," he sneered. "They always lie and deceive! Tani is no different. You think he cares about you? You think he *wanted* to be with you?"

"What are you saying?" TOM 23 was agitated and growing increasingly confused. Sensing that the machine was befuddled, Lavosi continued his poisonous rhetoric.

"Tell me, did Tani ever ask you to do things for him? Things that you didn't understand?"

Thinking for a brief second, TOM 23 recalled the scholar's strange request that he smash through the vault wall protecting the nuclear warhead. "Yes…"

Rubbing his hands together, Lavosi brought it home. "Tani only cares for himself. He used you. He betrayed you. Tani never wanted to stay with you. He doesn't care about your needs. That worthless wretch betrayed me too! He took what I want most in this world! He has betrayed you and me both!"

The words resounded inside the machine, resulting in a flurry of rage. The feeling of betrayal had to be satisfied. TOM 23 wanted revenge and Tani was at the root of his anger. Smashing his fist into the floor of the tunnel, the robot was quickly losing control.

"Follow him and teach him a lesson! Catch him and make him suffer! Betrayal should be dealt with swiftly. You cannot allow someone to treat you so horribly!"

"I will find Tani and make him suffer."

"Excellent..." Lavosi smiled. His new plan was already taking shape. The machine would track Nova 7 and kill them. After their slaughtered corpses were nothing more than cold memories, Lavosi would take back what was rightfully his. Smiling, he knew that the road to the nuclear warhead was going to be a reality.

His wild elation was to be short lived. Having heard the rat speak about how to look for boot prints in the snow, the machine was convinced it could track Tani on its own. Looking at the vermin, TOM 23 had a strange idea. What if the rat had also lied? What if the fleshling had betrayed him too? Viewing the skeletons in the tunnel, the idea became a concrete action. Throwing his hand forward, he grasped Lavosi once more. As he was lifted into the air, the monarch of Verminhold was stunned. Being captured by the machine again was not part of his plan.

"What are you doing?" he asked frantically, his blood-red eyes filled with terror. A nasty feeling of despair filled him. His sixth sense had kicked in, foretelling impending doom.

"Fleshlings cannot be trusted. You are a fleshling. You cannot be trusted." Grabbing a bundle of thick, corroded wiring, TOM 23 began to bind the rat king by wrapping the wire around him.

Terrified, Lavosi wailed in terror as the steel wiring dug into his flesh. Ignoring his pleas, TOM 23 continued to wrap layer after layer of wire around him. The elated robot observed his captive squirm less and less with each layer of wire. The fleshling would not escape his clutches. Using the entire bundle of wiring, the machine labored for many minutes, ensuring escape would be impossible.

"Let me go! I beg you! I will take you to Tani!" Lavosi wailed in fear, unable to budge a muscle.

"I don't need you to take me to Tani. You told me how to find him. I do not need you for now."

The plan had failed. Lavosi was a master of manipulation, but TOM 23 was unable to understand his subtleties and trickery. Where once he had been the king of getting his way, Lavosi was now in mortal danger. Whimpering, he pleaded again and again, but his entreaties fell on deaf ears. The ancient machine had already made up its mind.

Grabbing a spike of steel from the rubble in the tunnel, the machine drove it into the wall. Hoisting his defenseless captive into the air, TOM 23 hung Lavosi on the spike. Sheer terror was gripping the vermin king.

"What are you doing?" he cried out, unable to comprehend what was about to happen.

TOM 23 turned away from Lavosi's pleas without responding. Intent on satiating its anger, the machine wanted only one thing: to make Tani suffer for his betrayal. Determined to track him, TOM 23 left Lavosi and sought vengeance. The ancient behemoth strode quickly through the tunnels, soon leaving them behind.

In the silence of the empty tunnel, Lavosi whimpered and screamed in panic. As he wiggled around, the steel cables dug deeper into his flesh. Each panicked move made the restraints even tighter.

With madness already beginning to take him, Lavosi was filled with an all-encompassing terror. His blood-red eyes scanned the tunnel. In the flashing light, he could see the corpses, bound in wire, staring on with blank expressions. He screamed in desperation, but nothing responded. The tunnel was now just a tomb, an abandoned tomb. The entire rat expedition had been annihilated, sacrificed to the machine in a desperate act of greed so Lavosi could claim the nuclear warhead for himself. There would be no rescue party. There would be no one looking for Lavosi.

Though he didn't know it at the time, TOM 23 would never return. The machine would never make its way back to tunnel to rescue him from a slow, terrifying death.

Pinned to the wall, Lavosi gibbered and wailed in terror in the dark tunnel. His fate had been sealed. No one would save him and escape was not possible. Staring at the lifeless skeletons in the tunnel, Lavosi knew that he was the newest victim to be added to the collection.   He was now part of the sinister menagerie.   As his destiny sunk in, he screamed in terror again and again.   In time, his screams would stop.   In time, his pleas for mercy would end.   In time, he would be nothing more than a skeleton, bound in wire, forever entombed in the lonely tunnel.

Chapter 17
Representative Arthur Gallows

The hub of all life in the northlands of the Darken Realm was the great Iron Kai capital city of Stonen. Stonen's inhabitants lived in a unique environment. Nestled amongst miles upon miles of tunnels which had been burrowed out of the heart of a mountain, the majority of the city was secluded and protected by this massive underground network. A twisting series of discreet passages riddled the mountain in which the city was built.

Stonen was founded just a few months after the nuclear holocaust that had killed nearly all life on Earth. The remnants and survivors of a military base in the northern part of America had banded together and vowed to survive the harsh new world. The soldiers decided to build tunnels under the mountain to protect themselves from the harsh nuclear fallout. The city of Stonen was thus founded and served to protect thousands of survivors. The soldiers then struck out into the ruins of America to bring everyone they could inside their new mountain fortress. The survivors flourished inside the twisting tunnels and passages, which protected society's remains. Within a year's time, the Iron Kai Empire was formed and founded.

Generation after generation of Iron Kai was born in underground tunnels, and all of the inhabitants of Stonen had grown accustomed to the city life underground. Having spent their entire lives in such an environment, the citizens didn't know any better and felt right at home in the tucked-away metropolis.

Having survived the apocalypse, the new community formed a crude government to provide order to the inhabitants of Stonen. A complex caste system arose as the city grew. With each generation, more tunnels were burrowed inside the mountain to allow for the exploding population base. And with each generation that was born to the tunnels, the caste system grew more intricate.

The lower levels of the fortress city were completely dedicated to the military caste of the Iron Kai Empire. Subterranean hangars and bunkers were cleverly arranged to maximize the defenses of the city. There was only one way into the city, through the massive steel doors set on the lowest level of the mountain fortress. All of the barracks for the combat troops were set right beside the reinforced entrance. If Stonen ever came under attack, all of the forces would instantly mobilize at the entrance to the city.

Chiseled out of the rock were a series of machine gun bunkers and defensive positions surrounding the main gate on both sides. The bunkers were so perfectly engineered, they were impossible to take through an outside attack. All of the entrances to the bunkers could only be accessed from within the city. This defense had repelled countless invasions from hostile kingdoms and empires in the turbulent years after the apocalypse. Not one enemy soldier had ever survived the gate defenses to breech the mighty steel doors. Stonen was a fortress that had withstood both the test of time and aggressive enemy advances.

Just above the military district were the slums of the city. The poor section of Stonen was a commune of sorts. Giant rooms had been burrowed in the mountainside to provide housing for the underprivileged citizens of Iron Kai society. Personal quarters were nonexistent in this portion of the city. Instead, the giant rooms were filled with row after row of bunk beds. The mess hall and bathing areas were also communal. Public education in this portion of the city was non-existent; the Iron Kai government felt that this caste of citizens were typically not worth the time or trouble which a proper education would require. Most of the soldiers were born to this caste, and the government also felt that uneducated military personnel were typically easier to control, more likely to follow orders. The remainder of the workers from the lower caste of the

Iron Kai were typically manual laborers and servants to the higher castes in the city.

Just above the slums in Stonen, higher up inside the mountain, was where the middle class of the Iron Kai made their living. Though the accommodations were still based around communal living, each family had its own sleeping quarters. However, the dining areas and wash facilities were typically shared by three or four families. This caste in the Iron Kai society was comprised mostly of skilled crafters and struggling merchants.

As one climbed higher into the city, the great tech houses, merchants, and schools of knowledge could be found in its fourth section. Members of this caste had devoted their lives to the pursuit of knowledge or to the creation and sale of complex technical devices. The study of ancient technology and sites of innovation was centered upon this section of the city. An enormous library, even larger than the great library of Rasheed, was located in the district. The library was whispered to hold nearly fifty thousand books, most from the time before the apocalypse. This treasure was so closely guarded and protected that only a few hundred citizens even had access to it.

Finally, also located in this district were the centers for art and literature. A small number of positions in the arts, highly prized, were allowed to exist and support the advancement of entertainment. Musicians and theater workers were rare and as a result, emerged as highly sought professions. The governing council, led by representatives from each district, often used the theater district as a means to further their own interests and to spread propaganda. In stark contrast, most of the entertainers held opposing perspectives and radical views on political topics, often leading to brash feuds between the theater class and the ruling body. If it were not for Emperor Gunther's firm support of free speech, many believed that most of the theater professionals would have been imprisoned for their daring and harsh attacks against governmental policy.

Above this section of the city was the governmental district. The private residences of the city officials, as well as government buildings, were all situated in this district. Fabulous single family mansions and grand court houses lined the well kept byways and avenues.

The ruling body of the Iron Kai was broken down into several distinct branches. The military branch was under the control of the emperor, a birth-right title which was handed down through the generations. Every child of the ruling emperor had the right to lead the empire, but the representatives of the governing council picked which child was best suited to take on the role of leading the mighty Iron Kai armies. Fierce rivalries often resulted between the offspring of the ruling emperor. These intense family feuds gave rise to the strongest of the brood rising to power, an almost evolutionary way to weed out the lesser rulers. Although any new emperor had to be a direct blood descendant of the current emperor, selection of the strongest child allowed for a better process for the sustained advancement of leadership within the Iron Kai Empire.

The remainder of the government was made up of representatives and advisors. Each district of the city was represented by one advisor and two representatives. Oddly enough, the representatives and advisors did not have to be born from the castes that they represented. The majority of the governing body was born from the upper, wealthier castes in the city.

In determining matters of policy and lawmaking, each representative cast one vote to determine the outcome of a proposed issue. The advisors did not have any voting authority but were allowed to propose their views on an issue directly to the emperor. The ruling emperor's vote on any issue or law weighed fivefold, and thus was a very heavy vote. The ruling body had more power than the emperor, but the opposing viewpoints of its members often left the majority of all decisions in the emperor's hands. Although the Iron Kai Empire was not a dictatorship, it was often perceived as such since the emperor held so much power. This high level of power often made the emperor the target of politically motivated attacks and manipulative plots to sway public opinion.

*   *   *

Night had fallen over the mighty city of Stonen. The majority of the city was below ground, hiding within an enormous mountain, protecting its citizens from the harsh world. A custom within the city after nightfall was to dim the lights within the tunnels to give the inhabitants a physical way to perceive the passage of time. Without such conventions, subterranean life would be difficult.

Council Representative Arthur Gallows was looking out the window of his home at the city streets as the lights dimmed. Smiling, he felt a small amount of comfort seeing that night had overtaken the subterranean city. He felt a bit chilled, almost instinctually, as the light dimmed. Walking over to his study, Arthur grabbed his favorite sweater and pulled it on, then stepped over to the corner of the room and flipped a switch. The natural gas fireplace set in the wall sprung to life and orange flames rose from the tubing within. When the lights went out at night, so did the city's main heating system. It was up to each citizen to warm their living area after sunset.

Crouching down, Arthur warmed his hands by the fire. Lost in thought, he rubbed his balding head with his wrinkled hand. Representative Gallows was in his early fifties, having spent the last twenty-some years in public service, acting in various political positions. His current position was on the council, acting as a representative for the middle-class caste. A staunch opponent of Emperor Gunther, he had led an opposition force of politicians against Gunther for the last ten years. After Gallows had initiated dozens of nasty political attacks against the emperor, it was no secret that he and Gunther *hated* each other. Although Gunther viewed Gallows' tactics as cowardly, he always allowed him to speak his piece; former emperors of the Iron Kai had been much less forgiving of political opponents, often imprisoning or charging rivals as traitors to the empire.

Gallows crouched by the fire and watched the orange flames flicker in the artificial hearth. Smiling and comforted, he let the warmth wash over his body. Lost in thought, he never heard the frantic advance of a shadowy figure toward the front door of his home.

Suddenly, a loud bang sounded, a frantic knocking at his front door. Surprised by the commotion, he scrunched up his nose and called to his servant.

"Millie, can you get the door?" Gallows requested, somewhat irritated.

No response. Suddenly he remembered that his wife and servant had gone to market and would not return for another hour. With a loud sigh, he stood up and proceeded to the front door, but upon opening it, found no one standing there. Confused, he took a step outside and looked around. Just below the steps leading up to his home, a shadow moved from the darkness. It caught Arthur so off guard, he took a step back in alarm.

"Don't worry, it's me," a whisper rose. The shadow moved and became a form. A pale man dressed in fine clothes hunched forward and rested his hand on Arthur's arm.

Blinking several times at the man, his heart still pounding, Gallows remembered the person now standing before him. "Jackson, you gave me quite a startle. What are you doing here? It's night and you scared the hell out of me."

Jackson Mire was a merchant from Rasheed and had spent much of his life transporting goods between the northern empires and the southern reaches of the Darken Realm. It had been a great many months since the two men had last met.

"Can we go inside?" Jackson seemed worried and kept looking around as if they were being watched.

Concerned with his strange behavior, Gallows ushered him inside. Before closing the door, he looked around at the dark, quiet street one last time, half expecting to see someone lurking in the shadows.

"What's all of this about?" Gallows asked, worried, as he urged his friend toward the hearth.

"I'm not sure I can tell you. I'm not sure who to trust anymore."

"What? You're not making any sense. What happened?"

Breathing erratically, Jackson seemed under extreme duress.

"Sit down; let me get you some tea," Gallows offered and Jackson Mire sat down in his study. The tea kettle was still warm and Arthur poured a cup of tea for his long-time business acquaintance.

As he handed him the tea, Jackson was shaking uncontrollably, and the cup chattered on the saucer. Seeing his anxiety, Arthur grew even more distraught.

"Just calm down. I haven't seen you for many months. What happened?" Gallows asked. Calming down a bit, Jackson still seemed reluctant to speak. The representative of the Iron Kai high council tried to soothe him once more, eager to uncover the cause of the strange visit.

"Can I trust you?" Jackson spoke with worry on his face.

After blinking several times, Arthur gave a confident response. "Yes, you can trust me. We've known each other for many years. What happened? What is all of this about?"

A moment of silence rose between them. Jackson seemed to be undergoing a fierce internal struggle as he wrestled with his doubts about Gallows. Finally, he spoke, almost in a stutter. "It's my brother..." he shook his head in despair.

"Your brother?"

"He's dead." Jackson spoke in a matter-of-fact tone, with a distant look in his eyes.

"Dead? Your brother Jonathon is dead?" Arthur echoed in alarm. Like Jackson, Jonathon was a merchant, and both brothers had worked with Arthur Gallows for many years, importing exotic wares from Rasheed. Arthur's mind was spinning from the news. Collecting his thoughts, he asked, "What happened?"

"I'm not exactly sure. Last time I saw him was a few weeks ago. We were running supplies to refugees. One night, he came back to camp scared out of his mind. He said that he had run into a disjointed militia of sorts that had been making raids against Reaper Kai supply convoys. He told me that Rasheed soldiers and Steel Crag soldiers had been hitting Reaper Kai supply lines for many months. The militia told him that the last convoy they destroyed had secret communications from the Reaper Kai high command."

"The Reaper Kai high command?" Gallows was intrigued and eager to learn more. "What did the communications indicate?"

"I'm not sure I can tell you." Mire spoke in a frantic tone, turning around to look out the window of Gallows' study. The dark street was quiet and no one could be seen lurking beyond.

"You can trust me," Arthur urged.

Mire spoke in a near whisper, his expression distant. "The militia stated that the communications were to Emperor Gunther himself."

"What?" Gallows was stunned. "Secret communications from the Reaper Kai to Emperor Gunther? Our emperor?"

Shaking with overwhelming fright, Jackson looked as if he had just crossed some terrible line. "You cannot tell *anyone* what I have said! After my brother told me of this news, we found him dead the next morning at the edge of camp, his throat slashed. Ever since then, I've been on the run. I have been tracked for weeks and followed the entire time. I barely made it here!"

"You can't be serious!" Gallows' mind was spinning. "The emperor in league with the Reaper Kai? I've never agreed with his political views, but Gunther in league with the enemy?"

"I don't understand it either, but it must be true. Why else did my brother die? Why else have I been followed the last week? My life is in danger and there's a good reason for it."

"What else was in the communication? I need more information."

"The communication was telling Gunther that he is supposed to meet in secret with an emissary of the Reaper Kai, here in Stonen within the week."

"Reaper Kai? Here in the city? That's impossible!" Arthur spoke in distress.

"Not possible? Trust me. Trust my pain. My life is in danger and for good reason. Do what you wish with this information. I'm leaving. I can't risk being seen with you." Jackson stood up quickly. As he did, his tea cup fell from his shaky hand and hit the hardwood floor with a crash. The fine porcelain dish shattered and the frantic merchant stumbled, almost falling over. Arthur gripped his friend in an attempt to steady him. In a wild animal panic, Jackson pushed him away and ran for the front door. Flinging the door open, he rushed into the dark streets. Before Arthur could react, he was gone, leaving Arthur alone on his porch, staring into the lonely streets.

Charging away, Jackson moved down an alley behind the courthouses with a smug, devious look on his face. A mischievous feeling coursed through him as he thought about the chaos he had just unleashed. His intent was to misdirect the representative of the Iron Kai Empire, and he had been successful. When he reached the sanctity of the darkness he halted and caught his breath. As Jackson Mire stood in the shadows, a tremor of fear rolled through him. *Someone* was watching him.

Collecting his thoughts, he knew that he was no longer alone. He spun around; someone had joined him in the dark alley.

"Did he believe you?" the shadowy form questioned.

"What? Who are you?" Jackson responded. His hand dropped to his belt and grabbed a dagger, pulling it free from the sheath.

"Did he believe your lies? Did he trust your twisted tongue?" Still shrouded in the darkness, the shadowy form took a bold, aggressive step forward.

"You were watching us?" Mire asked, his voice contemptful, the knife quivering in his hand.

"Yes, I was watching you. Did Gallows buy your theatrics? Did he believe your lies? Gunther is to meet with a Reaper Kai this week? How are you going to fulfill this lie? Meet with Gunther *yourself?*"

"You know my plan well. I don't know who you are but this secret will die with you!" Mire declared spitefully. With a cry of anger, he charged with the intent to stab the mysterious man to death. As he swung full force at the shadowy form, the mysterious man sidestepped quickly, avoiding the attack. Jackson, confused in the darkness, suddenly felt a heavy blow strike him as a solid object connected with his skull. Dazed by the attack, Jackson swung around, trying to stab the shadowy form. He was too slow; another blow landed and Jackson fell forward face-first into the paved stone alleyway. With blood pouring from his wounds, he was on the verge of unconsciousness.

"Damn you!" Mire screamed and swung his knife again, trying to disembowel the mysterious man.

The mysterious man dodged the attack and counterattacked. With a grunt, the aged man struck Jackson Mire, the Reaper Kai agent, once more, this time in the throat, killing him instantly.

A final scream tore through the silent alley as the mystery man's attack ended Jackson's life. As the death cry slashed through the dark subterranean alley, it proceeded to echo in the tunnels. Arthur Gallows, still befuddled by the strange visit from his long-time business partner, was chilled to the bone as his friend's final utterance met his ears. With ice in his blood, he froze on the stairs of his home. He experienced a frantic urge to flee, but was too curious to ignore the strange event. Slowly, he moved down towards the alley. As he did, the mysterious man heard his footsteps and fled the grisly scene.

Crouching down, Representative Gallows tried to save his friend, but to no avail. Jackson Mire, a man who had been scared out of his mind only a few minutes earlier, was now dead. The strange events of the night stirred Gallows and chilled him to his very core. Jackson *was* being stalked. If Jackson was being stalked and was now dead, was the rumor about Gunther true? Was Gunther in league with the enemy? Did Jackson Mire die because of this information? The rumor was transforming into reality in Gallows mind. Looking at Jackson's dead body, Gallows was suspicious of Gunther. Shaking his head in disbelief, he wondered what further horror he would have to endure to uncover the mystery of Jackson Mire's death.

With a tremor of fear, Gallows knew that he had to save the Iron Kai Empire. Relying upon years of experience with attacking the emperor politically, Gallows vowed in that dark alley to avenge his friend at *any* cost. He knew that a tough road awaited him. Gallows knew that his new task was to bring down the emperor himself and to save the Iron Kai Empire at any cost.

Chapter 18
Dangerous Meeting

"I told you! It's my day off!" Gunther boomed from his mighty throne in the Truce Hall. Wiping a dribble of beer off his fiery orange beard, he was almost in a rage.

The guard who found himself forced to intrude upon Gunther's day of quiet had an odd, startled look upon his face. Unable to comply with the emperor's demand, he simply stood in the doorway to the Truce Hall, fidgeting a bit, trying not to anger his master any further.

"Are you deaf? I said it's my day off." Grabbing the stein of beer, Gunther sought to ignore the intruder. Rising from his throne, he turned his back to the guard and wandered over to the enormous windows that looked down upon the lakeshore below. Violent waves, driven by a powerful fall storm, had created white caps on the lake. In the distance, Gunther spotted a fishing boat bouncing up and down, bounding from wave to wave. As the small vessel tried desperately to escape the coming storm, the observer was positive that the boat would capsize before ever making it to shore. With each heave and surge, the bow of the small boat shot directly toward the wave trying to drown it. Rising high, the bow of the ship would crest the top of the wave and the captain would prepare for the next assault.

With stein in hand, Gunther slowly sipped the fine beer and watched in fascination as the boat slowly loomed closer and closer. Smiling, Gunther suddenly wished that he had lived the life of a fisherman. It would be so simple, devoting one's life to peaceful bliss, a profession that offered the outdoors and a way to live a serene life.

Thinking about his own condition, Gunther wanted to laugh out loud, tossed by a roiling mix of emotions. His face quivered as troubling thoughts passed into his mind. Screams echoed in his consciousness as he remembered the sounds of the radio, the horrid radio through which, for months, he had been monitoring the war in a faraway land as his soldiers fought desperate battles against the Reaper Kai.

The sounds of dying men resounded in his mind as memories flooded him. How many had died in the name of the Iron Kai war machine to protect the Darken Realm from the Reaper Kai? How many people had fought so that the evil taint of the Dark Order could be eradicated once and for all? As his thoughts lingered in a dark place, he felt a presence, someone watching him.

Thinking that his disobedient guard was still lingering in the entryway to the Truce Hall, Gunther spun around with the intent of giving his subordinate an unequivocal instruction to leave him alone or face a night in the brig.

Much to his surprise, the guard was nowhere to be seen. The doors to the Truce Hall had been shut, and an eerie figure was lingering only a few feet away from the emperor. An aged man, heavily balding, with a ring of gray hair around his sun-spotted head, rested heavily on a wooden staff used to support his old bones. With a calm, reserved look, he eyed Gunther in silence as if soaking in his presence.

Startled by the newcomer, Gunther fondled a revolver strapped to his belt. After pulling it free, he didn't point it at the strange guest. Instead, he simply held it in clear view to make a stern point. "I am not accustomed to rude intruders, especially in my throne room. You have a lot of nerve sneaking in here."

"I did not have the need to sneak in here. I was allowed by your fine soldiers into this place so that we could converse." The aged man's voice was confident, his gaze never wavering.

"Allowed in?" Gunther snorted. "Not by my guards!" They eyed each other, and the emperor was on the verge of training his weapon on the old man. Pulling the hammer back on the revolver with his thumb, he was ready for conflict. "Did you kill them?"

"Kill them? Your guards? Why, no!" The oracle spoke in a playful tone. "They were kind and gracious. I simply *empowered* them to see things my way. Humans are somewhat foolish in that regard."

"Humans? So what are you then? An assassin? Are you here to kill me?" Gunther gripped the handle on his gun tightly as a twinge of madness lit his eyes. The emperor was convinced the man before him was some sort of Reaper Kai assassin. How else could an old man get into the throne room of the most powerful ruler of the Darken Realm without being given so much as a second glance?

Pondering the question, the old man nodded in agreement to some of Gunther's words. "I guess in some circles I would be called an assassin, but then again, many would call me a savior, one that deals out punishment to assassins. And no, I am not here to murder you, simply to elicit your help in a task that I have been commanded to complete."

"Only a Reaper Kai could befuddle my guards."

"Oh, that is not entirely so." The aged man smiled. "You and I are so very similar, Lord Gunther, so similar that you have no idea."

"You walk in the shadows, sneaking in here like a common thief. I see no similarity between you and myself."

"Long ago, our races diverged. The great civil war was waged in this very city hundreds of years ago. Have you heard the stories? Do you know of the tragedies?"

"You think me a fool? Of course I know of our dark history, the times when the Reaper Kai emerged from the shadows and tried to overthrow this great empire," Gunther boomed back with a look of anger on his face. Still weary and mistrustful of his guest, he held the revolver at the ready. "What I don't know is why you think *we* are similar."

"It's simple: my ancestors are from this city, the homeland of the Iron Kai. *We* share common ancestors and that is why *we* are so similar."

"Common ancestors? You have Iron Kai blood in your veins?"

"Yes, Iron Kai blood is in my veins, but also Reaper Kai blood. The great purges split the empire, tore it in two. My order, an ancient order, was also expelled from the empire. Secluded within the heart of darkness, we grew silently, worshipping in secret to avoid the slaughter and vengeance of the Dark Order." Taking a shaky step forward, the man garbed in blue stared at Gunther, a look of wisdom gracing his features. With a labored motion, he extended his hand toward Gunther in a gesture meant to gain his trust. "My name is Matthew Moralis, descendant of Ceibla Moralis. I am here to begin the purges anew. The time has come for the witch hunts to begin once more in Stonen. The Iron Kai Empire is about to be attacked from within. Time is short and you need my help."

Taking a step back, Gunther's face turned bright red in both amazement and anger in reaction to what he had just heard. As he shook his head in disbelief, the beer stein clutched in his left hand fell to the floor and exploded into a pile of broken ceramic fragments. "I should kill you where you stand, old man!" he boomed in rage. Frustrated and shocked, he stared at Matthew's outstretched hand, a gesture of good will. Placing his gun back in his holster, Gunther was battling a war within his own mind. His intellect told him to kill the old man because logic indicated that this was some sort of Reaper Kai trap. But Gunther's soul, his gut instinct, told him to believe the old man. Standing still for a brief moment, he pondered the outcomes of the two possible actions. If the old man was correct, the Iron Kai capital was swarming with enemy saboteurs and assassins. All of the great empires that had already fallen were infiltrated and destroyed from within. Rasheed, the Steel Crag Mining Guild, and the Mord Tech Empire were all weakened internally prior to invasion. Was it so difficult to fathom that the Reaper Kai would try to destroy Stonen in a similar manner?

Thinking back to the invasion of Dakota Beach only a few months back, Gunther grew even more convinced that the old man before him was telling the truth. In that attack, several enemy landing craft had tried to breach the outer defenses of the city by means of a lakeside assault.

The pieces began to fit together and the attack on the capital city of Stonen seemed imminent. Returning his focus back to the old man, he looked at his outstretched hand once more. Giving in to his gut instinct, Gunther stepped forward and clasped Matthew's hand. Shaking it firmly, they stared into each other's eyes. Both were determined men and both were not to be underestimated. A silent oath had been spoken in that handshake.

With a sigh, Gunther pulled his hand away and moved over to the enormous wooden table. Pulling a chair out, he motioned for the old man to sit down. With a bow of respect, the Oracle of Justice took his place at the table. Ignoring rank and etiquette, Gunther avoided sitting in his mighty throne at the end of the table. Instead, he took a normal chair and sat right beside the old man, giving him another gesture of respect.

Collecting his thoughts, Gunther opened the dialog. "I am not sure exactly what you need from me."

"That is quite simple. I need a few troops and the ability to move throughout your city unhindered. I'm in no condition at my age to engage an army of Reaper Kai assassins and saboteurs. I have strong powers, but they are mostly useless. The Reaper Kai will be immune to my abilities, all except one. Although I cannot fight them, I can find them. I can locate them one by one in your city. The troops, your soldiers, will need to perform the attacks."

"Attacks? You mean kill them?" Gunther concluded.

With a nod, Matthew sighed. "These are dark times. Without stabilizing this city by eliminating the hidden operatives within, I fear you will be unable to withstand a full- scale invasion. I wish there was another way, but you cannot simply imprison a Reaper Kai. A fully trained war priest could not be held in a simple jail cell. I fear that killing them is the only way to stop their advance."

Gunther shook his head, feeling himself being led to a very dark place. "I am the leader of the military, but it is illegal for me to order a strike on hidden operatives within the city. Such a command must be given by the representative council."

"Will they agree?" Matthew's tone was skeptical.

"No, they will never agree. This law was enacted after the last civil war, and is meant to protect the civilian population from religious persecution. I would never be able to convince them otherwise. Hell, even telling them about you would cast serious doubt and suspicion on my ability to lead."

"Then what are we to do?" Matthew quizzed the emperor.

"I don't even trust you fully at this point. My instincts tell me that your words are genuine but I still cannot fully trust you. I need more evidence. I will send some of my own troops out quietly and try to verify your claims. If I find any supporting evidence, I will move to aid you and to aid this empire," Gunther concluded.

"With all due respect, we don't have the luxury of time. Each day that passes furthers the goals of the enemy."

"Let me remind you that I control this empire, not you. I need evidence before action."

"I have evidence."

Gunther eyed Matthew with a squint of suspicion. "What kind of evidence?"

"There was a Reaper Kai operative killed last night in an alley near the courthouses."

"What?" Gunther roared in alarm. "I have heard no news of this."

"Look into the matter. There are dark forces at work that have sought to conceal this fact."

"Conceal the murder of a Reaper Kai in this city? Who would do such a thing?" Gunther rumbled darkly. With a sigh, he shook his head in disgust at the old man. "So be it. If your claim is credible, we will move forward with a plan of action."

Standing, the old man bowed in respect to the emperor. "Just remember, time is not *our* ally. Each day the Reaper Kai saboteurs and assassins remain hidden within this city is one day closer to the doom of this empire." With that, Matthew Moralis left the throne room.

Making his way through the hallways of the palace, the old man never knew that he was being watched. A hidden lurker, closely monitoring Gunther's dealings, watched the old man leave with great interest. A statesman, a member of the council, dressed in regal clothes, lingered near the throne room, watching and waiting. Secluded in shadows, the figure watched with fascination as the strangely dressed man in blue robes exited the Truce Hall. As he shook his head in disbelief, the man's imagination and fears were set in motion.

"So it is true," the man whispered to himself. "Gunther is conducting secret meetings..." Although he was unable to comprehend what he had just witnessed, the event had given striking credibility to the claim of a dead man. Coming into the light, Representative Arthur Gallows eyed the Truce Hall in growing dread. *Something* sinister was at work within the city of Stonen. Gunther had met in secret with a strange visitor.

Convinced of his suspicions, the Representative sought to set things right. Charging through the palace, he exited and made haste to the criminal courthouse just a few blocks away. Rushing into the office of a high ranking judge, Gallows startled the man inside his office.

"Arthur? What is the meaning of this?" Magistrate Riches, the highest ranking judge in the Iron Kai Empire, spoke in alarm, confused by councilman Gallows' actions.

"We need to hold a meeting, an emergency meeting. We need to convene the council immediately."

"Meeting? What are you talking about?" Riches was still alarmed.

Turning around, Gallows shut the door to the office. Moving quickly towards the desk, he sat down and shook his head as if trying to return order to his thoughts. "I need to order a secret session of the high council. We need to convene the council, and without Emperor Gunther knowing about it!"

"What? That could be construed as treason!" Magistrate Riches' concern was rapidly increasing. "Slow down! What is all of this about?"

"If Gunther can hold *secret* meetings, so can we," Gallows responded abruptly. With a flurry of fear in his voice, the representative recounted the grim tale of the mysterious death of Jackson Mire and the clandestine meeting between Gunther and a mysterious holy man garbed in blue robes. Embellishing, he quickly drove a wedge of terror into the judge, the same judge whom Gallows had manipulated time and time again in the past.

Suspicion mixed with fear and soon became a reality for the two members of the Iron Kai government. Convincing themselves of the truth of Gunther's shadowy deeds and feeding each other's panic and paranoia, the two soon conceived a plan with a foundation built on lies and deception. A noose of falsehoods had been created, and Emperor Gunther was the now the target of a political lynching.

Guided by their panic, the two Iron Kai officials agreed to further investigate their emperor, seeking to usurp Gunther, who they were now convinced was in league with the enemy. With this secret plan at work, the Iron Kai government began to tremble.

Gallows' pent up hatred of Gunther due to past political differences, along with the mysterious death of Jackson Mire, had turned him into an inquisitor, seeking to bring down the mighty emperor. The Reaper Kai had devious saboteurs at work inside Stonen, but the worst threat to the empire was currently one of its own, a council member with selfish ambition and a misguided sense of suspicion.

Chapter 19
Treachery and Fear

"I don't like this one bit," a burly soldier with dark eyes declared tensely. His hand flexed repeatedly over the pistol holstered on his leg, his eyes shifting back and forth. He was anxiously chewing on a toothpick, shifting it from side to side in his mouth.

"Me neither. Something is not right. It's been several minutes already. We're going in and we're going in *now*," Gunther concluded, taking a bold step forward.

A guard moved to block the emperor's way with a strange look on his face, his hands outstretched. "It will be just another minute," he said nervously.

"Get out of my way. That is an order," Gunther boomed at the guard.

Scowling as his face turned bright red, the guard stammered and stuttered, "I don't report to you!"

Gunther felt anger roll down his spine in reaction to this preposterous statement. He gripped the guard tightly by the shoulder, allowing his fingers to dig in. With an iron hold, the emperor stared him down and the guard conceded defeat, allowing Gunther and his trusted captain to pass into the morgue. Almost crying out in pain, the guard was relieved that Gunther had let him go. Rubbing the bruised muscles in his shoulder, he slunk off quickly into the darkness, seeking to warn his master about the latest developments.

As Gunther and the captain burst through the door, a man in a long white coat stained in gore spun around with alarm. Apparently he had not finished his current task, working on a corpse with the scalpel he gripped in his hand. Striding forward, Gunther inspected the body on the gurney with suspicion.

"Is this him?" he boomed.

"Who? I don't know what you're talking about," the mortician lied through his teeth, an odd expression on his face. The disobedience first from the guard out front and now the mortician was making Gunther wonder who truly ruled the empire.

"Don't toy with me. Is this the Reaper Kai who was killed last night outside the courthouse?"

Blinking and trying to avoid his gaze, the mortician's eyes shifted uneasily to the bloody arm of the corpse on the gurney. The skin on the body's left forearm had already been removed. The purpose of this strange procedure was unclear at the moment.

Watching the mortician's concerned glances at the body, Gunther's trusted captain, a soldier named Maddock, took a step forward and eyed the mortician's handiwork.

"Doing a little creative work there, doc?" He spoke in a harsh tone, biting down on his toothpick, almost snapping it in two. "What the hell are you doing in here? I thought your job was to make the bodies look presentable for burial, not mutilate them."

Gunther was also suspicious. "Step away from the body."

The mortician didn't even try to disobey. Placing the scalpel on the gurney, he grabbed a rag and began to wipe the blood from his hands. With a sigh, he leaned up against the wall and stared at the two intruders with a solemn look etched upon his face.

Examining the body carefully, Gunther had a flash of insight as he looked at the corpse's left arm, now stripped of its skin. "Let me guess what I'm going to find on the right arm?" Gunther shot a hate-filled glance at the mortician.

Captain Maddock had a pretty good idea as well and moved forward to pull the sheet off the body. A black ink tattoo in the form of a snake, coiled around the man's forearm, was revealed in the dim light of the morgue. The snake tattoo branded on the corpse's body was a telling sign; all Reaper Kai were branded with the sinister snake tattoo on both forearms.

"Reaper Kai it is," Gunther concluded with rage filling him. There were dark deeds and plans afoot in Stonen. Angered by the revelation, he wanted to make sure that the mortician was at full attention. As he breached the distance between them in swift, determined strides, his fiery orange beard was quivering in rage. "Can you tell me why you were in the process of cutting the flesh from this man's arms? Can you tell me why you were trying to hide the fact that this man is our enemy?"

The mortician began to breathe erratically. Concerned for his own safety, he tried to back away, but Gunther countered every step, every move. He blocked the mortician's route of escape, his fury now uncontainable. Maddock also moved in and shoved the mortician against the wall. Alone and outnumbered, the mortician's bravery began to falter. Avoiding eye contact, he tried to ignore them.

"Disguising a dead Reaper Kai body after we have declared war is considered an act of treason. You know what they do to traitors?" Maddock taunted the man. "You are in some serious shit, aren't you?"

"Traitor?" the mortician laughed dryly. "I'm not sure who the *real* traitor is anymore!"

"What the hell does that mean?" Gunther rumbled.

The man ignored the question and tried to step away. Once more he was blocked.

"Let me remind you that I am emperor and your lack of obedience will land you in a jail cell. I am tired of the games. Why did you try to disguise this body and hide the truth?"

"I was ordered to!" he confessed.

"Ordered to? By whom?" Maddock pressed.

The mortician's gaze shifted uncomfortably.

"Tell me what I need to know or Maddock here will handcuff you and you can spend the rest of the day in a cold jail cell," Gunther warned. "My patience is gone, as is my trust in you. Tell me who ordered you to cover up this mess."

"I can't!" he moaned in fear.

"You can and will tell me. Who ordered you to do this?" the emperor pressed again.

"Representative Gallows..." the mortician admitted, shaking his head in despair.

Gunther and Maddock were both stunned.

"Did you say Gallows? Arthur Gallows?" Gunther needed confirmation, feeling as if his ears had played some cruel trick on him.

Nodding in consent, the mortician conceded the horrible truth.

"Why the hell would Gallows cover up the death of a Reaper Kai operative?" Maddock quizzed him.

"I don't know. I don't know." The man under interrogation was frantic, eyes darting back and forth. "He said it was in the interest of the defense of Stonen."

"This doesn't make any sense!" Gunther boomed, feeling betrayed. Unable to think, he shook his head back and forth. "Bag the body," he ordered the mortician. "Maddock, call two full squads of troops down here immediately. We are sealing up this place tight until I figure out what the hell is going on."

Maddock grabbed his radio and called in two full squads of loyal troops to secure the mortuary as the mortician encased the corpse in a black body bag. Zipping it shut, he stared at his two visitors in fear.

Within minutes, the mortuary was swarming with Iron Kai soldiers loyal to both the emperor and Maddock. As they burst in through the door, Gunther felt his control of the situation returning. Pointing at the mortician with disdain, Gunther ordered his troops to take the man into custody. "Seize him and hold him in one of the rooms in the palace. Do not let him out of your sight. Grab this body and transfer it to the palace as well. No one is to go near it; keep it under guard at all times."

"I think it's time we confront Gallows about this matter." Gunther's voice was harsh. "We're going to pay him a visit right now."

"That won't work." The mortician spoke in a matter-of-fact tone, panic having taken over his senses. Circumstances had caused him to regress into no more than a tattling schoolyard rat. He hoped in vain that the information he offered would invoke a feeling of mercy in the emperor.

"Why not?"

Every eye in the room turned to the mortician in expectation following Gunther's question.

"There is a special session of the high council being held right now. You can't speak with him unless you pull him out of the high council meeting," the frightened mortician squealed.

"There is no high council meeting today," Gunther responded with certainty.

"You are mistaken; Gallows has scheduled a high council meeting today," the mortician stood his ground. "He told me himself."

"That's not possible. I'm invited to all of the high council meetings…" A chill shot down Gunther's spine as the reality began to set in. All of the strange behavior at the morgue and the cover-up of a Reaper Kai operative slain in the city were the focal point of the suspicion. Something sinister was at work and it seemed that Gunther was somehow the target of this plot.

As he stared at Maddock with concern, his trusted captain looked back with a similar look. The intent was now clear. The high council, under the leadership of Arthur Gallows, was seeking to cover up a possible Reaper Kai attack within the city, and Gunther was purposely being excluded from the proceedings. His suspicion mounting, for the first time in what felt like forever, Gunther knew real fear. Somehow, a political action was mounting and Gunther was its target. With the threat of enemy invasion becoming a tangible reality, the danger for the Iron Kai Empire had never been greater.

Motioning to Maddock, Gunther and the soldier stepped away from the scene in the morgue, preferring to converse in private.

"What are we going to do?" Maddock asked his emperor.

"I have a pretty good idea what I'm going to do. Come with me, Maddock, I have a special task for you."

"Task?" he quizzed with some interest. "The kind of task that is going to get me killed?"

"Probably." Gunther smiled.

"Is this task illegal?"

"Yes, it is. Performing this task without the will of the high council could be considered seditious and an act of treason."

"What is the number of *illegal* actions I've been involved in? I've done so many now that I can't remember clearly. I bet this is the fifth, maybe sixth illegal covert action I've performed for you." Maddock smiled as he spoke.

With a sigh of resignation, Gunther shook his head. "I only do what I think is right. I only ask you to do these sorts of things for the good of the empire. If the average citizen knew what we knew, the world would be a very scary place. I break the law to save lives, plain and simple."

"I wasn't complaining," Maddock said with a spark of amusement. "You know me, I love killing Reaper Kai."

"I know you do. And speaking of Reaper Kai, I think you'll get your wish. That corpse in the morgue seems to be the tip of the iceberg. Come on, I have someone for you to meet."

"A special someone that is going to get me killed?"

"Of course." Gunther's smile reflected Maddock's own.

"Sounds fun," Maddock concluded. He snapped his jaw shut quickly, his teeth smashing into the toothpick in his mouth, which shattered under the force. Spitting out the fragments, he saluted Gunther crisply with a smile.

Chapter 20
The Oracle of Justice

"I can see you..." the man whispered, closing his eyes and drawing in the essence of his target. With a shudder, the soul of the sinister presence flooded his mind. A sickening feeling of loathing filled his senses. Whomever he was sensing was filled with intense hatred, a being born from pure evil. Squinting in the dark tunnel, the holy man sought his objective carefully. He breathed softly, extending his hand before him. As his fingers wandered in the air, his mind was rapidly beginning to focus in on the threat. His hand vibrated like a tuning fork, an odd sensation, as he tried to focus in on the demonic presence in the dark tunnel.

The aged man was deep below the surface of the earth, wandering Stonen's subterranean streets. Vaults and an endless series of twisting tunnels and passages made up the core of the city. The man was in the capital's lowest portion, below the military district, where the great furnaces and sewer pipes disappeared into a vast network of abandoned caves. Miles upon miles of dark rooms and hidden vaults were in this portion of the city. In the times of the apocalypse, great machines had dug trenches in the earth. This section of Stonen was the most ancient part of the city, a place where forgotten memories of a dark time had been entombed in the icy shadow. It was in these twisted tunnels and passages that a hunter stalked his prey.

"I think they are this way," the man intoned cryptically. Dressed in splendid blue robes with tinges of gold, the foreboding man held a wooden staff in his hand. His face was stricken with age. Wispy gray eyes opened and surveyed his surroundings with suspicion. White tufts of hair surrounded his bald, shiny head. "I can sense them close by. Be on your guard."

His companions, a squad of Iron Kai special forces under the direction of Captain Maddock, a trusted ally of Emperor Gunther, looked at the man with deep suspicion. Even though they had had strict orders to obey the strange man's instructions, they were less than receptive to his insane ramblings. The squad had been searching the lower tunnels of Stonen for more than an hour already. Every few minutes, the aged man would whisper that *they were close by* or *evil was near.* The constant ramblings of the crackpot had left the soldiers sullen and totally unresponsive to his orders. To them, he had cried wolf too many times already.

Even though the old man was not worth listening to, their leader, Mad Dog Maddock, was a force to be reckoned with. Maddock had given his squad direct orders to listen to the strange old man. Along for the ride, Gunther's trusted captain was watching his crew very closely. Whenever one of them began to whine about their current assignment, he shot them a bloodthirsty, maniacal look. A few seconds of Mad Dog Maddock's 'look' was more than enough to get them back in line.

Their current assignment was filled with mystery. Only Maddock knew the entire story. Rumor had it that the strange man had been allowed to travel about the city by the order of Emperor Gunther himself. Even though the man appeared totally insane, the lowly soldiers knew better than to question the orders of the emperor.

His hands shaking, the old man began to stutter as he tried to discern the squad's next course of action. As his hand flew around like a crazed hornet, the soldiers had to duck more than once to avoid being struck by his wild gestures. Coming to rest, the old man sighed and pointed down a nearby tunnel. "It's *this* way!"

"I think you're full of shit, old man," a private dressed in green combat attire scoffed. He would still follow orders, but didn't regret giving the old man a hard time.

Maddock was about to intervene once more but he didn't need to. As the soldier's eyes shot back toward the object of his scorn, he was taken aback by the old man's fierce gaze. Holding unwavering eye contact with the disrespectful soldier, the aged man stared directly into the soldier's soul. The soldier felt a strange wash of energy roll through him, and stepped back with a shudder. The old man had made his point, using his strange powers to stir the youth. As the bizarre sensation ebbed away, the soldier shot him a dirty look, grabbing his gun and holding it tight to his chest.

Smiling, the mysterious man whipped his head suddenly to the right. As if listening to a voice in his mind, his eyes moved toward the junction of tunnels only a few yards away. Stepping forward quickly, he used his staff to steady himself as he bolted down one of the tunnels.

Rolling their eyes, the Iron Kai soldiers gave chase with bemused looks. The old man was strangely quick and the soldiers had to run to catch up to him.

"I see you!" Matthew Moralis rasped, his gray eyes bulging. The old man stopped before a steel door in the wall of the tunnel and pointed at it with an unsteady finger. "In here!"

Not knowing what to think, the soldiers simply stared at him with sick fascination. "What the hell are you talking about?" one of them challenged him. "We have been down here for over an hour. Is this another one of your wild goose chases, old man? I'm getting a little sick of your crap. If it weren't for Maddock here ordering us to go with you, I would have left your sorry ass down here alone twenty minutes ago."

Undaunted by the soldier's stern words, the aged man dressed in splendid blue robes readied himself. He gripped his staff tightly in one hand as his other hand stretched toward the door knob. But the door knob held fast, having been sealed from within the room beyond. Matthew Moralis remained undaunted. He smiled as his hand began to quiver, only a few inches away from the knob. A strange vibration shuddered through the tunnel. The knob on the door began to rattle under the unseen force of the aged man. Although he did not even touch it, the object responded to his will, moving and dancing on its own, trembling and shaking.

The Iron Kai soldiers trained their weapons upon the aged man, jumpy and suspicious after witnessing the strange scene.

"Stand still, old man!" one of soldiers shouted, seeing the door vibrate though untouched. "Put your hands in the air!"

"Put your weapons down!" Maddock ordered his troops, but they were totally unresponsive to his orders after witnessing the old man's supernatural powers. Gritting his teeth, Maddock shook his head in anger as he chewed on a fresh toothpick, watching his crew fall apart.

The aged priest garbed in blue did not respond to the order; instead, he continued to concentrate on the door. The door knob was rattling back and forth violently under the strange force of his will. His psychic powers were strong and he was breaching the door without using a key.

"Didn't know that you were a damn Reaper Kai. I should shoot you dead where you stand, old man!" another soldier shouted in disgust, aiming his gun at the man's chest.

"Reaper Kai?" Matthew Moralis shot back in a nasty tone. "I am no Reaper Kai." With that, the door knob clicked open as the lock succumbed to his will and command. Preparing for the coming conflict, the man grasped his staff tightly. "I hope you have more than those guns to protect you."

"What are talking about?"

"It will take more than weapons to survive the conflict within." Matthew's voice was ominous. A chill shot down the spines of the soldiers as they surveyed him. With a deep breath, he prepared himself, focusing on the task at hand. Steadying himself, he knew that battle was imminent. The aged man took a brief moment to close his eyes and say a silent prayer, his lips moving and a whisper exiting his mouth.

"What are you doing?" another soldier spoke in alarm.

Without responding, the man garbed in blue robes flung the door open.

Rushing inside the room, the squad of troops was shocked by what they found. A group of five figures garbed in blood-red robes were crouched around a cauldron. A noxious smell greeted the soldiers' noses as they stared in horror at a black mass in progress. One of the men had exposed his wrist, which was cut in several places. The red-robed man was allowing the blood from his wounds to drip into the cauldron. Inscribed upon his wrist was a black-ink tattoo in the form of a serpent.

Spinning around, the host of red-robed men jumped to their feet.

The Iron Kai soldiers, accustomed to a sense of security inside their own capital city, were absolutely awestruck by the scene. The crazed old man had been right; Reaper Kai were hiding within the walls of Stonen. Shock turned to outrage, and immediately, they trained their guns upon the red robed priests. Without warning, gunfire ripped the air. The squad leader, having the quickest reflexes, was the first to open fire, knowing full well that a commune of Reaper Kai priests could destroy dozens of soldiers.

Maddock's bullets tore forward and struck one of the Reaper Kai priests. The force of the assault was intense, and the priest crumpled as the high velocity projectiles tore through his body. A spray of blood was torn free as he died in the shower of lead.

The return attack was fierce. Requiring only a brief second to act, the remaining priests began to channel energy through their demonic hearts. They screamed in primal rage as the demonic energy was unleashed. A crackle broke the air; a black jet of pulsing light spun around like a corkscrew from one priest's hands. The vortex struck a soldier in the chest. As the psychic energy bore into him, a grotesque noise erupted. The twisted spiral of power had devastating effects upon the man. His bones twisted, rotating around as the black energy cored him. The muscles inside the man's body, violently torqued, tore under the pressure. Finally, blood vessels strained and succumbed. The twisting power could not be stopped and the soldier screamed in agony. His body was wrenched around and around as bone after bone broke.

With a tortured grimace, the soldier crumpled, his internal organs pulverized and shredded by the shattered bones in his chest. He gasped in agony, only seconds from death. As the soldier died, three of his companions met similar fates. One of them clutched his throat, unable to breath. The second soldier was screaming as his body was burned by demonic fire. A third shuddered on the floor, poisoned needles imbedded in his chest.

Rising smoke and burnt flesh mingled in the air, creating a sickly odor. Chanting filled the room as an ominous language was incanted, prayers spoken to demons and creatures born from hell itself. A bright blast of flame arced across the room, its orange light erupting from the sinister Reaper Kai priest. Another soldier had been incinerated by hellfire. Screaming in pain, the man whose flesh was burning and whose clothes were aflame ran from the room, trying to escape the demonic attack. The squad was quickly losing steam, having been decimated in a matter of few seconds.

Stepping over the corpses of the slain, the aged man garbed in blue was undaunted by the display of evil power. He released his staff, which levitated off the ground. Floating in the air, the wooden staff began to shimmer. A blast of light emanated from the weapon with a bright pulse.

Seeing the strange display, the Reaper Kai priests knew that the aged man was no ordinary soul. They focused their wrath upon him, assaulting him with the will of their dark souls. Demonic energy rushed forth to slay the man.

A lance of fire erupted forward, a green glowing orb of energy enveloping him. He was assaulted by a spiraling corkscrew of darkness, and a crackle of electricity shot forth. Standing resolute, the man allowed the sinister psychic energy to strike his frail frame. Every demonic attack struck his body. In the blink of an eye, all of the pyrotechnics subsided. Standing tall and strong, the aged man was unscathed by the Reaper Kai attacks. Their demonic power had left him unwounded.

Stunned by the ineffectiveness of their attacks, the Reaper Kai each took a step back. A second of indecision was all the soldiers needed. Taking the initiative, the remaining soldiers opened fire. Firing as many rounds as possible, they rapidly turned the tide of battle. Mad Dog Maddock smiled in glee as his crack-shot aim mowed down the opposition. Expertly training his automatic weapon on his foes, he fired several rapid bursts of gunfire, spraying each Reaper Kai with multiple bullets. The priests, losing the life force in their veins by violent gunshot wounds, stared in awe at the aged man before them. As they collapsed to the ground, the last image to imprint itself upon them was the strange old man, a holy man, an oracle of a forgotten god.

"Who are you?" a dying Reaper Kai rasped, clutching his wounds, feeling the blood pour from his body.

"I am Matthew Moralis, the Oracle of Justice." With a look of dispassion, the man garbed in blue grasped his still-levitating staff.

"Moralis..." Gagging, the Reaper Kai finally understood. "A descendant of Ceibla Moralis..."

"The reign of the Dark Order is at an end," the aged man responded in a crisp tone.

A look of awe ignited in the priest's eyes as he looked upon a living legend. The lost tribe of Ceibla Moralis was no myth. There was truth to the legends of the ancient order. Breathing a final breath, the Reaper Kai passed into death; the last image he would ever see was a holy man, a true holy man, the descendant of a mythical hero.

Finishing the job, the Iron Kai troops put a few extra bullets into the Reaper Kai just for good measure. The survivors of the harsh battle within the secluded tunnels of Stonen stared in awe at the aged man. Grasping his staff, The Oracle of Justice eyed the remaining soldiers and considered them with a serious gaze. "I suggest we call for reinforcements; my job here is not yet done. There are more of the Dark Order infesting this city. We have much work to do."

The soldiers regarded him with stunned glances. Eyeing the dead Reaper Kai, Maddock grabbed his radio. Contacting other members of his covert unit, he asked for additional assistance.

Maddock smiled and slapped Matthew Moralis on the shoulder. "I've met some strange people and done some strange things for Gunther over the years, but you, old man, are the most unusual of them all." Chewing on his toothpick, he gave Matthew Moralis a bemused look.

The evidence of war was everywhere within the room. Dead soldiers and Reaper Kai alike littered the premises. Blood had pooled on the floor around the corpses and gore was spattered on the walls. Exchanging quick glances, the survivors knew that this was a day to be remembered. The Dark Order had infiltrated the most powerful city remaining in the Darken Realm. Looking at Matthew Moralis and Captain Maddock, each of the remaining soldiers felt that they had a profound duty to perform. Returning his men's gaze, Maddock spoke to them.

"Can you understand now why this mission is top secret? Can you see why I couldn't tell you why we were following this crazy old man around the bowels of this city?"

Nodding in respect, the soldiers saluted their leader and gave Matthew encouraging looks.

Shaking his head in despair, a soldier viewed the bodies of the slain Reaper Kai. "It's happening again isn't it? The purges and witch hunts? It's just like the stories my father told me about the civil war when I was young. We're living through it again, aren't we?"

Without a word, Maddock simply stared at the soldier and nodded in agreement.

The reality hit them hard. Each and every one of them, including Matthew, knew the history of the great purges and the civil war that had almost destroyed the city of Stonen. The inquisition had begun once more. The capital city of Stonen was no longer safe. As in days of old, the witch hunts were beginning again. Led by the enigmatic chaplain, the Oracle of Justice, the Iron Kai were about to embark upon a sinister holy war within the streets and byways of their beloved capital city. The Great Purges had begun again, a secret war that would force Maddock's troops to act as a cleansing force, driven by violent action and an iron will to survive.

Chapter 21
Twisted Guilt

Holding the parchment in her hand, Marion Toil, the Queen of Rasheed, was trembling, feeling a mixture of emotions. Her servant stood at attention, purposely avoiding eye contact with the dark queen. Resting both of her hands in front of her, she allowed the contents of the parchment to sink in.

"Leave me!" she commanded the servant, her voice cracking, overwhelmed by her conscience. Seeing her distress, the servant immediately made haste to escape her possible wrath and retribution. The queen was obviously in a dark place, a much darker place than usual. Everyone in Rasheed who had survived the invasion knew to steer clear of any Reaper Kai, especially when gripped by any sort of passion.

Leaving the area with the intent of self preservation, the servant hurried away, and Marion Toil was left alone in the western garden of the palace. A chill wind was riding the air pushing in from the harbor. The breeze was refreshing, and for good reason. Recently, the dungeons of Rasheed had been 'cleaned.' Over one hundred victims had met their deaths at the hands of Reaper Kai priests within the dungeons, forced to endure the cruelest forms of pain and punishment until they succumbed to the torture. The corpses were deposited in the western garden, just outside the guest quarters within the palace walls. The sickening piles of broken, rotting bodies emitted a horrid smell. The gentle breezes pushing from the harbor cleansed the air, pushing the majority of the smell out of the courtyard.

Opening the parchment once more, Marion allowed her emotions to get the better of her. The parchment was a clandestine communication from Metalweaver Flats, the secret Biogtech production facility in the desert region northwest of the city. The message revealed that Globulus, former body guard of the Toil royal family of Rasheed, had been captured and was being transferred to the city. The intent was to allow Marion the pleasure of torturing her former friend and protector.

Thinking about the events that had led her to that point in her life suddenly filled her with a deep sense of guilt. She had betrayed everyone she had loved and everyone who had loved and cared for her. A tear rolled down Marion's cheek as she surveyed her broken empire. As she stared toward the wall, the piles of dead bodies filled her with a sudden sense of revulsion. A swarm of flies were buzzing over the bodies, laying fresh eggs, adding to the already hideous swarm of maggots that covered the corpses. The revulsion turned to nausea. Bending over, Queen Toil let the sensation overtake her. Rising bile filled her throat. Giving in, she retched on the ground. As she threw up, tears welled up in her eyes. She staggered back, weak from the ordeal, then moved over to a bench in the garden.

Wiping the cold sweat from her brow, she touched her face. Only a mere year ago, she had been a graceful beauty. Now deep trenches and wrinkles scoured her once-pretty complexion. Grabbing her hair, she stared at it in horror. Once she had glorious golden locks of blond; now her hair had turned jet black with strands of gray. A lump of flesh had expanded on her shoulder as the bone beneath was warped by demonic magic. All of the physical transformations that Marion had endured had been the result of immersion in evil. The dark forces that gave her power required a tithe. That tithe was intended to mark the servants of darkness with physical malformations so that all could know that the price paid was in full and that the soul of that person was forever bound to evil.

Thinking about her condition, she began to sob. Her life had once been so simple, so filled with vitality. She had a loving father and a kingdom that loved her family very much. In time, Marion would have risen to power, being the only offspring of King Toil. But reckless ambition and a secret pact with Father Vertigo had

changed the fate of an entire empire. Instead of waiting for her
father to pass gracefully and assume leadership, she plotted and had
him killed at the hands of an assassin. As was law, Marion was
crowned queen after his passing.

At first it was a strong victory, and she felt triumphant. The
entire kingdom was hers to rule as she saw fit. But in the wake of
war and mass murder, the charm of ruling had changed from that of
a positive goal to something truly twisted. The once-beautiful
palace had been stained by conflict and carnage. The servants who
had lovingly spent their lives building the beauty were now gone,
swept away by death and war. Instead of a peaceful garden filled
with exotic songbirds and flowering plants, the garden was now
littered with rotting bodies. The songbirds had been replaced by a
murder of crows, a horde of black squawking menaces that were
growing fat feeding off the carrion.

The grass in the garden had withered and turned gray, having
been deprived of water for so long. The rose garden had died off
save for the most hearty, enormous rose bush, which grew in the
shadow of the western wall. Brilliant yellow flowers sprung from
the plant, in stark contrast with the rest of the garden. Catching
sight of the wonderful plant, Marion's gaze was transfixed upon it.

She rose in a trance, staring at the soft yellow petals.
Thinking about all that had transpired, she walked toward the
flowering plant and dropped to her knees. Crouched before it, she
bent forward and smelled the aroma from the yellow flowers. A soft
melody greeted her nose and she smiled for a brief moment through
the tears and sorrow gripping her.

After the fall of Rasheed, Marion had been too elated by her
success and new role as queen to even consider the consequences of
her actions. As time went on and her further actions caused the
murder of others, she began to reflect on the situation. A deep sense
of guilt began to overwhelm her senses. She had not just betrayed
her own family; she had betrayed an entire nation. Her emotions
began to take hold and the guilt became a crippling sensation.

Father Vertigo could sense her anguish and knew that he
needed to get her under control. Marion was, after all, in charge of
the covert actions in the Reaper Kai Empire. A compromised
Marion could lead to possible exposure of those operatives. Trying

to comfort Marion in his own unique manner, Vertigo told her that in order to escape her guilt, she needed to remove everything that had been part of her old way of life. In his eyes, there was no guilt if everyone you had betrayed was dead.

His philosophy was twisted, but somehow it made sense to her. Having killed her own father by ordering his death, Marion had removed King Toil from the equation. The treacherous palace guards who had helped her overthrow the empire had all been purged as well. Over a dozen guards who had survived the siege of Rasheed found themselves imprisoned and tortured to death. Marion's philosophy on this matter was somewhat chilling. If the guards would betray the king to help Marion, they were not to be trusted. If the guards were not to be trusted, they must be killed. Everyone she had known or loved was dead. Everyone she had betrayed was gone, everyone except one…

Still gripping the parchment, she looked at it once more. Globulus, the loyal and noble bodyguard of the Toil family, the closest thing she had to a brother, had been captured and was being transferred to Rasheed. He was the final piece of baggage from her former life. Once Globulus was dead and gone, the cycle would be complete. All of those who had been betrayed would be purged. If everyone was finally dead, her sense of guilt could abate. Vertigo's postulate was correct in her eyes; there was no need to feel guilty if everyone you betrayed was dead and gone.

Thinking about the situation, she did not fear killing him, but she still felt dread. The coming confrontation would tax her soul. Globulus was the exact opposite of Marion. The hippo warrior was a noble, selfless creature who lived to serve the greater good. Marion, on the other hand, was a deceitful, selfish soul who cared only about personal gain. Any confrontation between two such souls was something to loathe and fear for someone gripped by evil; a kind-hearted soul would rise to the challenge as a way to possibly bring back someone who has fallen into darkness.

Unable to comprehend what she would say to the noble hippo when they would finally meet, she began to tremble and sighed, shaking her head. The confrontation would be frightful. Thinking further, she resolved that it was the end of the cycle, the end of the destructive set of events set in motion so long ago. If she could endure the final one whom she had betrayed, she could survive anything.

The thoughts about betrayal and the upcoming confrontation with Globulus gripped her with anxiety. Wanting to escape the disturbing feeling, she looked for an effective diversion. She crouched near the rose bush, gripping the stalk of the plant with both hands. As her hand closed around the stalk, thorns, tiny needles, pricked her flesh. Feeling a light pain, she paused and looked at the yellow flowers intensely. A wave of guilt washed over her. Sorrow and despair flowed through her. Tears began to stream down her face once more as images flashed through her mind. She could still see her loving father clutching his chest as he bled to death. The last thing King Toil had asked for was to see his little girl as he died. She remembered how loving his eyes were as he stared at her while his wounds took his life, wounds that would never have been inflicted if it weren't for Marion's orders to have her father killed. The images were raw and overwhelming.

Trying to escape the thoughts, she remembered the sounds of the citizens of Rasheed as they died by the hundreds, gunned down by Biogtech troops as they tried desperately to flee the city. The wails of anguish seemed to reverberate in her mind over and over again. The tears turned into helpless sobbing and she breathed heavily as her soul was wracked with guilt.

"What have I done?" she whispered, trying to escape the feeling. As guilt battered her being, a twinge of anger rose within her. The prideful, reckless evil that caused her to do unspeakable things reared its ugly head. It appeared in the pit of her stomach at first and then rose through her body like a wave of heat. Her face turned red and she was overcome by hate. Shaking in rage, she screamed. A tantrum filled her. "To hell with them!" she whispered and a crooked smile graced her lips.

Still touching the thorn-covered husk of the rose bush, she looked at it and grasped the stalk with all of her might. The thorns pierced her flesh and a flash of pain erupted in her hands. Feeling the thorns pierce her body rekindled the hatred in her soul. Filled with destructive intent, she ignored the pain and pulled with all her might, trying to uproot the plant. The thorns dug deeply and blood seeped from between her fingers. The pain was agonizing but it felt wonderful to her. As she gritted her teeth, a sneer covered her face. She tugged with all her might, but the roots held fast and she began to lose her grip. The blood made the stalk slippery and her hands slid along its length, thorns ripping into her flesh and cutting deep gashes in the palms of her hands. Pulling away, Marion Toil looked on in horror as she surveyed the damage to her body.

Blood flowed freely from the wounds as she stared at her injured hands. She smiled, and then began to laugh dryly, watching the crimson blood drip. All she wanted was to destroy something beautiful, but the rose could not be destroyed.

"I am glad that you have returned your emotions to where they need to be. It would be troubling and dangerous to your very life if you began to have second thoughts about your place in my empire," a sinister rasp cut through the air.

Spinning around, Toil was stunned to see that Father Vertigo had crept up behind her during her emotional ordeal. His pasty white form was especially glaring in the warm light of the sun. His hands were folded behind his back and his rotten black eyes stared directly at her without any reservation.

"How long have you been standing there?" she asked him.

"Long enough to give you the emotional boost that you needed." Vertigo spoke in a commanding tone, his voice booming from his frail frame with frightening intensity.

"Emotional boost?" she echoed, mystified by the response.

"Indeed. I am a leader. To lead my empire, I give my subjects emotional clarity. When I sense that they are troubled, I can influence their emotional state. Take yourself for instance. You were feeling guilt and sorrow. Guilt and sorrow are on the road to weakness. I cannot allow you to feel such things. I simply gave you back what your soul *truly* yearns for. I want you to hate. I want you to cause suffering. One cannot truly hate if they are gripped by indecision. I gave you focus because I care about your growth in this empire. Do not trouble yourself with sorrow; replace it with hate and let the bitterness rule you."

Bowing before him, she acknowledged his teachings with a respectful demeanor.

"There, you see? You are already back to the way you were *meant* to be," Vertigo sneered as he stroked his forked, pasty white beard.

"I appreciate your charity in helping me back to the proper path, master."

"Now we will converse about your operatives in Stonen, the capital of the wretched Iron Kai empire. Are we well under way for the preparations for invasion?"

"Yes, master. My operatives are in the final phases of the plan and are ready to destroy the infrastructure and kill off the ruling body." Marion's tone was confident.

"I had a dream, and a dark dream at that. In this vision, a demon appeared to me, a demon sitting upon a mighty throne forged of human bone. The shadowy creature told me to be wary, wary that old enemies were now undoing our plans of conquest. It only lasted a brief moment but I pay high attention to such visions, since they are rare and I believe the demon was real." Vertigo was still staring at Marion, his black eyes submerged in his skull.

Taking a brief moment to ponder the strange vision, a look of concern gripped her features. Returning her focus to the lord of evil, Marion spoke with hesitation. "I am not sure if this is an issue, but I have lost contact with Brother Mire; he did not check in last week."

"Jackson Mire?" Vertigo grew silent, appearing to be meditating, as if probing the universe for guidance. Shaking his head, he declared, " I have a subtle sensation lingering at the edge of my consciousness and I cannot decipher the feeling. I believe that our operatives in Stonen are in danger."

"I commonly have operatives that do not check in; either they are unable to without being detected, or they were killed. Perhaps we should wait; the operation is set for execution in less than a month's time."

"No!" Vertigo's tone was harsh. "You will order the operation for six days from now. I will instruct Brother Feral to proceed with the attack on Stonen. I do not think the dream that was sent to me was merely a dream; I believe it was a message to ensure our victory."

"Six days will not be enough time to complete all of the operations. We still have not been able to penetrate the defenses around the city's water and air supply. We will not be able to let loose a plague upon the city prior to invasion." Marion took care to maintain a respectful attitude, as her master was clearly agitated.

"I don't care! Something is not right! If the demon was correct, old enemies are aiding the Iron Kai. I suspect the lost tribe of Ceibla Moralis has finally entered the war. I have not heard from Sister Nightshade, so the destruction of these dissidents has probably not come to pass. You will order the operation for six days from now. I will order Brother Feral to begin the siege on Stonen to coordinate with your attack order."

"Yes, master." Queen Marion Toil bowed before her lord.

With that, Vertigo left the courtyard and returned to his tower within the palace. Marion was left alone in the courtyard. Looking at her hands, she saw that the blood had clotted, but she was now a gory mess. She stared at the rose bush that had inflicted the horrid wounds, noting that it had survived her assault upon it. The roots had held fast—it was a true survivor. This thing of beauty, the last of its kind in the garden, had withstood the attack and had left her a bloodied mess. Pondering the strange events, she thought about Vertigo's lesson: guilt could be cleansed by killing. Next she stared at the rose, and another lesson filled her mind: it takes more than reckless hate to kill a thing of true beauty. Considering both lessons, she felt a sense of dread wash over her. If a simple plant, a flower, could survive in such a harsh environment, one filled with death, it would be nearly impossible to destroy all hope and create a paradise built on hate and suffering. True hope and beauty were eternal.

It has been said that good cannot exist without evil. The contrary is true as well. Even in a world gripped by death and war, evil cannot exist without good. In times of strife and suffering, there is always hope.

Chapter 22
The Fallen Emperor

Touching her gently, his rough hand caressed the soft skin around her neck. The maiden shivered under the attention, beginning to feel her pulse quicken and her heart race. Sensing her vulnerability to his gentle touch, Gunther moved closer and tenderly kissed his beloved on the lips. She smiled, feeling warmth spread through her, and responding ardently to the loving attention.

Stepping forward, she grasped his shoulders, then flipped her long hair so that the flowing locks draped over his face. Gunther reacted to the sensation of her long hair against his face with a jolt of adrenaline. Running his hands through her abundant tresses, he could smell a faint scent of perfume. Breathing heavily, he began to kiss her over and over again.

Lost in each other, the emperor and his mistress enjoyed a secret mid-day rendezvous. The emperor was not married and it was a fiercely guarded secret that he and his servant had spent the last four years as lovers. A liaison between a noble and a person of a lower caste was scandalous in Iron Kai society. It was an unwritten rule for a leader of the Iron Kai to avoid becoming romantically involved with a servant. Gunther didn't seem to mind this rule much. Instead, he had a lasting relationship with his mistress, Juliana, and they were both quite happy with the arrangement.

The lovers were nearly naked and utterly caught up in the moment; however, their mid-morning rendezvous was about to be cut short. The sound of angry shouts in the hallway outside his personal quarters instantly put Gunther on edge. His personal body guard was yelling for assistance. Hearing the ruckus, Gunther jumped to his feet, pulling his shirt back on in a hasty manner. Rushing across the room, he grasped a pistol from his belongings and burst into the hall.

Members of the council guard, the personal police force of the Iron Kai high council, were assembled in a sizeable force within the hallway. Gunther's personal body guards all had their weapons drawn and were in an intense stand-off with the council guard forces.

"Drop your weapons!" Maddock screamed in alarm, training his submachine gun on the invaders of the royal palace.

The council guards, also brandishing automatic weapons, were tensely moving these weapons from target to target. They were badly frightened and severely outmatched. Trained solely to keep the peace in a relatively civilized city, the council guard had never seen real combat. Gunther's forces, on the other hand, were combat-hardened, battle-ready troops who had served in some of the worst military campaigns in which the Iron Kai army had been involved over the last ten years.

"We're not backing down," a sergeant of the council guards replied in a weak voice, quaking in his boots. Though the council guards were twelve strong, Gunther's guards, numbering only four, were still intimidating the hell out of the green guardsmen.

"This is an act of treason," Gunther boomed loudly, holding his pistol tensely, preferring not to train the weapon on anyone in the room.

"Treason?" A snide voice ripped through the hallway as a statesman dressed in fine clothes burst in. Arthur Gallows, representing the council, crossed into harm's way to address the tense crowd.

"I say we waste them," Maddock sneered, pointing his gun at Gallows. "Let's kill you first."

"You have got a lot of nerve coming in here with weapons drawn, Gallows," Gunther declared, staring at the intruder who was apparently leading the insurrection.

"Nerve? You're the one with a lot of nerve, conspiring with the enemy!" Gallows accused him with a mad look in his eye. The councilman was clearly out of control and the situation was turning from bad to worse.

The council guardsmen were retreating, sweat pouring down their faces. The standoff was not going well. Fearful for their lives, several of the men were mere moments from fleeing the tense scene.

"Stand your ground!" Gallows ordered the guardsmen, sensing their panic. "Take him into custody!"

"I don't think so!" Maddock roared with his trigger finger tense. He was only a few seconds away from opening fire. He was completely loyal to the emperor, and there was no way in hell he would allow his beloved leader to be captured.

"Hold your fire," Gunther urged. He knew that the situation could end in disaster if things got much worse. Trying desperately to unravel the mysterious intrusion, he reached forward and clutched Maddock's shoulder in reassurance. Moving forward, he put himself between all of the guns in the room, placing himself between all of the possible combatants. It was a wise move. Gunther's troops would not open fire with him in the way and the council guards were relieved, no longer the target of Gunther's crack-shot combat veterans. "Let's all just calm down."

"By the power of Iron Kai high council, I hereby charge Emperor Gunther with one act of murder, conspiracy to commit treason, and seditious consultation with an enemy power. As dictated by our laws, Emperor Gunther is remanded into custody until a trial can be concluded. Take him!" Arthur Gallows called out harshly.

"Murder? Treason? Have you lost your mind, Gallows? What is all of this about?" Gunther questioned, enraged.

"You know all too well what this is all about. Your acts to weaken and destroy our empire are at an end. Your reckless greed to station yourself within the Reaper Kai Empire has failed. You will be tried for your crimes and punished accordingly."

"You think me a traitor? You are a fool! The only traitor in this room is you, Gallows! I know of your plot to hide the evidence of the Reaper Kai operative. I know you have been consulting in private in order to overthrow this empire. The only traitor is you." Looking at the council guards, Gunther gave them an order himself.

"As your emperor and sovereign, I command you to take Arthur Gallows into custody."

The council guards were stunned and did not know what to do. The entire fate of the empire was resting in their hands. By law, they were only to answer to orders from the high council; but Gunther was their sovereign, their mighty ruler. Indecision gripped them and most backed away in confusion. They were about to break rank and follow Gunther's orders.

As Gunther was on the verge of winning the stalemate, fate intervened. Over twenty additional council guards stormed into the hallway, shifting the balance of power back to Gallows. Severely outnumbered, Gunther knew that his influence was failing. The situation could have only two outcomes in his mind. Lawless violence could erupt, and Gunther knew that he and his loyal soldiers had only a slim chance of surviving at best. The other option was to surrender himself and spare the lives of his men. Shaking his head in anger, Gunther knew what must be done. With a sigh, he decided caution would be the better road.

"So be it, Gallows." Gunther's expression was fierce. "I will submit, but only to spare this empire from madness and dark deeds."

Handing his pistol over to a council guard, he held his hands in the air as an act of submission. Seeing his opponent submit filled Gallows with a wash of pride. The reckless emperor had finally been defeated in his eyes. Smiling in elation, Gallows ordered, "Seize him."

The force of numbers could not be ignored. Surging forward, many hands gripped and grappled the emperor. They twisted his arms behind his back, forcing him to his knees. Binding him in chains, the council guards quickly restrained the emperor, then pulled him forcibly to his feet. Fully restrained, Emperor Gunther swallowed his pride and stared at his enemy, Arthur Gallows. Gallows, thrilled with his capture, moved forward to confront the confined emperor.

"This is a great day in our history. Our empire, almost on the brink of ruin, has labored and struggled to survive the coming darkness. All the time we battled and fought, our own emperor was conspiring against the people of this mighty nation, meeting in secret with emissaries of darkness. This will be marked in history as the day that our empire was saved from destruction and it was done by me! History books for generations will sing my praises."

Gunther was disgusted by the councilman's bravado. Shaking his head in revulsion, he locked eyes with the out-of-control government official. "I hope your act won't be remembered as the day that the enemy won the age-old conflict. Yes, we have battled the enemy, but I am not one of them. Your actions have severely compromised the defense of this nation. Who will lead our great armies?"

"Leading our troops will not be an issue. The ineffective attacks upon the enemy capital will end with your capture. I can lead our troops to victory once your poisonous influence has been removed," Gallows erupted in a haughty burst.

Shaking his head, Gunther was unable to rationalize what was happening. Trying to salvage as much as he could of the dire situation, he looked over at Captain Maddock with a serious look. His eyes remained focused on Maddock as he spoke in a confident tone, his gaze never wavering. "I have served this nation with the best intentions. Here, this day, I am doing my part in defending this nation. All I ask is that you do your part to defend this nation as best you can. Save this nation, Maddock."

Returning his gaze with a deep understanding, Maddock responded, "It has been the greatest honor of my life to serve with you. I will defend this nation." He spoke in a solemn tone, understanding the unspoken order. Saluting Gunther, he stood at attention until the council guards ushered the emperor from the hallway of the palace, leading him to prison.

After the situation had abated, Gunther's loyal men stood in the hall and stared at each other in alarm. Gunther's beloved, who had overhead the entire event, entered the hallway with a look of shock on her face. With tears mounting in her eyes, she shuddered and tried to keep from weeping.

"Why is this happening?" she asked, her voice strained, as she tugged nervously at her long black hair.

"I don't know." Maddock's voice conveyed his dismay. He was staring down the hallway, secretly hoping the strange events were some cruel ruse, but to no avail; the emperor had been captured and was now on his way to a jail cell.

Gunther's five loyal friends stood motionless, pondering the strange, almost unbelievable events that had just transpired. Many moments passed and still they stood stunned, unable to vocalize their emotions. After several tense, strained minutes of silence, the calm was broken by a meek voice.

"Now what?" one of Gunther's bodyguards asked, utterly perplexed.

"We complete the mission." Maddock's tone was matter-of-fact. "You heard Gunther; he asked *me* to defend this nation." Shaking his head in disbelief, he let out a sigh. "I can't do this alone. Gunther wanted *us* to defend this nation. Our task is far from over. This city is still infested with covert operatives, enemy agents lying in wait. We're running out of time. We must finish the job and slaughter any remaining Reaper Kai within this city. With Gunther captured, the enemy will surely find out and order a full-scale invasion, knowing that our military leadership had been compromised. Our empire is collapsing and we must do our part to protect this nation."

"I'm scared." Juliana's voice was desolate.

"I am too," Maddock admitted, and moved forward to console Gunther's beloved mate. Placing his hand on her shoulder, he tried to reassure her. "Don't worry. He is strong and wise. It will take more than that fool Gallows to bring him down. In the end, Gunther will make it through; he always does."

Nodding in agreement, Juliana tried to smile.

Maddock stepped away from her to examine the remaining loyal guards. With a mad look in his eye, he gave an order. "Get your gear and get the others. It's time we finished our duty. Let's go kill some Reaper Kai."

With that, the secret team formed by Gunther moved off into the palace and towards the cellar, which concealed a secret weapon. In a war of secrets and hidden assassins, the ultimate weapon was truth. The Oracle of Justice, a man born from an ancient tradition which had long preserved its own truths, was a way to reveal the true nature and identity of the enemy agents. Coming before

Matthew Moralis, the team made ready to finish the fight and defend the nation against the threat festering from within.

Chapter 23
Collateral Damage

"Come to your senses!" Matthew Moralis spoke in a dark tone, eyeing the soldiers with disgust as his brow creased with clear agitation. "The heavy burden of our task does not include open, reckless slaughter. Innocent civilians could be killed!"

"We do not have the luxury of time on our hands. This mission will continue," Maddock replied harshly, taking a step towards the Oracle of Justice. As he attempted to stare down his opponent, the old man remained undaunted.

For many moments they locked their gazes, neither willing to retreat or concede defeat. Finally, still engaged in the bitter struggle for supremacy, Maddock spoke again, his eyes remaining fixed on Moralis. "You have your orders, corporal. Go in there and get the job done."

A soldier dressed in black combat attire stared at the two opponents with concern, reluctant to carry out the orders that had just been handed to him. Shaking his head in reservation, he grabbed a black mask from his belt. He pulled the mask over his face, leaving no part of his face visible but his eyes. The ensemble was now complete; the corporal was garbed in black from head to toe and his identity was totally concealed.

Grabbing his submachine gun, the masked soldier pulled the slide back on the weapon, chambering the first round of the magazine into the firing chamber. Clicking off the safety on the weapon, he was good to go, ready to make war. Turning back, he shot his leader, Mad Dog Maddock, one final glance of hesitation.

Trying to reassure him, the veteran officer gave him a nod of approval. The Oracle of Justice countered with a look of anger and shook his head in staunch disagreement. "The liberators are now the butchers," he observed in a tone of revulsion, purposely trying to agitate Maddock.

Not giving an inch of ground, Maddock retaliated with a dour series of jagged comments. "He has his orders. Let him carry them out."

"So be it, fool. You are walking a dangerous line, a line that should not be crossed," the old man warned ominously.

Leaving the bickering leaders of the covert operation behind, the corporal dressed in black emerged from the alleyway. He closed his eyes for a brief second, breathing in and preparing himself for the coming conflict.

Holding his weapon, he could feel his hands trembling. The previous operations had been in complete secret; the enemy forces had been the only onlookers involved, and all of them had died in the attacks.

Opening his eyes, the operative looked toward his destination. He left the safety and seclusion of the alley with some ambivalence, sucking in a full lungful of air. Trying to stop from trembling, the soldier focused on the task at hand. He moved forward, and finding himself exposed in the open, charged down the subterranean streets of Stonen, garbed in black, ready for the kill.

Moving swiftly, he passed a man and woman holding hands, walking down the street in the dimly lit tunnel. Night had fallen and the environmental controls in the underground city had dimmed the lights to simulate the night. At first the couple seemed indifferent to the man charging down the street garbed in black, holding a submachine gun at the ready. Their indifference rapidly turned to alarm as they processed the attire of the sinister-looking man.

The woman let out a yelp of alarm as her date pulled her behind him in a crude attempt at protection. Staring in awe, the couple was elated to realize that the gunman never even gave them a second glance. Bursting forward, the soldier opened a door to a popular restaurant.

The hostess had a warm smile on her face as she prepared to greet the sinister man. As she took in the soldier, her eyes widening, she retreated a step, cowering and holding her hand over her mouth. She was so surprised that she found herself unable to make even the feeblest noise. Gasping for breath, she ducked behind the counter.

Never wavering, the soldier entered the dining hall. It took a brief second for the patrons to become aware of his presence. First looks of alarm were exchanged. Next, several patrons cried out, many screaming: "He's got a gun!"

The frenzied reaction startled the soldier, who grew distracted, eyes darting back and forth in an attempt to find his target. The alarm was more than enough to bring the hidden Reaper Kai to his feet, stunned by the brazen gunman. Knowing that a fully armed soldier would not bust into the restaurant without a good reason, the disguised Reaper Kai knew that the fight was being inescapably brought to him.

The motion of the man standing from the table moved the gunman's focus directly to that man. Their eyes locked and the soldier knew that he had found his target. Training his weapon upon his chest, he opened fire.

Anticipating the attack, the Reaper Kai was already on the move, launching himself away from the table at great speed. The movement was so distracting, the soldier lost control of his weapon. The out-of-control gun sprayed a volley of bullets which ricocheted through the dining hall. A scream rose as an innocent patron was struck, his chest absorbing the brunt of two gun bursts. The force of the attack was so severe, the innocent patron was thrown back and his chair tipped over, throwing him onto the floor in a shower of pain. He clutched at the wounds on his chest, the crimson horror of blood seeping from the injuries with sinister fury. Choking on the blood filling his mouth, the innocent man died immediately, felled by the random gunfire.

After witnessing the slaughter of the man, the rest of the patrons were gripped with panic. Many screamed, and some dove for cover under the tables. Others sought to escape the chaos and fled through the front door of the restaurant.

The soldier saw the damage he had wrought with such indifference and was stunned by the mistake. He had lost control and as a result, a harmless patron, a civilian, had perished in the attack. As he stood with the barrel of the weapon still smoking, it took a second for the gunman to regain his composure. He blinked several times, the original purpose of his mission resurfacing in his mind; there was still a dangerous Reaper Kai priest on the prowl.

The sound of pots clanging and broken dishes clamored through the air as he stood looking around him. Training his ears on the sound, the gunman traced the noises to the kitchen. He snapped out of his trance abruptly, eyeing the dead man on the floor one last time before rushing into the kitchen.

Stumbling through the doorway, he was instantly shocked to find a knife hurling toward his face at breakneck speed. Instinct took over and he tried to duck under the deadly projectile. However, he was too slow, and the blade struck and imbedded itself in the side of his head, its point sticking into his skull. The attack was successful and the blade dug in. The gunman's last-minute maneuver, however, had deflected a straight shot. The blade barely punctured his bone and he was still able to function.

Pulling the knife out, he threw it to the floor and turned to look for the source of the attack. The soldier saw that the cook had been killed, his slashed throat exposed. No motion of any kind stirred the kitchen; the Reaper Kai had concealed himself somewhere inside. Panning his weapon around the room, the corporal's trigger finger twitched as he sweated profusely, his head bleeding relentlessly from the brash knife attack.

Breathing heavily, he rounded the edge of the stove, training his weapon on the possible threat. He whipped the gun down swiftly, but saw nothing before him.

Thud! A jagged pain tore into the soldier's back, evoking a tortured gasp. Another knife had been hurled at him and stuck in his shoulder blade. Whirling around, he yelled and sprayed the kitchen behind him with gunfire. His bullets rammed into the steel cabinets with a jangle. The unknown attacker was still hidden and well concealed.

Backing into a corner, the gunman resolved not to be ambushed again. He scanned the room in suspicion, leaving the knife imbedded in his flesh for the time being. The soldier knew without a doubt that he had to focus on the conflict at hand. Letting his guard down even for a second to remove the blade was all the

Reaper Kai needed to end his life. With a frantic posture, he scanned the kitchen for any sign of his enemy.

An odd sight greeted his eyes. A knife on the counter rose from the surface. Hovering in the air, the blade seemed to dance. It spun around in the air several times, controlled by an unseen force. Mystified, the soldier hit the deck and none too soon. The blade hurled quickly through the air and imbedded itself in the wall behind him. Only a split second longer and the soldier would have another blade stuck in his body, perhaps even ending his life.

Angered by the continual psychic attacks, he knew it was time to make a move. With a war cry, he charged across the kitchen towards the opposite side of the room. A form flashed into his field of vision as he rounded the corner, a man crouched near a counter top. Without thinking, the soldier trained his weapon on the person and fired upon him. The submachine gun hummed as a burst of weapon fire broke the air with crisp snaps. His aim was true and the bullets slammed into the target with frightening results. The target of the attack was no Reaper Kai. Instead, another cook, who was cowering behind the counter, was torn by gunfire. Pierced by several well placed shots, the cook was killed instantly.

The soldier was completely broken by the effects of another senseless killing, his morale shattered. Not just one innocent man had died in the attack. Two dead civilians were now the price of a botched assassination gone horribly wrong. Shaking in fear, he moved away from the dead cook with panic setting in. The attack was a failure.

Just as his qualms and sense of defeat were taking him to a dark place, the Reaper Kai moved in for the kill. Clutching a knife, he moved in swiftly and jammed the blade into the soldier's back. Screaming, the soldier flung himself forward, away from the blade. Turning around, he was too slow and the Reaper Kai was on him immediately, blood-stained blade in hand.

The gunman found himself unable to respond, and forced to assume a defensive stance. Throwing his arm forward, he barely managed to block a vicious swing. The knife dug into his forearm as he stumbled backwards, and the Reaper Kai jumped onto him like a lion ready to feast. The blade was aimed at his chest. Dropping his gun, the soldier garbed in black screamed as he grappled with the evil priest. He was severely wounded, barely able to hold his own, and strength was leaving him. Holding on with all of his might, the soldier fought to keep the blade from piercing his flesh. Blood was pumping from his open wounds as he struggled against a swift death.

The edge of the blade inched forward as both combatants struggled with all their might. Grunting with effort, the Reaper Kai was also smiling, as the blade was only a mere inch away from cutting the soldier's flesh.

Dizziness washed over the gunman as the loss of blood began to take its toll on him. The tip of the blade bit flesh, and the Reaper Kai tried to force it deeper. Losing strength, the corporal was on the verge of being slaughtered by the covert Reaper Kai operative. Just when things seemed most dire, a crash erupted from behind the combatants.

The back door to the kitchen, which led into the alley, had been breached. With a forceful kick, the door frame was torn loose as splinters of wood erupted in all directions. Maddock, garbed in a black mask of his own, burst through and moved swiftly into the kitchen. Drawing down on the Reaper Kai in the act of killing his countryman, Maddock never hesitated and opened fire. Bullet after bullet erupted from his pistol, and the hot lead rammed into the sinister Reaper Kai. After six shots, the Reaper Kai crumpled over, dropping the knife.

Gasping for air, the mortally wounded Reaper Kai stared up at the ceiling, his eyes rolling back and forth. Maddock walked over to hover above him with a look of dispassion, training the gun on his head. Pulling the trigger twice, he executed the Reaper Kai. He holstered his weapon, then leaned over and grabbed his companion. Pulling him to his feet, he steadied the wounded man and assisted him in escaping into the alley.

Making haste, they darted across the street and into another alley across the street. The rest of the covert strike team were assembled and waiting. They quickly escaped into the night, disappearing into an access tunnel. As they fled the scene, troops now controlled by Arthur Gallows flooded the area, having been summoned to the scene of conflict.

The attack had been both a success and a failure. On the one hand, a sinister Reaper Kai agent had been slain and his murderous plots to kill and destroy were now put to rest. On the other hand, the rash action had cost the lives of two innocent men, slaughtered by acts of irreverent violence, their lives lost due to reckless actions inspired by fear.

War has many costs. The cost of human life can often seem indiscriminate and random. Although casualties are a dire consequence of war, many often ignore the unseen consequences. What of those that witness such horror? What of those survivors who must bear psychological scars, having withstood the attack and survived by luck alone? It is these unseen forces and many more that tear at the hearts and souls of all those who pass the perils of battle.

War is a horror unmatched, but to hurl oneself into the fray without any regards for the innocent is a display of unconscionable action which has forsaken any trace of civility. In dark times filled with indecision, it is easy for good people to lose their way and blatantly disregard simple morals. Maddock and his team had crossed this sacred line, shifting from heroes into murderers as the result of a poor decision driven by frantic fear of the coming darkness.

Chapter 24
The High Tribune

The courtroom was crammed to the gills with hundreds upon hundreds of people. Every nook and niche contained either a concerned or a fascinated citizen of Stonen. The trial of all trials, an event never preceded in the history of the empire, was taking place. The emperor, who occupied the highest political position in the Iron Kai Empire, was being tried for treason, a crime punishable by death. It was the biggest political event in Iron Kai history since the great witch hunts and civil war against the Reaper Kai.

Every politician from the high council was present, along with a host of high- ranking officials from every affiliation. Whispering amongst themselves, the crowd of patrons sounded like a room of hissing serpents. Frightful glances were exchanged as fearful theories were disseminated. The rumor mill was in full swing, churning out confusion and ill-fated postulates. Everyone in the courtroom knew that the entire fate of the Iron Kai nation was hanging in the balance. With open war raging between the Iron Kai and the Reaper Kai, the situation was dire.

Every one of the spectators knew that Gunther was a capable leader and ran the military and armed services with distinction and precision. First and foremost, the emperor was a soldier and a skilled tactician. There were very few who had doubted his military prowess before the insidious allegations of treason and consorting with the enemy. After the charges surfaced, dissidents immediately jumped on the bandwagon, preferring to go against the popular emperor.

Within two days of Gunther's imprisonment, the entire empire was rocked with indecision, having been split down the middle. One faction felt that Gunther was guilty of consorting with the enemy, while the other felt he was innocent. Even though there was no tangible evidence, the media was swarming over the story, filling the gaps of knowledge with rampant speculation that stirred up a fury of fear. The other half of the populace was staunchly supportive of their beloved emperor, feeling that the charges were a ruse, and a crude one at that. With the opposition falling under the leadership of Arthur Gallows, a politician who many felt was corrupt, the stories about Gunther's betrayal seemed more like a tactic for the council to gain power. Many simply felt the council was trying to overthrow the government and that Arthur Gallows was attempting to rise to power.

With tensions still running high, everyone in the room was staring at the emperor. He was reserved and calm. Sitting with perfect posture, he carved an impressive figure, completely ignoring the jeers and sneers from those who did not believe in him. Not wanting to give an inch of credence to the charges, he sat in a confident manner, focusing on the task at hand.

The trial was a circus. The prosecution had spent the entire morning painting a bleak picture which cast Gunther as the mastermind of an intricate plot to overthrow the government and hand over the keys to the empire to the Reaper Kai order. A flurry of shaky accusations was being thrown at him, in false statements based upon pure speculation. The trial was more about theatrics than truth. Arthur Gallows, having suffered a bruised ego during Gunther's arrest, chose to make personal attacks directly against the emperor without any evidence to support them. All the while, the accused sat motionless and indifferent to the rants. This lack of interest in the charges enraged Gallows further and he stepped up the attacks, painting Gunther as a sinister ruler interested only in treason.

Throughout the entire process, the spectators were looking at their leader with severe scrutiny, as if inspecting some mutant creature under a high-powered microscope. Some in the audience wanted to see Gunther exhibit weakness, which they could then interpret as evidence of his guilt. Others were elated by how strong and resolute he was. His verdict rested largely on his ability to maintain his persona in the trial.

Gunther was a masterful tactician and political leader. He had a real knack for maintaining control of any situation. No matter how desperate the cause, he always strove to take charge so that his subordinates would have faith and confidence in his actions. This trial was no different. He maintained a stoic presence and remained in control of his emotions the entire time. Even though his mind was screaming inside, he kept this panic under control and to himself.

The trial, based on shaky facts, was proceeding quickly. The presentation of the charges was complete and now it was time for the emperor to take the stand. This was an excellent opportunity for Gallows' prosecution to take the lead and directly attack Gunther with no holds barred.

The council guards brought the emperor to the stand, to which he walked confidently. Knowing he was being fully scrutinized, he maintained perfect posture. As he sat on the stand, he took a brief moment to collect his thoughts and scan the room, focusing upon the trial's spectators. Many were unable to look him in the eye as his gaze swept across the room. As his eyes passed over these onlookers, they uneasily shifted their own eyes, averting their gaze. He could sense immediately that these spectators were against him. Sizing up the room, he knew that the fate of the Iron Kai Empire was hanging in the balance. If he was stripped of his position and convicted, the empire would disintegrate into two factions. This splitting of ideals and power during a war would be deadly. The dissention would give the Reaper Kai a sizeable advantage that would ultimately lead to all of their deaths.

Taking a deep breath, Gunther collected his thoughts. At that moment, he made a silent oath not only to himself but to his people and to all of the citizens of the Iron Kai Empire. *"I vow to make it through this. I vow that my actions will be honorable and to act only in the best interests of this nation and its people."*

With that, he nodded to the magistrate that he was ready. The magistrate nodded back with an inscrutable look, and the interrogation of Gunther began.

A member of Gallows' prosecution rose and shot Gunther a contemptuous look, a look that declared, *I will destroy you.* Gunther simply ignored him.

"Can you please tell the court how you knew Jackson Mire?" legal counsel Hayes questioned.

"I never knew of Jackson Mire until his death," Gunther boomed back.

"Interesting. You never knew of Jackson Mire until after his death?" the prosecutor shot back sarcastically, spinning around to look at the crowd. "That is a very strange story indeed. So the first time you knew of Jackson Mire was after his death?"

"Yes, that is correct."

"Jackson Mire was a prominent businessman who traded goods between Rasheed and Stonen for a great many years. For anyone in this court who has not heard, this noble businessman was being followed and tracked by a host of assassins. In good faith, he traveled to this city with the intent of giving crucial information needed to defend this nation against the attacks of the Reaper Kai order. He met with representative Gallows and was then found brutally murdered in an alleyway." The counsel spoke in a methodical tone, trying to weave a sinister tale. "I will ask you again, you never knew of Jackson Mire until after his death?"

"That is correct, I did not know of Jackson Mire until after his death," Gunther repeated.

"Well, Jackson Mire seemed to know of you. It seems that prior to Jackson Mire's death, he received information about a certain high-ranking member of our government who was receiving secret communications from the Reaper Kai order. Before his death, he confided this fact to a member of the high council. Do you know who was implicated in this conspiracy?"

"Objection. This testimony cannot be corroborated. It was given and not recorded in any manner. Who was this witness?" Gunther's counsel rebutted.

"The testimony was received by the honorable Arthur Gallows only minutes before Jackson was murdered in the street near his residence," the prosecutor shot back. "The admission is given by a high council member in good standings."

"The admission may be admissible but there is no way to verify the accuracy of the statements," Gunther's counsel objected.

The two combatants looked to the magistrate to resolve the issue. The magistrate overseeing the trial was Magistrate Riches, the same man in whom Gallows had confided upon Jackson Mire's death. The magistrate had been convinced of Gunther's guilt from the beginning, having bought into all of Arthur Gallows crazed theories. Taking a brief moment to ponder the situation, he ruled in favor of the prosecution, feeling confident that Gunther was guilty.

"The testimony will be presented as accurate. Please continue," Magistrate Riches concluded.

Gunther's defense was stunned and shocked. They looked at each other in alarm. They could instantly sense that the proceedings were tainted and corrupt. It seemed that the emperor had already been convicted, and that the trial was a mere formality to appease the public.

"I will state the question again. Do you know who was implicated in the conspiracy by Jackson Mire prior to his cruel murder?"

"No I do not," Gunther replied, although he knew full well what the answer was.

"You, Gunther, were implicated in the conspiracy. Before he was brutally murdered, Jackson Mire stated that the Reaper Kai were communicating in secret with you!" The prosecutor spoke in a commanding tone, pointing directly at Gunther.

A tremor of whispers erupted from the audience.

"Silence," the magistrate commanded, and the audience complied instantly.

The accusation did not seem to agitate Gunther, who remained stoic and did not even respond.

"Do you still deny knowing of Jackson Mire before his death?"

"Yes, I never knew of Jackson Mire before his death," he repeated once more.

"It's time to come clean." Arthur Gallows rose to his feet, his tone contemptuous.

"*I* have nothing on my conscience," Gunther said, his intonation subtle, locking eyes with Arthur.

"How can you deny this?" Gallows tore into him, taking the lead.

"There is nothing to deny. I never knew of Jackson Mire before his death."

"After his death, his body was moved to the morgue in secret. No one but myself, two members of the council guard, and the mortician knew of his death! The murder was a complete secret." Gallows approached the stand. "And yet one day after his death, you appeared at the morgue and knew that he was dead. How is it that you knew of his death?"

Falling silent for a brief second, Gunther could feel the noose tightening around his neck. The Oracle of Justice, Matthew Moralis, had told Gunther of the murder. To protect the covert operation of killing the Reaper Kai imbedded within the city, Gunther knew that he could not disclose who had told him of the murder. If he disclosed the information about Maddock's strike team, it would compromise the mission and the Reaper Kai would survive to carry out their acts of sabotage and murder. Stonen would be defenseless, and the enemy operatives would cause severe damage, possibly enough to spell ruin and defeat for the entire Iron Kai Empire. Gunther had to keep the secret; the fate of the empire depended upon his silence.

The enraged Gallows felt that he was making good progress and saw the emperor's lack of response as a chance to pounce. "I ask again, how were you informed of the murder of Jackson Mire?"

"I cannot disclose that fact," Gunther said in a subdued voice.

Hearing that the emperor refused to answer the question made the entire courtroom erupt into a frenzy of suspicion. His inability to respond shifted the focus of blame directly to him. The emperor of the Iron Kai Empire was hiding something. His response had been perfect—just what Arthur Gallows needed to convict him.

"Isn't it strange? Jackson Mire appears here in Stonen claiming that you, Emperor Gunther, are conspiring with the enemy in secret. After meeting with me, a member of the high council, he was assassinated in the street. Only a handful of people knew of his death, but you showed up at the morgue the next day. Now you cannot disclose who told you of his murder? All of these facts show that the reason you knew of the murder is because you ordered the murder of Jackson Mire. It's time to come clean. Did you order the killing of Jackson Mire?"

"No," Gunther replied, observing the crowd in the courtroom shift toward convicting him. "I did not order the killing of Jackson Mire."

"Come clean!" Gallows roared.

Many in the audience rose to their feet and began to shout that Gunther was guilty. The circus was coming alive and the crowd hungered for blood. Many in the crowd wanted Gunther to be fed to the lions.

"I did not order the killing of Jackson Mire," Gunther boomed back. "But can you tell the court, Gallows, why you ordered the snake tattoos on Jackson Mire's arms to be removed? Why did you order the mortician to remove evidence that he was a Reaper Kai?"

The courtroom exploded once more and now they stared in horror at Arthur Gallows. Shaking his head defiantly, he gritted out a scornful reply. "I am not on trial; I am not answering any of your questions."

The magistrate was shocked. He had been told by Gallows about the strange events, but Gallows had never mentioned that Jackson Mire was branded with the mark of the beast, the mark of the Reaper Kai. Indecision was beginning to mount in his eyes. Maybe there was something more to the story? Magistrate Riches was instantly on edge. He shook his head, suddenly feeling felt that he had been played by Gallows.

"Silence!" Riches yelled and the crowd grew quiet, but remained unsettled. After the courtroom was returned to order, Riches stared at Gallows and spoke directly to him. "Is it true? Did Jackson Mire have the brand of the Reaper Kai?"

Unable to respond, Gallows turned bright red with rage. "I am not the enemy here. Gunther is in league with the enemy."

His lack of response drove another flurry of whispers throughout the crowd. It was apparent that Gallows himself was trying to conceal something sinister as well.

"I ask you again. Gallows, was Jackson Mire branded with the mark of the Reaper Kai?"

With much hesitation, he answered, "Yes, he was marked with serpent tattoos."

The crowd was shocked and stunned. Gallows' admission sent a tremor of fear into every member of the audience. Reaper Kai were inside the city, inside the walls of Stonen.

Magistrate Riches sat back in his chair with a look of defeat on his face. The trial had turned into a diabolic scenario. Both Gunther and Gallows were hiding secrets and the chaos inside the city over the past week was beginning to make sense. Shaking his head, the magistrate knew that the empire was under attack and it was clear that multiple plots were playing out inside his courtroom. Looking at the rabble of people staring down at the two combatants, he knew that a terrible line had already been crossed. Many members of the public knew now that two leaders of the government were hiding something. If he expelled the public from the proceedings at this point, the entire city would tear itself apart with rumors and wild theories. Riches knew that in order to maintain organization within the city, the public needed to be involved with the resolution of this dire trial.

With a sigh, Riches looked at Gallows. "You knowingly concealed information about enemy forces within this city. You admitted to lying to the government about enemy movements within our empire. Arthur Gallows, I hereby charge you with obstruction of government processes and conspiracy to commit treason. You are remanded to custody." Looking at the council guards, he pointed at Gallows. "Take him into custody and shackle him. Leave him in the courtroom; I may have further need for him."

"What?" Gallows screamed in rage. "This is insane! Gunther is the real threat not me!"

"Councilman Gallows, you are a threat to this empire. You lied to a high ranking magistrate and knowingly sought to misinform and possibly overthrow the current government by a deceitful act of coercion," Magistrate Riches concluded in an enraged tone.

The council guards obeyed the order and handcuffed Gallows, forcing him to sit.

Riches then turned his attention to Gunther on the stand. "I need to depart from common courtroom proceedings since it is now evident that these events are not common. I feel very strongly that the events that have transpired today could spell the doom of our great nation. I will now consult and question Emperor Gunther directly in an effort to discover the truth in these matters."

The courtroom was completely silent; no one moved or dared to breathe.

Gunther turned to the magistrate and bowed his head in respect.

"Emperor Gunther, over the past few weeks, twenty three people within this city have disappeared. Last night, an armed gunman dressed in black combat attire burst into a restaurant and killed several civilians and a man marked with the sign of the Reaper Kai, who appears to have been a Reaper Kai agent. We now know that Jackson Mire, as both you and Arthur Gallows admitted, was also a Reaper Kai agent. It appears that this empire has a real crisis on its hands. Would you agree?"

"Yes, we are in mortal danger," Gunther concurred, still calm throughout all of the proceedings.

"Are the disappearances of the twenty three people, the death of Jackson Mire, and the man in the restaurant last night related?" Riches was intelligent and he had successfully put all of the pieces of the puzzle together.

"Yes, all of the events are related," Gunther confirmed.

The audience was stunned. A sinister plot was unfolding within the city and their worst fears were being realized. Just like Rasheed, Rust Spire, and Markov, Reaper Kai agents had infiltrated the city. The similarities were chilling. Everyone in the audience knew that if multiple Reaper Kai agents had been killed within the city, the enemy was close to a full-scale invasion of the Iron Kai Empire.

Riches sighed and shook his head in dismay. Gallows had played him and he had fallen into the trap. Looking back at Gunther, he asked another critical question. "The twenty three people that have gone missing over the past weeks, were these also Reaper Kai agents?"

Gunther responded without hesitation. "Yes, all of them were Reaper Kai agents."

The audience was now in full panic mode.

"That's twenty five Reaper Kai agents?"

"Yes," the emperor confirmed.

"All of these strikes were ordered by you."

Taking in a full breath of air into his lungs, he exhaled, knowing where the line of questioning was going. "Yes, I ordered all of these killings."

Magistrate Riches was stunned by the admission.

"You realize that ordering covert strikes without the knowledge of the high council is an act of treason?"

"Yes, I fully acknowledge that I broke the law. I knowingly ordered multiple covert strikes within this city without the knowledge of the council. If given the opportunity to do it again, I would order these strikes without hesitation."

Riches was stunned. Shaking his head in dismay, he looked at his leader and did not know what to think. "You realize that you just admitted to treason? You could be put to death for your actions!"

"I would willingly give my life to protect this empire and the people of the empire. If my actions cost me my life, I am proud to have done what I have done. My duty, my obligation, is to this empire and its people. I knew of this enemy threat and knew that if it were not dealt with swiftly, it could lead to the death of many within this city. If these Reaper Kai operatives were allowed to remain, they would have caused horrendous damage to our infrastructure. We have seen this type of tactic occur against Rasheed, The Steel Crag Mining Guild, and the Mord Tech Empire. In each case, enemy operatives caused massive damage to the infrastructure and killed key leadership personnel prior to invasion. If given the opportunity again, I would willingly risk being charged with treason to ensure the safety of the citizens of this empire."

Standing up, Gunther spread out his hands and looked at his people. He smiled up at them, displaying the shackles on his wrists. As he addressed the audience, his voice quivered with passion. The emotion he was feeling was not lost on the audience. "I leave my fate in your hands. I am proud that I have served you, the great people of this empire. My love for this nation is so strong, I am proud of what I have done to defend it. The laws of this nation see me as a traitor and that is a title that I will wear with distinction since I fully admit to my actions. I admit to breaking the laws of this great nation, but I did it to save this nation. Treason is punishable by death and if death is my sentence, know that I go toward that fate with a proud heart. I know that I did the right thing even though my life is now forfeit. If given a chance to defend this nation again, I would do so. Our troops and soldiers have fought with distinction on the battlefield, giving their lives to defend us all. I did the same; I risked my life to save this nation and empire."

As tears streamed down his face, he spoke with his heart and soul pouring down his cheeks. "I love the people of this nation with all of my heart. I would sacrifice anything to keep this nation safe from tyranny and reckless hate. I believe so strongly in my actions, I will not disclose the members of the covert action cleansing this city of evil. I know that my inability to divulge their identities is further defiance of this country's laws, but I cannot risk failure of this mission. I am fully aware of my actions and knowingly await their consequences. My fate rests in your hands."

The audience was silent and many had tears of their own streaking down their faces. A noble leader, a hero who had risked his very life to ensure the safety of his nation, was shackled, awaiting his sentence. The fate of Emperor Gunther was hanging in the balance. After a day of emotional events and sinister plots, the entire nation was exhausted. With war looming on the horizon, tough choices would have to be made. The valiant emperor of the Iron Kai had admitted to treason and he would have to face those consequences.

Confused and exhausted, Riches ordered a recess in the trial. Both Gunther and Gallows were led away to the court jail. As the shackled leaders were led away, the stunned crowd broke into uneasy whispers. The controversy caused by not one but two government officials involved in secret plots was almost too much to handle.

As the crowd spun fanciful tales and was swayed by various rumors, Riches let out a sigh and stared at the gavel on his bench. Grabbing it, he gripped it tightly, wanting to break it in two. His courtroom was supposed to be a place of justice. Instead, Gallows had turned it into a circus and a farce. Shaking his head in anger, he felt guilty and used. Vowing to set things right, he slowly stood from the bench and retreated into his chambers.

While the Iron Kai Empire was gripped with indecision and chaos, the Reaper Kai plotted the demise of their age-old enemies. As emotions ran high in the courtroom, legions of enemy troops, the largest army that the Reaper Kai had ever assembled, were marching on the city of Stonen. Led by Brother Feral, ruthless Reaper Kai general, the army had but one purpose: destroy the last free empire in the entire Darken Realm. With chaos gripping the Iron Kai leadership, the coming conflict could spell the ruin of all.

Chapter 25
Target 47

The time had finally come. After years of preparation, an intricate plan was about to be set in motion. Anxious for the call, the Reaper Kai operative looked at his pocket watch with growing fascination. He eyed the minute hand on the watch as it slowly moved forward, edging toward an important point in time. Breathing heavily, the operative opened his satchel and inspected its contents.

A bundle of six sticks of dynamite with a digital timer were resting at the bottom of the satchel. Beside the explosives was a radio handset that was emitting a light static twang, occasionally screeching like a scratchy record which had somehow survived a sand storm.

As he touched the explosives, the operative was thinking about his objective, going over the mission plan in his mind. The plan was relatively simple. At five past eight in the evening, he was to leave his dwelling within the city of Stonen and travel to the power station near the center of the mountain. He was to infiltrate the fence line around the station and plant the explosives with a five minute delay. After completing his primary objective, he was to travel into the lower district and kill a lieutenant of the Iron Kai army.

Holding the watch to his ear, he listened to the device tick away as the seconds passed and the time grew ever closer to the predetermined strike. Thinking about the carnage he was about to unleash filled him with a deep pride. The Iron Kai were the Reaper

Kai's most reviled enemy. Centuries of hate and mutual casualties had led to a bitter animosity that could never be quelled with simple diplomacy. To end such aggression, the complete eradication of the other faction must take place.

Tick tock. The clock ground away. Pulling the timepiece from his ear, the operative watched the minute hand come to rest on five past eight, the time of action. He jumped to his feet with a demented grin, grabbing his satchel. Leaving his abode, he ran down the staircase of the subterranean apartment building and jumped into the street below.

The environmental controls had dimmed the lights in the city as they did every night. The dark streets were noticeably more empty than usual. A rash of recent disappearances and murders in the city had driven most people into their homes. With doors barred, the citizens of Stonen huddled in the dark and wondered what the strange sounds outside their homes signified. Evil deeds were afoot and a flurry of wild fantasies had been sparked after their leader's admission that Reaper Kai agents had been found inside the city.

Smiling at the quiet street, the lone Reaper Kai operative peered into a nearby alley. He saw nothing to deter him between the two buildings, and proceeded to bolt into the darkness. Rushing forward past garbage cans, he huddled near the end of the alley, crouching near a grate set in the ground. He had cut the lock off the grate on the previous night, and now opened it effortlessly and jumped into an electrical access tunnel. Moving on all fours like an animal, the saboteur progressed quickly through the tunnel. After thirty yards, he found another metal grate in his path. Stealthily, he popped the grate loose and pulled it into the access tunnel.

The perimeter of the power station was silent as he dropped to the ground. Amazed with the ease of his progress, he felt unstoppable, and rushed on with exhilaration, pulling the watch from his pocket. Only two minutes were left until his scheduled planting of the explosives. *Tick tock.* He eyed the watch in fascination. The other operatives were probably on their way to their targets as well. If the plan went off successfully, the hidden Reaper Kai operatives within the city were about to unleash a torrent of chaos meant to disable the infrastructure of Stonen and to kill many of its leaders. Being part of such a diabolical plan made the young Reaper Kai proud to be serving his race.

Tick tock. It was time to strike. Pushing through a hole in the fence, the operative moved towards the power station and silently slipped inside, dropping to one knee and pulling the bundle of explosives from his satchel.

"I wouldn't do that if I were you," an ominous voice rang out in the darkness of the power station.

Dropping the explosives in terror, the Reaper Kai operative took a step back and peered into the darkness. *No one* was supposed to know of his plot, or of the general plan. A bright surge of fire lit the darkness. Flashing light erupted and bathed the access tunnel in an eerie glow; a soldier with cold eyes was holding a military flair aloft in his hand. The white light danced in the darkness, illuminating the room with a pale hue. Blinking several times, the Reaper Kai agent was stunned to find that he was not alone; in fact, he was completely surrounded. A host of soldiers were training automatic weapons on the lone saboteur. As the flare flickered, the leader of the covert strike team threw the glowing spike of fire on the floor beside the Reaper Kai. The hissing torch spat white sparks on the floor as it burned down.

Stunned by the ambush, the Reaper Kai trembled, the explosives resting on the floor next to him. One of the soldiers took the initiative, grabbing the bundle of explosives and disarming them by pulling the digital timer and detonator out of the dynamite. Within moments, the plot to destroy the power station had ended.

The lonely Reaper Kai was young and poorly experienced at that. He had little power when it came to open conflict. His powers were based around divining past events and had nothing to do with combat. Essentially defenseless, he scowled at the swarm of soldiers surrounding him.

"What is all of this about?" he hissed in defiance.

An aged man moved forward from the darkness into the flickering light of the flare. In the dim light, his wrinkled face made the man look truly ancient. He stared at the Reaper Kai with an expression of solemn contempt. The Reaper Kai looked back and sneered.

"Who are you, old man?" he spoke again.

"I am a dagger, an instrument used to scourge and kill a tumor growing within this empire. I am happy to say that this is a great day indeed and this meeting between all of us is a happy event," the Oracle of Justice replied.

"A happy event?" The Reaper Kai operative was mystified.

"Yes, it's a happy day indeed," Maddock pitched in, chewing on his habitual toothpick. Seeing the Reaper Kai scum before him made the captain agitated, and he bit down on the toothpick, snapping it with his teeth. Angrily, he spat the remnants of the toothpick at the Reaper Kai, spraying him with wood fragments and saliva. "We're about to throw a party."

"A party for what?"

"A party for you. You are lucky number forty seven," the Oracle of Justice replied in an eerie tone.

The number hit the Reaper Kai operative with ominous intensity. When the original operation was set in motion, all of the operatives had been briefed that a total of forty seven Reaper Kai were to infiltrate the city in order to cause acts of murder and sabotage. Forty seven Reaper Kai had been allocated to destroy the infrastructure of Stonen. Shaking his head in dismay, the operative could not believe his ears.

"You lie!" he screamed in rage.

"It's no lie. Your little rampage is at an end. You are the last operative in this city. With your death, we are insuring the future of our empire." Maddock almost laughed at the insolent agent.

Pulling a knife from his belt, the young operative prepared to charge the Iron Kai soldiers in an insane display of homicidal rage. He raised his blade with a desperate war cry. Muzzle flashes from numerous guns flashed in the dim light. Popping, several bullets broke the silence of the power station. The weapons struck true and the Reaper Kai, the last and final enemy agent, was shot several times. Falling to the floor, he looked up at the soldiers in the flashing light of the flare. They watched him bleed to death with cold, merciless expressions. Operative forty seven gagged but once before breathing his last breath.

As the final Reaper Kai in the city of Stonen died, a sense of fulfillment warmed the team of covert Iron Kai soldiers. They had risked their very lives over the past weeks and many of their countrymen had died in the operation to eradicate the tumor that had infected the city. At last, the enemy operatives were all gone, all dead. The mission had been insane to contemplate, and without the help of the Oracle of Justice, a descendant of Ceibla Moralis himself, the mission would have ended in ruin. The enigmatic old man had protected countless soldiers during the witch hunts and had led the covert strike team to the doorstep of every Reaper Kai hidden within the city. The mission had been a complete success.

Rummaging through the satchel of the dead Reaper Kai, an Iron Kai soldier found the radio in the bag. Throwing it to Maddock, the soldier smiled.

As he held the radio, Mad Dog Maddock understood the smile on the soldier's face. He depressed a button on the device and spoke into the radio with a taunt in his voice. "Anyone out there?" Static was his only response. "Mission complete," he spoke into the radio again, trying to illicit a response.

Finally a raspy voice responded from the other end of the radio. "Why is it that I don't believe you?"

"The mission is complete," Maddock toyed with his adversary. "I didn't say *whose* mission is complete."

"Who is this?" the raspy voice responded, somewhat curious.

"They're all dead. It's really sad. Forty seven dead Reaper Kai. We just killed the last of them and it looks like it was just in time. Your little plan has failed. None of your poor little agents made it to any of their targets. *Our* mission is a success, *your* mission is a complete failure," Maddock taunted the mysterious voice at the other end of the radio.

"Failure?" A sinister laugh broke across the radio. "You have only a few days left to live. Cherish your victory while you can. By the end of the week, the Reaper Kai order will be dancing on your broken bodies, pissing on your corpses. Enjoy the happiness. Enjoy your *success*. Your lives are forfeit. You are all going to die."

"Do your worst. The age-old feud will come to an end and we will show you who the *superior* race is. In the end, we will be dancing on your broken bodies." Maddock's tone was brash. "I can't wait to meet you on the battlefield."

Laughing dryly, the evil voice responded, "I will cherish that meeting as well."

With that, Maddock threw the radio to the floor and stomped on it. The device shattered immediately under his weight. As the members of the strike team stared at the broken radio, they felt utterly alive and completely defiant. The team had done the impossible and killed a small army of enemy agents. However, the cost of war had been harsh; twenty three soldiers had lost their lives in cleansing the city of the hidden menace.

As the flare burned out, the team emerged from the power station. Looking at the dark city around them, they knew that the enemy would not lie silent for long. Even as adrenaline filled them at the thought of their success, they looked to the future with apprehension. The coming conflict would not be easy.

Chapter 26
Invasion

The Truce Hall was buzzing with activity. All of the Iron Kai high council members, save Arthur Gallows, were crammed into the room, listening to a horrifying series of communications that were blasting over the air waves. A battle line some twenty miles wide had formed along the southern rim of the Iron Kai Empire. A large army, the largest ever fielded by the Reaper Kai, was on a full-scale offensive. Twenty thousand Biogtech soldiers, led by over two thousand Reaper Kai battle priests, were attacking three Iron Kai cities. The cities of Green River, Three Forks, and Harper's Way were currently under heavy assault. Each city had a small number of troops, numbering close to one thousand per city.

The defenders of the three cities were fighting a desperate struggle, holding back the flood of enemy troops long enough for the civilian populace to evacuate. Streams of thousands upon thousands of refugees were fleeing northward towards the mighty capital city of Stonen. Having wiped out all other enemies within the Darken Realm, the sinister Reaper Kai order had set its sights on their final enemy.

All of the leaders stared in horror at each other as they listened to the chaotic radio transmissions. The full-scale invasion of Iron Kai Empire was under way. With the majority of the empire laid out north of Stonen, everyone in the room knew that the battle would soon come to the capital city. Unable to comprehend what to do, the leaders were completely ineffective. Most were bureaucrats and knew nothing about war and battle. Their emperor, Gunther, had been imprisoned after opting to plead guilty to treason. Arthur Gallows, the politician more obsessed with his own ego than the fate of the Iron Kai Empire, had also earned a prison stay after admitting to lying to government officials and concealing a Reaper Kai plot within the city of Stonen. Unfortunately, the brazen official had turned to suicide, hanging himself within his jail cell only a mere hour after admitting to trying to overthrow Gunther. The remaining members of the Iron Kai leadership were too unsure of themselves to make a solid strategic decision. The empire needed strong leadership, and it needed it now.

As the leaders stared at each other, dumbfounded, things grew from grim to dire. A flurry of new communications broke over the radios, intercepted by a squad of alarmed technicians. Three fishing vessels sailing upon the great lake on which Stonen bordered had just sent in frightening radio transmissions. The communications indicated the presence of enemy landing craft, dozens and dozens of boats laden with enemy troops heading directly toward the city of Stonen.

"Can you repeat?" the technician spoke into the radio, wide-eyed fear taking root upon his face.

"I say again, I count over forty enemy ships inbound. I repeat, over forty Reaper Kai landing craft are headed directly towards Stonen," a frantic fisherman reported.

"Can you identify what the boats are carrying?" the technician stuttered, nearly overcome by fear.

"All the ships are loaded with Biogtech infantry. Several of the ships are also loaded with larger forms on board. I can't tell what exactly the forms are. There are tarps covering the cargo."

"Estimate the number of troops on each boat," the technician commanded.

"I can't tell for sure, maybe three or four dozen troops per boat, maybe around fifty."

The revelation sent a panic through the Truce Hall. If the estimates were correct, there were forty-some odd ships inbound with fifty enemy troops per ship. Doing some quick, dirty math, everyone in the room figured that over two thousand Biogtech soldiers were about to hit Dakota Beach, the heavily fortified beachhead just below the capital city. With two thousand troops inbound and twenty thousand more within fifteen miles of the capital, the nation's doom could be imminent.

Running over to the windows of the Truce Hall, the politicians and bureaucrats stared in horror at the great lake just below the capital city of Stonen. In the distance they could discern a swarm of landing craft, filled to the gills with enemy soldiers. The ships were pushing hard and fast across the lake; it would be only a matter of minutes before they unloaded their deadly cargo. Fear was ripe in the room and no one had a solid plan of action.

Even the commander of the Stonen defense forces, Field Marshal Patrick, was on overload. He was a courageous military leader but the army assaulting the core of the empire was too much for him to handle. Fighting a battle on one front was one thing, but four battles occurring simultaneously close to the capital was too much for his mind to process. Taking a shaky stab at national defense, he ordered troops to Dakota Beach with the intent of trying to repel as many enemy forces as possible. If the beachhead fell, it would be impossible to defend the exterior of the capital city. Enemy forces overrunning the beach would allow the Reaper Kai to endlessly reinforce their assault against the capital city.

Watching the swarm of Iron Kai soldiers hit the bunkers above Dakota Beach gave the onlookers little solace. The advance of the enemy was too intense and the observers were cringing, knowing that a battle would soon be raging below.

"What are we doing?" A high council member was trying to collect his thoughts out loud. He stared at his companions with a look of shock and horror as his brain was shutting down. "We need to do something," he whined.

"We don't have any time to do something. We're being invaded and no one in this room has a damn idea what to do!" another councilman replied in a frantic tone.

"Marshal Patrick!" Magistrate Riches urged the commander, who was sweating profusely. "What are your orders?"

Shaking his head, Patrick wiped the sweat from his brow and shook his head in dismay. "It's too fast. It's too quick. I don't know what to do. I'm only trained in defensive tactics, there are too many attacks taking place. I don't know what to do."

"Well, do something quick!" A lieutenant pointed at the beach below. The enemy was drawing close, so close that the Biogtech soldiers were now visible in the landing craft, their pasty white bodies reflecting enough light to make them resemble tiny beacons of dread, drawing ever nearer.

Someone needed to do something quickly, and Magistrate Riches knew that this was his time, his place to act for the betterment of all. Collecting his thoughts, he stared in horrified wonder as the enemy boats came closer and closer. He shook his head as his stomach knotted with dread and a shot of adrenaline rolled through him. He barely understood what he was doing, but he knew he needed to act. Rushing to the podium near Gunther's empty throne, he waved his arms around like a maniac trying to draw the attention of everyone in the Truce Hall. His feeble tactics were nothing more than a distraction in the extreme chaos.

Irked by the irreverence of the rest of the room, Magistrate Riches felt something snap inside him. A feral, inhuman scream rose in the air as the man seemed to lose his mind. The sound was so unnerving, it caught the attention of everyone in the room, which grew eerily silent. The only sounds were the crackling radios, transmitting the screams of dying men on nearby battlefields. With all eyes on him, Riches knew that the group had to come together and to act quickly.

Taking a pause, he stared at the frantic crowd before him, trying to calm himself and focus his thoughts. Breathing heavily, he collected himself and spoke with the intent of fixing the mess for which he felt partly responsible.

"We are on the brink of ruin. At this moment, we are standing on the precipice of destruction. The entire southern edge of our empire is under attack and now our capital city is minutes away from a full-scale lakeside assault. If we do not act quickly to resolve this, there will be no more empire. We need to calm down and figure this mess out right now." Riches spoke methodically, staring at the crowd.

"Over the past few days, our nation has been rocked with scandal. Two members, two trusted members of our government, have betrayed the confidence of our nation by breaking its laws and seeking to hide these truths from us. I don't know what kind of world we live in and why these things have happened, but I do know one thing; I know that sometimes hard choices have to be made in hard times. I believe now is such a time, a time where we must put aside our differences and our ideals and focus on survival. Yes, we have been betrayed from within, but we hold the answer to our survival, in the form of the leader who has led us through this terrible war to this point."

The officials were restless, but their gazes grew dreamy, almost hopeful, as they watched the speech unfold.

"I don't know who was telling the truth. Gallows claimed Gunther is in league with the enemy but Gunther claimed Gallows was in league with the enemy. We can make only a few choices at this point. We can choose not to trust either man for they have both admitted to breaking our laws and betraying our trust. If we choose this option, we are on our own. We must survive this attack and persevere. Two other choices present themselves. We can choose to trust either Emperor Gunther or the words of the late Representative Gallows. If we put our trust in Gallows, we must still try to weather this invasion without a seasoned military leader." The room looked on and pondered the reasoning.

"Or we can put our trust in our emperor, a man who has admitted to ordering death and slaughter. Even though he betrayed his position and abused his power, I feel that he did so to protect us all. The burden of leadership is a tough one. In order to save us all, he chose to lie to us, to spare us the horror of war. If Gunther is truly in league with the enemy, we are lost. But if he is as noble and courageous as I believe, a man who willingly put his life at risk to save us all, I believe he is the man who can lead us to victory. I ask you all to put your trust in our leader, our emperor. He will not let us down; he will never surrender. I say we pardon his misdeeds and put our trust in him once more."

As Riches looked out at the crowd, many nodded their head in agreement. Most believed that Gunther was a wise and noble leader. The nods quickly turned to growing consent. Fear and a will to survive had changed many of their minds. Sure, the emperor had broken the law, but he had done so for the greater good. The growing agreement ignited in a powerful fury of hope. The hope broke into chanting and soon everyone in the Truce Hall was chanting Gunther's name.

Magistrate Riches had a smile on his face. With a sigh of relief, he ordered the release of their mighty leader. Rushing into the cell blocks, the council guards drew near Gunther's cell as the sounds of artillery fire roared to life with thundering booms. With death and despair on the horizon, hope was rekindled as the cell door opened and Gunther stepped out from the darkness. With a serious look on his face, he assessed the sounds of combat booming in the air, and knew what needed to be done. Gritting his teeth, Emperor Gunther stroked his fiery orange beard and then gripped his hands together tightly.

Trumpets blared in the distance. The enemy landing craft crashed onto Dakota Beach. Gunfire roared to life. Charging from the dungeons, Gunther hurried into the fray. The siege of Stonen had begun.

Chapter 27
The Siege of Stonen

"Fall back!" an officer yelled as a host of Goat Minions poured into the trench with frightening speed. Garbed in blood-red robes, the sinister agents of evil jumped head-first into the trench. Thirty Goat Minions had survived the machine gun fire, a fact which evoked utter terror in the defenders. Black, beady eyes looked for targets. Driven by the smell of blood, the dark minions of evil hungered to kill and slaughter. Needing blood and death, the Goat Minions went into a berserk fury, savoring the taste of slaughter and misery.

Confronted with these horrific creatures in the midst of their ranks, the Iron Kai soldiers tried to flee. Screams of pain rose in the trench as the Goat Minions began to butcher the defenders. Blood was flowing freely as the insane killing machines crushed defender after defender. Relentless gunfire was exchanged inside the trench. Bullets raced through the ranks, killing attacker and defender alike as the stunned soldiers tried desperately to survive the assault. Terror had now crippled the entire rank of soldiers.

A man yelled in agony as a Goat Minion continually struck him with a knotted club. Another man gagged, trying to pull an axe out of his stomach. No direction in the trench offered a refuge from death. The sound of the Goat Minions baying in sheer ecstasy created a gruesome clamor. Elated by the carnage, the creatures were driven by the smell of blood into a trance in which killing was their only focus. They swung time and time again, ignoring pain and damage to their own bodies. With supernatural fortitude, they withstood gunshot wounds and continued to kill. Drenched in blood, the Goat Minions severed limbs and shattered skulls, butchering the hapless victims of the trenches.

The officer screamed again. "Fall back!"

His words were cut short. Like a smear of fog, a shimmering wraith glimmered in the morning sun. Something had moved behind the trench, into the core of officers trying desperately to rally their troops. Blinking, the officer took a step back. Emerging from the shifting light came a Reaper Kai priest. Once invisible, Brother Feral, sinister general of the Reaper Kai, now stepped into plain view. He smiled smoothly, muscles rippling. Breathing in, he recoiled, tensing back to strike using a gore-stained, curved blade with saw-like teeth. The black weapon swung forward, cleaving into the officer and killing him immediately.

Another officer witnessed the attack and drew his pistol. By the time he took aim at the Reaper Kai priest, his opponent was already gone, disappearing into a shimmering wave of distorted light. The war priest had mastered the art of bending light around himself, and was able to disappear completely from sight. The shocked officer never knew what hit him. Appearing behind him, Brother Feral decapitated the officer quickly. Before the man's severed head hit the ground, the sinister general had disappeared from sight once more, blending into his surroundings.

The reckless and aggressive war priest had already claimed the lives of seven Iron Kai officers. His ability to turn invisible was causing chaos as all of the leaders on the ridge above Dakota Beech rapidly died in droves. Without solid leadership, terror filled the trenches as hope failed. The troops found themselves on their own, trapped in their individual, desperate struggles to survive. Many soldiers had fled already, utterly demoralized by the specters of death.

The front line, the trenches behind Dakota Beach, was beginning to buckle. As the Goat Minions slaughtered the defenders, an entire army, comprised of just over five hundred Biogtechs slowly plodding up the hillside, made its advance. The beachhead assault had been a disaster for the defenders of Stonen. Over forty landing craft had deposited two thousand Biogtech soldiers onto the beach. The defenders could have held the beach if it weren't for the brutal Goat Minion assault led by Brother Feral. The bunkers defending the beach had been overrun quickly by Feral's swift and brutal tactics. The assault was so quick and vicious, mere minutes had passed before the enemy had taken fifty yards of territory, and heavily fortified territory at that.

As the shattered army tried to hold the beach, a second army assaulted the city just outside the mountain fortress of Stonen. A sprawling suburb of homes and shops was now the staging ground of heated urban warfare. A defense force of two thousand troops was trying to hold back a flood of nearly ten thousand enemy troops. The fierce fighting was a testament to a strong will to survive. The Iron Kai forces were bitterly trying to hold back the flood. Block after block of the suburb was being taken by Biogtech soldiers as the defenders slowly retreated towards the city defenses. The shops and houses made the retreat easier, providing excellent cover from the gunfire.

The shattered remnants of refugees and soldiers were still pouring in from the three southernmost towns in the empire. Half of the troops had been killed in tense conflicts, but one thousand soldiers still remained and were making their way back to the capital city. A battlefront had erupted in the lush farmlands and forests as well. Over a twenty-mile front, soldiers were desperately fighting for their lives as the twenty thousand invaders spread across the same lines.

The invasion was a tactical nightmare. There were now seven distinct battles taking place near the city of Stonen.

*   *   *

Charging into the Truce Hall, the newly liberated Emperor Gunther had walked into a hornets' nest. Panic was ripe and there was considerable chaos as multiple military leaders argued about the next course of action. Instead of acting decisively, each leader was terrified and was unable to come up with a solid plan. The members of the high council were stirring up more trouble, trying to give orders that few were listening to. Bureaucrats are ill equipped for war but it doesn't seem to matter. Politicians are always eager to give orders even though they have never stepped onto a battlefield. This was the case in the Truce Hall. Bickering politicians were trying to run an out-of-control war.

Still dirty and reeking from the jail cell, Gunther assessed the situation as he entered the Truce Hall. Focusing on one of the soldiers in the room, he charged over and brashly commanded, "Give me your pistol."

The soldier obeyed immediately. Clicking off the safety, Gunther pointed the weapon at the ceiling of the Truce Hall. He fired the weapon three times, the bullets harmlessly hitting the ceiling. The pops of gunfire caused a tremor and most everyone in the room hit the deck, instinctively trying to avoid the gunfire. A silence broke over the room as everyone stared at their newly exonerated leader.

"First order: only military personnel are to be in this room. Everyone else is to leave!" he shouted. The high council members held their ground like deer caught in the headlights of a car. Acknowledging their lack of response, Gunther increased the pressure. "Any person in this room ten seconds from now who is not military personnel will be shot, and I mean it." His tone was brash, and the message was received loud and clear. The bureaucrats shuffled out of the Truce Hall with frightening speed.

Rushing over to the window of the Truce Hall, Gunther could see Dakota Beach below. The defenses had been shattered and enemy troops had all but taken every defensive position.

Turning to the stunned officers in the Truce Hall, he boomed, "All troops stand at attention!" Training kicked in and the officers formed lines and fell into rank quickly, till all of them were standing at attention.

Seeing order begin to return gave each of the officers hope. In mere seconds, their leader, their true leader, had restored continuity amongst the soldiers. "Are the helicopters in the air?" Gunther quizzed his troops.

"No, sir!" an officer responded.

"Get them airborne now. Continually strafe the beachhead. Get those Biogtechs driven far enough back to retake the bunkers. I want those machine gun nests back up. If additional landing craft approach from the lake, the choppers are to immediately attack these boats. I don't want any additional troops landing on the beach," Gunther ordered, setting the officer in motion. He charged over to one of the radio technicians and the order was sent out.

"Radio the forces in Detro Tech city. Order all of the helicopters back immediately. Order them to attack any enemy boats on their way back across the lake. Keep these choppers focused on giving support to any soldiers fleeing south of the city. I don't want our forces cut off before they get back to the city." Another officer acknowledged the order and rushed over to the radio.

"I can see lots of smoke to the south. Are we being invaded from the south?" Gunther quizzed his officers.

Field Marshal Patrick stepped forward and gave a quick summary. "We are estimating enemy troop levels of about twenty thousand. Attacks along the entire southern edge of the empire are under way. Green River, Three Forks, and Harper's Way have all been overrun. The city defense forces were unable to hold back the flood of troops. Over one thousand soldiers have been killed already and the enemy is on full advance. We have reports that enemy armor formations, the same ones seen in Markov, are on the outskirts of Green River. We have confirmed sightings of at least fifty heavy Biogtech assault rigs inbound. Thankfully, they're slow."

"What about the refugees? Are you posting guards to prevent Reaper Kai from slipping inside the city in all of this chaos?" Gunther questioned the leader of the Stonen defense forces.

"No, my lord." Patrick spoke with hesitation. He had not thought about Reaper Kai trying to breach the city defenses masquerading as refugees.

"Maddock!" Gunther boomed.

Mad Dog Maddock made his way to stand before the other officers and acknowledged the emperor.

"Are their any more Reaper Kai in the city?" Gunther quizzed. His question sparked a look of concern on many faces within the officer corp. The reason Gunther had been imprisoned was for ordering an illegal covert strike within the city against these hidden operatives.

"All enemy operatives, forty seven strong, have been neutralized, my lord." Maddock spoke with a look of pride on his face.

"Excellent. I want you to get Moralis, the oracle that helped us purge the city of Reaper Kai. Stage him and a commando team near the front gate. With all of the refugees pouring into the city, I don't want any Reaper Kai priests slipping in during all of the chaos. Use Moralis to identify any Reaper Kai trying to pass inside the city. You have full authority to kill anyone suspicious. Go now!"

Maddock smiled at Gunther. "It's good to have back, sir," he said with a crisp salute.

"It's good to be back," Gunther boomed with a fierce look in his eyes, smiling at Maddock. Maddock charged out of the Truce Hall, ready to make good on the orders.

Returning his attention to Patrick and the inbound invasion, Gunther moved on to another set of orders. "We have fourteen tanks inside Stonen. Get them out quickly and punch through the battle line. I want you to initiate a surprise attack on those enemy Biogtech assault rigs moving on Green River. Take out as many as you can, then fall back to the outskirts of Stonen. Use the mobile artillery to harass the Biogtech invaders."

Patrick acknowledged the orders and pointed at one of his officers to ensure they were carried out. Another officer rushed off to the radios, setting another plan in motion.

"Mobilize our own internal forces. Send five thousand troops to bolster the defense of the lands just south of Stonen. I want all of the civilians supported as they evacuate. Send orders that everyone evacuating should bring as much food and supplies as they can carry. We have substantial food reserves but I want everything we can get if we are forced to retreat inside this city. Bring all of the survivors into Stonen. We have more than enough room for them, especially in some of the older tunnels and sections of the city."

"Yes, sir." Patrick motioned to another officer.

"Pull troops out of the northern cities. Half of their defense forces are to rally to Stonen. Since we now have a defined battle front, I want to shore up our defenses and prevent any enemy troops from pushing into our northern cities. If we can prevent the spreading of enemy troops, we can continue to rely on supplies from the north. If our empire gets split in two, we cannot support the Stonen defenses since our supply lines will be shattered." Gunther spoke calmly and methodically. He was a masterful leader, able to take care of multiple crises without even breaking a sweat.

Watching their leader confidently give orders set most of the soldiers at ease. Having a tough and strong leader who was able to function under extreme stress was reassuring to the fledgling leaders. Within a few minutes, there was a definitive course of action and the plans were sound. Confidence was beginning to build in the Truce Hall. The thoughts of the enemy being successful in their invasion were pushed from their minds. Everyone in the room looked at Gunther with passion building in their hearts. A man who had been imprisoned only a few minutes prior was now calmly leading an army. Gunther was an inspiration to all of them. Sensing that his actions made a positive impact, he focused on boosting their morale further.

"We have all been through one hell of a morning, haven't we?" His voice conveyed a quiet dignity.

The rest of the officers crowded around him nodded, feeling more at ease.

"Know this: our empire has withstood centuries of strife and war. The actions of the Reaper Kai should not worry us. Our military and its leaders are the best in the land. We have suffered a minor setback by being invaded. Even though the enemy has quickly pushed forward, we will hold them back and win the war. The enemy sought to murder our leaders and destroy our infrastructure with hidden saboteurs and assassins. You all heard Captain Maddock; forty seven hidden Reaper Kai priests were slaughtered and destroyed within our city. Their plan to murder us has ended. This is the first time an empire has survived a surprise attack by the Dark Order. We are no ordinary foe. We are the strongest empire in the land. We have the bravest soldiers and in the end, we will dance on the corpses of our enemies. In the end, we will be the victors. I say to you all, I have never seen a finer army, a more courageous band of warriors. I am proud to lead the best army in all the land. Here is to all of you!" Gunther, dressed in reeking clothes, stood at attention and saluted all of his gallant soldiers. The vision of their proud leader, only a few minutes prior imprisoned due to his fierce convictions and need to protect his people, was a powerful sight.

Smiles covered the faces of his officers and a spark of fire lit their souls. An aggressive surge of power rolled through them. Gunther had turned chaos into order. Gunther had turned panic into power. The soldiers who had lost hope found new strength. The surge of courageous aggression they were all feeling against the enemy could turn the tide of battle. Gunther's inspiring force would in turn surge downward through the ranks of the troops. A confident leadership would evoke confidence in each and every soldier. While fear is infectious, so are hope and gallantry.

"There is no fear!" Gunther boomed. "There is no chaos! We will beat them back and forever purge them from this land. We fight today not just for our empire and our loved ones. We fight for all the countless generations of our people who bled and died for freedom against dark tyranny. You are the army that will forever silence the Dark Order. Death to the Reaper Kai!" he bellowed.

The fire had been lit in their hearts. War cries and battle chants erupted amongst the soldiers. Raising their fists in the air, they chanted and praised Gunther. He held his own fists in the air and chanted with his men.

As the battle raged on in the trenches, courage and order had been restored. Panic was no longer ruling them; instead, a powerful emperor had taken charge. The battles were far from over, but the Reaper Kai would be hard pressed to continue their reckless advance. A bitter confrontation was being waged trench to trench, city to city. The fate of freedom was at stake in a battle against an enemy without any regard for peace and dignity. As this fate hung in the balance, hope roared from the radios and the troops were inspired. Fighting with their hearts, the Iron Kai soldiers held their ground and the battle for Stonen raged on.

Chapter 28
The Tide of Endless Death

A butane lighter erupted in the darkness. A flame, orange at the tip, blue in the middle, sprang to life in the midst of the ruins. Bringing a cigarette forward, the soldier lit the tobacco. Eyeing the wonderful object in his hand, the man smiled, then covered the tip of the cigarette with his hand, concerned that the glowing light from would draw unwanted attention.

It had been three hours since sundown and the remnants of the city were quiet at last. For the past two days, a Reaper Kai invasion force had been assaulting the suburbs around the mighty mountain fortress of Stonen. The above-ground dwellers had already fled into the city, abandoning their homes for the sake of safety. An invasion force of twenty thousand Biogtechs had slammed into the suburbs and ground to a bloody halt. Though significantly outnumbered, the valiant battle-hardened Iron Kai soldiers were not about to give up any additional ground. The defenders of Stonen reinforced this urban battleground quickly, preferring the cover of abandoned buildings to the open fields of wheat beyond the safety of the buildings.

Over one thousand Biogtechs had been destroyed in fierce fighting in a single day of combat. The courageous defenders had lost just over one hundred soldiers in the exchange, a minimal amount considering the circumstances. Dakota Beach and its defenses had been overrun by Brother Feral and his substantial military forces. Having lost the beach, Stonen was now open to an endless supply of enemy troops transported directly across the lake to reinforce the already large number of enemy troops.   Brother Feral and his army had ground to a halt on the eastern edge of the suburbs as well, his forces jammed up as the ferocious defenders held their ground.

After two solid days of combat, the quiet engulfing the suburbs of Stonen was a welcome relief. Most of the soldiers were exhausted and completely strung out. While the death machines of the Reaper Kai did not require any rest, the human soldiers of the Iron Kai army were not so lucky. Some sections of the city had seen ferocious firefights lasting close to ten hours straight.   The seemingly endless horde of robotic soldiers streamed into the city relentlessly. From time to time, the enemy would order the assault to stop as they tried to concoct another plan of attack.

This was such a time, a time where the Reaper Kai commanders had halted the attack long enough to regroup.   The calm was much needed. Many of the human soldiers had taken the opportunity to scarf down a vital meal and then take a break to sleep for a bit.

The soldier grasped the cigarette, smiling once more as he drew it near his lips. Sucking down a full drag, he felt the smoke tingle as it settled into his lungs. After a few seconds, he could feel the nicotine enter his blood, and it felt wonderful. The anxiety seemed to diminish as he continued to take drags off the cigarette. Within a few minutes, he was at peace. Looking around the ruined house, the soldier was glad to be alive. His unit had been the first to reinforce the suburbs and was the first to make contact with enemy forces. Within the initial few minutes of combat, his good friend from childhood had been gunned down and left for dead at the south end of the city. The defenders had been driven back quickly by the ferocious attack, and the soldier was unable to recover the corpse of his dead friend.

Thinking back to the events of the past few days, the soldier shook his head in dismay; it had been hell on earth. He finished the first cigarette and grabbed another to light from the pack. Pressing his back against the back wall of the building, he laid his head back and stared at the ceiling in the darkness. As the nicotine flowed through his blood, he looked around with a dull gaze, lost in thought and gripped by exhaustion. His lazy daydream would be short-lived.

Movement somewhere close stirred the soldier. Placing his lit cigarette on the floor, he grabbed his assault rifle and made ready to defend himself. Having taken up a defensive position on the second floor of a civilian residence, the soldier had a great view of the surrounding area. Trying to find the source of the sound, he peered out the window quickly and glanced at the street below. A host of Biogtech soldiers were passing a few blocks down, moving away from the battle front, an imaginary line of death drawn just a block away. The robotic soldiers moving away from the scene of combat were an odd sight. For the past few days, the enemy had been relentlessly attacking, always pushing forward. It was completely out of character for the Reaper Kai forces to be retreating instead of reinforcing.

Concerned, the soldier moved quickly down the staircase and alerted the survivors of his broken squad.

"Hey, check this out," the soldier whispered excitedly.

Following him, several members of his crew ascended the staircase and peered out the window toward the strange sight. By the time the soldiers had reached the second floor again, they saw hundreds of enemy troops moving away from the scene of the most recent conflict. The rapid withdrawal of hundreds of troops is never a good sign. Pulling troops out of an area is a reliable indication of something wicked about to hit the area.

"This is not good," another soldier stated in dismay.

"Where the hell are they going?" Grabbing his cigarette, the watchman took a puff and shook his head in confusion.

Not only were Biogtechs retreating, but their sinister masters were, as well. Reaper Kai priests were also rushing out of the area. This further evacuation drove a wedge of fear into the soldiers as they watched in sick fascination. What was the enemy about to unleash? What horrid attack was about to be revealed?

It took several minutes for the troops to fall back. The entire front line of the enemy had withdrawn. An eerie silence washed over the city, interrupted only by the blast of the radios as many soldiers tried to figure out what the hell was happening.

The Truce Hall was no help. Emperor Gunther was also mystified by the withdrawal, especially after two heated days of bloody combat. Pondering the action, he was unable to react with an appropriate plan. He was fearful to pull his own troops back, thus possibly giving the enemy free ground, but was also terrified not to pull them back.

Taking another drag off his cigarette, the soldier stared at the silent street below. Nothing was stirring and many soldiers had come out to examine the 'front line' with suspicion.

The darkness they scanned hid an unseen horror. Invisible in the dim light, something wicked edged near, a potent enemy weapon.

The sound was the first discernible sign of the attack. A skittering noise echoed faintly in the distance. It sounded almost like the light patter of rain at first. The skittering grew in intensity, beginning to sound like hail hitting the concrete. Startled, the soldiers braced themselves, weapons at the ready. The racket increased, now almost resembling a host of locusts closing in on their position.

In the dim light, they came quickly, rushing across the ground like a living wave of metal. A frightful sight broke the cover of darkness as thousands upon thousands of silver disks rushed across the earth. Now only thirty yards away, the host of Splicers rushed quickly towards the defenders, tentacles probing the air for any sign of life, any hapless victim. The robotic disks had but one purpose: find a host and take over its nervous system. Once the Splicer had control of the host, a series of powerful Reaper Kai computers would coordinate the spliced slaves to do the will of evil.

Skittering and clambering, the metal wave rolled forward with a clatter. The Iron Kai soldiers trained their weapons and opened fire. Keeping back the horde was a losing battle. Only a few soldiers managed to open fire before the entire front line of the defenders was overrun. Several Splicers were blasted to rubble but the counterattack was futile at best. Rushing forward, dozens of metallic disks grappled the hapless warriors in the street. The soldiers, completely covered with the insidious invaders, screamed in terror as the metallic parasites sought to enslave them. There were so many of the Splicers, the primitive machines were actually battling one another to take control of the host.

An entire squad of troops collapsed and was pinned to the ground. As each soldier fought to stand, the legs of the machines pressed into their flesh, boring into their spinal cords while coppery tentacles pierced their skulls. Powerful surges of electricity were pulsing into the victims, crashing their nervous systems, allowing the machines to integrate directly with their brains. Even as they convulsed, the soldiers were already becoming the enemy. Rising from the ground, the spliced soldiers grasped their weapons and began to march down the street in search of their own countrymen to brutally murder.

Perched on the second floor of the building, the soldiers watched in horror as their brothers in arms were converted and subverted. The watchman kneeled, the cigarette still in his mouth, puffing on it as he shot at the metallic disks. He fired repeated bursts of gunfire, his aim true, and blasted a Splicer to a pile of rubble. His two companions fired as well, and shattered a few more robotic spiders. The Splicers were so thick, the soldiers did not even have to aim very well; firing in the general direction of the oncoming mass would kill many of them.

As they gunned the Splicers down, the swarm reached the bottom of the building. The metallic disks broke against the side of the building like a wave of water, several of them crashing against the wall with a thud. Firing desperately, the defenders knew it was almost over for them. Grasping hand grenades, the soldiers threw the projectiles out the windows into the midst of the Splicers.

Dull booms echoed amidst the skittering as the grenades detonated, shattering many of the silver disks. Screams rose from the first floor. The soldiers defending the first floor were covered in the metallic disks. Piercing flesh, the Splicers sought to rule their souls and steal their minds.

Skittering up the stairs, over a dozen Splicers launched onto the three soldiers. The soldiers fired in a frenzy, but were soon overcome and pulled to the floor. The machines bored into their flesh with their needle-like legs, puncturing muscle. With vice-like grips, the tiny disks began to integrate them into the Reaper Kai army.

Feeling pain, the soldier gritted his teeth. Knowing that it was the end, he took several strong drags on the cigarette in his mouth. The burst of smoke flooded his lungs and his spine began to tingle. Shocks of pure electricity were jolting his body. With all his might he tried to resist, but the machine was too strong to ignore. Coppery tentacles pierced his skull. The lights began to flicker for the soldier as he puffed away on the cigarette. Bright blotches of light filled his vision as his body began to convulse. The Splicer nuzzled up against his shoulder blades as it finished taking control of him. His spasms and convulsions subsided and the soldier stood, a blank expression upon his face. As he looked around, the Splicer controlled his actions. He walked slowly over to the staircase, while his two companions rose from the floor as well, metallic disks nuzzled up against their backs. With equal looks of dispassion, the new slaves of evil sought to kill their own countrymen.

As the soldier walked down the stairs, the cigarette fell from his mouth and hit the floor. The glowing embers of the tobacco were still smoking as he walked away, seeking to kill and murder against his own will. Moving into the street below, the three slaves looked drearily at the scene of chaos gripping the urban battlefield. More of their friends and fellow soldiers were falling in combat, being harvested by the army of silver disks skittering about.

The swarm of spider-like machines marched on, flooding the buildings. As they crawled in through the windows, the human defenders fired their weapons, destroying many. For each Splicer that fell, however, three more rushed inside to enslave the defenders. All along the battlefront, screams pierced the air as soldiers were overrun and enslaved, becoming unwilling servants of the Reaper Kai.

In the dense buildings and twisting streets, the defenders barely had any time to react. The enemy could be contained by hiding within the buildings, but this cover actually caused devastating results to the Iron Kai army. Since the soldiers were unable to see the Splicers until it was too late, only a small percentage of the diabolical machines were destroyed before acquiring hosts. The results of the attack were obscene to witness. Nearly five hundred soldiers once in the service of the Iron Kai had been subverted and were now slaves of evil, walking through the streets, guns in hand, ready to kill for the Reaper Kai army.

A cry of alarm broke across the radios as the defenders prepared to face their own countrymen in combat. A new battlefront had formed seven city blocks closer to the city of Stonen. Troops had orders to kill their own, and braced themselves for the horrid battle. Gunfire erupted as brother killed brother. Spliced slaves killed their own men, under the hateful control of the metallic implants invading their consciousness. Walking like an army of zombies, they brandished their guns and shot down and murdered other Iron Kai soldiers.

A heated battle, a losing battle, was being fought. As the Iron Kai slaughtered their own spliced soldiers, the Splicers themselves would detach from the corpses. Still functional, the Splicers would charge the battle lines, hungry and eager to enslave a new host. Covered in blood, the metallic disks looked like horrific spiders drenched in gore. As they pushed forward, the secondary battle line began to falter as freshly spliced soldiers became slaves to evil, and members of the same squads were forced to fight their own friends.

While Splicers openly fed upon the hapless defenders, Brother Feral ordered a full attack on the city. Unwilling to sacrifice any of the Reaper Kai priests, Feral ordered a complement of ten thousand Biogtechs to lay waste to anything in their path. Legions of robotic soldiers pressed into the suburbs, cackling and pushing towards their center.

Within only thirty minutes, twelve hundred Iron Kai troops were pinned, unable to escape, unable to flee. The cords of the noose began to tighten. Unable to withstand the attack, the battle lines buckled and a massacre was fully underway. The ten thousand Biogtech soldiers slowly plodded onward and could not be contained. The combination of the Splicers mixed in with the massive numbers of Biogtech soldiers caused horrendous results. After another fifteen minutes of combat, all of the soldiers had either been killed or spliced and made unwilling servants of darkness.

The battle for the suburbs had ended. The Reaper Kai had taken all of the surrounding area just outside the city of Stonen. Dakota Beach was under constant reinforcement, with several landing craft depositing fifty troops every five minutes upon the beach.

The capital city of the Iron Kai Empire was completely cut off from all aid. Boats and ground units were unable to reach the city. Seeing the enemy troops marching towards the front gate, the Iron Kai barred the doors and prepared to defend the city itself from an endless army of troops. As the mighty doors slammed shut, hope was beginning to fade and the fate of freedom hung in the balance.

Chapter 29
Never Surrender

The front gates crashed to the ground after the explosion rocked the city. A superheated plume of fire and debris rose into the air, causing a shower of explosive destruction. A split second after the blast, the armies of darkness marched into the mighty city of Stonen. The radios were buzzing with activity as the gates collapsed. Soldiers, demoralized and filled with fright, began to flee in terror, deeper into the city. All that remained of the Iron Kai army had taken defensive positions, desperately trying to hold back the flood of invaders.

As the demise of Stonen was under way, Gunther, the true last leader and bastion of freedom, took a quiet moment to ponder the ill-fated events. Alone by the window, he looked down from the Truce Hall. From his vantage point, he stared at the lake and dropped into an almost trance-like state.

Heavy winds of near gale force rushed across the lake with an intense fury. The mighty surge of rushing air broke across the water, creating powerful and violent waves. It almost looked like the ocean, pitching and rolling with a natural fervor. In that moment of time, Gunther smiled and remembered his childhood.

When he was young, Gunther's room in the palace was near the enormous air ducts that brought clean air into the subterranean city of Stonen. In times when violent winds raged, the air ducts would rattle and high-pitched screeching caused by the wind echoed as the violent air pushed inside the ductwork. He always hated the wind since it kept him awake long into the early hours of the morning.   He hated the sounds that the wind made as it rushed through the pipes.

The city of Stonen was on the verge of ruin.   Enemy troops were now pouring into the city and all hope seemed to be lost. There would be no retreat; the enemy had cut off all routes of escape.   Hearing the military personnel behind him shout orders into the radios should have startled Gunther, but it did not.   He continued to stand calmly, staring at the violent waves on the lake below with a somber look.

An enormous wave broke on the shoreline.   As the tumbling water hit the beach, it had a sudden, startling effect upon Gunther's mind.   Blinking several times, he stared at the beach and then back at the water.   The shoreline had been taken by enemy troops, but no new enemy troops had landed on the beach; the storm was so violent that no additional enemy reinforcements could land there.   A natural event was working in the advantage of the Iron Kai.   Seeing this natural event unfold, he smiled dreamily, his mind working feverously to concoct a course of action.

As he stood at the window looking at the beach, Gunther's military advisors were shouting, unable to fathom what was happening.   The Iron Kai Empire was arguably the most powerful empire in the entire Darken Realm, and it was now being overrun and destroyed by enemy forces.   Several military advisors were shouting at Gunther for direction but he didn't even look at them. Instead, the emperor was lost in his own world.

Thinking about all of the enemy forces now engaged within the bloody war, the gears of his mind put the pieces of a puzzle together.   Thinking about other forces, Gunther was suddenly aware of their armored troops, tanks and other battlefield support vehicles. As he looked at the lake once more, a concrete idea flowed through his mind and a plan of action came into reality.   He returned to his frantic advisors, looking calmly at them and at the wild chaos sweeping the room.

"Quiet!" he shouted, and the order sent a shockwave through the room.   Everyone closed their mouths and stared at their leader with wide-eyed fear and trembling.

"We are being overrun!" a radio operator called out with such despair that Gunther was taken aback.   Sizing him up, Gunther sighed and closed his eyes for a brief moment. Collecting his thoughts, he opened his eyes and stared around him. There was not a single person who did not feel fear or think that the end of the Iron Kai Empire was at hand.

"Everyone listen to me." Gunther spoke with a powerful booming voice. "I want you to radio all of the troops in the city. Tell them that when the enemy breaks and begins to flee, they have standing orders to give chase and kill at will. Tell the troops they have a standing order to kill any Reaper Kai and give chase until the entire army that is laying siege to this city is eradicated."

The order was so absolutely shocking and counter-intuitive, his military personnel simply stared at him dumbfounded. Was he kidding? The enemy was on full advance and there was no way in hell that the enemy forces would be retreating any time soon.

"Sir! We are being overrun!" another officer said in exasperation. "This city will fall."

Snorting at the foolish man, Gunther continued to give orders. "Contact the tanks battling on the western edge of the suburbs. Tell them to break through the enemy lines and head directly toward the front gate. Run over anything that gets in their way, don't even waste the ammunition."

Still dumbfounded, his troops began to feel either hope or madness had taken him.

"What are you thinking?" Field Marshal Patrick inquired, seeing the strange look on Gunther's face. The emperor had a concrete idea and this piqued Patrick's interest.

"What am I thinking? We're only minutes away from destroying the entire Reaper Kai army laying siege on us," Gunther boomed.

His staunch confidence sent a wave of pure hope through the shattered ranks of the fallen and failed. Craning their necks to see him, everyone felt a twinge of fire light their souls.

"Where are Maddock and Matthew Moralis?" Gunther quizzed.

"Somewhere by the front gate. They were behind the battle lines after we closed the gates to the city," a radio operator responded.

"Contact them immediately. Tell them to get several squads together and await *our* arrival." Gunther spoke in a crisp tone, staring at his officers as he spoke.

"*Our* arrival?" Patrick echoed, blinking in awe.

"Our troops are failing, the have lost their nerve." Pulling a pistol from his belt, the emperor checked the clip and removed the safety. He looked to his officers with an almost manic smile. "How many times have we been subjected to murder at the hands of the enemy? How many times have our loved ones been slain and brutalized? It ends now! It ends here!" With a crazed look, Gunther scanned the crowd. His officers were trembling, feeling a bloodlust build in their hearts. Bringing the speech home, Gunther powerfully commanded, "Bleed with me."

Stunned, they looked at each other as chills ran down their spines. Unable to speak, they looked at their valiant leader and began to understand. Gunther himself was about to charge into the front lines and bleed with his troops, risking his life to set an example and to inspire them. Holding his pistol ready, he smiled at them and his voice boomed again. "Bleed with me! Bleed with your troops! Bleed for the freedom of this great nation! Bleed in defiance of tyranny!"

Grabbing their weapons, their hearts soared and they felt courage wash over them. Chanting broke the air in the Truce Hall as the officers made ready for war. Seeing their fearless leader strong in the face of such adversity made all of them know that the day was not yet over and the battle had not been lost. His officers had been rallied and they were all ready to charge into the meat grinder to give their lives for something bigger than themselves. They were all ready to battle against reckless aggression.

The radio operators understood the order to engage any fleeing enemy troops. Gunther's madness was beginning to take shape. A series of commands were issued, stunning the troops in the thick of combat. Knowing that *something* was about to happen gave them the extra will to push on. Holding their ground, the front gates became a killing ground, a place where many lives were lost in fleeting moments of unchecked anger and hatred.

Booms and explosions made the very air tremble. Biogtechs, some thirty ranks thick, continually marched onward, pressing deep into the city of Stonen. Machine gun nests had been hastily thrown together and manned. The broad city street at the base of the mountain was a scene of great carnage. As the ranked soldiers marched onward, the defenders fired at will, piercing many ranks as the machine guns hummed away, crushing rank after rank of enemy soldiers. Splashes of hydraulic oil were filling the streets, mingling with pools of blood from the human defenders. In the span of a few minutes, the dead littering the street grew numerous. As the machine gun nests shredded Biogtechs by the dozens, a pile of broken plastic and mangled robotic soldiers accumulated on the ground. As more were blasted, the pile grew in size. Soon, fresh Biogtechs had to climb over the pile of debris to get into the street beyond. Although the defenders remained valiant, the tide of enemy troops was too powerful and was able to press on with the strength of sheer numbers alone.

As the ranks of Biogtechs moved closer to the machine gun nests protecting the streets of Stonen, a gibbering rose in the ranks of Biogtechs. A flash of movement caught the eyes of the defenders. Red-robed forms were pushing through the Biogtech units. Dozens and dozens, nearly one hundred cloaked forms in all, were rushing to battle. A crackle of yellow energy pulsated at the hub of these forces. Brother Feral was leading over ninety Goat Minions into the middle of the battle, using the Biogtechs as a shield against the gunfire. As the sinister Reaper Kai general drew close to the scene of battle, shimmering light surrounded him and he blinked out of view, disappearing into a swirl of shifting shadow.

When the Biogtech troops were a mere thirty yards from the machine gun nests, the red-robed Najaszim, the hated Goat Minions, broke from the forward ranks. Slavering and hungry for blood, the twisted demonic minions raised weapons over their heads and grunted and screamed war cries in the language of the devil himself. The chanting and raving sent a tremor of panic into the gunners. Training their weapons quickly, they opened fire and a stream of bullets roared forth. Many of the Goat Minions were hit, rending flesh. A spray of blood erupted as the machine gun fire tore the servants of hell into a gory mess. Several fell but many were too quick and were able to breach the battle lines. Jumping head-first into the nests, the Goat Minions grappled the defenders and began to pummel them with jagged weapons. Screaming in rage, they began to butcher the gunners trying to maintain the nests and defend the street from further enemy advance.

The charge of Goat Minions could not be held back. Within minutes, all of the gunners had been brutally slaughtered, most dismembered beyond recognition. The feral killing machines were now covered in blood, ripe with the scent of death, and seeking more carnage and misery. Driven by sickening instinct, the Goat Minions charged onward, ready to end more life with brutal fury.

Many demoralized soldiers broke rank and fled, horrified by the sounds of their brethren dying in droves. Having initially been driven back, the enemy had now pushed to the first junction in the city. Streets sprawled before them and the heart of Stonen itself was now exposed. Victory was close at hand for the evil forces on the attack.

Biogtechs gunned down Iron Kai soldiers as they fled. Goat Minions butchered valiant defenders. Reaper Kai war priests channeled dark energy and plumes of hellfire incinerated battle-hardened soldiers. The fall of the Iron Kai Empire was near.

Deep Grotto Plaza became the site of the dramatic conflict. A collection of many streets within the mountain fortress ended at Deep Grotto Plaza. The protectors of the city spread out and took up defensive positions. Many soldiers had broken and were rushing away to escape. As Reaper Kai priests, Goat Minions, and Biogtechs advanced on the plaza, an equally important set of Iron Kai officers approached the scene of combat from the opposite direction.

"Death to the enemy!" Gunther boomed as hundreds of fleeing soldiers stopped dead in their tracks. The mighty emperor of the Iron Kai Empire was headed into combat to kill the enemy. Seeing their own emperor take to the field of battle made all of them stop. The fleeing soldiers felt the fire in their hearts rekindle. If the leaders of the empire were willing to give their lives, the soldiers could do the same. Feeling a flame illuminate their souls, they echoed Gunther's cry. Surrounding their leaders, they flanked Gunther's war party and began to chant and shout war cries and taunts.

Matthew Moralis, the Oracle of Justice, dressed in fine blue robes, stood in the center of the street leading into the plaza. Mad Dog Maddock stood beside the holy man with a look of dispassion on his face. Dutifully, they remained and awaited Gunther's instructions for the coming conflict.

Seeing him charging to battle, the two approached and joined the war party. Hundreds of troops had joined the emperor's personal war band. As they proceeded, rallying all they saw, thousands of Iron Kai soldiers answered the call and clambered into the enormous plaza to do battle.

Brother Feral was standing in the center of the street, flanked by Goat Minions and Reaper Kai priests. Hundreds of Biogtechs were slowly plodding onward, giggling as their red eyes targeted human defenders. Gunfire roared as the defenders fired back.

"Give me strength," Matthew Moralis prayed as a gentle breeze broke over Gunther's war band. A holy glow rose around them as the Oracle of Justice raised his staff into the air with both hands. The aged man looked up as he prayed, and the powers of heaven responded. The war party moved onward.

Seeing the holy glow, Feral sneered. The Reaper Kai general could sense that Gunther himself had taken the field of battle. "Kill them all!" he screamed in rage, pointing at the war party. Feral's war band rushed forward to slaughter Gunther's party.

Seeing them rush, Gunther ordered an attack of his own. The Iron Kai soldiers charged while firing their weapons at Feral's troops. Bullets from both sides sliced through the air and cut into both ranks. Biogtechs and soldiers alike fell as the projectiles shredded into them. Rushing over the dead, the two war bands sought to engage each other in close quarter combat, in vicious hand-to-hand melee. Dark prayers were uttered as demonic psychic attacks sought to kill the Iron Kai. Matthew Moralis held his ground and his heavenly prayer dissipated the evil energy, leaving all of the troops unscathed. The holy energy had prevented even a single soldier in Gunther's war band from falling victim to enemy psychic attacks. Seeing the lack of effect of their psychic powers, the Reaper Kai priests brandished hand weapons and charged as well.

Wielding bayonets as they charged, the Iron Kai soldiers were eager for the kill. Shouts and yells broke over the plaza. Screams of rage erupted. The two charging war bands met in the center and crashed together with frightening results. Many screams rose as the priests clad in red were impaled by bayonets. Iron Kai soldiers were pierced by bloody weapons as the Goat Minions bayed and beat them without mercy. Small-arms fire from pistols increased the chaos as the Iron Kai officers shot Biogtechs at close range.

"Feral!" Gunther yelled, wielding a pistol in one hand and a hunting knife in his other hand. The emperor had spotted the Reaper Kai general and wanted to engage the enemy leader himself.

Seeing the defiant emperor of the Iron Kai, Brother Feral smiled and raised his black saw-like scimitar over his head. With yellow energy crackling around him, the Reaper Kai general disappeared from sight.

Knowing Brother Feral had turned invisible, Gunther focused on the imminent attack. Matthew Moralis, still surrounded in a holy glow, rushed to Gunther. The dark magic was strong, but not strong enough for the Oracle of Justice. Throwing his staff forward, the aged man could see the evil general rushing Gunther. His aim was true and the long staff struck Brother Feral in his stomach. The attack was not deadly but was strong enough to make Feral lose his concentration. As he blinked back into view, Gunther could now see the enemy's dark general. Without hesitation, he charged forward and slashed him with his hunting knife.

A deep gash opened on Brother Feral's arm as the blade bit flesh and tore muscle. Stunned by such a brazen assault, Feral took a step back and looked at his ruined form. Vanity was his weakness and seeing his perfect body marked with his own blood drove Feral into a killing frenzy. He cursed loudly, a hate-filled look covering his face. "You will pay for you insolence!"

"Do your worst!" Gunther boomed back, raising his pistol. Taking hasty aim, he fired as Feral charged him. The shot missed, and he braced himself for an attack.

Swinging with all of his might, the Reaper Kai priest hurled the blade at the emperor's head. Gunther ducked down swiftly. The black saw-toothed blade whistled through the air only a few inches above his scalp. Seizing the advantage, Gunther slashed at Feral's stomach, but the lightning-quick general managed to avoid being disemboweled.

At that moment, Maddock and a Reaper Kai priest came in-between the two leaders. They grappled with one another as Maddock's knife grew dangerously close to the priest's throat. Though struggling fiercely, the red robed man was outmatched. The captain, stronger and much more capable, made short work of the Reaper Kai. Grunting, he jammed the knife into his chest. The Reaper Kai fell to the ground with a tortured gasp, and Maddock charged toward a Goat Minion in the process of mutilating an Iron Kai officer.

Gunther caught the end of the bloody exchange, momentarily losing his concentration. When he sought to continue his attack on Brother Feral, he found his opponent *gone*. The sinister Reaper Kai general had disappeared during the distraction. Spinning around, Gunther was just in time to see that Feral had moved in behind him. The crackle of yellow energy dissipated as the priest stepped into view and swung his scimitar again with the intent of killing Gunther. Unable to fully react, Gunther stepped back and tripped over a dead soldier. Feral tried to change the position of his weapon as Gunther fell backwards, but was too slow, and the tip of his scimitar merely nicked Gunther's chin.

Lying on his back, Gunther steadied his pistol and took another hasty shot at Brother Feral. Although his aim was cursory, the bullet rammed into the side of Feral's face, shattering bone and tearing a bloody swath through his cheek bone. Reeling from the wound, Feral staggered backwards. Never had someone come so close to ending his life. With adrenaline and fear filling him, he wavered. Seeing his confusion, Gunther fired again. This time, the bullet grazed his skull, tearing a chunk of his scalp loose.

Another moment was all Gunther truly needed as his wounded opponent staggered back. Holding his breath, he took solid aim at his chest and pulled the trigger. The gun jammed and the emperor looked on with stunned frustration and disbelief. Cursing fate, Gunther rose to his feet and holstered his weapon. He charged Brother Feral with a blood-curdling war cry with his hunting knife in hand.

Seeing the angry emperor charge brought Feral back to the reality of combat. Recovering his focus, he raised the black saw-toothed scimitar above his head and charged as well. The two combatants screamed like wild animals, seeking to kill one another with a terrifying fervor.

As they crashed into each other, Feral swung the weapon downward, trying to chop Gunther's head in two. Accustomed to battle, the wily emperor of the Iron Kai blocked the attack by grabbing his arm mid-swing. The blade was held fast in the air. Locked in close combat, the two leaders stared at each other for but a brief moment before the tide of battle drastically changed for one of the gladiators. While holding Feral's arm steady, Gunther brought his other hand in for a killing blow. Clutching the hunting knife, he grunted and drove the weapon into Feral's stomach. The blade hit flesh and Gunther's strength drove the entire length of the blade into Brother Feral.

The blow was horrendous, but Feral seemed initially unfazed. Throwing Gunther back, he took a step away and clutched his stomach. Crimson blood, Feral's blood, covered his hand. As he stared at the red smear of gore, a primitive howl rose in his soul. The pain and blood would make most soldiers terrified and desperate to flee, but Feral was no ordinary combatant. Gunther had besmirched his perfect body and disfigured the Reaper Kai general. Vanity was Feral's one true focus in life. Feral was obsessed with his appearance, and the blood dripping from his body was the most egregious sin that anyone could commit against him. Shaking in rage, he screamed at Gunther.

"How dare you! How dare you ruin my perfect form! The demons in hell will sing my praises as I slaughter you!" Feral began to hack away at Gunther.

The blood rage which overtook Feral was so aggressive, the emperor was unable to dodge the first attack. Even as he held up his arm to shield himself, the blade tore into his flesh. Jumping back, Gunther was awestruck by his opponent's berserk fury. The Reaper Kai general screamed in rage and slashed at him with repeated, vicious strokes.

Gunther's knife was still stuck in Feral's stomach and his pistol had jammed, leaving him totally defenseless against the brutal attack. Moving back quickly, the emperor tried to avoid the assault long enough to obtain a weapon.

The battle was so intense, he had taken a mere few steps backwards before crashing into a Goat Minion. Grabbing the sinister creature, Gunther pulled it into Brother Feral's path. The evil general was so enraged, he hacked indiscriminately, slashing the Goat Minion to bloody ribbons in an effort to kill Gunther.

As the creature screamed and died, Gunther grabbed the bloody hatchet still clutched in its quivering hand. Not wasting a second, he sidestepped around the eviscerated Goat Minion and swung full force, striking Feral at an odd angle. The hatchet hit Feral's shoulder and glanced off his bone. With strong momentum, the hatchet continued forward and rammed into his throat. A nasty wound opened and Brother Feral staggered back as blood pulsed from his throat in a crimson spray.

"How dare you..." he whispered as his eyes rolled back into his skull. "Give me strength, dark spirit, I live only for your gifts of pleasure and to serve your evil majesty."

Taking full advantage of the situation, Gunther let out a deafening war cry before he moved in for the kill. "Death to the Reaper Kai!" His voice was so loud, many of the combatants turned in time to see him swing the bloody hatchet. With a series of wild swings, Gunther struck Brother Feral repeatedly. Again and again he smashed him with the hatchet, and Brother Feral was too dazed to even protect himself. Falling to the ground, General Feral of the Reaper Kai order tried to stand. Gunther did not falter, nor did he show any mercy. Raising the blood-stained weapon, Gunther slammed the hatchet down on Feral's forehead. The weapon struck, shattering the evil Reaper Kai's skull. Brother Feral, fierce leader of the Reaper Kai army, died before the might of Emperor Gunther.

As their general died in a horrifying manner, indecision filled the remaining Reaper Kai war priests. Their powerful general, a general who had led them to countless victories, had been slain in violent combat. The sight of their leader lying dead upon the ground turned their hearts to ice as panic rolled through them. Turning to flee, the Reaper Kai priests tried to escape the bloody melee.

The Iron Kai soldiers now had a clear advantage. They screamed out gleeful war cries, sensing victory close at hand.

Surrounding the last remnants of the war band, Gunther's men began to butcher the Reaper Kai. Many were gunned down or hacked to pieces as they ran for their lives. Within a few minutes, the entire enemy war band had been completely eradicated.

The butchered Reaper Kai served as a beacon of hope to the defenders of Stonen. Standing tall and proud in the center of the carnage, perched upon the corpses of their enemies, were the valiant leaders of the Iron Kai army, officers and emperor. The dark vision was an inspiration. Feeling proud that their leaders had come to their aid, the Iron Kai soldiers rallied and pushed forward. The Biogtech army was still in full advance but it didn't matter; the Iron Kai troops had been fully motivated and nothing would stop them from crushing the enemy.

Taking aim, the defenders of Stonen, with vigilant hearts and courageous souls, repelled the invaders. By the droves they fell, Biogtech soldiers and Reaper Kai alike, killed by expert marksmanship. As rank after rank fell, the edge of the plaza became a mountain of shattered robots and slain priests.

Confusion gripped the invading army. Their general had been slain and now chaos had gripped the Reaper Kai forces. Taking advantage, the Iron Kai continued the attack and the battle became theirs. As the stalwart defenders maintained their supremacy of the conflict, a rumble hit the streets of Stonen. Tanks, the glorious tanks of the Iron Kai army, had broken through the gates and enemy lines. Driving down the streets of the underground city, they simply ran over anything in their path. The diesel-powered behemoths clogged the streets, taking great pride in squashing the enemy. Driving so that nothing could escape their wrath, the tanks ran over Reaper Kai and Biogtech alike, leaving a trail of blood and oil in their wake.

The two blades of a scissors, the Iron Kai soldiers and the tanks, came together at last, catching the Reaper Kai in the middle between them. Over eight thousand Biogtechs and seven hundred war priests were trapped between the two progressing forces.

The battle inside the city of Stonen lasted only a few hours after the defeat of General Feral. In the end, the majority of the Reaper Kai army had been crushed. Due to the storm raging on the lake, the enemy was unable to reinforce their troops. Once the Iron

Kai had retaken their city streets, the front gates looked like a hornet's nest as the victorious troops rushed out to sting and attack. The enraged Iron Kai soldiers had but one standing order: give chase to any fleeing troops and slaughter them without mercy. The order was taken very literally and within the span of twenty hours, the remnants of the enemy invasion force had been routed and scattered into small bands of fleeing forces.

Courage can take on many forms and can have many outcomes. Gunther's empire had been tottering on the brink of ruin. To have a vision of hope in such desperate times and to enact such a daring plan required careful leadership. Gunther was a leader of both intellect and action. To come up with great plans is one thing, but to act on such vision is another. The emperor of the Iron Kai had but one single vision: unite his troops with daring leadership and drive the enemy to their graves. Both this vision and its execution had been perfect.

History is written by true leaders, those who deny the inner fear clawing at their fragile minds and see their vision through to the end. Freedom and justice are two ideals worth fighting for, and it takes great leaders to protect such virtue. Gunther was such a person, a courageous leader who would do anything in his power to protect the ideals of an entire nation.

The siege of Stonen had ended, but everyone knew that the war was far from over. The Reaper Kai had suffered a defeat, but they would return. For the time being, the last two remaining empires were at a stalemate, both licking their wounds until the drums of war would sound again.

Chapter 30
Reflections of a Dying Nation

His hands still warm from the fire, Emperor Gunther moved away from the great hearth, toward one of the enormous windows of the Truce Hall. He stretched out his warm hand to place his palm on the cold window. As his fingers were chilled by the cold glass, cooled by the freezing winter night, he gave out a loud sigh. Many moments passed and finally, all of the warmth had faded from his palm. Pulling his hand away, he looked at his handprint, formed by moisture and condensation upon the glass. As he watched the natural mystery unfold, the condensation slowly evaporated and began to disappear. Within seconds, his handprint was gone and nothing remained but the memory of the event.

Reflecting upon the phenomenon he had just witnessed, Gunther felt very strongly that his faded handprint represented his great nation, his great empire. The Iron Kai had sustained heavy casualties and losses against their ancient arch-enemies, and the war thus far had been costly indeed. Although the Reaper Kai had been driven from the capital city, Gunther knew they would return. As he watched his handprint fade from existence, he wondered if his nation would also cease to exist and eventually fade out of memory, crushed by the Reaper Kai.

Feeling a sense of dread wash over him, he looked down and viewed Dakota Beach, the city's great lakeside line of defense, illuminated by torchlight. Although many weeks had passed since the Reaper Kai invasion, the dead still had not been buried and laid to rest. The soldiers had been toiling tirelessly trying to bury more than thirty thousand soldiers and civilians who had perished in the previous battle. Their bodies had frozen in the winter chill and many had not yet been attended to.

Having seen and experienced the horrors of war, the troops were beginning to lose hope as they buried the endless mass of corpses. Even though it was demoralizing to continually tend to the dead, especially with their mental state still fragile following the invasion, it was even more demoralizing to leave thousands of slain countrymen littered about the streets and familiar sites of the Iron Kai Empire. And so, by torchlight, Gunther's troops toiled throughout the night to lay their brethren to rest.

From his vantage point at the height of the Truce Hall, Gunther had an eagle's eye view of the scene. He watched for a great many minutes. With each passing moment, he grew more disturbed by the activities, barely able to comprehend that so many of his people had lost their lives. And although the Iron Kai had survived the invasion, Gunther knew deep down in his heart that his empire could not survive another attack.

This fact he had kept to himself. Despair is a disease that can spread and rampantly destroy even the mightiest of civilizations. Gunther had serious doubt that his empire could survive the war. He wondered if anyone in the future would even remember his culture and his people. As he watched his soldiers toil endlessly with the dead, he wondered who would be left alive to bury the next rank of slain soldiers. Would anyone honor their memory? Would anyone survive and pay tribute to their sacrifices, or would the enemy leave his countrymen dead upon the earth to rot? Shivering, he felt fear in his heart, dread lingering in his soul like a festering wound that invaded the mind, continually poisoning its host. His people felt uneasy but Gunther felt worse. He knew more than anybody the state of his nation and knew that it was weak, ripe for slaughter and submission to the enemy.

"I cannot bear this any more," Gunther said in a voice leaden with bleakness. Turning away from the windows of the mighty Truce Hall, he looked over to the hearth. His beloved, his secret mistress, was wrapped in a blanket near the flickering flames. Seeing his concern, she looked at him with serene compassion, the flames of the fire reflecting in her soft eyes.

"Sit with me, by the fire. Warm your chilled bones," she invited with a soft smile.

"It's not my bones that are chilled; it is my heart that has grown cold."

"Then come by me, maybe my heart is warm enough for the both of us."

Stepping over to the hearth, he settled by his beloved, reaching out to caress her head and run his fingers through her long flowing hair. She responded instantly to his touch, grabbing his hand. Kissing it gently, she placed his hand on her chest, beside her heart. He could feel the blood pumping through her and the warmth beneath. Feeling weak, he leaned in to her and she clutched him tightly. He buried his head within her chest, breathing hard and erratically fighting off the urge to weep. As turmoil gripped him, she consoled him and held him tightly. Rubbing his back with her right hand, she kissed the top of his head repeatedly.

"What am I going to do?" he asked his beloved with concern that could no longer be contained.

"I am nothing more than a commoner, you know that. I know nothing of war," she responded, still embracing him.

"That is why I love you so much. The taint of battle and bureaucracy has not left a mark upon you."

"Yes, but neither have the glories of victory or triumph, either. I'm a commoner and although I don't know the terror of war, I will never know the exhilaration of success, the exalted feeling of succeeding against insurmountable odds. I know that you have seen much and bear a heavy burden, but I'm proud and a little jealous. I am too timid to lead, too scared to believe in myself, and that's why I envy you so much. You have taken on the mantle of leadership, no matter what the consequence to yourself may be. Do you remember being imprisoned for your actions? You believed so strongly in the defense of your people that you risked your life to do so. You were charged with treason for your beliefs and risked death for those beliefs. In the end, you were hailed as a savior; in the end, you saved this empire. No bureaucrat or politician saved this nation — you did, and you did so by following your heart."

Hearing her kind words, he was still gripped with inner turmoil, and shook his head, slamming his fist down upon the floor of the Truce Hall. He was so frustrated and wanted nothing more than for the war to end and for his people, and all people, to be free and safe from the taint of carnage that had overtaken the Darken Realm.

"I've tried so hard to save this nation. I fear that in the end, it will not be enough. The enemy is too strong, too resilient. Already they linger near our borders once more, growing stronger by the day, amassing fresh troops for another assault. We're running out of time and I don't have a solid course of action."

"You'll find a way," she reassured him.

"I'm not so sure."

"You'll find a way, you always do."

"If I cannot?" Despair had taken him again.

"Failure is not an option, not for you. That's why I love you so much. You can take a disaster and turn it into a parade. You can grasp victory from the seeds of defeat. The reason I know that you will not fail is because I love you. I would never give my heart to someone who is weak. I would never give myself to someone that I did not respect above all and trust in completely. I know that you will succeed because I am not weak and I would not give myself to a weak person. My love for you is a testament to your strength and resolve. You will not fail and you will bring this nation from darkness."

Hearing her words had inspired him once more. Looking up into her serene eyes, he felt weak before her love, but strong in spirit. Grasping the back of her neck, he pulled her forward and kissed her gently on the lips. She responded to his affection and returned the sentiment. He pulled away from her lips and stared into her eyes for a long moment. As he did, he smiled and felt his heart lift. She was a born a commoner and he born to royalty; their love was forbidden by their culture, but it was a most perfect love. He was a valiant leader and she was a loving free spirit. Together they could endure any hardship and celebrate any victory.

"I love you," Gunther said to her.

"I know." She smiled back.

Suddenly, he grew distant and she could tell that he was disturbed.

"What is it?"

As he looked over to the windows of the Truce Hall, his thoughts were lingering with his soldiers, toiling with the dead upon the beach below. Blinking several times, he knew what must be done.

"I'll be back," he said in a cryptic tone.

She shook her head in confusion. "Where are you going?"

"Down to the beach. I'm going to help my men bury the dead. I need to help them move on from this tragedy. I need to help myself move on from this tragedy. I won't be much help, but it's something I need to do for them and for myself."

"I'm proud of you." She spoke with tears in her eyes.

"I know," he responded with a wicked grin.

Gunther moved away from the warmth of the hearth and his beloved. Stepping out of the Truce Hall, the emperor of the Iron Kai sought to help his men bury their countrymen. His presence was welcome, and the soldiers who had been feeling dread in their hearts were overcome by the sense of honor that accompanied serving with such a great man as Gunther. Seeing him help with the most discouraging of tasks made each of them feel that they mattered, and in Gunther's eyes, each person did matter.

As he toiled in the darkness with his men, Gunther's heart was not laden with sadness, pity, or defeat. Instead he was invigorated and enlightened. When each casualty was buried, he did not respond with tears of despair; instead he honored the dead by saluting them, paying them one last tribute, one last honor for making the ultimate sacrifice.

Chapter 31
Stalking Prey

The sniper breathed softly as the sights of her rifle came to rest on the chest of a Reaper Kai priest garbed in blood-red robes. She made a conscious effort to quiet her breath even more, resting the rifle firmly against her shoulder. The barrel of the weapon was positioned on a rock, lovingly secured in a nook between the stones. A light breeze was blowing out of the northwest. Feeling the wind against her face, Carla made a mental note about its intensity and direction. As she adjusted her weapon in consideration of the wind currents, the gun sights drifted slightly.

Her small form was pressed against the earth, concealed in a specially made suit covered in brown and tan swaths of dirty fabric. Patches of small desert plants had been painstakingly added to the outfit. The camouflage was extremely effective, so effective that one would have to be a mere few yards away to even be able to detect her presence. Avoiding detection and killing at long range were Carla's specialties, skills that she had mastered more out of necessity than out of desire.

As the breeze beset the young woman garbed in desert camouflage, she could feel the air dry her sweaty skin. She had already been lying uncomfortably on her stomach for more than half an hour, watching her prey in the valley below. The amount of enemy soldiers was intimidating and Carla was beginning to waver regarding the idea of attacking them. Killing a squad of Reaper Kai was a daunting task. The primary target would always be the Reaper Kai priest. Taking into account the priest's formidable psychic powers, it was a real gamble to survive a battle. Some priests could even use their powers to find a concealed attacker. The young sniper had spent many months battling evil, and their tactics were well known to her. She would only get one chance to save her friend and failure would mean her death.

Scanning the makeshift camp below in the setting sun, she found that most of the inhabitants were inside tents, concealed from view. Carla shook her head in frustration; the attack was not a sound choice. A half dozen Reaper Kai priests were in the camp. She could kill one, maybe two before they detected her, but it would be a sure death sentence as the others came looking for her. In addition, the formation had a considerable amount of Biogtech soldiers surrounding the camp. Taking a quick check of her ammunition, she knew that there were more enemies than bullets. Even if she made every shot, she would never be able to kill them all. Scowling in frustration at the prospect, she rolled onto her back and took a break from surveying the enemy camp.

"This isn't going to work," she whispered to herself. Keeping behind the rock face, she grabbed her pack and fumbled through it. She found her canteen, drank several swigs and wiped the sweat from her face. As she lay on her back, she stared at the blue sky above her. She looked up lazily, caught in a sudden daydream brought on by weariness. For a few moments her mind wandered and she thought of a peaceful world.

The only thing that the young woman had ever truly wanted was to find a quiet town in the wasteland and settle down. She was the only child of parents who had died long ago in a freak accident in the mountains. After that, she had grown up with her grandfather before her entire village had been ravaged by plague. His death ushered in a frantic life for young Carla. She then fell in with gun runners and worked as a mercenary until the start of the war against the Reaper Kai. Shortly after the start of the war, she had a chance encounter with the war master of Rasheed. Since then, she had been traveling with the noble hippo warrior Globulus and had led an adventurous and arduous life.

But Carla was merely a victim of circumstance. She had not *chosen* her current life but rather followed the simplest path, walking the road that was presented to her. Although she was an extremely effective mercenary, she longed for a simpler time and place, a place where she could live her life and raise a family.

The concept of family was a fragmented one for her, but it was the thing that she craved most. Having a rough past without a firm family in her own life, she longed to have a family of her own, something which she would fiercely guard and treasure. If she had her way, she would relive her own childhood through her own family, patching up the holes in her heart with kindness toward her own children. She also longed to have a husband, a man who would hold her tight in the darkness of the night, someone who was courageous and strong. The thoughts of such a simple life were what kept young Carla going in the most desperate of times, in times such as her present circumstances.

Carla had been tracking the slave convoy for many weeks, trying to find a chance to ambush it and ultimately liberate her best friend from certain death. During their travels, Globulus and Carla had stumbled upon the secret of secrets: an enormous foundry and production complex in the desert, controlled by the Reaper Kai, in an area known as Metalweaver Flats, was churning out a nearly endless supply of robotic Biogtech soldiers. If this facility was left unchecked, it would eventually mean the ruin of the entire Darken Realm. The Reaper Kai order could easily overwhelm the defenses of any kingdom or empire that remained by sheer numbers of enemy troops. After discovering this hidden menace in the desert, Carla and Globulus sought to reach the safety of the northlands to alert the Iron Kai forces gridlocked in a desperate war against the Reaper Kai order. But before they could reach the safety of the Iron Kai Empire, Globulus had been captured by Reaper Kai priests and his fate was to die at the hands of sadistic dungeon keepers in the city of Rasheed, tortured by his former foster sister, Queen Marion Toil.

And so for the past few weeks, Carla had been tracking the slave convoy through the wasteland, hoping for a time when she could liberate her treasured friend. But as the convoy passed through the wasteland, it grew and grew. At each town they passed through within the Reaper Kai controlled territory, more slaves and enemy troops were added. In the last week alone, two additional Reaper Kai priests and two full squads of Biogtech death machines had joined the convoy. Her chances of saving Globulus before reaching the city of Rasheed were becoming more and more remote.

The decision to rescue Globulus was also a reckless choice. If Carla were to be captured or killed, her knowledge of the secret Reaper Kai production facility would be lost. The smart choice would be to abandon her companion and warn the Iron Kai, but Carla was blessed with unwavering compassion. She could not stand to abandon her friend to a death of torture, no matter what the cost. Carla would do anything in her power, even sacrifice her own life, to save him. This fierce conviction was hazardous in a time of war, but such ideals were the only thing keeping humanity from splintering into an utterly barbaric society.

Just the thought of her beloved friend in danger made Carla's blood boil. Grabbing her rifle again, she rolled onto her stomach once more to check the camp. Maybe, just maybe, another chance would present itself.

Staring through her scope, she scanned the hapless victims of the Reaper Kai war machine. A gangly gaggle of lost souls, exhausted beyond belief, had collapsed around the perimeter of the tents. Many looked on the verge of death, effectively starved and massively dehydrated. Panning her weapon around, she finally caught sight of her noble friend. Globulus' enormous form was resting on the ground. The one-ton hippo hybrid was clutching his right leg with a grimace of pain on his face. Panning her scope downwards, she could see the wound on his leg, a wound that had been caused by a savage Goat Minion during their travels. His wound had festered before his capture and a considerable infection had taken over.

Seeing his condition filled Carla with fear. He had been battling the infection for many weeks already and it was still an issue. Shaking her head in concern, she watched as Globulus took his shackled hands and pressed on the wound. As he did, pus erupted from the wound and he quickly wiped it away with a severe look of discomfort on his face. Shaking her head in distress once more, Carla knew that if the infection was not controlled, he would probably die before reaching Rasheed.

Panning the scope of the weapon upwards, she looked at his face. Strangely enough, despite the infection and the initial effects of starvation, Globulus looked remarkably well. His complexion was usually a coppery brown when healthy and he didn't look any worse for wear. Oddly enough, he looked better than the last time they had actually been in contact. In reality, the mighty hippo hybrid had a stern stamina and fortitude. His gruff will and tough body were more than enough to withstand any injury or infection.

Smiling, she looked at his face and felt mildly relieved. Her concerns about his survival were beginning to wither. As she stared at her friend in the valley below, the sun passed beyond the western edge of the world and the desert began to darken. Seeing that night was falling, Carla grabbed her pack and unfurled her sleeping bag. She found her supplies, chewing on the tough jerky and washing it down with some warm water. As the chill air settled over the wasteland, Carla clutched her rifle, wrapping her arms around it. Thinking about her life and her friend in the slave camp below, she fell into an uneasy slumber.

Chapter 32
The Long Road Home

As his right foot hit the ground, a spike of pain flared, rushing through his thigh like a jolt of fire. The valiant soldier looked straight ahead with an unflinching gaze in an attempt to avoid the pain. Taking another step forward, the hybrid soldier sighed and forced the thought of pain from his mind. Step by agonizing step, he focused on just surviving, just moving onward.

The towering form of the giant took the lead in the formation of slaves and war prisoners. He was a hybrid life-form, a creature that was the descendant of an animal which had been genetically fused with a human. Currently, he was fighting back the pain engulfing his body and moving on as a stubborn hatred burned in his heart. The mighty creature was Globulus, a hippo hybrid of pure legend. Standing taller than two men, his mighty muscles rippled underneath a coppery brown hide covered in jagged scars. Splotches of an almost purple tint covered the mighty hippo warrior's arms. He wore gigantic camouflage pants that had been cut and torn on his right leg. Beneath the gash in his clothing was a festering mess. A battle many weeks ago had left Globulus with an infected leg, a persistent infection that would have claimed a lesser life-form.

But while weakness was an option for many, the mighty hippo soldier was undaunted by such foolish trivialities. Globulus was built for one thing alone: survival. In such a harsh world, he was a seemingly perfect creature, able to withstand enormous damage and to survive horrible infections. Although his leg was still infected, his body was doing a fantastic job at mitigating the polluted wound.

With each step he took, the pain flared and sent a shiver of agony through him. Instead of whimpering from the duress caused by his injuries, Globulus had another thought. If he was in pain, it meant that he was still alive, still able to fight and defy the enemy. He gladly accepted the pain. With each step, he focused his eyes on the Reaper Kai priests leading the formation of slaves. With each bolt of pain that gripped him, he stared more intently at his foes, focusing his pain into rage against his enemies. He loathed them, he hated them, and if given even a small opportunity, he had resolved to end all of their lives.

Whereas Globulus had found strength in the horrible conditions, the other prisoners had succumbed to despair. Hope had faded and many had simply given up. They plodded on quietly, eagerly awaiting their deaths as a way to stay the terror that had gripped their hearts and fragile souls. The formation was for the most part a convoy of despair, a group of slaves on a death march through the wasteland.

The blistering sun shone down on the convoy with ominous intensity. Hundreds of slaves and shackled war prisoners plodded along in silence. Since there was no way to feed and provide water to *all* of the prisoners, many were starved and dehydrated beyond belief. Every mile or so, another would begin to lag behind the rest of the group. At first they tried to keep up but in the end, fatigue and exhaustion took over. Seeing them lag behind, the sadistic priests would charge over to the fallen prisoners and begin to club them, prodding them to get up and continue by chastising their bodies with pain. It didn't take long before the body and mind of the prisoner were broken. Most would collapse to the ground and begin weeping, a miserable-sounding wail that assaulted the rest of the formation. As hope dwindled even further, the priests would beat the prisoners to death or so horribly mangle them that death was not far behind.

As the miles amassed, many had fallen, consumed by the bloody road into the southlands. Since the death march began, the initial formation of two hundred prisoners had dwindled to barely one hundred. Half of the prisoners had died and were left to their grisly fate in the abandoned wasteland.

A sickly swarm of buzzards and desert vultures had tracked the formation of prisoners. The avian scavengers knew that all they had to do was follow the slave convoy for a fresh meal of broken flesh. Having grown brazen, the carrion feeders would even attack the living as they were left for dead behind the brutal death march. The living served as a meal to the vultures, and many lost their lives being pecked to death as swaths of their flesh were torn free by ravenous birds.

After several weeks of such sickening visions, many prisoners who fell behind begged the priests to kill them. Truly malicious to the core, the priests denied the request and preferred to listen to the screams as the vultures feasted upon their victims.

The formation of prisoners was being channeled to the city of Rasheed. The palace had become a notorious interrogation center where the cruelest of the Reaper Kai could practice their sinister skills on a nearly endless supply of victims. Most captured military personnel were sent to the dungeons of Rasheed to live out the remainder of their lives in agonizing pain, reluctantly divulging secrets and attack plans crucial to a defense against the Dark Order.

As the formation plodded on, three of the priests stopped dead in their tracks. One of them spun around and scanned the desert wasteland. Holding his hand above his eyes to block out the burning sun, he scanned the surrounding area with a wary gaze. Something had unsettled the Reaper Kai priest and he was viewing the surrounding area attentively, half expecting some sort of ambush.

"What is it?" another priest rasped, eyeing his companion with suspicion.

"I am not sure…" he replied, scanning the horizon. "I keep feeling that we are being watched. But every time I stop and try to use my powers to search the area, I cannot seem to pick up on anything."

"Perhaps it's just your imagination," the third priest intervened.

"Perhaps…" The lead priest motioned to several other war priests at the back of the prisoner formation. They came forward with quizzing glances, pulling back their crimson hoods to better view their leader.

"You sense anything?" he quizzed them.

None of them sensed anything, and they shook their heads.

The priests did not realize they were being stalked by a silent predator. Young Carla Reins had been following the formation, spying on it, hoping that she would have a shot in a million at liberating her companion from the slave convoy. But while the priests could sense her presence, Carla's instincts and experience instructed her to stay back, far away so that the priests could not locate her. And so the game of cat and mouse continued through the wasteland. As the priest lost his psychic lock on Carla, his attention shifted back to the slave formation.

With a sigh, he noticed the noble hippo staring at him with intense disgust. Looking back at the enormous prisoner, the Reaper Kai grew bold and taunted Globulus. "What are you looking at, you filthy animal?"

"I am staring at a dead man." The hippo spoke with venom in his voice, staring at him with intense loathing.

"You are damn lucky that Queen Marion Toil wants you alive. If it weren't for her orders, I would have killed you long ago."

"When she is gone, I will come for you, then your companions, and then anyone I can find that wears those damn red robes. You have underestimated not only me, but the resolve of anyone in the trenches still fighting for freedom."

"Freedom?" the priest laughed dryly. "Freedom is an illusion. Freedom is a term that you use to conjure mirages of happiness. You do not have freedom. We have freedom, true freedom. We have no bonds of morality to keep us hindered from living full lives, lives filled with carnal pleasure and endless fulfillment of our desires. You have shackled yourselves with chains, bound yourselves so that you cannot truly embrace what you really want. We are nothing more than animals, creatures with selfish wants and lustful desires. Where you fail to act upon your impulses, we embrace such want as power. You will never have true freedom until you cut the bonds holding your selfish wants from ruling you. To give in to desire and lust is the only true freedom."

With a dismissive shake of his head, the mighty hippo countered his rival's sadistic argument. "Where selfish want turns to greed, there is nothing that can satiate your empty hearts. You live on, consumed by an endless hunger of want that you can never satisfy. Where you have lust and desire, we have honor and kinship. You find strength in carnal pleasure, we find strength in companionship. As your greed and lust overtakes your senses, it consumes you, utterly enveloping you in a shroud of confusion. Power is not the fulfillment of hateful desire; power is the ability to concede part of oneself for the greater good. I will never be drawn to your definition of freedom and you will never understand my beliefs. In a world where colliding ideals cannot be satisfied by diplomacy, war is the only option, and I gladly take up the banner to defy your entire empire."

The argument was a strong one. Knowing that the hippo had gained a small victory by maintaining his sense of freedom, the priest gave in to anger. Grasping his club, he walked over and began to strike the mighty hippo repeatedly. Gritting his teeth, Globulus never acknowledged the pain; he simply stared the priest down. Finally, the temper tantrum had broken and the enraged priest conceded defeat.

The procession continued onward, closer to the city of Rasheed. As the familiar sights at the edge of the wasteland came into view, Globulus knew that they were getting close to the city. To the east of their position, he could see the Coal Wastes. The enormous quarries were home to open-pit mining operations in which raw coal was harvested from the earth. Slaves, hapless victims of the Dark Order, had been recruited for the job. Thousands of Spliced slaves, humans under the control of mechanical implants spliced into their nervous systems, plodded along slowly, harvesting coal from the pits. A line of slaves were marching single-file toward the city, each carrying a basketful of coal, with blank expressions lining their faces.

The scene was hopeless. In the past, the citizens of Rasheed had lived peaceful lives and prospered under the rule of the Toil family for centuries. In one single act of greed, the daughter of King Toil, the treacherous Marion Toil, had usurped her loving father's throne by having him assassinated. After the assassination, the new

Queen Toil took over the empire and handed it over in one night of reckless bloodshed to the Reaper Kai Empire. If it weren't for the hateful actions of Queen Toil, the city would still be under the rule of a courageous ruler.

As Globulus thought about his past, events began to rush through his mind. Scenes and images began to fill his consciousness as his feet plodded thoughtlessly onward. The death of King Toil filled his mind like a flood of ill will. He could still see the look on King Toil's face as an assassin's bullet struck his body and pierced his chest. King Toil knew that he had been mortally wounded and that he had only a mere moment left to live. Globulus could still see the loving father reach out his hand to his daughter. The dying king's last wish had been to hold his daughter in his arms and say goodbye to her. Pulling her close, he lovingly bid farewell to Princess Marion.

Tears began to form in Globulus' enormous beastly brown eyes. The image of the blank expression on Marion's face filled his mind's eye. That hateful wretch, that sinister animal of a daughter could not even look her own father in the eye as he died in her arms.

Betrayal can take many forms. For Globulus, King Toil was more than his king; he was his surrogate father and family. Marion was his sister, his sibling after coming to Rasheed. To be betrayed is to feel both loss and hatred. One cannot be betrayed by a mere stranger. In order to be truly betrayed, there must be a loving bond. This loving bond is used to manipulate and create chaos. This is exactly what Marion Toil had done: used a bond of love to lure both her own father and the noble Globulus into a world of deceit. In the end, the betrayal had destroyed Globulus' entire foster family. After King Toil's death, the hippo didn't just lose his father; he also lost his sister. Marion had been a trusted sibling and a loving member of the family. The betrayal had cut Globulus to the very core of his soul. The more you love, you more you lose when betrayed. Globulus had loved with all his heart and lost it all as a result.

The betrayal he felt sparked a sickness within him. A flutter of anxiety filled his heart. The sickness grew and his body felt weak as his thoughts lingered on sorrow. With his soul bouncing around, he was an emotional wreck. From sorrow came hatred. The two dark emotions battled within him, mastering his heart as he thought about the dark deeds of Marion Toil. Giving in to the sorrow, he wanted to weep. Giving into the anger, he wanted to kill.

There was only one outcome to such a mixture of emotions. He hated her. He loathed her. Globulus wanted nothing more than to see her suffer. Yearning with dark thoughts, he wondered what he would do to her if he caught her alone. The tears turned to rage. Wiping them away with his chained hands, a sneer covered his face. The sorrow was washed away and only an empty feeling remained. Globulus knew that the only thing that could bridge the gap and remove the empty guilt within him was to confront her. Resolute, he knew that before his death, he had to confront Marion about her treacherous deeds. As his thoughts were eclipsed by darkness, he fought to remain in control. With a conscious effort, he forced the darkness from his mind, and the evil malaise dissipated.

The daydream was wearing off. Looking around, he was suddenly aware of the mighty city of Rasheed just ahead. The eastern gate of the city was a mess. The enormous doors leading inside had been shattered in a past conflict and now survived only as debris around the gate. The once-pristine marble walls of the outer defenses had been tarnished. The citizens had lovingly washed and cleaned them in times of peace. Now they were marred and stained with blast marks and dried blood.

The towers had once held the banners of Rasheed and guards clad in purple walked the parapets. Now, Biogtechs swayed in the ocean breeze, pasty white bodies standing over the once-proud city.

The prisoner formation moved beyond the gate of the city and all of them beheld a ghastly sight. The entire eastern end of the city had been burned during the invasion many moons ago. Skeletal fragments of the once-prosperous markets and homes were now nothing more than burnt rafters and piles of white ash.

In that moment, Globulus stared in horror at the city that was once his home. To be betrayed is to once have loved. As the mighty hippo stared at the ravaged ruins of Rasheed, his sense of betrayal grew stronger. Globulus loved not only his king and foster sister; he had loved the entire city and nation of Rasheed. The noble hippo had loved the people of Rasheed, their customs and culture. Staring at the ruins and charred timbers, he knew that his heart belonged to Rasheed and its entire people. In that moment,

Globulus finally understood how much he loved what he had lost. This overwhelming emotion quickly turned to a heavy loss, an equally overwhelming feeling. The more you love, the more you lose. The more your soul has invested, the harder the fall. In that moment, Globulus finally understood how much he truly loved the nation of Rasheed and how much he truly hated Marion.

Progressing deeper into the battered city, Globulus let his newfound sense of hate envelop his mind. As the servants of evil marched Globulus inside the battered palace and into the dungeons below, he shook his head in rage. He vowed in that moment that before he died, he would make Marion pay for what she had done.

Chapter 33
The Price of Failure

The lord of the Reaper Kai sat upon a throne made of human bone, with a look of pure hatred on his face. Standing before him was a collection of priests who had survived the horrific battle of Stonen. The battle-torn band had seen some of the worst fighting that had taken place thus far in the war, and the siege of the Iron Kai capital had ultimately been a complete disaster. Eighteen thousand Biogtech soldiers, forty heavy assault rigs, and fifteen hundred war priests had been laid to rest on the field of war. The remnants were still trickling out of the northlands, licking their wounds and trying desperately to reorganize.

As Father Vertigo sat upon the vile throne, his displeasure began to grow with each passing moment while the survivors recounted the battle. It would take many months to restore a full army large enough to *attempt* another attack on the Iron Kai. Months did not fit into Vertigo's timetable very well. According to his own plan, Father Vertigo should now be performing clean-up operations, killing off the residents of any remaining villages and subjugating the rest of the Darken Realm. But instead of sitting upon the field of victory, the Dark Order had sustained a terrible loss, and this failure could compromise its total domination of the continent.

The Reaper Kai priest ended his retelling of the tale with a respectful bow. Fuming, Vertigo stepped to his feet and a howl of anger crackled from his frail form. "Leave me now!"

The priest scurried away quickly to escape his wrath. Stepping out into the hallway, the man shut the door behind him with a sigh of relief. Many who had failed Vertigo would often find themselves in difficult situations, if not outright dead. Rushing into the secluded hallways of the Rasheed palace, the priest hurried to escape any other possible repercussions of his actions. He knew that the last person he wanted to encounter was the queen of Rasheed, with whom Vertigo was enraged following the priest's own revelation about the battle of Stonen.

A black swirl of energy rolled around the room as Father Vertigo paced back and forth, the lifeless white husk of his body shaking with rage. With each passing moment, he became more frightfully out of control, his body wracked with tiny tremors, miniature seizures. The demonic entities kept inside his frail body were growing stronger as Father Vertigo lost his grip. Soon the tremors erupted into violent twitching as many voices filled the room. The demons were speaking, trying to gain control over the lifeless husk in which they resided.

The whispers grew in intensity and the swirl of black energy increased. Shades and faces grew visible, rotating around Father Vertigo. Standing amidst the evil energy, he mastered his own emotions and sought to set things right.

A complement of Goat Minions lingered near the entryway to his chamber. They were now cowering submissively, baying at their master as they nervously watched the black demonic energy swirl around the room. Slinking against the wall, they averted their gazes from him and whimpered like hurt animals. Seeing their cowardice and fright only enraged the lord of the Reaper Kai even more. As he held his hands forward, the swirling black mist increased tenfold, absorbing most of the light in the room. Although it was mid-day, the room was plunged into unnatural shadow as Vertigo unleashed additional power. The whispers grew to audible voices and the forms revealed themselves in the mist. Skulls and other misshapen forms were outlined in the dim light, riding the swirling waves of darkness.

Staring at his bodyguards, Vertigo forced his thoughts into the minds of the Goat Minions, commanding them with mental telepathy. *"Bring that worthless wretch of a Queen to me! I want to converse with Marion about her failure!"*

Bowing submissively before him, the three Goat Minions understood the wordless order and rushed off into the palace to fetch Marion.

It took but a brief moment for the creatures to capture her. Dragging her into Vertigo's room, they threw her to the floor.

"Stand up," Vertigo hissed in displeasure. As he spoke, the black swirl of energy grew in intensity. Almost all of the light in the room around Vertigo had vanished. The only thing that she could see was his pasty white face staring out of the shadow with an ominous look of hatred. Barely able to stand his disdainful glare, she averted her eyes out of a mixture of both fear and respect.

"What is your will, my lord?" Marion Toil inquired in a meek tone, feeling that her life could very well end in the next few moments. She had never seen her master so agitated.

"Tell me, how many Reaper Kai operatives were placed inside the walls of Stonen prior to Brother Feral's attack?" A booming voice erupted from somewhere in the middle of the room. It was an odd sensation to hear his voice, since it did not seem to even emanate from his body.

"Forty seven Reaper Kai were inside Stonen prior to the attack, my lord." She spoke softly, shifting her gaze nervously about the room.

"How many of these agents completed their objectives prior to the invasion?"

She could not speak. The answer to the question was complete failure. Vertigo was irritated and focused his thoughts on the Goat Minions standing beside her. One of them struck her in the face with its gnarled hand.

"Speak!" An echo of Vertigo's voice boomed in the darkness, this time to the right of her.

Stuttering, she blurted out a terrified response. "N...n...none, my lord."

"None?"

The Goat Minion struck her again in the mouth, this time forceful enough to draw blood.

"None, my lord, all of the operatives were killed prior to any of them completing their missions. The Iron Kai had help. The last communication of the operatives indicated that a man known as Matthew Moralis, the Oracle of Justice, led a covert killing team against our operatives. This team managed to kill all of our spies and assassins prior to invasion." Letting her wound bleed unattended, she answered hastily, trying to regain her composure. Marion was now in grave danger and she knew it.

"Who will lead my armies in the northlands?" he quizzed her.

Unable to comprehend the strange question, her heart began to race. Stuttering again, she tried to respond. "I know not, my lord."

"You don't know? Maybe you should have thought of that before your completely ineffective operatives failed to destroy the infrastructure of the city prior to invasion. Since the defenses of Stonen were fully intact during the initial assault, the Iron Kai had enough time to wage an effective counterattack against our troops. The northern army was shattered and Brother Feral with his entire command group were annihilated. Not one of our seasoned military war priests survived the battle. Your failure allowed the Iron Kai a sizeable victory. We should now be standing inside the Truce Hall dismembering Gunther and his entire staff. Instead, our army is in full retreat. It will take months to rebuild the army for another attack."

The fear was rising in her soul.

"Feral is dead?" she asked as the warmth in her body seemed to fade.

"Indeed! Feral was killed in close combat by none other than Gunther himself. An old man was said to have protected Gunther's entire war party from our psychic energy. Without the aid of the dark powers, the war band was outmatched and slaughtered. This Oracle of Justice, Matthew Moralis, must be a direct descendant of Ceibla Moralis. This turn of events is something that I could not even foresee. The lost tribe of Ceibla Moralis is beginning to mobilize and as a result, is an enormous threat." His temper had abated a bit and this was a good sign. Her life was swaying in the balance, resting precariously upon a precipice where but one single poor response to Vertigo's banter would lead her to a swift death.

"What is your will, master?" Marion questioned humbly, trying desperately to salvage her own life.

Laughing, he looked at her with disgust. "My will?" he boomed, still laughing dryly. "My will is that you suffer greatly for your failure! We are strong, and in order to stay strong, you must punish your subjects greatly. Weakness is not an option. Failure is a sign of weakness. To remove weakness, you must suffer and suffer you shall! I will purge the sin of weakness from you with pain. The only reason that you still draw breath is that you were successful in the invasion of Rust Spire and the Mord Tech Empire. Your previous actions have spared your life, but I warn you, another failure and your life is forfeit."

"But the Iron Kai had help. I would not have failed if it weren't for this Oracle aiding them," she whined.

"I suggest you hold your tongue!" he boomed as the Goat Minions began to pummel her with their bare hands, striking her repeatedly. "Test my patience again and you will die!"

Understanding the lesson he was conveying, she trembled, feeling that she had crossed the line.

"I willingly accept your generous act of punishment. I will pray to the demons as my body is purified and my soul is made whole by torture." Marion bowed before the dark lord.

"Not just your body will suffer for this outrage, Marion," he hissed. "The city of Rasheed is no longer yours to rule. You are no longer Queen. I am granting control of the city to someone more capable. Your failure has resulted in the loss of your kingdom. You will have no power. You will have no subjects, not even a servant. You will be nothing more than a lowly minion of mine."

Marion blinked as she tried to take in the punishment which, for her, was worse than death. The ambitious and treacherous young Marion had sold her soul and betrayed her entire empire so that she could become Queen and rule it. Now, her title and rank had been stripped away. She was nothing, not even a princess. All of her servants had been taken as well. She had lived a blessed life being the focus of power. Her entire life, she had commanded and given orders. Now she had lost all power and the entire focus of her dark obsession.

"No!" she wailed. Tears began to flow down her face. She had betrayed an entire empire so that she could rule. Now she had lost it all. Everything that she had done, all the dark deeds to feed her reckless ambition, had been in vain. The gains she had made had been erased in a single moment.

Smiling in the darkness, Vertigo was amused by her suffering. He had taken everything from her and it felt wonderful to the lord of evil. "You will learn your true place, Sister Marion."

"You can't do this," she wailed. "I did unspeakable things to please you. I did unspeakable things to my own family so that I could rule this empire! You can't do this to me! I am queen! I am the ruler of Rasheed!"

"You are nothing. You are powerless." Vertigo smiled as he soaked up her anguish. "Can you still see him?"

"What?" she asked, tears on her face.

"Can you still see your father? Can you see the look on his face as he died? Think of what you did to him. You murdered him. You betrayed your own subjects and killed their noble king and you did it to become queen. Now you are nothing. Tell me Marion, do you feel empty?"

"I hate you!" she cried out as guilt conquered her soul. Vertigo was right. Marion had betrayed everyone in her world to gain power. The sickness she was feeling could never end. There was blood on her hands and it would never be washed away.

"You hate me?" Vertigo boomed. "Hate will make you strong. Let it consume you; let it invade your senses. Let that hate drive you. Let your suffering guide you to victimize the helpless. Take your hate out on our enemies. Let the suffering inside you mold and sculpt you into a twisted visage of the devil himself. Your destiny is to cause reckless slaughter. Use this hatred to become what you yearn for most, a dark disciple. I want you to hate me. I want you loathe me. You think you hate me now? You know nothing of what dark pleasure I will make you feel. We are just beginning, Sister Marion."

"Damn you!" she wailed.

"Take her!" Vertigo called out, looking at the Goat Minions. "Take her to her own dungeon. Take her into what was once her palace. Punish her, torture her. Make her suffer!" He looked back at Marion. "You will spend many days in your own dungeon for your failure. I will make sure you survive the torture. I will make sure that death does not take you. To have death take you would diminish the suffering."

"No!" she screamed and flailed about.

Soaking up her anguish made Vertigo feel alive; he enjoyed torture and making others feel powerless and worthless. Beating her and pulling her from Vertigo's tower, the Goat Minions drug her through the palace as she screamed on. Her servants looked on in terror as she was pulled into the dungeons beneath the palace.

Chaining her to the wall, the Goat Minions began to torture her.

Screams of pain rose in the dungeon. Her wailing could be heard in every cell. As their former queen was tortured, the captives became still and listened to her suffering.

Just a few cells away, a noble warrior was chained to the wall. The sounds and screams chilled him to the bone. Globulus knew the voice all too well. The screams were those of Marion Toil.

Her whimpering broke the air again and again. The bone-chilling screams echoed in the dark tunnels. At first, the hippo warrior kept telling himself that she deserved it. The empty hole in Globulus' heart needed to be filled with something, anything. He kept telling himself that the screams and the punishment were a way to heal the sense of betrayal that he felt due to Marion's actions.

But with each scream, his heart hurt more. With each whimper, he felt pain in his soul. His thoughts returned to their childhood. He could remember running through the gardens with her. He could remember all the good times and fun that they had as children. Another scream broke and Globulus shook his head in confusion. She had betrayed the hippo's foster father and betrayed an entire nation. He wanted to hate her, he wanted to loathe her.

Another whimper cut pitifully through the air. A tear rolled down his face. Marion was a sinister creature who had caused tremendous suffering, but the sound of her torture was too much to bear. Another scream rose out. Giving in to his instincts, Globulus yelled out and tried to free himself from the chains. "Don't touch her! You leave her alone!"

The booming voice of the hippo echoed through the dungeon. Marion, in her cell, heard the noble voice of Globulus. The pain of guilt filled her. She had done unspeakable things and despite all of them, the noble Globulus was still trying to protect her. The strange display of love filled her with a sensation that she had never felt before. With tears streaming down her face, she called out to him. "Globulus!"

Hearing her voice made his heart jump. The misdeeds seemed to be cleansed and his soul leapt. He wanted to hate her but he couldn't do it, he just couldn't let her be tortured. Compassion is a beautiful and strangely resilient emotion. He still loved Marion deep inside and although she had done terrible things, he wanted to protect her; he wanted to save her. The noble Globulus could not stand to let her suffer, despite all her evil acts. "Marion!" he yelled back at her. All of Marion's past transgressions were wiped away and the slate was clean. He couldn't hate her. He needed to save her.

"Help me!" she screamed in agony.

"Marion! You leave her alone, you savages! You hear me? Leave her alone!" Globulus screamed back.

"Globulus! Help me!" Marion wailed as the evil creatures tortured her.

He grunted and pulled at the chains on his wrists. The cold steel dug into his flesh as he struggled to free himself. Yelling in a fury, he strained with all his might, but the chains held fast. Again and again he fought to free himself and to rescue Marion from the sadistic torture. The more he struggled, the more the chains tore his flesh. Even while bleeding profusely, he didn't falter, and never wavered. More than anything, Globulus wanted to save her. Tears rolled down his face as he tried to escape his bondage.

His mind was awash with wild plans, trying to figure out some way to end her suffering. In his desperation, the noble warrior tried to plead with the servants of evil punishing her within the cell. "Take me!" he screamed. "Torture me instead. Please leave her alone. Please take me instead of her! Torture me instead!"

Globulus would have willingly given himself to torture to save Marion, even after everything she had done.

Hearing his voice and his courage drove a deep wedge of sadness into her. As she blinked through the pain, an image of her father flashed into her mind. She could see his gentle face smiling at her. She could still hear his happy voice singing her to sleep at night. Blinking again, she could see him, dying in her arms after the assassin's bullet had torn his body, an assassination ordered by Marion herself. She could still see his face as he said goodbye to his little daughter. The series of images in her mind mixed with Globulus' compassion and filled Marion with a deep sorrow. As the Goat Minions punished her body, the world seemed to grow numb around her. The emotions she was feeling were raw and powerful. No longer did she weep from the pain; instead, she wept for what she had done. She wept for all the pain she had caused others.

Chapter 34
Infiltration

The wave broke and crashed. Sputtering and coughing, the young woman gasped for breath as another wave surged forward, overtaking her. The second wave was more intense. As it hit her, she spun around, head dropping below the water line. As the cold sea water stung her eyes, the young woman tried desperately to keep from drowning.

Although not the best swimmer, she was strong, healthy, and very determined. Kicking her feet, she reached the surface of the water and blinked several times as she coughed once more. She spit out the mucus-like sludge from her airway, and could finally breathe again.

Kicking her feet, she continued to swim toward her objective. The harbor of Rasheed was treacherous for ships, let alone a swimmer, especially at night. The once- mighty city had been taken and secured by enemy forces many months ago and had become a haven for the Reaper Kai in the southern reaches of the Darken Realm. The woman fighting her way across the harbor was none other then Carla Reins, Globulus' loyal friend and talented mercenary.

In the dim light of the night, Carla was breathing heavily, swimming slowly across the harbor toward her destination. Knowing that her companion had been taken inside the city to meet a fate of torture, Carla was determined to sneak into the city unnoticed and attempt to rescue him. The task was daunting indeed. Several hundred enemy troops were stationed at both of the gates leading into the city. Without the aid of a sizeable military force, it was impossible to breach either of the gates. The alternative was also dangerous. As Rasheed's harbor was open to the ocean, it took considerable fortitude for an individual to swim across it to reach the city docks. The waterfront was still protected, but only by roving patrols. The enemy didn't imagine a lone infiltrator slipping in by means of the harbor, and the city's defenses were geared more toward a full-scale assault.

Using this fact to her advantage, the sniper was nearing the city's docks. From her vantage point, she took a brief moment to bob up and down in the surf, eyeing her objective carefully. She was heading into the lion's den and caution was required. One mistake would lead to her death.

As she surveyed the waterfront, she could see small squads of Biogtechs roving amongst the docks and broken buildings along the harbor. Carla could easily detect over twenty troops milling about. The prospect was grim and she knew that slipping into the city by way of the docks was extremely unlikely. Trying to consider other possible options, she scanned her surroundings while treading water. The cold ocean waves were sapping the warmth from her body and her strength was beginning to wane. If she did not act quickly, Carla would have to retreat and make another attempt at a later time.

As she scanned the docks and waterfront, a curious sight greeted her eyes. A sewer pipe rested partially in the surging waves, only a few feet above the water line. A drizzle of sewage was leaking out of the open pipe into the harbor. Looking cautiously at the opening, she knew that it was large enough for her to fit into. She shook her head in dismay, trying desperately to find another route into the city of Rasheed, to no avail. Swallowing hard, she gave a loud sigh and knew what she must do. Finding fortitude within herself, Carla resolved to infiltrate the city by means of the sewer.

As she swam closer to the pipe, the water around her began to stink. Human waste and a light petroleum smell emanated from the harbor water around the open sewer pipe. Trying not to gag, she whispered, "You owe me big time for this, Globulus."

Once she reached the pipe, she stopped inhaling through her nose and breathed strictly through her mouth. Trying not to throw up, she carefully swam through a field of floating junk and waste. She chose to ignore her surroundings and moved on quickly to the sewer pipe.

Reaching the edge of the pipe, she grabbed its sides and hoisted herself into it. As she did, her camouflage pants brushed against the slippery brown sludge lining the floor of the tunnel. Almost gagging, she held her breath for a moment, just long enough to collect her thoughts. She pulled a bandanna from her pocket and wrapped the water-logged rag around her face, using it as a crude filter to block the smell of the sewer pipe.

The pipe was small, a mere four feet tall. Although Carla was small herself, she still had to crouch down and proceed carefully. Turning on a flashlight, she peered into the tunnel. Grotesque debris littered the pipe, causing her to shake her head in dismay. "I cannot believe that I'm doing this." With a sigh, she continued onward into the passageway.

She moved excruciatingly slowly. Each step was agonizing since she could not fully stand in the pipe. Instead she had to crouch and inch forward, one step at a time, bracing herself to avoid slipping and falling into the sewage. Her rifle, which was strapped to her back, was so long that it continually scraped along the top edge of the concrete pipe.

The pipe continued for about thirty yards before it ended at a junction. The stench of the sewer had increased dramatically and she pressed the bandanna against her mouth in a doomed attempt to purify the air. Taking a moment to get her bearings, Carla rested at the junction.

All around her, the pipe seemed to move. A carpet of cockroaches skittered along every surface. It was a disconcerting sight to witness a host of skittering insects moving all over in seemingly random directions, thousands strong. A shiver ran down her spine as she stared at the insect infestation. Looking up, she caught sight of the ceiling of the pipe. The mass of insects was also above her. Overcome by a creepy sensation, she decided that any place was better than her current one. Hastily making a decision, Carla chose to press on down the left tunnel.

As she did, the muzzle of her rifle brushed against the ceiling of the pipe once again. The mass of cockroaches were disturbed and many fell from the top of the pipe. Dozens landed upon her back. With a primal scream, she shook in disgust as hundreds of tiny legs prickled her skin. As they rushed across her bare skin, she began to tremble uncontrollably, and then bat and swat at the bugs. While brushing them off, she lost her balance. Instinct kicked in as she was falling, and she threw her hands outward and struck the side of the pipe. She had managed to keep from falling face-first into the sewage, but her hands were now in contact with the swarm of insects. Dozens more of the cockroaches moved off the wall and skittered down her arms. Trying not to scream, she steadied herself once more and brushed away the insects, removing most of them from her arms.

She kept moving, dazed by her revolting and terrifying surroundings, and wanting to put as much distance as possible between herself and the cockroach colony. She pushed down the left tunnel, which became larger and larger the further she progressed. Soon, the pipe was large enough to stand in and a crude brick walkway ran along the trough of sewage at its center. With a sigh of relief, she stood to full height and brushed off any remaining insect hitchhikers. She drew in a calming breath, thanking her ancestors for escaping the hideous tunnel.

Moving deeper into the catacomb of sewer passages, Carla greatly enjoyed the use of the brick footpath. The further she pressed into the dark tunnels, the deeper and wider the flow of sewage became. Now she was staring at a flowing sludge of waste several feet deep and three feet wide. She was horrified by the murky water, and the stench had increased tenfold. Trying not to vomit from the smell, she thought of other things, focusing on her captured friend, and found solace. It gave her peace to know that she had braved so many challenges already to aid her friend. She only hoped that her bravery would be enough to rescue him from a twisted death.

Taking a brief moment to collect her thoughts, she pulled the bandanna from around her face. Carla's small hooked nose came into view as she wiped the sweat away from around her nose and mouth. Sighing, she rolled her head from side to side, then rubbed her tense neck muscles with her fingers. The light massage was comforting for the moment. The noxious fumes of the sewer, however, were too much, so she placed the bandanna over her face once more. Still a little nervous about her adventure in the sewer, she tugged anxiously at her short brown hair. The nervous twitch was somewhat comforting and it distracted her enough to regain her composure and continue exploring the tunnel.

She was somewhat distracted and not paying close attention to her surroundings as she moved on through the pipe, looking for a ladder or some way to access the street above, which led into the city of Rasheed. Her perceptions of her circumstances should have been more careful. Lurking in the shadows in the passage just ahead was an unseen menace.

The sewer pressed hard to the right and when Carla rounded the corner, she literally ran into someone crouched in the tunnel. Stumbling over the filthy man, Carla collapsed to the ground. Her flashlight tumbled from her grasp, across the brick walkway. Instinctively, she rolled onto her back.

The filthy man was on top of her in a flash. He was dressed in a dirty green coat, his face obscured by a thick beard and a coat of black filth. As he grappled with her, a crazed look illuminated his hooded eyes.

Carla kicked him with all her might, and he grunted, taking the force of the attack in his stomach. Collapsing backwards, the derelict landed on his rump. Carla backed away, moving across the dimly lit tunnel like a crab skittering for safety. Jumping to his feet, the man charged her, grunting like a wild animal. Knowing that every second counted, she grasped desperately for the pistol on her belt. The weapon had barely cleared the holster when a deep pain erupted in the back of her head. A blunt object had struck her from behind and her skull was throbbing. She blinked, a wave of colored lights filling her vision as she almost blacked out from the blow and succumbed to her dizziness. The filthy man was instantly on top of her, grasping and pulling the pistol from her hand. Lying on top of her, he struggled to subdue her.

Carla screamed in panic, pinned to the ground by the weight of the grotesque man pressing down on her. Still dizzy, she fought to free herself. In a matter of seconds, another person came into view. A similarly grungy man, dressed in a brown coat and clutching a club, rose from the shadows behind her. With an equally disconcerting look on his face, he knelt down and placed his hands on her in an attempt to assist his companion in overpowering her.

Carla was terrified. Pinned to the ground in a sewer way, she was now trapped by two dirty men pressing down on her.

"What do we have here?" the bearded man said, almost jittery about finding young Carla in the tunnel.

"I'm not sure." The other creepy man smiled in glee. "Maybe we should investigate her further."

Screaming again, Carla was gripped by sheer panic, unable to move, restrained by the two foul-smelling men. She tensed her muscles, trying to wiggle free, but to no avail. The harder she struggled, the tighter they gripped her. Panic turned to all-out terror. Tears streamed down her face as she wailed in horror, "Let me go!"

They did not respond and continued to hold her down on the floor of the foul-smelling tunnel. As she struggled for her freedom, fear ruled her senses. Unable to discern the intentions of her captors for certain, she nevertheless had a sinking suspicion of what was about to happen. Not wanting to submit, she fought with all her might. Another scream broke through the tunnel as she wailed in desperation, echoing off the walls as she fought the two men. Extreme anxiety had kicked in and Carla was rocked with pure terror, not knowing her fate, not knowing what was about to happen to her at the hands of her filthy captors.

Chapter 35
The Rescue of Carla Reins

"What the hell are you doing? Get off her!" A booming voice rocked the tunnel, echoing off the walls with resounding force. An enormous dark-skinned man, easily six foot seven, charged forward from the darkness of the sewer and grabbed the bearded man, throwing him backwards. The bearded man hit the ground hard. As the enormous dark-skinned man moved quickly toward him, the bearded man made a hasty retreat.

The other man who had restrained Carla retreated as well, backing up with his hands in the air in an act of submission. He was concerned with the newcomer's possible reaction, his eyes darting back and forth in apprehension.

"I said, what the hell are you doing?" the dark-skinned man asked angrily. Avoiding eye contact with him, the two men did not respond; they simply ignored him.

Seeing the disheveled woman, armed to the teeth yet still terrified, on the floor of the tunnel made the newcomer restless. Leaning down, he quickly grabbed her weapons, and Carla didn't even try to stop him. She was still rattled by the two men, and was in a state of near-shock. Breathing in quick gasps, she simply stared at a nearby sewer grate.

The enormous man secured her weapons, then reached out his hand to her. Tensely, she looked back, jaw trembling. Her eyes moved up and met his. As their eyes locked, she felt more at ease. The feral, crazed look that the other two men had exhibited was missing from the newcomer's expression. Trusting in him, she reached out her own hand. He steadied her and helped Carla to her feet.

Standing in the tunnel and still frightened, she was unable to look at her assailants. Instead, she looked only at the newcomer. Seeing her lingering distress, the dark-skinned man shot a hate-filled glance at the two pasty white men who had attacked her. "You still haven't answered my question. What the hell were you two doing to her?"

Avoiding eye contact with him, the bearded man shuffled his feet before speaking. "We saw a light in the tunnel and came out to investigate."

"That doesn't explain why you had her pinned to the ground."

"She's a spy!" the other foul-smelling man called out with a frantic look in his eye. "We can't let a foul Reaper Kai spy rat us out!"

Not convinced by their answer, the newcomer turned to Carla. "You need to come with me," he commanded.

Carla would normally have resisted the order, but complying was better than the possible alternative of spending any more time in the tunnel with the two foul-smelling men. She nodded meekly in agreement.

Turning back to the two dirty men, he spoke to them without even opening his mouth; his glare spoke volumes, telling them that they were unwanted and had better not follow. They understood his communication clearly. Shifting their gazes to the floor of the sewer, they conceded defeat and remained in the passageway.

The tall man led the way with a lantern in hand and Carla's rifle in his other hand. Pressing deeper into the catacomb of tunnels, they moved further into a vast network of twisting passages. After a few minutes of travel, Carla was beginning to return to normal and the grim circumstances to which she had been subjected only a few minutes prior were also beginning to fade. Breathing softly, she glanced at her guide a few times before speaking.

"I wanted to say thanks." She spoke in a truly appreciative tone. "I'm not sure what would have happened if you hadn't come along when you did."

Stopping in his tracks, the enormous man turned to her. "I think we both know what would have happened if I didn't come along when I did."

Inhaling sharply, Carla acknowledged his dark assessment of the situation as true. He was correct; both of them knew what the outcome would have been. "I'm still thankful."

"I know." He nodded his head to her with a deep look of respect. "These are dark desperate times and humanity is a few gallons low on morality as of late."

She chuckled dryly, nodding in agreement.

Blinking several times, he realized that a formal introduction had not yet been made between them, and tilted his head downwards in a slight bow. "My name is Byron Clay, a former resident of the city of Rasheed." With a sweeping motion towards the ceiling, he gestured to indicate that he once lived above ground, somewhere over their current location in the sewer.

"Carla Reins." She smiled, already warming up to Byron.

"Pleased to meet you." He nodded again in her direction. Sensing a conversation about to erupt, he motioned her onwards; their journey would not take them too much further.

"How did you find me? How did you know that those two men were attacking me?" Carla was amazed by her fortunate circumstances.

"I didn't know, at least not directly. I saw John, the bearded man that attacked you, rush inside and grab his buddy Chris. I didn't know exactly what he was up to but I'm always suspicious of those two. They haven't done anything like this in the past that I know of, but I still don't trust them. I followed them out since I didn't have confidence in them and I'm glad I did."

"Me too." She felt nervous again, thinking back to them pressing down on her, pinning her to the floor with their hands touching her. She became anxious as she thought about the attack, and grew silent.

Passing only twenty yards further down the tunnel, the two travelers came to a steel door in the left wall of the passage. Byron rapped on the door with a pattern of short quick knocks and a few open-palmed smacks. A few seconds later, a clunking sound rumbled within as if a draw bolt or lock was being opened. The steel door creaked open a few moments later, and a pale man with glasses stuck his head out with an inquisitive look. Seeing Byron, the man opened the door fully.

The warden initially viewed the newcomer with suspicion, then glanced at the weapons held in Byron's hands. Without a second look, he stepped out of their way so they could move inside.

The sound of the door bolting behind them made Carla uneasy once more. She was now a captive of sorts, whose freedom was hanging in the balance, resting in the hands and upon the intentions of Byron. Sucking in a heavy breath, she sighed, trying to release some of her pent-up tension.

"Welcome to Refuge," Byron announced in a cryptic tone as they moved down the passage.

With Byron still in the lead, they continued down a curving passage. Ahead of them, they could see light beyond a bend in the tunnel. As they approached it, Byron extinguished his lantern.

Pushing into the light beyond, Carla was shocked by what she saw. An enormous room filled with machinery had become a haven of sorts. Dozens of pale people were crammed into the room. A collection of dirty pillows and bedding covered the floor. Crates of supplies and other garbage were unceremoniously strewn about the room. In the midst of all the refuse, people were trying to cling to life, barely holding on in the grim circumstances.

As they pressed into the room, the citizens of the sewer shantytown turned to regard Carla with deep suspicion. Hateful glances mixed with greedy ones. All of the people in the room were poorly dressed and malnourished. Even though her clothes were not in perfect condition, Carla was better off than most of the people surrounding her. Even though she had been tracking Globulus southward for many weeks, she had managed to scavenge and live off the land. She was far from starvation, and her wholesome appearance angered the citizens. They could all remember a better life, before the ravages of war came right to their doorstep.

Seeing their condition made her feel self-conscious, and she understood their plight. Not knowing what to do, she tried to avoid their hostile glances, and kept her eyes on Byron as they made their way down a crude path, cutting through the refuse of the shantytown. Passing out of the main room, they came into a hallway with two more exits. One of them led into another room, larger than the first, with even more people crammed into it. The other exit led into an electrical closet.

Seeking privacy, Byron chose to move into the electrical closet. He opened the door to reveal a room filled with a collection of guns and other weapons resting up against the wall. Breaker boxes and electrical cabling piled up to the ceiling filled the back end of the room. A sleeping bag and a pile of books were on the floor near one of the walls. Three dirty folding chairs surrounded a wooden crate. Atop the wooden crate were a tattered deck of playing cards and a crude set of poker chips.

Resting her rifle up against the wall with the other weapons, Byron motioned for her to sit at the makeshift table, and she complied, sitting down in one of the chairs. He joined her at the table, resting her pistol on top of the wooden crate, well out of Carla's reach. As he placed the gun on the crate, she eyed the weapon with a quick glance. Her fear had abated and her normal senses were kicking back in. She was already paying attention to her surroundings, and the handgun on the table was a tangible road of escape from the strange shantytown.

Seeing her expression, Byron knew that she was eyeing the gun. He could tell that she was formidable and accustomed to combat. "So tell me, young Carla Reins, are you a soldier?"

Blinking several times, she formulated her thoughts carefully, knowing she was now being interrogated.

"I'm no solider," she replied in an almost derisive tone.

"Not a soldier?" he almost chuckled. "You seem accustomed to combat. This rifle of yours here is very uncommon. Before Rasheed fell to the Reaper Kai, our soldiers didn't even have weapons this nice. So tell me, if you're not a soldier, what are you?"

"I'm a mercenary," Carla responded, sensing where his questioning was leading.

He responded with a chuckle of utter surprise. "A mercenary?"

"What's so funny about that?"

"Oh nothing, it's just you're kinda petite for a mercenary, don't you think?"

"I don't have to be big to kill someone at two hundreds yards with a rifle, do I?" she snapped back in irritation.

Smiling at her bravado, he nodded in agreement. "No, young Carla, you don't have to be very big to kill someone with a sniper rifle." He had only known her for a few minutes, but he liked her spunk and guile. It wasn't very often that he encountered someone so fiery, especially someone so small with those traits. "So tell me then, why is a mercenary sniper creeping around in the sewers underneath the city of Rasheed? What is your target? Who are you here to kill?"

"I'm not here to kill anyone."

"But you said yourself that you're a sniper, and a mercenary sniper at that. You must have a target."

"There is no target."

Her resilience to the questioning was rapidly irritating the large, dark skinned interrogator. Growing very serious, Byron stared at her with a commanding gaze. "I don't think you understand me clearly. Just because I saved you from getting raped back there, that doesn't make me your friend. I can hold you down here for as long as I want and no one will know a thing about it. You're in my domain and you need to answer my questions if you ever want to see sunlight again."

"You are their leader?" She asked a question of her own, trying to gauge the severity of her circumstances.

"Yes, I am their leader." Byron conceded a little information as well. He could sense that she was not totally unreasonable and could also sense that she required some information of her own before divulging the reason for her presence in Rasheed.

"Why are you here? What is this place?"

"Refuge was founded the night that the Reaper Kai attacked this city. I was a soldier, one of the Rasheed militia, but I had worked as a maintenance man for the city prior to my tour of duty and had worked in these tunnels for many years. The night Rasheed fell, I rounded up a dozen other soldiers and we grabbed as many people as we could and hid down here. For weeks, we would go out at night into the city and search for other survivors, bringing them here. We managed to save a few hundred people and they all live here, in the sewer."

"That was so long ago. Why don't you make your way into the harbor, and escape the city?"

"It's too late for that. Most of us are starving and are too weak to survive the swim across the harbor. Add in fear, and the result is little hope. Most everyone down here has lost everything, their families and loved ones, their homes. Hate has taken everything and fear is all that remains. Most are too frightened to escape and leave this place. They are paralyzed and barely have the will to live on. We go out into the city at night and scavenge what we can. We also fish from the harbor out of the sewer pipes at night. It's a tough life but it's all we have left."

The story was grim and Carla was fully absorbed by it. A heartfelt look of concern shaded her face as Byron recounted his tale. He had given some information to Carla, and now it was time for him to ask the questions.

"Now it's your turn." His voice was confident. "You are a mercenary sniper creeping around Rasheed. What or who is your target?"

She was beginning to trust him more and more. She could tell that he was no friend of the Reaper Kai and that his people had suffered much under their tyranny. Consequently, she began to open up.

"I have no target in the city. I'm not here to kill anyone; I'm here to rescue someone."

"Rescue someone?" he pressed.

"My friend was captured by the Reaper Kai and I've vowed to save him from a death of torture at the hands of the Reaper Kai priests."

"You've vowed to save him, alone?" Byron was mystified. "You came to break a prisoner out of the dungeons of the palace by yourself?"

Carla knew he was right to be skeptical. It was a reckless act of suicide to try to break a prisoner out of the palace by herself.

"Yes, I'm here to save him and I don't have anyone else to help me," she replied, then felt somewhat foolish. His responses thus far and his obvious skepticism made her feel that the task of breaking Globulus out of prison would be impossible.

"You are either totally insane or the most selfless person that I have ever met. Charging into the dungeons would be a death sentence for you."

"I don't care. He's my friend. I won't let him suffer death by torture, not while I can still help. I have to try." As she answered confidently, Byron could tell she was someone who should not be underestimated. Her courage and loyalty to her friend were inspiring. For so long his people in Refuge had been without hope, without courage. Now, a tiny, petite mercenary was willing to risk her life to save her friend. The turn of events was beginning to lift his heart. She was a role model, someone who had embraced selflessness to achieve an act of good in a dark world. Her commitment to her companion was something that Byron needed in his life after witnessing endless despair around him. He shook his head in disbelief. Carla was truly an icon of hope.

"Your courage is refreshing, Carla, but breaking into the palace to rescue your friend is nearly impossible."

"I have to try," she responded, more defiant than ever.

"Who is your friend? Who is worth your very life?"

She became extremely uncomfortable after he asked the question. Silence was her only response.

"Who is your friend?" he boomed, intrigued by her silence. She had opened up considerably about the rest of her journey, but her silence about the subject of her rescue efforts in Rasheed was beginning to irritate him.

"I cannot tell you."

"You will tell me or you will never leave this place."

"I cannot tell you."

"You must."

"No." She was almost on the verge of tears, knowing that her chance to rescue her friend was beginning to slip away. Frantically, she looked at the gun on the wooden crate. She was becoming desperate and Byron could tell. Seeing her look at the gun, he grabbed it and looked at her in surprise.

"You need to trust me. Why won't you tell me?"

"I can't tell you because he's from Rasheed. I can't risk something this important to me."

"He's from Rasheed? The captive you are here to rescue is from Rasheed?"

"Yes." She looked him directly in the eye, trying to size him up, wanting to trust him but not knowing if she could. As she looked into his eyes, he looked back with compassion, aware of her terror. With consoling eyes, he reached out his hand and placed it on her trembling one.

"You can trust me," he said emphatically, looking into her eyes, rubbing her hand gently. "Trust me."

She stared back, looking into his eyes intently. Feeling his goodness and his integrity, she conceded defeat and revealed her secret.

"I am here to rescue King Toil's warmaster. I am here to rescue Globulus from a fate of torture."

As she uttered her words, Byron's heart skipped a beat. He blinked several times, thinking that he was hearing a dream unfold. His heart raced and it felt like fire in his blood. There was not a nobler warrior or a stauncher defender of justice than Globulus of Rasheed. He was a beloved icon for Rasheed, a hero of legend, a creature that embodied loyalty and courage. Unable to comprehend that Globulus had been captured and would suffer a death of torture, he stuttered, his eyes bulging in disbelief. "Wh…what?"

"Yes, Globulus is my friend, that's why I'm here in Rasheed. I'm here to rescue him."

Awestruck, Byron, a former soldier of Rasheed, grabbed his hair with both hands and tugged on it in disbelief. A fire lit his heart and it felt wonderful. Strangely, Byron felt that he had a purpose once more. Their beloved hero Globulus, a warrior of renown, needed their help. It all made sense; everything made sense. No longer did his people have to fear the darkness; no longer were they without hope. A glowing symbol of hope, their valiant leader Globulus, had returned to Rasheed, and he needed help. Shaking his head, he knew what must be done.

"*You* will not save Globulus from a fate of torture." He spoke in a booming voice, standing up from the chair, eyeing her with a fiery gaze.

"You don't understand. I *must* save him," she countered, standing tall, her eyes piercing him with a flash of anger.

"No, it's you who do not understand. *You* will not save Globulus—*we* will save him!" he boomed. "Come on, we have plans to make."

Rushing from the room, he charged into the main living quarters of his people, the sewer shanty. Standing at the front of the room, his words rang out fiercely. "All soldiers, all warriors of Rasheed, come to attention! We have a purpose! We have a mission! Our glorious hero, our glorious leader, needs our help! Rally to me, rally to war! The noble Globulus, our courageous warmaster, is in need! He has been captured by the enemy, and Globulus needs out assistance. Grab your weapons and rally your courage!"

Byron's booming voice rang true and many of the hopeless felt a spark of light rekindle in their hearts. Their leader Byron was excited, and his excitement had set off a chain reaction amongst his people. Clambering to the room, all in Refuge came to hear what he had to say.

As he recounted the tale, Carla stood and smiled as she saw hope return to the broken people. They now had focus; they now had a primal optimism rekindled in their hearts. As she stared at the rabble, a fire leapt in her own heart. No longer did she have to save Globulus alone; Carla now had help, and significant help at that.

Whispering to herself, she uttered an inaudible vow. *"Hold on, Globulus, just hold on! We are going to save you!"*

Chapter 36
Prison Break

"Five seconds!" a grungy man declared in an excited but somewhat muted tone. His eyes flashed feverishly as he stared intently at his watch. The second hand moved forward quickly and he smiled directly at Carla Reins.

She looked back with trepidation and then closed her eyes.

In the distance, by the harbor, a massive explosion tore the air. An enormous plume of fire leapt into the night sky and the city was awash with red flames. A split second after the first explosion, another tremendous blast erupted, a few piers down from the first blast. The entire waterfront of Rasheed was bathed in an orange blaze.

Looking over to the leader of the raid, Carla could see a confident expression on Byron Clay's face. He nodded to her with a look that said, 'It's gonna be alright.' Acknowledging his silent words, she nodded back at him and said 'thanks' with her eyes. Clutching their weapons, they looked into the darkness of the night toward the harbor, at the scene of the explosions they had caused.

Within seconds after the blasts rocked the waterfront, loud sirens ripped the air. The whine of the alarms echoed through the abandoned city of Rasheed like a haunting wail. The burnt-out husks that were once homes stood silent. The once-bustling shops did not respond to the alarm. A foreign presence was the only entity that responded to the fiery attack. Shambling from the shadows came an entire host of Biogtech war machines. Cackling with blank expressions in their red robotic eyes, the machines tottered forward with weapons in hand. Reaper Kai priests, garbed in blood-red robes, hung behind their robotic counterparts, allowing the machines to investigate the explosions first.

The response to the demolitions attack was massive. The majority of the city's defenses were sent to the waterfront. The city of Rasheed had been heavily fortified at the gates leading into the city; an attack from the harbor, however, was not anticipated, and the defenses against it were weak. After the explosions, most of the garrisons protecting the city were routed to the harbor to repel a possible seaside attack.

Smiling in the shadows, Byron was pleased with the response. Motioning to his men, he signaled that the assault was on. His men, several of whom were former Rasheed militia, acknowledged his command and rushed through the alleyway. Byron and Carla brought up the rear of the formation and followed the motley assault team through the abandoned byways of the once-great city of Rasheed.

As chaos reigned in the harbor, the team managed to penetrate deep into the city without hindrance. The enemy's focus was on discovering the cause of the explosions and not necessarily on protecting the center of the city. This gave Byron's assault team a much-needed reprieve from enemy scrutiny.

A frenzied soldier was looking at his watch intently. "We have eleven minutes before the next charge goes off!" he whispered to the rest of the team.

Hearing his warning, they picked up the pace and bolted towards the palace gates. Within a few moments, the strike team reached the perimeter of the Rasheed palace. Their objective was to reach the dungeons below the palace and save the noble Globulus from a tortuous fate.

Raising his hand, Byron halted the advance of his team as they reached the edge of the palace walls. He moved to the head of the formation and assessed the gate defenses, which consisted of two Reaper Kai priests and six Biogtechs. Completely oblivious to the team's presence, the two priests were looking toward the fire curling into the air near the waterfront. Their lack of attention would prove fatal.

Byron turned to his team and pointed at his eyes, indicating what he was seeing ahead near the gate. He then raised two fingers, indicating that two primary targets were in sight. He motioned to another soldier, who came forward with a pair of pistols, both with silencers mounted on the barrels. He handed one to Byron and kept the other for himself. Sneaking forward, Byron and another soldier rushed across the street in the dim light, avoiding detection. Now a mere fifty yards from the front gate, they crawled on their hands and knees across the ground, closing quickly on the two Reaper Kai priests.

Both priests were still distracted by the flames and destruction from the first two blasts, and neither of them was aware that they were in mortal danger. Although psychic, neither guard could sense the impending doom, as their powers were based upon combat and the ability to make war.

Calmly the two soldiers rested in the darkness. Looking back to the rest of the team, the soldier with the wristwatch motioned that only one minute remained until the next set of demolition charges were set to blow. Both soldiers crouched in the darkness and took aim with the silenced pistols; each of them had his own mark and target.

The signal was simple. When the next demolition charge detonated in the distance, the Reaper Kai would be surprised beyond belief. The time ticked away, each second passing at an agonizing length. Growing more anxious by the moment, both of the soldiers breathed more heavily, nerves twitching in anticipation. A thin trickle of sweat rolled down Byron's forehead as he waited. He wanted to wipe it away but didn't want to miss his shot. Letting it roll down his face, he focused on the gun sight of his pistol and the target in the crosshairs.

Boom! Another explosion rocked the waterfront. A split second after the detonation, Byron and the other concealed soldier opened fire. Their silenced weapons were unleashed as they fired a volley of bullets at the Reaper Kai. Focusing on the newest explosion, neither of the enemy soldiers saw what was coming. The guard nearest Byron was hit first. Three well placed shots slammed into his chest. The other soldier was a split second behind Byron and managed to tag the other Reaper Kai in the face with two shots, another in the throat, and one final shot in the chest.

Both Reaper Kai fell to the ground without a sound, both dead before hitting the ground. The Biogtech soldiers were too slow to react. Though they were already under attack, their robotic brains had barely comprehended that they were engaged in battle. Two Biogtech soldiers fell before the other four were able to respond. Scanning the darkness with their night vision, the Biogtechs finally caught sight of the two soldiers, a second too late. Continuing the attack, the two men quickly gunned down the remaining gate defenders.

The assault was breathtaking to witness. Within half a minute, the two gunmen had killed two Reaper Kai priests and six Biogtechs in complete silence and without raising an alarm. Seeing their success, the rest of the strike team surged forward and reached the gate with weapons ready.

After receiving the signal to proceed, the commando team breached the palace gates and surged into the courtyard beyond. With weapons ready, they moved stealthily and quickly into the palace.

The interior was dimly lit. Torches placed at irregular intervals were reflecting off the black and white marble walls with dull intensity. The floor at the main entrance was still littered with the dead. The corpses, left to rot for many months, were an unsettling reminder of the harsh battle that had raged inside the palace the night Rasheed fell to the Reaper Kai. Ignoring the carnage, the soldiers stepped over the bodies and held their breath for a few seconds, just long enough to escape the stench. The team rushed forward and reached a massive spiral staircase in the center of the palace. Climbing into the darkness, the soldiers trained their weapons upwards. Nothing, absolutely nothing, was visible at the top of the staircase. The palace was strangely quiet and devoid of activity. With a chill running down his spine, Byron shrugged off the eerie feeling invading his senses as he stared into the darkness above them. Motioning them onward, he pointed to the other end of the massive hallway, at the spiral staircase leading down into the depths of the palace.

The team advanced deftly, rushing down the spiral staircase. As they reached the bottom, the smell of worn paper filled the air. An open archway extended into the darkness. To their right, the entrance of the great library of Rasheed was revealed. To their left, a steel door leading into the wine cellar and the dungeons beyond was set in the wall. The team assembled around the door and trained their weapons upon it. One of the soldiers reached forward and opened the door quickly. Taking aim, the rest of the team made ready to kill anything beyond the void. However, nothing was beyond the steel door but a series of torches flickering in a dull breeze rolling out of the lower corridor.

As the door opened, the stench of death rushed forth. The smell was so overpowering, one of the soldiers gagged repeatedly and finally vomited upon the finely crafted marble floor. Shaking his head in disgust, Byron shot Carla a look of concern. She was equally horrified, her sense of apprehension turning to fear; she could not believe that such a horrible place existed, and that her noble friend Globulus had been imprisoned in such a cruel environment.

Breathing through their mouths, the strike team continued the assault. They continued down the hallway, then advanced to the wine cellar and halted. Closing the steel door behind them, they all felt as if they had stepped into a tomb and the door had slammed shut. As the steel door closed, Byron said a few words to his team.

"Now that we are inside and the door is closed, the sound of our gunfire will be muffled. No one outside the door should be able to hear it. These tunnels up ahead are a maze. There are multiple attack points and since the cells are not a continuous hallway, you can travel in almost any direction when you hit the cell blocks. There are passages and more passages leading off into every direction. You can be ambushed and attacked from almost anywhere. Any hostile forces we see in here will be extremely difficult to flush out. Keep focused and keep another soldier at your back at all times. If you get into a firefight, watch yourselves and don't get separated. If you get separated, you die. Everyone got that?"

"Yes, sir!" the rest of the troops replied staunchly.

"Ok, let's do this!" Byron exclaimed. He motioned to his troops, who started to funnel past the wine cellar and into the cellblocks.

The smell of death increased and the air was thick and warm. A moist, humid stickiness clung to their skin as they pressed onward into the dungeons. Passing out of the wine cellar, the team came to a network of passages. Ahead of them, the corridor continued into the shadows. To their right and left, other passages pressed into the inky blackness. Torch light lit the passages and flickered as a sickening breeze circulated. Moving forward, they encountered a section of wall with dozens and dozens of keys on enormous brass rings. The collection of keys opened all of the cells in the dungeon. Byron motioned to the keys, and several soldiers grabbed all of them. As they moved down the primary hallway, they heard whimpering from within the cells.

Coming to the first set of prison cells, they shone a light into the cage. A man had been torn to pieces and his dismembered body was littering the cell floor. Rats scurried away from feasting on the rotting flesh as the lights passed over the horrific scene. Stunned, the soldiers felt a primitive sadness fill them. Such barbarism was frightening. They shook their heads, the sadness turning into a simmering rage. Seeing such madness and evil made all of them feel that retribution would be easy to unleash on the sadistic dungeon keepers. Encountering the enemy within the cell block would be something to cherish, a chance to kill the enemy and make right some of the misdeeds they were all now witnessing. Shaking her head in dismay, Carla said a silent prayer that she would not find Globulus in a similar condition.

As they stared at the mutilated man, the lights flickered at the end of the hallway. A flash of red rushed across the hallway in their peripheral vision. Spinning swiftly to point their weapons down the passage, they were all just in time to see several of the torches go out. The end of the tunnel was plunged into an icy blackness.

"Did you see that?" Carla whispered in horror.

"Yeah, yeah I did," Byron replied as a chill ran down his spine.

As he spoke, a gibbering rose from the darkness. Beasts of evil, foul Goat Minions, now concealed by the darkness, bleated in unison. Their sick war cries echoed off the walls and passages, creating the impression that the entire team was surrounded. In reality, they were. As they rushed around, more torches went out. The Goat Minions managed to extinguish all light. Relying on their keen sense of smell, the feral beast creatures stormed forward, driven into a frenzy as they fantasized about the smell of fresh blood.

"Ahhh!" A scream broke the darkness. A soldier near the rear of the formation cried out in terror as something pulled him into the shadows. Whirling around, the team was just in time to see a red form pull the soldier around a corner. Frightened and wanting to protect their comrade, two men rushed into the darkness to save him. As they ran around a corner, the sound of gunfire echoed in the darkness. Screams of agony pierced the shadows and finally ended in pitiful whimpers and pleas for mercy. Within a few seconds, silence gripped the cell block once more. Three soldiers were dead and the rest of the assault team was now being stalked.

Listening to their own hearts beating in the eerie silence, the remaining team members were awestruck by how quickly the Goat Minions had killed three of their companions.

"Hold your ground!" Byron spoke in a frantic tone. "Do not get separated."

Gibbering wildly, with madness flashing in its eyes, a Goat Minion rushed down the hallway with a bloody axe raised over its head. It screamed in rage as it came forward, guided only by bloodlust, bent on causing suffering and hungering for more soft flesh. Carla recoiled from the sight and brought her rifle upwards just in time to parry the viscous attack. The axe struck her weapon and she avoided a grisly fate. Swinging the butt of her sniper rifle around, she struck the creature in the face, shattering its jaw and knocking it back. She swung her weapon around, brought it to her shoulder and took hasty aim. The high caliber round tore forward and slammed into the beast's chest. The attack was severe and a jagged wound was torn in the monster's flesh.

Even though it was mortally wounded, it crawled across the floor, bloodstained axe in hand, swinging it wildly. Jumping with all her might, Carla avoided the wild swings. She dropped her rifle, swiftly pulled a pistol free from her belt and opened fire. Firing wildly, she struck the crazed creature several more times before it finally died.

As adrenaline pumped through her overwrought mind and stung her muscles, she became aware that the entire team was under attack. Spinning around, she gasped in horror as a soldier screamed in terror. A Goat Minion was on top of the man, repeatedly stabbing him with a jagged knife. Blinking and dazed, she stared down the passage. Another soldier was clutching a bloody stump where his arm had been sheared off at the elbow; a dead Goat Minion was twitching at his feet.

Frightened beyond belief, she screamed out in terror. "Globulus! Where are you?"

From amidst the sounds of the raging battle, the noble hippo immediately recognized Carla's shrill scream. "I'm here! Carla, I'm here!"

Straining with all of his might, he tried to break the chains holding him to the wall. Try as he may, he could not break free.

Seeing several of the key rings that had been hastily discarded on the floor, she grabbed them and rushed down the dark passage towards the sound of his voice. Holding a flashlight and the key rings in one hand and her pistol in the other, she could hear the sound of her friend's voice echoing in the tunnels. The ongoing sounds of battle ricocheted around her as her friend's voice led her deeper into the sinister dungeon, completely alone.

Finally she came to a door. Peering inside, she could hear Globulus' voice ringing out. She fumbled with the keys, jamming the first one into the lock, her heart pounding. It would not open.

"Carla, be careful!" Globulus urged, knowing full well from the sounds of battle that she was in mortal danger.

"Damn it!" she cursed furiously as she lost her grip on both key rings. Dropping down to one knee, she heard a shuffling noise from behind her. She turned her head and caught sight of movement very near her. Rolling onto her back, she kicked her legs forward, and just in time. A charging Goat Minion was bearing down on her. As she kicked her legs, she caught the beast in its stomach. The creature's momentum carried it forward and the Goat Minion landed on top of Carla. Screaming, she dropped the flashlight and struggled with the creature.

It smelled like death. The monster had spent so much time in the dungeons, the foul smell had permeated its bristly fur and embedded itself in its very skin. Breathing heavily, she brought her elbow around and struck it in the face. This act only enraged the beast further. Gibbering in fury, it smashed its forehead into her own, head-butting her. She pressed her pistol into its flesh in a daze and began pulling the trigger. Bullet after bullet erupted from the weapon and into its body. Screaming desperately, it grabbed her throat and began to choke her.

Gasping for air, she continued to fire into the Goat Minion. Bullet after bullet shredded the foul-smelling evil creature. Within a few seconds, she had emptied the entire clip into it, but still it attacked her, trying to crush the life out of her. Coughing, she dropped the pistol and grabbed the Goat Minion's claws, which were still around her throat. The world began to dim. Bright flashes of light filled her vision as the flow of blood into her head began to diminish with each agonizing second. Struggling, she fought the beast with all of her might. She knew that she had inflicted horrible wounds upon the monster, but she was beginning to doubt whether she would survive.

"Hold on, Carla!" Globulus roared from inside his cell. "Don't you touch her!"

The beast's grip began to falter. The blood loss from a dozen gunshot wounds had finally taken its toll. Its grip grew lighter and lighter each second. Finally, the Goat Minion died. Shaken from the attack, Carla grabbed the key rings, still in a daze, and began to jam each one into the lock. As she did, the sounds of combat continued around her. The Rasheed soldiers were battling valiantly against the forces of darkness. Ignoring the sounds, she focused on liberating Globulus.

Finally, one of the keys rotated in the lock. She pulled the door open triumphantly. Staggering inside, still weak from battle, she collapsed beside the mighty hippo warrior. She inserted the same key which had opened the door into the chains on his wrist lock and it opened immediately. The chains slid free and the mighty hippo warrior threw the restraints to the floor.

"Are you okay?" He assessed her for a brief second. She nodded in confirmation, and a fire lit the hippo's eyes. Standing tall in the cell, he flexed his enormous muscles and stepped into the hallway. "It's time for some payback!"

Rushing down the hallway, he caught sight of the nearest Goat Minion and charged. Like a freight train he came, thundering forward with a ferocious gait. He roared out a war cry which stunned every combatant, friend and foe alike. Crashing into battle, the enormous hippo hybrid grabbed a Goat Minion by the neck. He lifted the creature off the ground with both hands, twisting the red robed minion. Spiraling his hands around its subdued form, he broke most of the bones in its body. A grotesque snapping filled the air as the pressure from his attack splintered bone. Gasping in agony, the Goat Minion died immediately. Globulus threw it to the floor as if it were a mere toy, searching immediately for another victim.

Elated that their beloved hero was free, the Rasheed troops rallied and defended themselves with violent fury. Holding back the Goat Minions was all they needed to do; Globulus had been unleashed and nothing could stop his brutal fury. Rushing forward, he grabbed another Goat Minion and lifted it high above his head. With a grunt, he brought the monster down on his right knee, breaking its back like a twig. Throwing its lifeless body against a nearby wall, he charged onward, killing again and again.

Within minutes the cell block was silent. All of the Goat Minions had been put to rest, mangled by the forceful battle prowess of the coppery-skinned warrior known as Globulus. The exchange had been bloody. Six of the Rasheed soldiers had been killed and two horribly wounded. Now in control of the cell block, the liberators went from cell to cell, freeing the remaining captives who were still alive.

A rabble of soldiers and freed captives recovered weapons from the scene of conflict. Charging out of the dungeons, the team sought to escape the palace before reinforcements arrived.

As they fled the prison, a shadowy form lingered near the top of the spiral staircase, brought to the scene by her acute senses. She knew something was afoot in the dungeons, a place in which she herself had spent the past few days, tortured for her failures. Garbed in blood-red robes, the former queen of Rasheed lingered.   A confrontation was about to take place between a queen and her foster sibling, a confrontation that had been a long time in the making. Marion Toil was ready to confront Globulus.

Chapter 37
Confrontation

As she closed her eyes, a tendril of spiritual energy rushed out of her body. She bowed her head, shuddering as the raw demonic power flowed through her fragile frame. The sensation rose in intensity and for a brief moment, she fought back a wave of panic and the urge to vomit. Shaking her head, the red-robed woman fought to remain in control as she harnessed her psychic abilities.

As her thoughts extended beyond herself, she caught the scent of something familiar. Focusing on the thought, Marion Toil refined her powers and let her subconscious merge with her conscious thoughts. A wave of emotion flowed through her and it felt sickening. A flash from her childhood flowed into her mind. Blinking through the vision, the sinister Reaper Kai saw her foster brother. A vision of Globulus, a small beastly hippo laughing, stung at her mind. Shaking, she felt a wave of guilt roll through her, but she fought back the emotion, knowing that Globulus was drawing near. With a sigh and an anxious feeling inside her, she knew that a confrontation was about to take place between herself and her foster brother.

She emerged from her trance to look toward the great hallway beyond her current position. With a certain hesitation, she took a shaky step forward, moving into the great hall. At the far end of the expanse, a giant staircase descended into the depths of the palace, ultimately leading into the dungeons of Rasheed. Gripping her hands tightly, she squeezed all the blood from them so that they

were a pasty white.   Again and again she flexed her hands
nervously.

An image of her father flickered into her mind as she waited
patiently above the staircase.   Blinking, she could she her father's
loving face, wracked in pain but still compassionate.   In that horrid
vision, King Toil clutched his chest, blood pouring from the gunshot
wound.   Even through all the pain and terror, King Toil's final wish
was to see his daughter one last time before he died.   Desperately he
called for her over and over again as each passing second brought
him closer to death.   In that fateful moment, his daughter came to his
side with a blank expression on her face, an expression mingling
reckless ambition and hateful guilt.   In that moment, Marion Toil
said goodbye to her father and farewell to her humanity.   As she
watched her father die of an assassin's bullet, a bullet that was
ordered by Marion herself, she was tormented by a host of emotions.

So much suffering was caused by that one hate-filled act.
Looking down at her hands, Marion found that she was trembling
violently.   She shook her head back and forth as tears welled up in
her eyes.   Her body was wracked with spasms as she coughed.   The
guilt was overwhelming.   Shaking with an overwhelming self pity,
she tried to regain control.

An ominous vision then filled her psyche.   As if dark storm
clouds had washed over the great hallway, all the light in the area
seemed to dim.   Trembling, Marion looked around as shadows
seemed to dance on the walls, shattered forms drifting through the
room.   Marion's feeling of self pity had aroused something dark and
sinister.   As her soul was tortured with remorse, evil was stirring and
infusing her with other visions.

A greedy, self righteous vision filled her.   Marion could
remember how good it felt to sit upon the throne, the throne of her
father.   The sensation was almost intoxicating as Marion could recall
the first time she took the crown and placed it on her head.   She
could remember all of the shattered souls, the once-proud subjects of
Rasheed, looking upon their new monarch in sheer horror.   Making
them bow before her, she rose to her feet and threw her hands into
the air in an act of triumph.   Sure, she had partaken in the murder of
her own father, but to rule an empire and have everyone look at you
as their leader was a powerful reward for vicious deeds.   All Marion

ever wanted was to rule without question. All she ever wanted was absolute control and power over Rasheed. The guilt was beginning to slip away as her greedy soul found pleasure in its dark reward. Smiling, her body ceased to tremble. How wonderful it felt to be queen. The emotion was almost erotic to her. Thinking back to her dark mentor, another vision flashed in her mind.

"Guilt is nothing to a pure soul. To remove guilt, one needs to remove all the sources of guilt from one's life. Purge anyone, slaughter anyone that makes you feel guilt. One can only be truly pure if one is devoid of guilt." The dark vision of Father Vertigo invaded her mind. For the wicked, guilt is nothing more than an irritation, a thing to be endured until every source of guilt is destroyed and removed from the picture. Such a dark and evil philosophy had ruled young Marion's senses. And now, there was only one person remaining between Marion and this guilt-free existence. With a twisted sneer, she felt a tremor of anger fill her. She could sense Globulus was drawing near, charging up the staircase in an attempt to escape the palace of Rasheed.

Dark fantasy filled her mind. She would now have to make a tough choice; exist with guilt and remorse for the rest of her life, or try to cleanse this feeling by killing Globulus. Warring back and forth, each side of Marion sought to control the other. She was not always wicked, and the good and just side of her soul clashed with the reckless, ambitious evil side of her.

Closing her eyes, she let the horror of her existence flood her soul. Trembling again, she shook her head back and forth in terror.

"What have I done?" she whimpered. "What have I done?"

As she was lost in dark thoughts, the sounds of hurried footsteps charging up the marble staircase in the room brought her back to reality. With each thud, she trembled more and more. She knew that Globulus would soon be standing before her. As she readied herself, Marion's pulse began to quicken and she breathed erratically.

The sounds of footsteps increased and drew near. With no sense of what awaited them, the assault team that had liberated Globulus stopped dead in their tracks as they reached the top of the stairs.

A woman garbed in blood-red robes stood silently in the center of the great hallway. Though her appearance had been ravaged by the throes of evil, everyone could still tell that Marion Toil, the great betrayer, was now standing before them, the last obstacle between them and freedom.

The assault team looked at Marion in horror, paralyzed. Everyone knew of the dark deeds she had committed, and they all knew that her psychic powers were extremely formidable. Fighting her would be a credible death sentence. Her reputation alone was formidable enough to deter everyone in the assault team from combat. As the team members pondered their deaths at the hands of Marion, an enormous form pushed into view, placing himself between his comrades and Marion.

Globulus stood at the front of the pack and stared uneasily at Marion. As he did, their eyes locked and an emotional bond, an enduring link, seemed to form between them. With an unwavering gaze, Marion stared at Globulus and time seemed to stand still. The longer she looked into his compassionate eyes, the less anger she felt. Her lower lip trembled and she was on the verge of breaking down as sadness began to override her senses. Shaking her head, she brought herself under control long enough to issue an order to the rest of the assault team. "Leave us."

The rest of the team, shaking with fright, stared in disbelief and did not respond to the command.

"You don't have much time. It won't be long before the prison break is discovered. If you value your lives, leave now. You have nothing to fear from me on *this* day." Her words, which emerged into the air with a cold rasp, seemed to confound them. Unable to believe that Marion Toil was letting them go, they moved slowly at first until her message sunk in.

Once the command was fully understood, Byron motioned the rest of the assault team toward a passage that led into the once-beautiful gardens of the Rasheed palace. "Let's go!"

The remnants of the assault team and all of the freed captives followed without question, except one. As the mass of them rushed from the room, Carla remained and came to Globulus' side. Staring up at him, she grabbed his enormous hand. With tears in her eyes, she rubbed his hand gently and tried to smile. Fighting the tears, he looked back at his courageous friend and tried to return her smile. "Go now, Carla, I'll be fine."

Eyeing Marion, Carla shot her an uneasy glance before rushing off with the rest of the team.

And so they stood, alone in the hallway, staring at each other with a bond between them stronger than any chain.

"Don't say anything," Marion said as the tears began to roll down her face. Shaking her head in despair she began to weep uncontrollably. Through all the tears, she spoke in a calm tone to her foster brother. "Please don't say anything. I'm the only one who needs to speak."

"Marion…" Globulus shook and began to weep as well.

"Please, let me speak," she whimpered. "I'm so sorry for what I have done. I'm so ashamed of everything that has happened. I betrayed my people, my family, but most of all, I betrayed you. You were my brother, my kind-hearted friend that would have given his own life to help me. I hate you; do you know that I hate you?"

"Marion, please…" He took a step forward. Even though her dark deeds had caused suffering, he still could not stand to see her in pain. He wanted to console her.

"No matter what I have done, no matter how much death and bloodshed I have caused, you would still try to help me. That's why I hate you. I hate you because I want you to abandon me. I want you to hate me!"

"I cannot," he replied, and the tears streamed down his face. "I want to hate you. But I cannot. I just cannot hate you. I have spent every day since the fall of Rasheed thinking about how I wanted you to suffer, how I wanted to kill you. I let my anger rule me and I wanted to punish you."

"Then punish me!" she cried out. "Please just end this twisted existence of mine."

"I cannot." He shook his head, barely able to comprehend his own emotions. She had betrayed an entire empire and killed King Toil, a man who was more than just a beloved friend; he was Globulus' foster father. "When I heard you crying out in the cell when you were being tortured, everything inside me changed. I can't fathom why you've done the things that you have done, but I want no part in your suffering. When I heard you cry out in pain, my entire perspective changed. At first, I wanted you to suffer and be in pain. But the more you hurt, the more you screamed, I realized that I still love you. You are my sister and that will never change. We grew up together and in the end, I can never forgive you for what you have done, but I cannot stand to see you suffer."

Clutching her face with both hands, she wept and shook her head in despair. "I cannot forgive myself for what I have done either. I wish you would hate me, it would make it so much easier."

A tense silence ensued. Both of them looked into the other's eyes and the bond between them was still strong. Smiling, Globulus took a step forward to console her further. She shook her head and took a step back. "I don't deserve your compassion or your charity. Just go."

"Come with me. Leave this place of death," he urged. The suggestion seemed almost insane. But in that single moment, a twinkle of hope lit her face. In that one moment, she was no longer a dark presence, but rather swept up in her lingering imagination. She imagined freedom from her own dark thoughts. She imagined a world where her father was still alive. She imagined a world where she was a child, running through the gardens of the palace with Globulus chasing her. She imagined the warm sun on her face and the smell of flowers. Through all the duress and through all of her unhappiness, the single suggestion of freedom from evil made her heart soar and her soul surge.

But even though she wanted things to be the way they were, she could never go back. Her dark deeds could never be undone. The endless suffering she caused could never be washed away. Smiling at Globulus, she let the image of a peaceful world linger between them as she stared into his face.

"I can never go back. No matter how much I want it, I can never go back. I crossed a line that should have never been crossed. I have done unspeakable things and I do not deserve your compassion."

"Come with me. Leave this place," he urged again.

"It's too late for me." Marion looked back with a somber face. "You need to go. It's not safe. You need to go now and escape."

"Marion…" he shook his head.

"Globulus." Her tone was solemn as she looked at him.

He stared back with an equally intense, serious demeanor.

"You were brought here because you know about Metalweaver Flats?"

"Yes..." he seemed confused.

"If the production facility is not destroyed, the Reaper Kai will win this war." Marion spoke without breaking eye contact with him. "Make sure you make it home alive. Tell all that are still fighting the Dark Order about Metalweaver Flats. It is our darkest secret. Thousands of Biogtechs are being produced. Even our capital city cannot rival the production capabilities housed at Metalweaver. If Metalweaver Flats is not destroyed, the Reaper Kai will claim the entire continent and create a paradise of evil for all time."

"If you let me go, it is an act of treason against the Reaper Kai," Globulus said somberly.

"I know." Marion's voice was resolute. "My life is already forfeit, it has been since the first day I put on these robes. Now go."

Globulus looked at Marion one last time and she looked back. They would never meet again. Hearing the sounds of hurried boot steps, Globulus knew that enemy reinforcements were on the way. Charging out of the hallway, he ran to escape the palace. As he stormed into the distance, Marion stood alone in the palace, pondering what she had just done. Marion had let Globulus, a known enemy of the Reaper Kai Empire, escape with critical information vital to the success of the war against the Dark Order. She had crossed the line once more, this time betraying the Dark Order. Even as conflicting thoughts waged a battle in her mind, she felt at peace. For the first time in what seemed like forever, she was truly at peace.

Chapter 38
Atonement

With a vicious, cunning look, the mercenary known as Guillotine left the tower of the lord of evil. Having spent the past few minutes in the council of Father Vertigo, the opossum hybrid now made his way through the Rasheed palace. His new orders were simple: track down and kill Globulus and the soldiers responsible for the prison break.

Guillotine had a reputation for success and had completed many missions for the Dark Order. He was responsible for assassinating King Toil, capturing Mineera in Dune Station, and tracking Nova 7 to the Concrete Barrens; clearly, he was not to be underestimated. He was dedicated to the cause of evil and made a healthy profit performing dark deeds. It was always said that Guillotine was the most dangerous mercenary in the Darken Realm, or rather *had been* the most dangerous mercenary. After Banion O'Neil's return from retirement, Guillotine moved to the number two position.

His latest mission would bring him into hostile contact with the Rasheed dissidents and Globulus. Vertigo had ordered a death sentence upon the recently released prisoner, and he wanted satisfaction. The order was quite clear: bring in the head of the hippo hybrid, and the bounty was enormous. The greedy Guillotine smiled a broad toothy grin as he thought about the reward from such a mission. He also relished the thought of killing a hero of legend. Globulus was a well respected soldier and was known throughout the Darken Realm for daring deeds and acts of heroism. Taking down such a mark would gain Guillotine prestige and legendary status of his own.

As Guillotine made his way through the Rasheed palace, he caught sight of a shadowy form lurking near a passageway ahead of him. Squinting in the darkness, he was unable to discern who was waiting for him. He came to a halt, the hair standing straight up on his neck. Uneasy, the mercenary went for his weapon and trained the pistol on the shadowy form.

"Come to me." A thought entered his mind and he felt powerless to resist. The suggestion placed into his consciousness was hypnotic. Blinking several times, he felt a strange desire to obey the order. As he tried to resist, the thought entered his mind again, pricking his brain like a dream. *"Come to me, Guillotine, I want to reward you for your service."*

Unable to resist, the mercenary tottered forward through the dark palace. Moving ever closer to the shadowy figure, his numb mind recognized none other than Marion Toil. As he approached her in a dim daze, he caught sight of her face. Her once haggard visage had softened. The deep lines and trenches had dissipated. Her murky, gray eyes had tinges of blue in them once more.

Looking at her, Guillotine felt uncomfortable. She stared back with a sinister, almost hungry look, like a cat eyeing its next meal. As she smiled at him, the hair on the back of his neck stood on end once more. Guillotine's conscious mind screamed that he was in danger, but his subconscious mind had been taken over and Marion was controlling him with her formidable psychic powers.

"Come inside with me. There is nothing to fear," the voice erupted in his mind once more. He tried his best to resist, but found himself powerless in her presence. As he stepped inside the room, she slammed the door and drew the bolt, ensuring that no one could enter and that they would be left completely alone.

Hearing the draw bolt slide into place sent a tremor of fear into the mercenary. Trying desperately to defend himself, he attempted to raise his pistol and fire at her. His arms would not respond; he was powerless.

"I wanted to have a conversation with you." She smiled and never broke eye contact with him. *"Sit down!"* The words stung his mind.

Moving with a slow reluctance, the hybrid opossum complied and sat down in a chair at the center of the room. Marion Toil moved behind him and ran her finger across the bristly hair standing on end upon his neck. This sent a further shiver of fear down his spine. Seeing his reaction, she gave a dry laugh.

Resting upon a chair of her own, she stared at him with a wicked smile. Guillotine was now aware of the chamber that they were in. Looking around, he could see that the entire room was shrouded in webs, enormous spider webs. All upon the sticky strings were thousands of spiders. His eyes traced the edges of the room and found thousands of large spiders swarming, like a moving wall. Everywhere he looked, spiders the size of a human hand skittered and moved about the webs in frantic motions. Within a few seconds, several dozen of them had crawled onto Marion's robes. Smiling, she grasped one of the enormous hairy spiders and began to pet it lovingly. Her fingers ran across the furry menace and it responded to her touch by flexing its fangs. Shooting outwards, the black fangs were now exposed and dripping with venom. Marion collected a drop of spider venom on the tip of her finger, then licked it off with a wicked grin.

"My pets are so loyal and so beautiful." Smiling, she allowed the enormous spider to crawl back onto her red robes. Staring in horror, Guillotine could see several spiders descending from the ceiling above him, spinning webs as they dangled precariously above his head. He was frightened beyond belief.

"What do you want?" Guillotine stuttered in wide eyed terror as several of the furry beasts dangled above him.

"What do I want?" A cloud of rage and contempt crossed her face. "What do I want?" she screamed at him. "I want my life back!"

"I was following your orders! All this time, I was following your orders!" he whined, almost pleading with her.

"Do you know what this is?" she quizzed him, splaying her hands upwards, motioning to the hundreds of spiders now descending from the ceiling and skittering across the floor toward him.

Shaking his head, he was terrified. "No..."

"This is atonement. I am setting things right. Father Vertigo taught me that to quench and destroy the guilt in your life, you need to purge the things from your life that make you feel guilt. I'm sick of his twisted perception of this law, but I do agree with his thinking. I will not kill Globulus, the only thing that still remains from my past life. Instead, I've found a new way to shackle my guilt."

She pointed at him with a wordless instruction. The spiders had finished their descent and were now crawling upon his flesh. Dozens more moved from the floor up his legs, coating him in a living carpet of certain death. As the wicked spiders crawled over his body, their hairy legs pricked and tickled his skin, sending Guillotine into an almost coma-like state as his mind screamed in fear.

"I was following your orders!" he called out again.

"I know you were." She smiled. "I have another question for you."

"Anything! I will do anything you ask, just don't kill me!" he begged, shaking in terror.

"Did Vertigo order anyone else to track Globulus?"

"No, my lady!" Guillotine pleaded with her in a submissive voice as the spiders skittered across his body. Several dozen more crawled onto his helpless form. Every part of his body, including his face, was now covered by the creepy arachnids. "I was supposed to gather a team to track them. I was the only one in the room when he spoke to me. No one else has been ordered to track Globulus."

"Are you certain?" she rasped impatiently.

"Yes, my lady. I was the only one ordered to track him."

"I want to die," Marion said in a strange tone. "All I want to do is die..."

"If you hate the Reaper Kai order, why don't you attack them? It would mean a sure death. You can let me go, you don't need to do this!" he beseeched as one of the enormous spiders wedged itself in his mouth. He could now taste the hairy invader crawling into his mouth. Gagging, Guillotine tried to breathe as the spider pushed its way into his throat. Trying not to enrage it, he attempted to push it aside with his tongue, with little success. He even considered biting the spider but the thought of it biting his mouth and plunging its venom-filled fangs into his tongue was a horrifying prospect.

"I learned very early on that to destroy an empire, you must send spies and operatives to destroy it from within. I will make amends for what I have done. To openly attack the Reaper Kai is certain death. I can cause much more damage hiding within, like a cancer." She smiled, her expression radiant with loathing.

"Just let me go!" Guillotine whined, trying to speak with the enormous spider still crawling around inside his mouth. "I won't tell a soul!"

"I will set things right," she said with a wavering smile. Tears formed in her eyes and she stared at Guillotine with hatred. "You killed my father. You killed my father!" she shouted in anger. "I want him back!" she screamed at him. "I hate you. I hate you for what you have done. I'll hide my guilt. I will quench its hate-filled thirst, and I'll do so by claiming your life. If Globulus survives and makes it to the northlands, the secret of Metalweaver Flats will be exposed. All I want to do is die, all I want is to end my suffering, but I will endure and help bring the about the ruin of the Dark Order. I have done horrible things in the name of greed and ambition. I will pay for my sins with blood! I will pay for my sins with the blood of others."

Pointing at Guillotine, she addressed him one last time. "Do you have anything to say?" The enormous spider was still wedged inside his mouth. Seeing his condition, she smiled. "Or course you don't have anything to say."

As she flexed her fingers, her loyal pets heard her psychic command and obeyed without question. The living carpet of spiders upon Guillotine exposed their fangs. Piercing his flesh, the host of arachnids plunged their poison-tipped fangs into him. As their venom pumped into the vile mercenary, he began to twitch, trying in vain to scream. Within a few seconds, Guillotine slumped in his chair and the pistol fell from his hand. The weapon hit the floor with a clatter.

Guillotine, the sinister mercenary who had killed King Toil, captured Mineera in Dune Station, and tracked Nova 7 to the Concrete Barrens, was now dead.

Seeing the hundreds of spiders upon him, Marion smiled and felt her twisted heart soar. She had killed a wretched thing and had done so to protect Globulus. As she surveyed Guillotine's corpse, she became concerned about his remains. Looking at her spiders, she flexed her fingers once more and commanded them, "Feast on him, my pets. Leave no trace of him."

The spiders responded and began to regurgitate toxic enzymes upon the corpse. Beginning to feed, the host of spiders set to destroy any evidence of the vile mercenary. Pleased with her success, Marion sat back in her chair and watched her pets consume the corpse of Guillotine.

Chapter 39
The Road North

Crouching down, Globulus sparked a fire using a lighter he had borrowed from Carla. As he set the flame to the kindling, Carla seemed excessively concerned by his actions.

"Are you sure that's a good idea? Setting a fire could bring scouts or others to our camp," she added emphatically, watching the orange flame erupt in the dim light of the nighttime sky. "We barely made it out of Rasheed and I'm not sure the risk of a fire is worth the warmth it will provide."

"We'll be fine. The Rasheed soldiers that aided in our escape have hidden underground once more. They're smart enough to keep hidden until ill will begins to die down inside Rasheed. As for Marion, she will *not* betray us," Globulus responded in a dull tone, still crouched over the fire. His brown eyes stared with a distant look, almost as if he were looking past the fire instead of directly into it. He became increasingly sullen and distant as the silent, tense moments passed.

Sighing, Carla crawled across the ground and kneeled before her enormous friend. As she looked up at him, she could tell that he was under duress and that his mind was lost in another place. Trying to get his attention, she moved her head into his field of vision. At first he simply ignored her. The more he tried to pay no heed to Carla, the more obnoxious she became. She pressed her face further into his vision, until the only thing in his view was her face looking up at him. In a clear attempt to irritate him, she started to make weird faces.

A small smile broke upon the hippo's lips as he stared back at her. Finally the smile erupted into a faint chuckle.

"Ha! I knew you were still here with me," she concluded and backed away from him. Rubbing her arms to ward off the cold, she drew close to the fire.

"I'm sorry; I have a lot on my mind."

"I know. I'm just concerned that we may have mercenaries or Reaper Kai tracking us. We did just break you out of a prison, after all."

"No one will be following us. Not now, not ever."

She simply looked back and didn't say a word, still only half believing his assertion. Seeing her reservation, he sighed and shook his head at her. "You really are relentless, aren't you?"

"I didn't say a word," she defended herself with a coy smile.

"You don't have to. I know what you're thinking."

"Then talk to me."

"I don't want to."

"You do want to, you just don't know it!"

"Damn it, just leave me alone!" he growled.

"You know I can't do that. You're torn up inside and I'm your friend. Talk to me."

He maintained his silence, his gaze becoming distant once more. Staring into the fire, he watched the orange flames consume dry brittle grass near the fire pit. Slowly the cinder sparked the fuel and began to consume it. As the grass caught flame, the brittle stalks curled in the fire. Within a few seconds, the grass had been utterly burned, leaving only a smoking husk. As his gaze remained locked on the flames, he began to speak in a low tone, almost as if he was in a trance.

"Marion will not be sending anyone after us. She gave me her word."

"Her *word*?" Carla almost snorted outright. "She gave you her *word*? That woman killed her own father, betrayed you, and gave the entire kingdom of Rasheed over to the Reaper Kai. She gave you her *word*?"

Globulus shot her a menacing look, which jolted Carla. "Yes, she gave me her *word,* and I believe her."

"Why on earth would you believe her?"

"Because I looked into her eyes. She is tormented by what she's done. Marion is trying to atone for her sins and I will trust her. I can't explain it, I just can't explain it. She finally understands that a horrible line has been crossed, and she wants to set things right."

"So she's just going to let us escape and warn the Iron Kai about Metalweaver Flats? If we get back, it will mean the end of that production facility and the Iron Kai will have a sizable chance at surviving this war. It doesn't make sense that she would simply let us escape."

"It's complicated."

"Yeah, it is!" she exclaimed in exasperation. "Usually you're more rational than this."

"Just stop it!" Globulus shouted at her. Backing off, she shook her head in dismay. "Just leave it alone," he grumbled again.

"What would you do if you were hearing all of this from me?"

He did not respond.

"This is too important, Globulus. How many lives are at stake here? All you can tell me is that it's complicated?"

"Back off!" He shook with rage and his voice boomed like a cannon.

"No!" Carla stood up and flailed her arms backwards, pushing her head forward. Her lower lip was curled over her upper lip in an expression of defiance.

"She is my sister. All I want to do is believe that there is good still left inside of her. I looked into her eyes and she promised me that she would help us bring about the end of the Reaper Kai. I've known her almost my entire life. I looked into her eyes and believed her. She won't betray us, not now. She has lost too much and is in too much pain. I believe her because she wants to die, she wants to die and escape all this pain."

He was flustered and frantic as he spoke. Seeing the duress on his face, Carla shook her head guiltily. Feeling that she pushed him too far, she knelt down beside him again and placed her hand on his enormous forearm. Rubbing him gently, she tried to make amends.

"I'm sorry. I went too far."

"Yeah, you did. I don't know what I should feel. Part of me hates her. I hate her for what she did. King Toil was my father! Even though we're not blood relatives, hell, not even the same species, King Toil raised me as his own. I can never forgive her for what she did to him. She took my father, a man that I admired for his strong will and fierce moral convictions. He is gone and nothing can ever replace him." He slammed down his hand in a gesture of frustration.

"But the other part of me cannot abandon her. We grew up together and she was my sister. We spent our childhood playing in the gardens of Rasheed. That small innocent child is still inside of her! Even though she has been utterly seduced by greed and ambition, there is still that gentle, heartfelt side of her. I cannot simply abandon that. Deep down, I still love her. And deep down inside Marion, she still loves me. That's why she didn't stop us from escaping. She now knows that she has crossed a terrible line. Marion can never step back over that line, but she can lend aid to us. She won't betray me again. We have a deep bond that can't be broken or severed."

Looking up at him, she rubbed his arm again and smiled up at him. "I'm sorry for what I said. I'm sorry to have made you feel pain."

Smiling back, his eyes grew soft and kind. "Don't apologize. You were right, I had a lot on my mind and deep down, I needed to talk about it. Thanks for putting up with my crankiness."

Her eyes bright with emotion, she said, "Anytime, anytime you need me, I'll be there for you."

"Can we stop all of this gushy bullshit? I'm really tired of exploring my feelings."

Laughing, she nodded in agreement. "Let's talk about our next plan of action."

"We need to press on quickly. We have a long road ahead of us. Making it into the northlands won't be easy. Even though Marion won't send anyone after us, we should still be wary as we get close to Iron Kai territory. I suspect the war is still raging and that means we will have to avoid enemy patrols and break through enemy battle lines."

"I wish we had another alternative. I wish there was a way to raise the alarm by radio."

"Even if we had the capability to alert the Iron Kai by radio, I'm thinking that would be a bad idea. I'd rather not risk the Reaper Kai hearing the transmission and knowing that their little secret in Metalweaver Flats is out. I would rather alert the Iron Kai in secret, which would allow a full-scale surprise attack on the installation. Allowing the Reaper Kai to reinforce the facility would compromise a full-scale attack."

Carla nodded in agreement. "That is a wise thought."

"Let's get some sleep. We have a long road ahead of us and my damn leg still isn't completely healed."

As Globulus leaned back to get some rest, he was assaulted by young Carla. She rushed up to him and grabbed his enormous right arm. She hugged it with all of her might in a heartfelt expression of her appreciation. Stunned by her act, he chuckled and slapped her on the back affectionately with his left hand.

"It's good to have you back." She smiled and released his arm.

"Thanks, thanks for everything. It's good to be free and in good company."

"You really are becoming a refined hippo. Now we just need to get you a bath sometime soon. You smell worse than the sewer I had to crawl through."

He swung his arm forward to grab her, but she jumped back too quickly. "You little brat!" he growled.

"Have a good night." She smiled and crawled into her sleeping bag.

As the camp grew quiet, Globulus stared into the night sky and looked at the distant stars with a smile; it felt good to be free again. As his eyelids grew heavy and drowsiness took him, his soul lifted. It was the first time in a long time that he could spend a night as a liberated being, free of shackles, free to live again.

Chapter 40
Homecoming

"Banion..." a female voice broke through his quiet solitude.

Blinking in confusion, Banion looked around and found him self sitting in a wooden rocking chair. He grasped the armrests with his calloused hands, finding the wood worn and extremely familiar. Looking around, he was shocked to find his surroundings intact. Last time he had seen his home, his real home, it had been burned and destroyed.

Near the wall was a black piano with ivory keys. Staring in awe, he could see sheet music open on the piano. He shook his head in disbelief, rising from the rocking chair and moving over to the instrument. Reaching out, he grabbed the pages and inspected them. The bars and measures were all handwritten, and Banion smiled as flashes of recognition flowed through him. The title was written in flowing cursive, the handwriting of his beloved wife.

Glancing all around him in astonishment, he caught the scent of cookies and rushed forward, bursting into the kitchen. On the wooden table near the back door was a piping hot plate of cookies. He grabbed one immediately and took a bite. The chocolate melted in his mouth. It tasted absolutely wonderful to him.

"Banion..." another whisper broke the air.

Spinning around, he caught sight of a wisp of white fabric near the screen door. He rushed to the door, bursting outside just in time to see the remnants of a flowing white dress disappear around the corner of the building.

"Lily?" Banion called out in a mystified tone, his brain working feverously to understand the strange image. It had seemed almost as if his wife had just passed beyond his view. Stunned, he hurried around the corner of the building.

As he moved around the corner, smoke stung his eyes and he stopped dead in his tracks. Flames were now engulfing the side of his house. The sounds of gunfire, automatic weapons fire, tore the serenity. Coughing, he covered his mouth with his sleeve and reached in alarm for his gun belt. His tattered hand closed around the hilt of a silver long-barreled revolver. As his hand grasped the weapon, a spike of anger roared through his volatile mind.

The vision of his burning house rapidly changed. He blinked, his vision blurry, and another set of images rolled through his field of vision as he was transported to another tortured part of his former life.

As the vision expanded, he caught wisps and images from his former home in Dune Station when Banion was a mere teenage boy. With the smoke leaving his vision, the images materialized around him. A cage made of barbed wire surrounded a host of people, mostly naked. The mass of people were prisoners, caged like animals, unwilling prey to the Reaper Kai order. The terrified crowd was wailing in fright, staring at a podium several feet off the ground. A familiar-looking man was pressed to the stage, staring directly at Banion. Fear welled up inside him as he stared helplessly at the events unfolding around him.

"Frank?" Banion yelled in terror, seeing red-robed priests backing the man forcefully into the wooden stage. A woman laughed maniacally and stood over him, pointing at him. Shaking his head back and forth, Banion was unable to even move. His entire body was frozen and there was nothing that he could do. The man who had saved the orphan Banion from his dark childhood was now being forced to the wooden stage, his face rubbed harshly against the platform.

"Uncle Frank!" he yelled, staring in wide eyed terror at his uncle.

"I love you, boy," his uncle said in heartfelt tone.

As he finished speaking, a club struck his uncle, hitting him again and again. Blood erupted from the wounds on his back as he winced in pain.

"No!" Banion yelled as the sinister Reaper Kai priestess laughed again and again. Smiling in glee, the priestess watched the man get beaten to death. The world began to blur once more and the only sensation that Banion could perceive was the insane laughter rolling through his unsettled mind.

Light began to stream into his consciousness once more. As he opened his eyes, the laughter continued, but it had changed. Instead of a woman laughing, the sound was mechanical and measured. Banion shook his head, his vision clearing gradually, and looked around him. Tall pine trees stretched above him. Staring upwards, he saw wisps of smoke rising into the air. Popping and crackling exploded in his ears as a fire raged in the distance. Sitting up, he looked around and saw the pasty white forms of robotic soldiers, Biogtechs firing on helpless citizens.

Suddenly the vision became clear. The village that was being burned was the one where Banion had been born. Standing up, he tried to run towards the village. With each step he took, the village grew further away. Panic had set in and he knew why. The vision he was now witnessing took place when his beloved mother had been slain by Biogtech troops, when Banion was only a boy.

"I have to get to my mother!" Banion yelled as he ran faster and faster toward the scene of conflict. The faster he moved, the further the village became. Stopping dead in his tracks, he panted, trying to catch his breath. As he stood there motionless, his mother passed into view, a look of terror on her face. She was running for her life.

"Mom!" he screamed, but no sound came out of his mouth. "Mom!"

She was running toward him but could not see him. Instead it was as if she was looking through him. Shaking his head in anguish, he wanted to close his eyes. He knew what was about to happen next. A burst of fire lit the scene. A stream of flame erupted from one of the Biogtechs. Lancing forward, the burning stream hit his mother and her body exploded into a burning mass. Screaming, she flailed about, rushing forward, engulfed by flames.

"No!" he screamed again.

In the distance, the mechanical laughter broke the silence. The Biogtechs giggled as they slaughtered the last remnants of the villagers. At the edge of his vision, a little boy ran from a burning building and charged into the tree line. Banion knew the boy well; it was him at a very young age, the only survivor of the attack. As the little boy ran, tears streamed down Banion's face. Shaking in frustration, he could remember the terror of seeing his mother die and escaping into the forest beyond. Even as the image made him weep, it began to blur once more.

The flames remained, as did the smoke. As the blur dissipated, Banion could see the town of Birthrock being laid to waste. Stumbling out of the smoke, he caught sight of his front porch. Standing in the flaming ruins of his former home was his beloved wife. The last time he had seen her, she was lying, lifeless, in a pool of her own blood upon the porch. Yet in the current image that Banion witnessed, his wife was full of life, staring at him with somber eyes.

Blinking, he stepped out of the smoke and stared at her. She was wearing a lovely long white dress. Her long black hair was flowing down her shoulders. Smiling, Banion walked towards her with a dreamy fascination. Looking back at him with her dark brown eyes, she smiled warmly at him.

"Banion..." the whisper sounded again. He finally acknowledged the voice. His beloved wife, sweet Lily, was speaking to him.

"Lily?" he called, and tears began to run down his face. Stumbling through the smoke and fire, he tried to reach her. With each step, the flames erupted further, barring his path to his beloved wife. The more he tried to reach her, the thicker the smoke became. Her pristine, beautiful smile was obscured by the smoke and flames.

"Lily!" he screamed.

"Banion..." she whispered. "Come back to me. I love you so much. Banion, Come home to me..."

The sound of her voice disappeared. The smoke and flames overwhelmed Banion and he was forced backwards, forced to flee. Screaming in rage, he fought to control himself. He wanted to be with her, he wanted to be with his beloved wife who had died at a time which felt so distant...

"Lily!" Banion screamed and sat straight up. The dark night had overtaken the land and Banion awoke from a horrible nightmare. Frantically he looked around the campsite for his dead wife. She was nowhere to be seen. Thinking about her, he grabbed his chest, pressing his fingers into his duster. He passed his hand over his chest with a sudden frantic intensity, as if searching for something. Pressing down hard with his hand, he tried to feel for an object hidden beneath the fabric of his coat; when he failed to find it, he grew even more panicked. Pulling his duster open, his hand fumbled around inside the lining of one of his pockets.

Finally his fingers touched a metal object in his long coat. He smiled as his fingers closed around the object and pulled it free from his pocket. In the dim light, he rushed over to the camp fire and opened his hand. Resting in his palm was a gold wedding band. He looked at the ring triumphantly, tears streaking down his face. Holding his wedding band made him feel at peace. Pushing it around the palm of his hand with his fingers, he stared at it dreamily. "Sweet Lily..." he whispered. As he stared at his wedding band, he felt the urge to put it back on his finger. But as he grabbed the gold ring to do so, something stopped him. Deep down, something clawed at his senses and he stopped. Instead, he simply looked at the relic of his former life with a deep sense of sadness. Unable to comprehend the emotion gripping him, he was lost in silence, staring at the ring.

"Don't be afraid." Mineera emerged from the darkness, her voice a whisper.

Blinking, Banion looked up, startled. Without thinking, he closed the palm of his hand so that she could not see his wedding band. "What?"

"I said don't be afraid; you seem frantic, terrified." She sat down beside him near the fire. Smiling at him, she reached out her dark skinned hand and clutched his closed fist, the fist that held his wedding ring. Looking at him with her bright blue eyes, she rubbed his hand gently. Normally, Banion would have pulled his hand away, but this time, he let her console him. He had grown to trust Mineera and wanted her to comfort him.

"Are you all right?" Mineera asked him in a soothing voice, still rubbing his hand. "You were yelling in your sleep."

"Yeah, I think I'm all right. I was having a bad dream," Banion replied, smiling at her. Reaching down, he placed his hand on hers and gently patted it a few times before pulling away the hand away which was clutching his wedding band. "What are you doing awake? It's your night off from guarding the camp."

"I was also having a bad dream," Mineera admitted, staring at him with a heartfelt, calming gaze. "What a pair we are! Neither of us has had a full night's sleep for the last ten years."

Laughing, Banion smiled and returned his wedding ring into the inside pocket of his duster. As he did, the sense of sadness that had overtaken him seemed to abate. Shaking off the feeling, he turned back to Mineera.

"Sleep is overrated. Why sleep when you can stay up all night, consumed by bad memories?"

His sarcastic tone was somehow refreshing to Mineera and she responded with a chuckle. "Maybe someday, we will both learn how to sleep a full night."

"Somehow, I doubt it," Banion responded.

"Me too." She laughed again.

"So, are you ready for the road home?"

Staring at Banion with her bright blue eyes, Mineera was lost in thought and took a brief moment to formulate her answer.

"Yes and no. Part of me wants to go home but part of me never wants to go back," she concluded. "I want to get this bloody crusade done with. I want the Reaper Kai to be purged from the land, but I also like being out here in the wilds and wastelands."

"I'll miss our travels too," Banion nodded in agreement.

"When we are out here, I'm just Mineera. I'm not a former Reaper Kai, I'm just myself. When we are in 'civilized' lands, I'm the traitor of the Reaper Kai and everyone stares at me in disgust. No one trusts me and no matter what I do, I'm an outcast. I don't miss those days one bit, and I'm not sure I even want to go back. It seems no matter how long I live on this earth, I can never escape my heritage."

"You are never an outcast in my eyes; you haven't been one in a long time. Your fierce compassion and need to do the right thing, no matter what the cost, set you apart from all others. I don't care what anyone else thinks, I know the real you, and there's a lot to like. Don't beat yourself up too much," Banion said honestly.

Smiling, she accepted his compliments. "Thanks."

"You're welcome."

"Are you going to miss any of this? Any of our travels?"

"I've been thinking a lot about that lately. All my life, I've been on the path of vengeance. It has defined my entire existence. Now that we have the weapon to eradicate the Reaper Kai, I feel somewhat empty. Once they're all gone, what the hell am I going to do?"

"I feel the same way. Once we return and use the nuclear warhead, I'll be the last of my race, the last of my kind. I have no home, no focus. We are two of a kind, Banion O'Neil, two restless souls whose only purpose is to destroy the Dark Order. I don't know what my purpose is beyond that."

"It's so strange to me. We set out to do the impossible and here we are, on the verge of reckless slaughter. I don't want to go back. In a strange sense, all I want is to keep the quest alive. I thrive on exploring the ruins of old with a gun in my hand and my friends at my side. I will miss this life, and miss all of you greatly. We have been out here a long time, and Jared, Tani, and you, Mineera, are my new family. I feel like I belong with all of you, and I'll miss our adventures."

"We have such a wonderful little dysfunctional family, don't we?" Mineera laughed. "A pyromaniac scholar, an arrogant warrior, an insane psychic, and a mercenary rancher."

"I wouldn't have it any other way." Banion laughed dryly.

"Me neither," she responded with a smile.

"I'm gonna *try* to get some sleep."

"Me too," Mineera said in a sarcastic tone. "*Sweet* dreams."

Laughing again, he tipped his black cowboy hat over his face and drifted off into an uneasy slumber.

Chapter 41
Stalked

A white mist had settled over the forest. Trembling in the cool air, Jared crept amidst a large stand of aspen trees. All around, the white giants towered above him, having lost their leaves several months ago as fall overtook the land. As he crept silently on the soft mat of fallen leaves, he examined his surroundings with wild trepidation. In his right hand the tribal carried a radio; in his left hand, the Scar Blade was clutched with white knuckles.

As he stared about the mist-filled forest, he could barely see more than twenty yards in any direction. Darting from side to side, his gaze frantically passed from one form to the next, anticipating some horrid ambush. As the mist flowed through the forest, different shapes presented themselves in the shifting fog. Jared knew that his entire team was being hunted, being stalked.

He came to a halt near the center of the aspen grove, feeling suddenly exposed, and crouched down defensively. Fear gripped him and he took cover. Scanning the misty tree line, he saw nothing. As his senses grew increasingly anxious, the radio clutched in his hand sprang to life. Startled by the sound, Jared almost dropped the radio.

"Any contact?" Banion's familiar voice erupted from the device. Fumbling quickly with the volume control, Jared decreased it; the tribal did not want his position to be given away by the sounds coming from the radio.

"No contact yet," he whispered back. "I can't see a damn thing out here. Any luck from the ridge?"

"No contact from up here, kid. Be careful. If you don't see anything soon, get back up here."

Banion and the rest of Nova 7 had positioned themselves several miles to the east on a ridgeline overlooking the mist-filled valley. Mineera had grown restless in the morning and claimed to have felt a primitive, angry presence in the valley below. Sometimes her perceptions were wrong, but mostly they were correct. Feeling that the team was about to be ambushed, Banion decided to camp up on the ridge and send the most stealthy of their team, Jared, into the foggy valley below to scout for any possible threat. For the last several hours, Jared had been creeping around the forest in an attempt to validate Mineera's perceptions of impending doom.

Just as Jared was about to give up on his search, the monster stalking them made its appearance. As the tribal crouched on the wet, moldy leaves, an enormous explosion of sound greeted his ears. An ominous snapping of wood traveled through the air. Concerned by the noise, Jared crept quickly out of the trees and into the middle of a rock formation. Obscured by the excellent cover the formation provided, the tribal bounced up the rocks like a cat on the prowl. Dropping down, he concealed himself and looked in the direction of the loud noises echoing through the misty glade.

As he waited in the rocks, the sound of wood breaking increased in intensity. Whatever the strange sound was, it was drawing closer, ever closer to Jared's hiding place in the rock formation. Blinking rapidly, his eyes strained to see what was approaching in the dense fog. With heart pounding, he drew his submachine gun and trained the weapon towards the sound.

Pop! A tree at the edge of his vision broke under enormous pressure, snapping like a toothpick. The tree was huge and its broken trunk fell to the ground with an ominous thud. Startled, Jared retreated back on the rock outcropping, nestling in a crevice within the stone. Concealed within the small opening, he sought to control his breathing. Gradually, he brought his heart rate under control, breathing softly. His head moved slowly from the crevice in the rock, scanning the misty surroundings, gun ready for conflict. Looking down the barrel of his weapon, he could see an enormous shadowy form in the fog. He kept his submachine trained on the unknown threat and shut off his radio completely, not wanting a transmission from Banion to give away his position.

Snap!   Another tree broke, but this time, the unusual shadowy form hurled the broken trunk several yards from its position.   Whatever the beast was, it was extremely large and exceedingly strong.

"Go scout the forest..." Jared muttered in an irritated whisper. "My ass, go scout the forest!"

As several minutes passed, Jared watched in awe and wondered why the creature was moving so slowly. It looked as if the beast was somehow confused. For each step it took, it would stop and remain in place for at least thirty seconds or more. After the shadowy form would take a break, it would take a single step and the process would begin again. Confused by this unusual behavior, Jared's curiosity got the better of him. "I know I'm gonna regret this, but here we go!" he mumbled to himself in a bemused tone.

Moving down from the rock formation, he landed on the moldy leaves and decided to skirt the tree line and move in from behind the creature. Progressing in absolute silence, the deft warrior bounded through the trees, pressing deeper into the ancient forest of aspen trees. He took a few minutes to safely skirt around the threat, then moved in from behind the shadowy figure.

Crouched upon the ground ahead of him in the fog was an enormous form. Clad in black steel armor, the crouching creature was roughly twenty feet tall. It was hunched over and its single, red robotic eye was scanning the ground intently.

"What the hell?" Jared whispered under his breath. Thinking back to the battle in the forest, he reached the conclusion that the strange creature was probably the sinister TOM 23, the same machine that had captured Tani, the same one that attacked Lavosi's vermin army in the forest.

Jared knelt down and stared in fascination at the odd scene unfolding before him. Standing upright, the robot took a step forward and then crouched again. At this distance, the tribal was unable to tell what exactly the machine was doing. A dense strand of fog pressed into the forest and obliterated Jared's view of the monstrous machine. The enormous form was cloaked in mist once more, and the tribal wanted to get a closer look at what it was doing. Ignoring caution, he stood up and moved in for a better look.

Pressing onward slowly, Jared drew close to the robotic creature. As he moved closer, he slowed his advance and raised his weapon, pressing the submachine gun against his shoulder. Walking with the gun sights leading the way, Jared was not watching his path very closely. Concentrating on a possible threat ahead of him, he was unable to avoid an extended root poking out of the mat of dead leaves. His right foot caught the root and he tripped, his momentum carrying him forward. Jared's index finger had been anxiously resting on the trigger. As he hit the ground, his finger spasmed out of fear and pulled the trigger on his gun. A second after he hit the ground, his weapon discharged and three bullets erupted from it, creating a loud ruckus as the clap of gunfire roared in the silent forest.

"Damn it!" Jared muttered in disgust, angered that he had been so clumsy and stupid. Knowing that his position was now apparent to the shadowy form in the forest, he jumped to his feet and began to run. He had not traversed more than ten yards before the monster in the mist responded.

Hearing a crackling noise, Jared never looked back. With a powerful surge, an enormous green beam of light ripped through the fog, accompanied by an ominous hiss. As the green laser tore the fog, the smell of ozone wafted up. Out of the corner of his eye, Jared could see the laser slice through several trees. Turning his head, he was just in time to see three trees collapse, their trunks falling directly towards him.

He leapt back a step, guided by instinct. The first tree crashed past his face, a mere inch away from hitting him. Responding with animal-like agility, he swiveled his neck and caught sight of the second tree crashing towards him. Not even thinking, he leapt forward and the second tree crashed on top of his former position a split second later. Having avoided two deadly trees crashing toward him, he knew the third was close, and dropped his gun even as the Scar Blade cleared his scabbard. With a grunt, he slashed upwards with the ancient blade, striking the third tree. The shimmering blue steel blade severed the tree in two just above the tribal's head; the two pieces of debris hit the ground without harming Jared.

Momentarily elated by surviving the attack, he now found himself under heavy machine gun fire, erupting in the trees behind him. As he hit the ground, dozens of machine gun rounds tore through the trees, splintering them and creating a shower of mangled tree limbs. Jared covered his head and cursed out loud as the shower of debris hit him. As soon as the sound of the gunfire subsided, he was on his feet again.

Having secured his weapons, the tribal grabbed the radio and flipped the switch.

"I have one heavy contact and I'm under fire. Request immediate instructions from your position. I repeat, I'm under heavy fire," Jared yelled frantically into the radio. Behind him, the youth could hear the sound of grinding metal as if a rusted freighter had collided with a stone jetty. The sound of trees popping and breaking gave him a shot of adrenaline as the monstrous assault robot scanned the fog for the foolish fleshing that had fired its weapon.

"The route to our position appears to be open. What the hell is happening down there?" Banion's voice crackled from the radio.

"It's TOM 23. It's chasing me!" Jared responded.

Hearing that his friend was in danger, Tani had commandeered the radio from Banion. "Jared, get the hell out of there now. Just run for it!"

Another blazing stream of green laser fire whizzed over his head.

"What the hell do you think I'm doing?"

Not wanting to look back, Jared ran as fast he could, vaulting over logs and fallen trees like a seasoned athlete. His advantage increased the further he moved, passing into the fog and beyond the sight of the combat robot. After another thirty seconds of full sprinting, he managed to elude his attacker. Slowing his speed, Jared found that the sounds of battle had ceased. No more gunfire was racing through the trees, no additional green lasers were incinerating the woodlands, and the sound of the metallic menace breaking through the trees had subsided.

A pristine silence once again graced the forest. Stunned by the sudden calm, he listened intently to the sounds around him. The eerie silence was maintained. Just a moment ago, the forest had been devastated by the war machine. Now it was devoid of sound once more. Straining, Jared's ears were eager for any sound to emerge from the sullen forest. There was a substantial thirty second lag before a noise ripped the silence.

Crack! A tree was torn asunder and then all was quiet. The pattern was repeating once more. Blinking several times, Jared found himself mesmerized yet again by the robot's behavior. Looking into the forest, he knew that he should escape and run, but he was too interested in what the machine was doing. Why had it given chase and then let him go? Why was it taking only a single step and then pausing?

Sighing, Jared knew that he had been sent to scout the forest. If he left without learning more about the robot's bizarre behavior, he knew that he would regret it.

"Damn it!" he mouthed under his breath and sought to discover the mystery of TOM 23. Breathing softly, he moved slowly through the forest, back toward the robot. As he drew closer to the scene of conflict, the smell of burnt wood filled his nostrils. Several trees were still smoldering where the laser had sliced through them. His eyes shifted back and forth quickly, knowing full well what the cost of failure was.

After a few minutes, he came into a path of mangled trees. Knowing that the machine had left the trail through the woods, he followed the tracks to their source. Creeping up upon the robot, he could see it once more in the fog. It was crouched and its single red eye was inspecting the ground closely. After studying the ground for half a minute, the robot rose and took a step forward, smashing two trees as it moved into the forest. It took a step forward, then crouched down again and inspected the ground.

"What the hell are you looking at?" Jared whispered to himself, staring in awe at the strange sight. After another thirty seconds, the beast rose up again and took another step forward.

Jared furrowed his brow as a whisper drifted through the trees; the machine was talking, muttering to itself as it studied the ground. At first he thought the almost inaudible voice coming from the machine was merely his imagination. But the longer he watched the robot, the more convinced he became that the robot was talking to itself. Tani and Jared had spoken many times about robots and other old-world technologies. His friend's geeky enthusiasm had rubbed off a little onto Jared, and the tribal was now extremely intrigued that a machine would be talking to itself while looking at the ground. Wanting to know more, he stalked ever closer to the robot, staying behind it but pressing dangerously close to it.

Standing up, the machine bashed through a few more trees then dropped to the ground to study it once more. As it did, Jared finally could hear what the machine was saying. In a haunting voice, it said over and over again, "Why did you abandon me?"

As Jared heard the machine reiterate the same phrase, he looked at the robot staring at the moldy leaves with great interest. With a startled blink, comprehension finally dawned on Jared's face. He looked down at his own feet, then at the moldy leaves behind him. Small indentations had been left in the leaves. Crouching down, he could see a faint trail where he had passed through the forest. He turned his gaze toward the robot, utterly stunned. Standing tall again, it moved forward then crouched, studying the leaves with great interest once more.

"It's tracking us." Jared spoke in a whisper. As he heard the machine cry out, "Why did you abandon me?" over and over again, a fright filled young Jared. The machine was much more than a pile of wires and circuit boards. Something profound had happened. Life itself had evolved from something inorganic. Shuddering in the cold fog, he knew that he had to make haste back to his companions.

As he slipped away from TOM 23, Jared knew that the road home would not be easy. They had survived countless ambushes by the Reaper Kai and Lavosi's hateful rat tribe, but the foe now tracking them was well beyond comprehension. Nova 7's toughest challenge was still ahead: escaping from the most advanced robot that had ever been constructed by mankind. As he rushed through the forest, Jared heard the machine breaking through the trees once more, tirelessly tracking the mercenary team, and shook his head in trepidation. The greatest challenges were yet to come for Nova 7.

Chapter 42
The Frost Barrens

"This isn't going to work!" Tani declared, frustrated, holding the long pole made from a broken sapling tree stalk. The ten-foot pole was deep in the snow, and the rest of the team members were looking at the panicked scholar uneasily.

Nova 7 had pressed on eastward from the forested regions beyond the military facility where they had recovered the nuclear warhead, and found themselves in one of the most isolated regions of the Darken Realm. The area in which the companions were now trapped was known as the Frost Barrens by the local peoples of the north. Where the center of the continent was a ravaged hell-blasted wasteland, the northlands were equally inhospitable. Hundreds of square miles of broken lands were covered in glaciers and thick snow pack, a landscape devoid of all life. It was more than a thirty-mile trek across the interior of the Frost Barrens, and Nova 7 was now in the middle of the expanse.

A continual snow blanketed the Frost Barrens, concealing various dangers beneath the soft fluffy white layer. Pressing through the middle of a glacier was extremely dangerous. As the massive ice flows moved, giant chasms and rifts would form in the ice, creating enormous pits and canyons. Covered in fresh snow, many of the pits and canyons would be virtually invisible, cloaked by the fresh powder. With one wrong step, a traveler could fall hundreds of feet and end up inside the glacier, frozen fast within, never to be discovered until the glacier melted thousands of years later.

And such was the dilemma of Nova 7. The mercenary team had been forced to pick up the pace and press quickly into the glacier in a desperate attempt to escape their pursuer. TOM 23 had fanatical patience and the most stubborn will that the mercenary team had faced thus far in their travels. Obsessed with a need for revenge, the insane robot was tracking the team in earnest with the intent of punishing Tani for escaping and betraying it. Fueled by the volatile semblance of life coursing through its wiring and programming, TOM 23 wanted vengeance.

Knowing full well that being captured by TOM 23 would mean the end of the entire mission, Banion had accepted Tani's recommendation to press on into the Frost Barrens in an attempt to move quickly towards their objective of returning the nuclear warhead to civilization. The only thing that Tani failed to realize was that once the team had entered the enormous snow fields and glaciers, TOM 23 had a much easier time tracking them by following their footprints in the deep snow. The gains that Nova 7 had made over the past week trying to escape the robot had now been diminished, and TOM 23 was closing in fast.

The first day in the snow fields had been extremely precarious. Jared had fallen into a crevasse within the glacier, miraculously catching himself before falling to his death. After that initial incident, the team turned back to the nearby forest to procure long poles made of small trees to probe the snow for additional pits within the snow field. After losing crucial time, they set out once more and made their way slowly across the snow field.

TOM 23 was so enormous that the fissures in the ice were mostly insignificant in slowing his progress. The team members had lost their lead quickly, and it was now apparent that the relentless machine would catch them somewhere in the snow fields.

"Damn it!" Tani was irritated and in a state of pure panic. "I just don't know! From what I can tell, we're at the edge of a huge fissure in the ice. Everywhere I probe the snow, the pole finds nothing but air underneath. It's almost as if we're on a peninsula of ice out here!"

"Calm down," Banion ordered, shouting at Tani who was forty yards away. He had also been probing the snow near his location and had come to the same conclusion. The team was trapped in the snow field and an enormous fissure was blocking their progress.

"We need to get out of here!" Tani yelled back, his face bright red with anger and fright. "It's gaining on us!" Earlier that morning, the team had caught sight of the robot still tracking them, its black armor showing in stark contrast against the white snow. All of them knew that time was running out. Soon the machine would catch them and they would have to make a stand.

"It's the same over here!" shouted Jared, who was standing near Mineera. Both had been probing the snow as well and both had found the edge of the enormous crevasse lurking underneath the powdery snow.

Assembling back near the center of the solid slab of ice, they conferred quickly.

"Banion, we're running out of time." Tani was quivering in fear thinking about the monstrous death machine confronting the team out on the ice shelf.

"We're cut off," Jared concluded, motioning to the holes in the snow every foot or so around the perimeter of their location.

"We can't head back; we're already too far into the snow field," Mineera concluded in a dark tone. Her usual optimistic approach had also been defeated and she sounded disheartened like the rest of the team.

"I should have never betrayed TOM 23. I put us all at risk," Tani lamented, shaking his head.

"That's nonsense, just knock it off. If it weren't for your quick thinking, we would have never liberated the nuclear warhead from the ruins. You did what you had to," Banion countered.

"Did I? I could have gone about it a different way. The reason we are all in danger is because of my actions," the scholar persisted bleakly.

"Stop beating yourself up. We need your brains right now, not your despair," Mineera added.

"My brains? I have no idea what to do. We saw TOM 23 this morning. By my estimate, we have only half an hour max before it catches us."

"Then let's think it through." Jared spoke in a confident tone, trying to get everyone to focus. "We've been through much worse."

"Yeah, we have," Banion agreed.

Tani sighed, his eyes shifting back and forth nervously. The gears of reason and creativity began to grind away inside his mind. Many options raced through his frantic thoughts. With a shake of his head, he formulated a desperate plan of survival.

"I have an idea," he declared, his face turning almost as pale as the snow around them.

Seeing his duress, the rest of his companions were already skeptical about his 'idea.' But they remained silent, staring at him with dread growing in the pits of their stomachs.

"I'll go back alone, right now. I'll face TOM 23 and the consequences of my actions. It's chasing us because of me, not any of you. If I go now, he'll confront me alone and all of you will be safe," Tani concluded in a resolute tone.

"No way!" Jared snorted. "You're not going back there by yourself. If it comes down to it, we'll all make a stand together, no matter what happens. I don't want to let you die alone and for nothing."

Nodding, Banion agreed with Jared. "Noble but stupid, bookworm. Jared is right, there's no way in hell I'm letting you go back to face that damn robot on your own. If it is a stand we're going to make, then we do it together."

"We will be unable to face it in combat," Mineera whispered, thinking back to the carnage of the military base. In those frantic battles, entire armies of soldiers had fallen in a matter of minutes to TOM 23. Fighting was definitely not a sound option.

Crack! The sound of ice breaking echoed in the distance. Stunned, the entire team turned around in the hazy light of the morning sun and peered anxiously toward the sound of the noise. About half a mile down on the snow field, an ominous red eye surrounded by black armor peeked over the ice shelf. TOM 23, the ancient terror, was closing on the team. There was now no way for them to go back; the robot had blocked any path of retreat.

As they stared at the machine, its red eye looked back and saw Tani. Shaking in rage, the machine slammed its fist onto the ice shelf, shattering large shards of ice. The temper tantrum was accompanied by angry, lonely rants. **"Why did you abandon me?"** it moaned in agony and anger. Seeing Tani, it felt betrayed. A fresh shower of sparks erupted from its back as the processor core tried to understand the primitive, raw emotions coursing through the battered network of tattered circuit boards.

Their eyes fixed upon the machine, the team members watched in horror as it pulled the enormous bulk of its body onto the ice shelf.

"Come on, bookworm! Think of something!" Banion said in a frantic tone.

Tani shook his head back and forth. Seeing his response, Banion charged forward and grabbed the tribal, shaking him violently till he responded to the aggression and snapped out of his daze. Staring into Banion's maniacal eyes made Tani forget momentarily about TOM 23. Instead, he was frightened beyond belief that Banion was about to beat the hell out of him. The threat polarized the youth and adrenaline hit his blood like fire. The flash of fury felt wonderful and it made the tribal focus. Looking at Tani with a stern gaze, Banion spoke softly to him once more. "Focus on the threat. Calm down and get us all out of this."

As he blinked frantically, Tani's mind was set ablaze with wild ideas. Staring around like a madman, he considered their options. Time was running out. The ancient robot was moving up the snow field with frightening speed. Even as he shook his head with indecision, he had a crazy idea. Dropping to his knees, he dug in the snow with both hands. Within a few seconds, he found what he was looking for. The layer of snow underneath was rock-solid.

"I wonder…" Tani said with a flash of recognition, the cogs in his brain feverously grinding away. Running over the edge of crevasse that they had probed, he moved a good twenty yards toward the incoming TOM 23, then dropped quickly to his knees and began to dig once more. Within seconds, he found solid ice underneath the layer of snow. He blinked quickly, a smile illuminating his face, and then stumbled back to the team, frantically searching for his backpack.

As the tribal fumbled with his gear, TOM 23 drew closer. The machine was obscured from their view once more, this time as it tried to climb onto the next ice shelf. As it dropped into a valley within the ice shelf, Nova 7 lost sight of the robotic monster entirely. In the distance, it wailed angrily, "Why did you abandon me? I know what to do to feeble creatures! I will make you suffer. I will punish, I will kill!"

Hearing the robot chant sinister death threats elevated the level of danger for the rest of Nova 7. Thankfully, Tani ignored the taunts and threats and focused on the task at hand.

"Help me with these, quickly!" he ordered and brought out several bundles of explosives from his backpack. "We have to be quick; TOM 23 can't see what we're doing. We have to finish before it moves over the next ridge."

"What the hell are you doing?" Banion seemed genuinely concerned.

"I'm gonna blow a massive hole in the glacier," Tani said in a triumphant tone.

Jared and Mineera were also shocked. "You're gonna kill us all," Jared whined.

"No I'm not..." Tani handed each of his companions a demolitions charge. "We're standing on solid *rock* right now. Plant the charges on the *ice*. Hurry!"

Suddenly his plan made sense. Obeying his command, they rushed away towards the edge of the ice shelf. Hiding the charges in the snow, Tani instructed them how to arm the devices. Cautiously, they obeyed and a series of charges were set on the edge of the ice shelf. Rushing back, they caught sight of Tani pulling the remote detonators for the charges from his backpack. Four detonators were carefully armed by the scholar. He motioned to the rest of Nova 7, who all assembled near the tribal. Looking down to the ground, they each eyed the spot where he had dug into the snow, exposing the rock. Taking deep breaths, they listened to him intently.

"We need to be extremely careful. To detonate the explosives, we each need to hit the trigger at the same time. If we don't detonate them at the same time, we risk that the charges will not be powerful enough to crack the ice shelf. Everyone got that?"

They all nodded back in agreement.

"We also need for TOM 23 to get real close. If we blow the charges too early, it won't be in the center of the charges. If we wait too long, it will kill us all. Listen to my command; when I say GO, blow the charges and hold on for dear life. I'm not entirely sure that the rock we are on is intact and that we will survive the blast."

Looking at him with bemused looks, they all felt they were seconds away from a fiery death.

"Are you sure this is going to work?" Banion asked in a dour tone.

Smiling, Tani looked back and replied with brutal honesty. "I have no idea if this is going to work."

"Damn it, Tani! If you get us all killed…" Banion stopped short of uttering his threat.

Thud! A tremor rocked the ground beneath them. A series of vibrations was making each of them tremble. Just below the ice shelf, an enormous black steel arm thrust over the edge. The grinding of steel resounded with a mighty groan as the robot pulled itself onto the ice shelf. Standing very near the companions, the robot blocked the sun itself. A shadow fell over the team as they eyed the monstrous machine with wide-eyed wonder.

Thud! It moved forward with an aggressive motion. A series of sparks erupted from the machine's back and it paused, overcome by an electrical seizure. As it shook uncontrollably, the primitive emotion of abandonment filled the robot. It stared at Tani, knowing pure rage, pure hate. It wanted to punish Tani for his betrayal and would do so by claiming his life. Regaining part of its composure, it took a shaky step forward onto the ice shelf.

Wailing, it screamed in a mechanical tone, "Why did you betray me, Tani? Why did you abandon me?"

Holding his ground, Tani felt his stomach lurch. "I am so sorry." He was honest in his reply.

"Sorry?   You   will   die   for   your betrayal!" the robot screamed, its voice synthesizer cracking as another seizure of rage overtook it. TOM 23 was so consumed with rage, it never noticed the demolition charges hiding underneath the snow. Moving forward, the team tensed and all of them took a step backwards.

"Hold!" Tani whispered, reassuring his companions.

Thud! TOM 23 moved forward. As it did, a whirring noise erupted from the machine. Motors and gears were grinding away inside it. A steel tube erupted from the machine's arm. A light green glow began to emerge from the steel tube and a popping sound erupted from the weapon.

"Hold!" Tani urged again under his breath, just loud enough for Nova 7 to hear.

`"I spent an eternity in terror, longing to be saved from the shadows of my own suffering. At last I am saved from the darkness and this is how you treat me? You betray me, you abandon me!"` The speaker crackled as the robot's enormous red eye focused on Tani.

Watching its position closely, Tani felt the hair on his neck stand on end. Was this it? Was this how they would all die? Killed with the most powerful weapon imaginable in their possession?

Thud! TOM 23 took a step forward and the laser on its arm hummed, filling with energy. Tani knew that the time had come. Looking up at the monstrous red eye of the machine, Tani said compassionately, "I am so sorry..."

TOM 23 stopped dead in its tracks, seeing the duress upon his face. In that single instant, the machine understood regret. Seeing its former friend looking up at it with somber eyes, the machine felt anxious. Something was horribly wrong. For a brief moment they looked at each other, one born of flesh and the other born of steel. Not knowing what to think, the machine could not understand the new emotion it was experiencing. The anxiety turned to fear a split second before Tani gave the order.

Never averting his gaze from TOM 23, Tani shouted, "Go!" and pulled the trigger on the detonator. The rest of Nova 7 followed suit; each of them pulling the trigger on their detonators.

A series of harsh explosions ripped the ice shelf with tremendous force. A split second after the charges blew, a plume of icy shards were thrown free. Squinting, each of them felt cold shards of ice strike them, feeling almost like needles of cold scouring their faces. The explosion was massive and threw them back. Regaining their equilibrium, each of them perceived loud cracking. The ice shelf had splintered and broken. All around the robot, cracks formed and spread out like the remains of a shattered mirror.

Looking around, stunned, TOM 23 was barely able to comprehend what was happening. It lurched to the left, the laser beam erupting from its arm as its left foot broke through the ice. The green stream of light intended to kill Tani instead pierced the ice, further ruining its integrity. As the mighty robot struggled on the ice shelf, the damage caused by the explosives weakened the ice shelf to such an extent that loud sharp popping noises pierced the air as part of the glacier itself collapsed.

Staggering, the machine that knew life, knew fear. Staring in horror at Tani for what he had done, it tried to steady itself upon the ice shelf. Another series of groans mounted as massive fissures formed in the ice. Lurching downwards into an icy abyss, the machine stared at Tani and cried out in fear. "What have you done? Why have you done this to me?"

Tani was unable to respond, his heart heavy within him. Even though it was a mere machine, Tani had breached and broken a trust between himself and the robot once more. The robot was new to life, new to learning about emotion. As Tani watched TOM 23 disappear into the crevasse within the glacier, he felt pity for the machine. It was feeling fear, and in that moment of panic learned about mortality. To ponder and understand one's existence is to fear the unknown and to fear death. As the machine slipped deeper and deeper into the glacial rift, it struggled, and Tani had to look away. For a brief moment, he wanted to charge to the edge of the icy fissure in some feeble attempt to save the machine. Fighting back the emotion, he had to turn away.

"Tani! Help me!" TOM 23 pleaded in terror, panic having found its way into the machine's brain. It was initially able to grip the ice shelf with its arms, but gradually, the metallic claws slid free, and the ancient robot fell into an icy crevasse beneath the glacier. As it fell into the dark abyss, it screamed again and again, wailing for Tani to save it.

In the blink of an eye, it was gone. TOM 23 had fallen hundreds of feet into the center of the glacier, lost to the ice, lost to the darkness. In the solitude of the icy crypt, fear was consuming the machine. All was dark, all was silent. Thrashing in the darkness, it could see nothing. The only thing the machine could perceive was the thick ice around it and the inky blackness of its frosty tomb. As the glacier creaked and groaned, the robot was wedged in the ice, stuck and unable to move. Trapped deep within the glacier, raw fear ruled its senses. Life had found a home within the machine and with each passing moment, TOM 23 was overwhelmed with fear and begged in vain for mercy in the smothering darkness. In the icy tomb of the glacier, nothing responded to TOM 23's pleas.

Chapter 43
A Reflection on Conscience

"There is nothing else that you could have done. If it weren't for your actions, we would have died and the warhead would have been lost. The Reaper Kai order would have won a huge victory, leaving the Darken Realm in the clutches of pure evil. You did what you had to. Stop beating yourself up." Mineera spoke in a calm tone, draping her arm around the tribal scholar.

Shaking his head in anguish, Tani could still hear TOM 23 uttering his name over and over again, asking for mercy. He tried to escape his guilt-ridden thoughts, but quickly threw his hands up in the air in a gesture of defeat. "There's always *something* that you can do. I should have come clean about my intentions at the beginning with that damn robot. I should have told it what our circumstances were and tried to reason with it. Instead, I took the easy way out and lied. Look at what happened! We had to kill an ancient wonder to survive. We had to trap something alive in a living tomb within the ice just because I was unable to reason with the machine."

"Why are you even giving this a second thought? It was going to kill all of us. You did what you had to not only to save yourself, but all of us. You're a hero." Jared spoke while jamming the pine branch into the fire. Impaled upon the stick was a fresh cut of elk meat from a forest denizen that the team had killed earlier in the day. After defeating TOM 23, Nova 7 had escaped the horrid glacier and found themselves once more in a forest stretching on for hundreds of miles. "Just relax and enjoy your dinner."

"I'm not hungry," Tani pouted.

"I say it's time to celebrate," Banion declared, moving out of the darkness of the night and advancing into the camp with frightening speed. His movements were so fluid, so confident, it was almost unnerving to watch him advance. Pulling a flask from his gear, he unscrewed the metal cap and sniffed the contents. The smell of potent whiskey wafted from the flask and he smiled. Moving towards them, he sat down on top of the case holding the nuclear warhead. The rest of the team eyed their leader uneasily as he sat on the potent weapon of the ancients. Seeing their discomfort, he smiled and patted the weapon with his left hand. "Here's to Nova 7; we've officially survived the last of our enemies here in the northlands!"

Taking a small swig, he quickly passed the flask over to Jared. The tribal warrior was not about to miss a shot of whiskey. Grabbing the flask, he took a small swig and licked his lips. Next, the flask passed on to Tani. He held it with a distant gaze, looking into the fire as guilt filled him.

"Just tell us about it. Let us know how you feel," Mineera coaxed him.

Banion snorted at the idea. With a sigh, he stood up and moved over to Tani, gazing at him intently. "Listen, bookworm, we're not out here for our health. We have a strict obligation to recover this nuclear weapon and get back alive. We're not doing anyone a lick of good if we die out here. It doesn't help the war effort back home one bit if we fail. The armies of the Reaper Kai will be able to overpower all that remain if we fail. It's not about you, Tani, it never has been. It's about giving a chance to all those poor bastards that are still fighting the Dark Order. I suggest you bury your feelings and just move on. There's too much at stake for you to be brooding about your little robot friend. That damn machine was only a few seconds away from killing all of us, and it would have done so if it weren't for you."

"Just forget it," Tani said defensively.

"My point exactly: just forget it." Banion smiled and was happy the discussion was over.

"Banion!" Mineera said in alarmed protest.

"Just let it out," Jared instructed his friend earnestly. He knew him well enough to know that not dealing with the issue would just eat at Tani. Jared also knew that he would be completely ineffective if he was fixated on TOM 23.

"It was my fault in the first place that he attacked. If I wouldn't have tricked it, TOM 23 would never have attacked."

"If you wouldn't have tricked TOM 23, you would still be trapped in that tunnel and the nuclear warhead would still be in the vault. You had to do it," Jared emphasized, trying to help his friend.

"I could have done something else!" he shot back in a frustrated tone.

"How? How do you know what the future holds? You could have done a dozen other things and we would be worse off. You took a chance and made a gamble. In my opinion, the risk was well worth the reward," Banion added.

"But what's the point in doing all of this if we're just going to cause pain?"

"Pain? We have a nuclear weapon that is going to be used to annihilate an entire race. Our purpose is to cause pain," Banion said in a wicked tone.

"Yeah, but that's different." Jared countered. "The Reaper Kai are not innocent, they've caused enormous suffering."

"Who cares about a machine? It's not alive anyway," Banion asserted.

"I disagree." Mineera interjected. "I could sense *something.*"

"It was alive. It had crude emotions and fear. It was so lonely. It had been isolated, tortured by sadness and abandonment. I knew that I could manipulate TOM 23 and did so to reach our objective." Tani spoke softly, engaged by the conversation.

"You had to do it, Tani. I know that it's tearing you up inside, but you had to do it. Banion is right; we are not out here on a mission of mercy. We're here to put an end to the worst empire that has ever existed in the history of mankind. I can appreciate how you feel, but you had to do it," Jared responded with empathy.

"Some of the hardest things that we have done in life are things that must be done. Even though you had to do what you did, I do admire your compassion. It's easy to be reckless. It's easy to

be heartless and to think about objectives from afar. You've done what you did and sometimes you can't forget what you've done. The only thing that you can do is hope that you are strong enough to do the right thing when such an opportunity presents itself. I commend you, Tani, for your heart, for your compassion. The road we are on is bloody and I'm glad that you have not lost yourself in the process." Mineera smiled at the youth with deep affection.

Shaking his head, he drummed his stumpy fingers against the side of the metal flask holding the whiskey. With a slow motion, he moved the flask to his lips. Finally, he opened his mouth and tipped back the flask, taking a swig. As the whiskey hit his tongue, Banion cheered.

"That's the spirit!" Banion nodded with a look of triumph.

Tani was not happy but he did need to move on. Taking the flask from his lips, he raised it in the air and declared, "To TOM 23."

The rest of the team nodded back with somber looks and responded in unison, "To TOM 23."

With that, Tani took one more swig and then passed the flask on to Mineera. Rolling her eyes, she grabbed the flask with a sigh. Nodding at the rest of them with a bemused look, she took a tiny swig then handed the flask back to Banion. Recapping the flask, he placed it back in his duster and moved back over to sit atop the nuclear warhead.

Everyone cringed as he did so and he laughed defiantly at their discomfort. For effect, he made a fist and rapped on the container.

"I wish you wouldn't do that," Mineera said nervously.

"I know." Banion smiled back and winked at her.

"Who wants the first steak?" Jared asked, removing the skewered meat from the campfire.

"I'll take it." Tani extended a shaky hand, holding out the dirty cup which he used as a crude bowl. Seeing him take the food made the rest of his companions feel better. The quest had taken its toll on everyone, but each of them felt obligated to bring each other back from the edge of despair. It was a solemn and unspoken pledge they had all made to each other. There was a certain amount

of magic in seeing one of their own triumph over adversity and begin to move on.

"Now what do we do?" Jared spoke while skewering another chunk of fresh meat on a new pine branch. As he began to cook the next elk steak, he looked to Banion for guidance. "We've run out of enemies. The Reaper Kai expedition has been annihilated, the rat expedition has been destroyed, and finally the robot guarding the ruins has been defeated. We're all out of enemies."

Banion looked at the naïve tribal with a chuckle. "Out of enemies, you say? I'm sure we'll find some more."

Laughing back, Jared agreed. "Yeah, we're good at making enemies, aren't we?"

"We now need to focus on getting back to the Iron Kai Empire. Even though we made a pledge to aid King Toil and the kingdom of Rasheed, our pledge will be honored by delivering the prize to the Iron Kai," Banion stated. "Rasheed was destroyed but our purpose still remains."

"Do we even know where we are?" Tani quizzed, looking at the enormous forest around them.

"I think so. The map that we got from the wilderness outpost is crude but it's detailed enough to lead us to this civilized area on the eastern edge of the map. Our goal is to press on through these forests and reach these towns and outposts. From there, we will try to work our way into the great wastes and hopefully back to the Iron Kai Empire."

"So what is the path to these civilized lands?" Jared asked, moving forward to view the strange map.

"We need to press through this forested region for about a week. After that, there's a mountain range to the southeast and this pass here labeled 'Death Drop Pass' with a skull. Beyond these mountains is a deep expanse known as the 'Great Shush Valley'. Near the end of that valley is a wilderness outpost known as the 'Red Mountain Inn'. All in all it looks like we have several weeks of travel ahead of us," the leader of Nova 7 concluded.

Nodding, the rest of the team acknowledged the plan. With a sense of relief, they looked at each other with silent glances. All of them were deep in thought. From time to time, each of them would

glance fleetingly at the black case resting near the edge of the camp; the black case, the horrid case, which contained the most fearsome weapon known to man. Although they had defeated countless foes and had obtained the nuclear warhead, the region of the world that they were about to enter was one of the most mysterious in the entire Darken Realm. Hundreds of travelers had taken the plunge to explore this vast wilderness, only to have their quests end in failure. The forest hid deadly peril beyond any comprehension. With weeks of travel ahead of Nova 7 through the dangerous wilderness, the road home would not be easy.

More information about the Darken Realm
can be found at
www.darkenrealm.com

www.ingramcontent.com/pod-product-compliance
Lightning Source LLC
Chambersburg PA
CBHW032239010726

47494CB00002B/556